THE BORDER EMPIRE

by

Ralph Compton

Daniel O'Donnell
O Donnell
901
1 503 D 1 4838
1 800 2 0 1 4838
Daniel O'DONNELL

BERKLEY
New York

BERKLEY
An imprint of Penguin Random House LLC
penguinrandomhouse.com

Copyright © 1997 by Ralph Compton
Penguin Random House supports copyright. Copyright fuels creativity, encourages
diverse voices, promotes free speech, and creates a vibrant culture. Thank you for buying
an authorized edition of this book and for complying with copyright laws by not
reproducing, scanning, or distributing any part of it in any form without permission.
You are supporting writers and allowing Penguin Random House to continue to
publish books for every reader.

BERKLEY and the BERKLEY & B colophon are registered trademarks of
Penguin Random House LLC.

ISBN: 9780451192097

Signet mass-market edition / July 1997
Berkley mass-market edition / October 2019

Printed in the United States of America
29 31 33 35 37 38 36 34 32 30

Cover art © Hiram Richardson
Cover design by Steve Meditz
Logo art by Roberto Castillo / Shutterstock

Ralph Compton Westerns

THE AMARILLO TRAIL *(by Jory Sherman)*
THE AUTUMN OF THE GUN
A WOLF IN THE FOLD *(by David Robbins)*
BLOOD ON THE GALLOWS *(by Joseph A. West)*
THE BLOODY TRAIL *(by Marcus Galloway)*
BLUFF CITY *(by David Robbins)*
THE BORDER EMPIRE
THE BOUNTY HUNTER *(by Joseph A. West)*
BRIMSTONE TRAIL *(by Marcus Galloway)*
BROTHER'S KEEPER *(by David Robbins)*
BULLET CREEK *(by Peter Brandvold)*
THE BURNING RANGE *(by Joseph A. West)*
THE CONVICT TRAIL *(by Joseph A. West)*
THE DANGEROUS LAND *(by Marcus Galloway)*
THE DAWN OF FURY
DEAD MAN'S RANCH *(by Matthew P. Mayo)*
DEATH ALONG THE CIMARRON *(by Ralph Cotton)*
DEATH OF A BAD MAN *(by Marcus Galloway)*
DEATH OF A HANGMAN *(by Joseph A. West)*
DEATH RIDES A CHESTNUT MARE
DEMON'S PASS *(by Robert Vaughan)*
DEVIL'S CANYON
DOOMSDAY RIDER *(by Joseph A. West)*
DOWN ON GILA RIVER *(by Joseph A. West)*
THE EVIL MEN DO *(by David Robbins)*
FATAL JUSTICE *(by David Robbins)*
THE GHOST OF APACHE CREEK *(by Joseph A. West)*
THE HUNTED *(by Matthew P. Mayo)*
THE KILLING SEASON
THE LAST MANHUNT *(by Joseph A. West)*
THE LAW AND THE LAWLESS *(by David Robbins)*
THE MAN FROM NOWHERE *(by Joseph A. West)*

NORTH TO THE SALT FORK *(by Dusty Richards)*

THE OMAHA TRAIL *(by Jory Sherman)*

ONE MAN'S FIRE *(by Marcus Galloway)*

OUTLAW TOWN *(by David Robbins)*

PHANTOM HILL *(by Carlton Stowers)*

RALPH COMPTON COMANCHE TRAIL *(by Carlton Stowers)*

RALPH COMPTON DOUBLE CROSS RANCH
(by Matthew P. Mayo)

RALPH COMPTON HARD RIDE TO WICHITA
(by Marcus Galloway)

RALPH COMPTON STRAIGHT TO THE NOOSE
(by Marcus Galloway)

RALPH COMPTON THE CHEYENNE TRAIL *(by Jory Sherman)*

RAWHIDE FLAT *(by Joseph A. West)*

RIDE THE HARD TRAIL *(by David Robbins)*

RIDERS OF JUDGMENT *(by Ralph Cotton)*

RUSTED TIN *(by Marcus Galloway)*

SHADOW OF THE GUN *(by Joseph A. West)*

THE SHADOW OF A NOOSE *(by Ralph Cotton)*

SHOTGUN CHARLIE *(by Matthew P. Mayo)*

SHOWDOWN AT TWO-BIT CREEK *(by Joseph A. West)*

SIXGUNS AND DOUBLE EAGLES

SKELETON LODE

SLAUGHTER CANYON *(by Joseph A. West)*

STRAIGHT SHOOTER *(by Marcus Galloway)*

THE STRANGER FROM ABILENE *(by Joseph A. West)*

STRYKER'S REVENGE *(by Joseph A. West)*

TEXAS HILLS *(by David Robbins)*

TRAIN TO DURANGO

TUCKER'S RECKONING *(by Matthew P. Mayo)*

VENGEANCE RIDER *(by Joseph A. West)*

VIGILANTE DAWN *(by Marcus Galloway)*

WHISKEY RIVER

Prologue

"Come in, Wes Stone," said Texas Ranger Bodie West. "I've been expecting you."

"You've heard, then," Wes said.

"That you're the son of Nathan Stone," said West. "I suspected as much the first time I ever saw you. You're the very image of him."

"A damned shame somebody didn't tell me about him before he was lying dead in the streets of El Paso," Wes said. "I've taken his weapons and his name, and before God, I'll track down the bunch that killed him. They're going to die. To the last man."

"I can understand your feelings," said West. "What became of Nathan's dog?"

"Empty's with my horse," Wes said. "He followed me from El Paso, but I still don't have his confidence. I reckon I'm a poor second to Nathan Stone."

"Give him time," said West. "He's an intelligent animal."

"I want to know everything you can tell me about my father," Wes said.

"It's strange that you should arrive at this particular time," said West. "Byron Silver is in town, from Washington. He probably knew Nathan Stone better than any man alive. I know he'll want to meet you. How long do you plan to stay?"

"As long as it takes to learn about my father," Wes said.

"Then you'd better take advantage of havin' Silver and me here at the same time," said West. "Many of the men who knew Nathan—King Fisher, Ben Thompson, Wild Bill Hickok—are dead. Why don't you have supper with Silver and me? Then we'll come back here to the office, make a pot of coffee . . ."

"I'd like that," Wes said.

"We'll be at the Star Cafe, at five," said West.

Bodie West stared at the door for a long time after Wes had gone, struck by the uncanny likeness of the young man to his father. West was familiar with the Sandlin gang, the outlaws who had gunned down Nathan Stone. The gang hung out below the border, in Old Mexico, and it was against international law for an American to venture there. Should young Wes cross the Rio Grande, his life wouldn't be worth a plugged *peso*, nor could he expect help from his own land. But Wes was the very image of his father, and Nathan Stone would have crossed the border without a moment's hesitation.

Texas Ranger Bodie West and Byron Silver got to their feet as Wes Stone entered the cafe.

"Silver," said West, "this is Wes, Nathan's son."

"My God," Silver said. "You're Nathan Stone all over again."

He offered his hand and Wes took it. He didn't

look in the least like Wes had thought he might. He looked to be in his late thirties, with gray eyes, and his black hair had some silver at the temples. His Stetson was flat-crowned, with silver conchos. The rest of his attire was that of a Texas cowboy, down to his run-over boots.

"You don't look much like I expected," said Wes.

Silver laughed. "I'm just a Texas cowboy at heart, but I just never took to wrasslin' cows. I'd heard of you, but didn't know how to reach you. It's mighty fortunate, me bein' here. I hope you'll be as much a friend to me as your daddy was."

"I hope so, too," Wes said. "I want to know as much about him as you can tell me."

"That'll be a lot," said Silver. "Do you have Nathan's watch?"

"Yes, sir," Wes replied. "That, his Colts, his Winchester, and his name."

"There's a story behind that watch," said Silver. "Nathan and me come within a gnat's eyelash of gettin' ourselves killed. I got ventilated, and Nathan finished the job alone."*

Silver talked for an hour. Bodie West, hearing the story for the first time, listened in rapt attention. Young Wes Stone sat spellbound, his eyes aflame with excitement. There was a long moment of silence when Silver had finished.

"I never got all the facts," Bodie West said, "because Nathan wouldn't talk about it, but we pieced the story together. Captain Sage Jennings, one of the finest Texas Rangers who ever lived, was shot in the

The Dawn of Fury.

back. He was left paralyzed, unable to move, but he still had one thing going for him. Nathan Stone was his friend, and Nathan went after the bushwhacker. We don't know how many weeks or months Nathan was on the trail, but we do know that the hombre that shot Captain Jennings paid with his life."*

"That explains the ranger shield my father had," said Wes.

"Yes," West said. "He never wore the badge himself, although I wanted him to. When Captain Jennings died, he wanted Nathan to have that shield, and I presented it to him."

Having finished their meal, the trio returned to Bodie West's small office. There, the two men took turns relating to Wes the legends that surrounded Nathan Stone. Far into the night they talked, until they were interrupted by a scratching at the door. When West opened the door, a gaunt hound trotted into the room. Empty, Nathan's dog, had been there before. He looked at West and then at Silver, for he knew them both. He then lay down beside Wes Stone's chair.

"He's beginning to accept you," said West. "Nathan would be pleased."

"I'm obliged to both of you," Wes said. "All I have of my father is what I've learned from those of you who knew him. I don't know when—or if—I'll see either of you again. Tomorrow I'm riding after my father's killers."

"The Sandlin gang," said Bodie West. "They'll kill you and relish every moment of it."

*The Killing Season.

"I know," Wes replied. "There's a price on my head. But Nathan Stone died for me, and if that's what it takes, I can do no less for him."

"I know how you feel," said Silver, "but I'm not sure Nathan would approve of that. I learned, over the years, that he came west riding a vengeance trail. I know he gunned down seven men, and they all deserved to die. But it changed Nathan's life in a way that he wasn't able to accept. He was lightning-quick with a pistol, drawing with either hand, but it was a blessing and a curse. He was blessed with a skill that kept him alive, but was cursed with the need to defend his reputation as a fast gun. He can't speak for himself, so I'm speaking for him. I don't believe he'd want that kind of life for you."

"I reckon not," Wes said. "My mother died the day I was born, goin' to her grave without me or anybody else knowin' my father was Nathan Stone. Somehow, he knew. But he respected her wishes and kept it from me. After he was dead, Molly Horrell told me the truth. I understand my mother's reasoning, and my father's respect for her, but when the trail forks, a man must make his own decision. I've made mine."

"Nathan Stone couldn't have said it better," Silver said, "but as you know, I represent the attorney general's office, and I have to warn you that it's a violation of international law for you to ride into Mexico for the purpose you have in mind."

"I know that," said Wes. "Bodie's made it clear enough. But how is the Sandlin bunch to pay for their crimes? Do you expect them to ride into Texas and surrender?"

"Hardly," Silver replied, "but there's that damned agreement with Mexico."

"We're supposed to respect their sovereignty," said West, "while their government sells out to thieves and killers who have only to cross the border to escape the law."

"That's the truth, if I ever heard it," Wes said. "I saw it happen in El Paso, and if it hadn't been for this sacred, one-sided agreement Washington has with Mexico, my father might be alive today."

"I can't argue with that," said Silver. "I'm only reminding you that, legally, our hands are tied. When you cross the border, there won't be a lot we can do to help you."

"I haven't asked for any help," Wes said.

"Under similar circumstances," said West, "neither would Nathan Stone."

"While I can't promise any help," Silver said, "I can be sure that you know all that I can tell you about the Sandlin gang and the power behind them."

"They're a bunch of thieves and killers," Wes said. "What more is there to know?"

"While Sandlin's bunch is primarily engaged in rustling and wanton murder," Silver replied, "they're only part of an unsavory crime ring that's protected by corrupt Mexican officials. There are ties all the way to Mexico City, where there are powerful men who are virtually untouchable. In Washington, this unholy coalition is secretly referred to as the Border Empire, because they operate on both sides of the border. They are engaged in white slavery, counterfeiting, smuggling, and you name it."

"There is no law in Mexico, then," said Wes.

"Oh, there's law," Silver said, "but it's sold out to powerful criminal interests. You'll be branded an outlaw, as much in danger from Mexican police and the army as from the Sandlin gang. In his prime, Nathan Stone never rode into a nest of rattlers such as you're considering."

"I'm obliged for what you've told me," said Wes, "but I don't aim to go after every sidewinder in Mexico. I only want the Sandlin gang."

"You still don't get the drift of what Silver's saying," Bodie West said. "While you're looking for the Sandlin gang, every thief and killer in Mexico will be looking for you. You can't go after part of the Empire without all of it coming after you."

"That's it," said Silver.

"Anybody comin' between me and the Sandlin gang does so at his own risk," Wes said. "If everybody's against me, I won't have to be picky about who I shoot, will I?"

"I reckon you'd better keep that in mind," said Silver. "You're closer to the truth than you realize."

"I'll do that," Wes said. "Bodie, Mr. Silver, I'm obliged."'

With that, he was out the door, the hound following.

"God, I wish there was something we could do to keep the young rooster alive," said Silver. "Somebody to watch his back."

"So do I," West said, "but we no longer have an informant anywhere south of the border. The last one had his throat slit last year."

Removing only his hat, gunbelt, and boots, Wes lay down across the hotel bed. Not to sleep, for he doubted that he could. Empty sat on the oval rug, his eyes on Wes. Already there was a little of the companionship between the two that the hound had shared with Nathan Stone. While Empty knew Nathan was gone, he was drawn to this young man who had Nathan's weapons, who rode the same trails Nathan had ridden, and was like Nathan in so many ways. Wes had taken to speaking to the dog, a habit that had been strong in Nathan, and it had done much to win Empty's trust. Wes sat up on the bed and ruffled the dog's ears.

"Empty, I reckon we left West and Silver on a sour note, but there was no help for it. I swore an oath on my father's grave, and I aim to keep it."

There was a rumble deep in Empty's throat that wasn't quite a growl. It was more a sound of agreement, of understanding. Wes stretched out on the bed, while Empty curled up on the rug beside him.

Wes and Empty had an early breakfast. Afterward, Wes stopped at a bootmaker's shop with a special request of the cobbler. Inside the top of his left boot, he had a sewn-in, all-but-invisible leather pocket in which he concealed the Ranger's shield and the watch that had belonged to his father. Inside the top of his right boot, he had sewn in a thick leather sheath for a knife. Into it he inserted a throwing knife, with a slender haft and a heavier blade. A friendly Mexican in El Paso had taught him to throw the deadly weapon, and he had mastered it to perfection. It appeared he was going to need every skill he possessed as he rode the vengeance trail south of the border.

Outside the bootmaker's shop, as Wes was about to mount his horse, a cold voice spoke from behind him.

"I'm callin' you, bucko. Turn around an' draw."

Carefully keeping his hands away from his Colt, Wes turned to face the challenger. The kid wasn't more than a year or two older than Wes, and his weapon was thonged down on his right hip.

"I have no fight with you," Wes said. "I never saw you before in my life."

"No, but I saw *you*," said his antagonist. "Struttin' around in Dodge, when you was with the railroad. I saw you draw, an' you ain't no great shakes with a gun. I know I can beat you."

Bodie West and Byron Silver had just left a cafe where they'd had breakfast, and were across the street. Other men, careful to stay out of the line of fire, had suddenly gathered to witness the deadly ordeal between Wes Stone and his unknown challenger. Wes tried one more time to avoid the fight.

"Back off," Wes said. "I don't want to fight you."

"Well, I ain't givin' you a choice."

Not a man on the street later remembered seeing Wes Stone draw. The challenger had pulled iron first, and his weapon had cleared leather before Wes made his move. Suddenly a flaming Colt was in his hand, and the foolish young man who had called him lay dead, his weapon unfired.

"He called me," Wes said. "I had no choice."

The men who had seen it nodded. Only Bodie West spoke.

"It was more than fair. Ride on."

Wes mounted and rode south, Empty following.

"He's Nathan Stone all over again," said Silver. "Right down to the curse."

"Yes," West agreed. "All our warnings to the contrary are too late. The die is cast."

Wes rode wide of San Antonio. In Uvalde, he bought a packhorse and a packsaddle. Deep in Old Mexico, where every man's hand might be against him, he doubted that there would be supplies when he needed them, and certainly no ammunition for his Winchester and Colts. He knew the risk of a well-provisioned packhorse, for Mexico was a poor land in which only a few did not live on the ragged edge of starvation. Even without a price on his head, men would kill him for the horse he rode, while a loaded packhorse added to that danger many times over. But there was no help for it. Leaving Uvalde, Wes rode west to Eagle Pass, where he would cross the border. He had only a crude map of Old Mexico. The same friendly Mexican who had taught Wes to throw a knife had also drawn the map, for which Wes had paid him a double eagle. It had only major cities and rivers, and there was a possibility, Wes decided, that it would be of little use to him. During his months in El Paso, he had heard continual references to Namiquipa, a village where the Sandlin gang reportedly corraled rustled horses and cattle. Wes knew that Namiquipa was somewhere to the northwest of the town of Chihuahua, which was some two hundred miles south of El Paso. That the Sandlin gang had men posted at strategic points along the border, Wes had no doubt. With that in mind, his plan was to cross the border near the village of Eagle Pass, where it was unlikely he would be noticed. He must then travel west. Rather than go directly to Namiquipa, he would first go to Chihuahua. He counted it unlikely that the Sandlin gang would expect an American enemy to approach from the south. But his edge—the element of surprise—would last only until Sandlin's bunch received word there was an armed *gringo* in town. But it was the only plan he had, and swallowing hard, he trotted his grulla across the stream that was the Rio Grande. His packhorse—a bay—had not become used to the packsaddle, and he fought the lead rope. He kept trying to snake his head around, to see what the contraption was that was roped to his back.

"Come on, boy," Wes implored. "The packsaddle won't hurt you."

Wes rode well beyond the border before turning west, careful to avoid the Rio Grande lest he encounter soldiers or sentries for outlaw bands. He had traveled only a few miles when he saw smoke ahead. He reined up, and the hound sat down, an inquiring look on his face.

"Empty," said Wes, "it's mighty early in the day for a cook fire."

On impulse, Wes pointed to the distant smoke, and to his total surprise, Empty took a few steps in that direction. He looked back, as though uncertain, and again Wes pointed to the smoke. Reassured, Empty disappeared in the brush. Wes took the opportunity to rest the grulla and the bay, wondering how

Empty—if he *had* gone to investigate the smoke—would convey his findings. He soon learned. Empty trotted within a few paces of Wes and paused. There was that sound—somewhere between a bark and a growl—and he turned back the way he had come. Wes mounted his horse and, leading the packhorse, followed. Occasionally, Empty waited until Wes caught up, and then went on. The clearing was just large enough to accommodate a small cabin, a shed, and a pole corral. Beneath the shake roof of the shed stood a mule, and when it sighted the two horses, the animal began braying a noisy welcome. Smoke trailed up from the cabin's stick-and-mud chimney. From behind the cabin a Mexican emerged. Apparently he was unarmed.

"*Buenos dias, señor.*"

"*Buenos dias,*" Wes responded. "*En paz.*"

"*Si,*" said the Mexican. "I am Pancho Gomez. It is only Maria and me. We wish no one harm."

"Nor do I," Wes said. "I am Wes Stone."

"*Bienvenido,*" said Gomez. "We are poor, *señor.* There is pulque and goat's milk."

"Señor Gomez," Wes said, "there's coffee in my pack, and I'll share it with you and Maria."

Maria's curiosity had gotten the best of her, and she stood in the doorway, her dark eyes on Wes. When she spoke, there was something akin to awe in her voice.

"Pancho, it is the *compañero* of the Señor King Fisher, but more the *niño.*"

Gomez removed his wide-brim straw hat and took a closer look at Wes.

"Madre de Dios," he breathed, taking a step backward.

"My father, Nathan Stone, was a *compañero* to King Fisher," said Wes.

"Espectro," Gomez said, still unconvinced.

"The *niño* of the Señor Stone," said Maria.

"Sí," Wes replied, pursuing his advantage. "The Señor King Fisher is *muerto*. So is my father, Nathan Stone."

Gomez crossed himself, removed his sombrero, and bowed. Wes dismounted, looping the reins of both horses around a pole that supported the cabin's stoop roof. Removing an extra two-pound bag of coffee beans from his saddlebag, he presented them to Maria.

"Gracias," said Maria.

All the furnishings within the cabin were crude and handmade, but the interior was meticulously clean. Maria stirred up the fire within the stove. She wrapped a handful of the coffee beans in a clean cloth and began crushing them with a wooden mallet. Gomez nodded toward the kitchen table. Wes drew out a chair and sat down, Gomez taking a seat across from him.

"Señor Gomez," said Wes, "what can you tell me about my father, Nathan Stone?"

"He come with the Señor King Fisher to hunt the wild horse," Gomez replied. "Per'ap you come to hunt the wild ones, also?"*

"No," said Wes. "I seek the *bandidos* who murdered my father, Nathan Stone. They steal and kill

The Killing Season.

both north and south of the border. You have heard of the Sandlin gang?"

"*Dios!*" Gomez said fearfully. "*Por Dios!*"

"You know of them, then," said Wes.

"They are everywhere, *señor*," Gomez replied. "The very walls of the *cantinas* are the eyes and the ears of these sons of *el Diablo*."

"I know them, Señor Gomez, and they know me," said Wes. "They have put a price on my head. I am riding to Namiquipa, where I have heard they may be found."

"*Sí,*" Gomez replied. "They are there, in Ciudad Juarez, Chihuahua, Hermosillo—"

"And Mexico City," said Wes.

The coffee was ready, and when Maria placed the tin cups on the table, her eyes met those of Pancho. The look of fear that passed between them wasn't lost on Wes.

"I have talk too much, *señor*," Gomez said hastily.

"Your words will go no farther than my ears, Señor Gomez," said Wes.

But they were afraid. Gomez gripped the edge of the table with his hands to stay their trembling. Maria peered out the kitchen's single window as though she expected the devil and all his minions to appear at any moment. Wes downed his coffee at a single gulp and stood up. He spoke to the old *Mejicano* and his wife as kindly as he could.

"For your hospitality and for telling me of my father," said Wes, "*gracias.*"

Wes made his way out of the humble cabin and mounted his horse.

"*Vaya con Dios*, Señor Stone," Gomez said from the doorway.

Wes lifted his hand in farewell and rode away. Having waited in the brush, Empty soon caught up to him, and they traveled westward. What Gomez had told him had come as no surprise. The man's obvious fear at the very mention of Mexico City said more than words could have. Wes recalled the legend that had arisen around Frank and Jesse James. Outlaws and killers, the very land through which they had ridden abounded with friends who had willingly hidden them from the law. But the James boys hadn't been able to buy the law, and that had proven their undoing. The Sandlin gang, however, had stacked the deck in the most diabolical manner possible. Empty ranged ahead, and Wes felt better for having the hound with him.

Wes chose a spring with good cover. There he built his almost smokeless supper fire, dousing it well before dark. He moved well away from the spring, spreading his bedroll near where his horses were picketed. While Empty would warn of any approaching danger, the grazing horses were an added precaution. An unfamiliar sound caused a grazing horse to raise its head, listening. To a trained ear, the absence of the *munch-munch-munch* of a grazing horse was as eloquent as a shouted warning. Wes slept, awakened once by the cry of a distant coyote. He waited until good daylight before lighting his breakfast fire, and then built it beneath a tree so that the leaves would dissipate the smoke. After breakfast, he saddled the grulla, loaded the packsaddle on the bay, and rode west. Ahead, he knew not how far, Wes could see a mountain range that seemed to run the length of the land, from north to south.*

"Empty," said Wes, as they approached a stream, "it's time for rest."

Troublesome though it was, when Wes stopped to rest the horses, he removed the packsaddle from the bay and unsaddled the grulla, allowing the animals to roll. It might soon become a luxury neither horse would enjoy, when Wes was forced to ride for his life, but he would allow them their simple pleasure while he could. He estimated that in a day and a half, he had ridden well over a hundred miles. He had no idea how far he was from Chihuahua or what he would do once he arrived, but it was a place to begin. Continuing to ride west, his keen eyes caught a series of black specks against the blue of the sky. The specks soon took shape, as they spiraled downward. Buzzards!

"Empty," Wes said, "something or somebody's had a bad day."

As Wes rode nearer, he could see wisps of dirty gray against the sky. Smoke, from more than a single fire. Again, this time unbidden, Empty forged ahead. He returned, and this time there was no approving grunt. He whined, distressed. It was enough for Wes to dismount, leaving his horses among concealing trees and brush. He continued on foot, his hand near the butt of his Colt. He came upon the clearing suddenly. Where once a house and small barn had stood, there was only smoldering ruins. But the charred re-

*The Sierra Madre.

mains of the buildings were only a small part of the tragedy. The Mexican couple—probably man and wife—lay facedown a few feet apart. Both had been shot in the back, not once, but many times, long enough ago for the pooled blood to have dried. But Empty had found something more. He whined once before trotting off among the trees to the west of where the house and barn had stood. Not knowing what to expect, Wes followed. On what might have been a door from the burned house, a young girl— maybe a year or two older than Wes—had been spread-eagled. Her ankles and wrists had been bound with rawhide, and she was stark naked. Taking the knife from his boot, Wes hastened to cut her bonds. First he freed her ankles, and the moment he loosed her hands, she came at him in a kicking, clawing fury. In her brown eyes was a look of madness, and her strength was such that she dragged Wes to the ground. She fought him for the knife, with every intention of gutting him if she got her hands on it. Wes fought his right arm free and drove a fist into her jaw. It stunned her long enough for him to get to his feet and return the knife to its sheath inside his boot. Finally she sat up and looked at him.

"Do you speak English?" Wes asked.

"Yes," she hissed, "but I hate it and the *gringos*."

"I freed you," said Wes, "and I had nothing to do with what happened here."

The sun was warm, but she began trembling, as though with a chill. Huge tears rolled down her cheeks, and she spoke through clenched teeth.

"They use me, defile me," she said bitterly. "I swear, by the horns of *el Diablo*, they will be sorry they do not kill me. I will find them, and they will die."

"Do you know the men who did this?" Wes asked.

"*Bandidos*," she said. "Seven of them. They have many horses. They demand food we do not have."

"So they murdered your parents," said Wes.

"Before my eyes," she said, the tears increasing.

"I'll think of some way of burying them," said Wes, "but first I must find you some clothing."

"No," she said, "it does not matter. They take everything but my life. Let us do the burying, before the *busardos* come. Even more terrible than their dying was having the *busardos* take them, while I am helpless and can do nothing."

Wes had known his share of women, but he suddenly felt awkward and self-conscious in the presence of this naked female who just didn't seem to care.

"Come on," he said. "You can wait with the horses while I figure out some way to bury your dead."

She came willingly, and Wes led her away from and around the clearing, so that she wouldn't have to see the dead bodies. Empty growled as they approached the horses, not trusting this stranger.

"You'll be safe here with my horses and my dog," said Wes. "You might as well know my name. I'm Wes Stone. Who are you?"

"Maria Elena Armijo," the girl said.

"Wait for me here, Maria," said Wes.

Beyond the remains of the cabin, much of the land had eroded, leaving deep gullies. One of them became the grave of the girl's parents. Wes placed them side by side and caved in the banks of the gully.

They should have had better, he reflected, but without a shovel, it was the best he could do. Suddenly Wes was startled by the frantic barking of Empty, followed by the patter of departing hoofbeats.

Chapter 1

The grulla was gone. Swiftly Wes removed the packsaddle from the bay, mounted the animal, and lit out in pursuit. He was guided by Empty's barking, and he soon caught up, for the hound had headed the horse. The confused grulla was galloping in a circle, and Wes, galloping the bay alongside, seized the grulla's reins. But again the girl's eyes blazed with insane fury, and she flung herself at Wes, shrieking and clawing. They tumbled to the ground in an ignominious tangle of arms and legs. Thoroughly angry now, Wes managed to slam a right to her jaw, and she went limp. From his saddlebag he took a pair of yard-long rawhide thongs. With one, he bound her ankles, and with the other, her wrists. He then slung her, belly-down, over the packhorse. Riderless, the grulla stood with the reins dragging. Empty kept his distance, regarding the horse with suspicion, until Wes was in the saddle.

"Empty," said Wes, "how did I ever get along without you?"

By the time Wes rode back to claim his packsaddle, the troublesome girl had come to her senses. Wes slid her off the bay and sat her down with her back against a pine. She regarded him in silence, and he found himself facing a dilemma. What was he going to do with her? He began with a question.

"While I was burying your kin, why did you take my horse?"

"I go after the *bastardos* who ruin me," she said.

"Naked, without food or weapons?"

All the defiance leaked out of her, and her eyes couldn't meet his. Clinging to her was dirt and bits of leaves, and she seemed pitifully thin. Wes couldn't help feeling sorry for her, because it seemed she was concealing her grief behind her hatred for the outlaws who had brought her world to an end.

"If I turn you loose," Wes said, "do I have your promise that you won't do anything foolish, such as stealing my horse or scratching my eyes out?"

"You have my promise," she said, and this time her eyes met his.

Wes removed the rawhide, freeing her hands and ankles. She sat there, her back to the pine, watching him. Wes spoke.

"What am I to do with you?"

"You have been kind to me," she said, "and you may do anything you wish."

"Damn it," said Wes, "I don't want your body."

"I cannot fault you for that," she said bitterly. "It has been violated by *perros*."*

"You are not the first to be violated," said Wes, "and I think no less of you. First, we will go to the spring, so that you may wash yourself."

She said nothing and, taking her hands, he helped

*Dogs.

her to her feet. She went ahead, and leading the horses, he followed. There was a runoff from the spring, the water flowing over some large stones. She seated herself on one of them. From his saddlebag, Wes took a small square of soap and presented it to her. When she seemed at a loss as to what to do with it, Wes took it and soaped her thigh. Getting the idea, she took the soap and finished her bath. She then slipped into deeper water and, submerging her body, washed her hair. Finally, dripping, she stepped out on the grass.

"Let the sun dry you," said Wes, "and I'll find something for you to wear."

He had two changes of clothes in his saddlebag. While they were only denim shirts and Levi's trousers, they would have to do.

"Get into these," Wes said. "I reckon they won't fit very well, but you can't go anywhere naked."

"Where I be going?" she asked.

"With me," said Wes. "I can't leave you here."

Wes almost laughed when she donned the shirt and Levi's, for they swallowed her. In the front of the shirt, she held her own, but the sleeves covered her hands. The legs of the Levi's extended well over her feet.

"*Gracioso*," she said, looking at herself. "*El tonto.*"

"No," said Wes, "you don't look funny, and you don't look the fool. Here, I'll roll up the sleeves of the shirt and the legs of the Levi's. Until you can do better, you'll get by."

She still viewed herself with some amusement, but with shirtsleeves and the legs of the Levi's rolled up, she could manage.

"Where you take me?" she asked.

"Where do you want to go?" Wes asked. "Do you have kin?"

"I wish only to find the *perros* who kill my *padre* and my *madre*," she said.

"How are you to do that?" Wes asked. "Had you ever seen any of those men before?"

"No," she replied. "I hear them speak of Chihuahua. While they are taking their turns with me, one of them laugh and say I am something they do not share with Sandlin."

"Sandlin," said Wes. "Maria, are you *sure* of that name?"

"I am sure," she insisted. "I can do nothing else, so I listen."

"We're goin' to trail that bunch," said Wes. "I have plans for them."

"For why do you want them?"

"Maybe I'll tell you later," Wes said. "Let's just say for now, I have as many reasons for wanting them dead as you do."

Wes lifted her up on the withers of the grulla and mounted behind her. The bunch had made no effort to conceal their trail. It led west, and there were tracks of at least twenty horses, all of them shod.

"They have steal many horses," said Maria.

"Yes," Wes said. "These will be driven across the border and sold in Texas. How long had they been gone when I found you?"

"They ride in at dawn," said Maria.

"We're a good five hours behind them," Wes said.

They rode on, traveling more slowly, for the grulla was carrying double. Empty ran far ahead, for he still didn't trust the stranger who had taken the horse. While Wes didn't confide in the girl, there was a chance they might catch up to the outlaws sometime after dark. Wes had no doubt that these thieves and killers were part of the Sandlin gang, so he would take no chances when he eventually faced them. He was a little uneasy, because he had no idea how Maria Armijo might react. If her fury again got the best of her and she gave away their presence, Wes might find himself outgunned. He might quickly become the hunted instead of the hunter if even one of the outlaws escaped.

"We're going to stop before dark, cook some food, and eat," Wes said.

"We be close enough for them to see the fire in the night," said Maria.

"Maybe," Wes said cautiously. He didn't want her getting ideas.

They reached a stream where the outlaws had watered their horses, and many of the tracks where the animals had left the water weren't entirely dry. The bunch wasn't more than an hour ahead, Wes decided, and darkness was only an hour away. He dismounted and helped Maria down. By the time he had removed the packsaddle and unsaddled the grulla, Empty had doubled back. His hackles rose, and he regarded Maria with anything but friendliness.

"The *perro* does not like me," Maria said.

"He hasn't forgotten you took my horse," said Wes. "Behave yourself, and he'll get over it."

Choosing wood carefully, Wes built an almost smokeless fire. Filling the coffeepot with water, he put it on to boil, while he sliced thick slabs of bacon into his skillet. Maria watched with interest.

"I reckon you're hungry," Wes said. "Sorry I didn't think of it sooner."

When the coffee was ready, he filled a tin cup and presented it to her.

"Coffee," said Wes.

"*Gracias,*" Maria said. "I have tasted it only once in my life."

Empty came near only to accept his portion of the bacon. Wes doused the fire before sundown, and when it was dark enough, he made his move.

"I'm going to find that outlaw camp," he said. "I want you to remain here until I return."

"No," she said defiantly. "I go with you."

"You will remain here," Wes said, just as stubbornly. "Empty will be scouting ahead, and you make him nervous."

Wes mounted the grulla and rode out, Empty taking the lead. Less than an hour's ride brought them close enough to the outlaw camp for Empty to double back. Wes reined up, dallying the grulla's reins about a convenient limb. There was no moon, but the starlight was sufficient for Wes to keep Empty in sight. While there was no sign of a fire, the smell of woodsmoke was strong. Wes moved on cautiously. The bunch had apparently holed up in an arroyo, for they had no reason to expect pursuit. Wes had his Winchester, but he suddenly wished he had brought the second of Nathan Stone's Colts, which he had buried among his provisions. The Winchester would have to do. Empty growled softly, his warning to Wes. Creeping to the rim of the arroyo, Wes could see the outlaws gathered around the fire. Suddenly they leaped to their feet, hands darting to holstered weapons. Just as suddenly, they relaxed, laughing. Into the mouth of the arroyo walked Maria, just as naked as the moment Wes had found her! Her hands were behind her back, and while still in the shadows, she paused.

"Well, by God," one of the outlaws exulted, "the little catamount didn't get enough of us this mornin'. She's follered us, wantin' more, an' I aim to be the first to oblige her."

He started toward her, and the rest of them followed, laughing in anticipation. Wes held his fire, fearing any move he made would be the death of the girl. But Maria Armijo had come prepared to take her revenge. Behind her back, she clutched the second of the Colts that had belonged to Nathan Stone. Four times she fired, the shots blending into a continuous roar. Four of the outlaws were down, and before the remaining three could pull their guns, the Winchester was blazing. The horses reared and nickered, but Maria Armijo stood there calmly, the Colt in her hand. Wes slid and half fell into the arroyo. Maria just looked at him, a half-smile on her lips.

"Why the hell did you do that?" Wes stormed. "You could have been killed."

"*Sí*," she said calmly, "but I do not know of your debt to them. I know only of my own. My regret is that I did not kill them all."

"Damn it," said Wes, "there was only five shells in the Colt. You couldn't possibly have shot more than five of them. If I hadn't been on the rim, one of them would have shot you dead. Where are your clothes?"

"I leave them with your other horse," she said.

"I reckon I'll have to give you some credit," said Wes. "What they got was the last thing they expected."

"What become of the many horses they steal?"

"We'll free them to return to their home corrals," Wes said. "We'll free the outlaws' mounts, too, except for that black. He doesn't seem to have a brand. We'll take one of the saddles, and the black will become your horse. We might as well see what else we can use, that this bunch of varmints won't be needin' anymore."

She crossed herself. "You would rob the dead?"

"I would," said Wes. "You accounted for four of them, so don't go preaching at me."

To his total surprise, she laughed.

"Do what you wish, Señor Wes Stone. I will tell the black horse that he is mine, and that I am his *bueno amigo.*"

Wes, going through the pockets and saddlebags of the dead outlaws, discovered more than a thousand dollars in gold coins. Several owned Colts whose shells were compatible with the two Colts that had belonged to Nathan Stone. Wes took extra saddlebags in which to carry the gold and the shells. Maria had managed to make friends with the black horse, and had chosen a saddle that had belonged to one of the outlaws.

"You can have a Winchester and a revolver, if you want," Wes said.

"I will take them," said Maria.

"I'll saddle your horse," Wes said, "and we'll ride away from here."

"Without burying the dead?"

"They rode away without burying *your* dead," said Wes.

Wes saddled the black, and from one of the dead outlaws who had owned a Colt, he took a gunbelt. The Colt was fully loaded, and he handed the rig to Maria.

"We'll have to cut some new holes in that belt so it will fit you," Wes said.

The saddle Maria had chosen had a rifle boot, and Wes shoved a Winchester into it. Empty, not liking the prevailing smell of death, hadn't entered the arroyo. Wes helped Maria to mount the black and, leading it, he started for the mouth of the arroyo, where Empty waited. Most of the freed horses, fearful of the smell of blood, followed the black.

"The horses follow us," said Maria.

"Let them," Wes said. "Once they're out in the open, they'll make tracks for wherever they consider home. I expect the horses belongin' to the outlaws will be goin' to Chihuahua or Namiquipa."

"What is the place you say?"

"Chihuahua or Namiquipa," said Wes. "Namiquipa is a village somewhere to the northwest of Chihuahua. From what I have learned, it's where the outlaws corral the horses they have stolen in Mexico, until they can be taken across the border and sold."

"Namiquipa," Maria said. "It is a strange sound. I hear them speak of it."

They reached the place where Wes had concealed

the grulla, and Wes mounted. Maria then directed
him to the bay, which she had ridden.

"Where did you leave your clothes?" Wes asked.

"In the darkness, near the horse," said Maria.

Wes fumbled around until he found the garments,
and handed them to her. He led the bay, while she
followed on the black. The packsaddle was where it
had been left, somewhat disheveled following Maria's search for the Colt.

"What gave you the idea there was a gun in my
pack?" Wes asked.

"I not know," said Maria. "I have only the hope."

"You'd better get back into your clothes," Wes
said.

"*Mañana*," said Maria. "Sleep *desnudo*."

"Suit yourself," Wes said, "but it'll be a mite cold
before morning. I reckon I can spare you a blanket."

Wes picketed all three horses and spread his bedroll near them. There were two extra blankets in his
pack, and he gave them to Maria. Wes removed only
his hat, gunbelt, and boots, placing the colt where he
could get his hand on it in a hurry. Maria rolled
herself in the blankets next to him, and before he
could close his eyes, she spoke.

"I wish to be with you. I am afraid."

"Afraid, hell." Wes snorted. "You just shot and
killed four men."

"Is *diferente*," she replied. "I am alone. I do not
wish to be."

"Maria," said Wes, "you are beside me. That's
close enough."

She laughed, but there was no humor in it. "What

can you do to me that has not already been done this day?"

"I don't aim to do anything," Wes said. "I have a woman waiting for me in El Paso."

"*Muy bonito*," said Maria. "Not ugly and used."

"Yes," Wes admitted, "she is pretty, but so are you. Damn it, stop thinking of yourself as ugly and used."

She said no more, and he thought she had fallen asleep, but she had not. She had only moved closer, and was determined to wriggle under his blankets.

"Maria," said Wes, exasperated, "if I let you under these blankets next to me, will you behave yourself and try to sleep?"

"Per'ap," she replied.

Beside him, she reached for the two blankets he had given her, drawing them across Wes and herself. But she had no intention of sleeping.

"You have not tell me why you hate these outlaws," said Maria.

"All right," Wes said with a sigh. "I'll tell you."

He told her, and until he had finished, she spoke not a word.

"Your *padre* be avenged. I kill them with his *pistola*."

"I wish it was that simple," said Wes, "but I do not know that the outlaws who died tonight are those who killed my father. The thieves and killers who ride with Sandlin are many, and I do not know where they are to be found."

"But you ride to Chihuahua, to Namiquipa."

"Yes," Wes replied. "I aim to gun them down to

the last man. It's the only way I can be sure of killing the men who murdered my father."

"*Madre de Dios*," said Maria, "there be many. Per'ap I help you."

Wes laughed. "You will walk naked into their midst with a loaded gun?"

"There be other way," she said, ignoring his sarcasm. "When you have the look of a *Mejicano*, per'ap they not be so quick to kill you."

"The look of a Mexican? How?"

"I show you *mañana*," she said.

Old Mexico. June 29, 1884

Upon arising, Maria had donned the baggy clothes. Wes started a breakfast fire, and when he had finished slicing bacon into the pan, Maria pointed to the knife.

"*Cuchillo*," she said, holding out her hand.

Having no idea as to what she had in mind, Wes handed her the knife. Without any explanation, she vanished into the woods, returning just before Wes had the bacon and the coffee ready. She returned his knife, and in one pocket of the shirt there was a quantity of reddish bark. Wes said nothing, and after they had eaten, Maria emptied the grounds from the coffeepot. Rinsing it thoroughly, she filled it with cold water and, stirring up the fire, put the pot on to boil. When it had begun to steam, she removed the lid and dropped all the shaved bark into the pot.

"When it's done," Wes asked, "what's that goin' to be?"

"I show you," said Maria.

When she judged it had boiled enough, Maria removed the pot from the fire. Removing the coffeepot's lid, she allowed the mixture to cool. She then fished out the slivers of bark and placed the pot before Wes. The brew looked like strong coffee.

"You're expectin' me to drink that?" Wes asked.

"*Por Dios*," said the girl in disgust, "put the hand into it."

Gingerly, Wes dipped his left hand into the still-warm liquid, and when he withdrew it, the skin was as brown as Maria's own.

"The hand of a *Mejicano*," Maria said triumphantly. "Dip the other."

Wordlessly, Wes did so, with similar results.

"You like?" Maria asked.

"Lord, yes," said Wes. "I can't believe it."

Maria went to his bedroll, removed a blanket, and spread it on the ground.

"The clothes," she said.

"No," said Wes, getting her message.

"The clothes," Maria said firmly, "or you be *Americano. Muerto Americano.*"*

Wes removed his hat, his gunbelt, his boots, and his socks. More slowly, he removed his shirt, and finally his Levis. She pointed to the blanket, and he stretched out on it. Into her cupped hand she poured some of the dark liquid, and starting with his already-stained hands, stained his arms all the way to his shoulders.

"Close the eyes and the mouth," she ordered.

Beginning at the hairline, she worked the dark

*Dead American.

stain into his face, his ears, and the back of his neck, well below where the shirt collar would ride. She then worked the stain carefully into the skin around his mouth and the underside of his nose. His chin and throat got similar treatment, and she darkened his upper torso well below the collarbone. Finally she started with his feet, taking the stain all the way to his knees.

"More?" she asked, eyeing what remained of his still-pale skin.

"No," said Wes hastily. "I'll just have to be careful not to strip at the wrong time or place. How long will this stuff last?"

"A week, per'ap," Maria said. "You look."

He found a place where the water had eddied, and looked at himself.

"Tarnation," he said, "I don't believe it."

"You already have the dark hair of a *Mejicano*," said Maria.

"I'm obliged," Wes said. "What can I do for you in return? Where can I take you?"

"I go with you," she replied. "Remember, the *Mejicano* wears off."

It was a sobering thought, for he could never stain himself as thoroughly as she had, even if he knew the kind of bark shavings from which she had created the stain. He had removed his clothes before this strange woman he had known only a few hours, trusting her after she had stolen his horse, disobeyed him, and had taken one of his Colts. Now he was genuinely surprised to find himself at ease with her, even liking her. Actually, he felt only a little guilt, recalling the faithful girl who had shared his bed for many months in faraway El Paso.* Quickly he freed himself of the guilt. This was the present, and it might be all he had. He might never see El Paso or the girl again. . . .

Namiquipa, Old Mexico. July 1, 1884.

A trio of outlaws pondered the six horses gathered outside the corral.

"I don't know what the hell to make of this," Shatiqua said.

"Me neither," said Boudlin. "They was seven men rode out. Where's Shag's black?"

"Damn it," Dantzler said, "when the boss gits back from Chihuahua, he'll want to know what happened to Shag and the hombres ridin' with him. Boudlin, you and Shatiqua mount up, back-trail these horses, an' git back here pronto. I don't want Kazman climbin' my carcass, an' me with no answers."

Shatiqua and Boudlin dropped the poles of the corral, allowing the six weary horses to enter. They then caught up their own mounts and saddled them. Shaking his head, Dantzler watched his companions mount and ride off toward the east. He had little doubt the seven missing men were dead, and he didn't relish breaking the news to Kazman when the surly leader returned.

Wes and Maria had stopped to rest and water their horses.

*The Autumn of the Gun.

"We ride to Chihuahua or Namiquipa?" Maria asked.

"Chihuahua," said Wes. "Namiquipa may be only a village, controlled by the outlaws. I hope Chihuahua is enough of a town for us to ride in without arousing suspicion. There's a chance, when those horses return riderless to their home corral, some of the gang may back-trail them. Once they find those seven dead men, they could easily begin tracking us. But we'll lose them when we reach Chihuahua."

"Per'ap," Maria said. "How well you speak the *Español?*"

"*Muy bueno, señorita,*" said Wes.

She raised her eyebrows, and he broke into a bawdy song in Spanish.

"*Bueno,*" Maria said.

She began firing questions at him in Spanish, and just as rapidly he fired back every answer in an accent as fluent as her own.

A little more than an hour before sundown, they reached a clear, deep-flowing stream. "We'll stay the night here," said Wes.

"Do you wish me to cook the food?" Maria asked. "It is woman's work."

Wes laughed. "It is the work of anyone who wishes to eat. But go ahead. Long as the fire's out before dark."

He unsaddled the horses and removed the packsaddle from the packhorse. Gratefully, the animals rolled and then made their way to the stream to drink. Wes took the time to divide the gold coins he had taken from the outlaws. Half of them he returned

to the saddlebag, and presented it to Maria. When
she looked at the contents, she caught her breath.

"I do not know there is so much in the world.
Why do you give it to Maria?"

"It's half of what I took from the outlaws," Wes
said. "If something happens to me or we become
separated, you will not be poor."

"Per'ap it be stolen from the poor."

"Maybe," Wes conceded, "but we have no way of
knowing, and no way of returning it to those from
whom it might have been taken."

"Is true," said Maria. *"Gracias."*

After supper, Wes picketed the three horses well
away from the stream.

"Why you take them so far from the water?"

"For the same reason we'll be spreading our blankets there," Wes said. "Indians, outlaws, bears, or
cougars all need water, and the farther we are from
it, the less likely we'll have to fight any of them."

"It still be light," said Maria. "You will go to the
stream with me while I wash?"

"I reckon," Wes said.

She slipped out of her too-big clothes, and Wes
followed her to the creek. She still had the bit of soap
he had given her the day before.

"You do not wash?" she asked as she began soap-
ing herself.

"I reckon I'd better not," said Wes. "It'll wash all
the *Mejicano* off."

She laughed. "I fix more. Come."

The water *did* look tempting, and having stripped
him to apply the stain, he decided she wasn't about
to be shocked now. Quickly he removed his hat, gun-

belt, and boots. He then slipped out of his shirt and
Levi's. Careful to leave his Colt within reach, he got
into the cool water. She immediately flung his face
full of water, and he retaliated. Following a pleasant
time in the water, they crawled out on the grass to
dry.

"We were like the *niño*," said Maria.

"*Sí*," Wes agreed. "Like the child that I never
was."

"Never?" said Maria wonderingly.

"I don't feel like I ever had a childhood," Wes
said. "My mother didn't want me, my kin were
ashamed of me, and I never knew who my father
was until he was dead."

Her eyes met his, and the bleakness and regret in
them stirred her to her soul. She crept close, put her
arms around him, and he responded. Their emotions
spent, they lay there in silence, watching the silver
stars bloom in the deep purple of the sky. Mosqui-
toes began to feed on them, and they arose.

"Come on," Wes said. "Let's get under those blankets before the varmints raise a mob and carry us
off."

Chapter 2

By the time Shatiqua and Boudlin reached the arroyo where their seven companions had died, the stench was unbearable. They stood on the rim and viewed the carnage below, speechless.

"My God," Boudlin said, "I ain't never seen nothin' like this. What you reckon was the cause?"

"Hell, how should I know?" said Shatiqua. "Maybe some hombres bushwhacked 'em and took the horses they was bringin' to Namiquipa."

"That don't make sense," Boudlin replied. "Why didn't they take the horses our bunch was ridin', along with the others?"

"We're gonna be needin' some answers for Kazman when we ride back to Namiquipa," said Shatiqua. "Them horses went somewhere when they left that arroyo. We'd better git down there and do some trackin'."

They studied the tracks of the horses as they had left the arroyo.

"Nobody's drivin' them broncs," Boudlin observed. "They scattered every direction."

"The shootin' could of been done from the rim," said Shatiqua, "but it would of took two gunmen to kill 'em all. They wasn't a bunch of shorthorns."

"That means they'd of left their horses back a ways and snuck up on foot," Boudlin said. "All we got to do is ride in a circle, an' we'll find some tracks."

"Hell, you'd have to be blind not to," said Shatiqua, "with all them horses wanderin' around loose."

"Suit yourself," Boudlin said. "Where I come from, a man reads sign well enough to know a horse with a rider from a horse without."

Boudlin began circling and soon found the place where Maria had left the packhorse. Following the tracks of the packhorse were tracks of a second animal, and finally tracks of a third. There was a profusion of tracks near the creek where Wes and Maria had spent the night.

"Three horses, three riders," Boudlin said triumphantly, "and they rode west. I reckon we'd better follow 'em and see where they went."

"They're headed straight to Chihuahua," said Shatiqua, "where these tracks will be lost among a thousand others. Besides, there'll be rain before we ride ten miles. No trail."

"You aim to tell Kazman that?"

"If I have to," Shatiqua said. "He'll never be the wiser. Besides, it's the truth."

"I'm a mite tired of bein' stuck in Namiquipa, never seein' nobody but that slicked-up varmint Kazman," said Boudlin. "I wonder where Sandlin is."

"I been with this outfit five years," Shatiqua said. "I ain't never seen Sandlin, and I don't want to. I know of at least one hombre that got curious about Sandlin, an' one day he wasn't around no more. Sandlin's bad medicine."

*   *   *

From beyond the mountains to the west, a rising wind swept in thunderheads, and for almost two hours there was a drenching rain. Wes and Maria took shelter beneath some trees, which did little to keep them dry.

"Tarnation," said Wes, "that rain just blew in from nowhere."

"*Sí,*" Maria agreed. "Is no rain in winter, but per'ap every day in summer."

"How long is summer?" Wes asked.

"Start in May, end in October," said Maria. "It rain again *mañana.*"

The clouds were soon swept away, and the sun quickly dried their clothing.

"What you do when you reach Chihuahua?" Maria asked.

"I haven't decided," said Wes. "I'll likely have to spend some time in the saloons, if I'm to learn anything about the Sandlin gang."

"Saloons?"

"Cantinas," Wes said.

"I go with you," said Maria.

"It's no place for a woman," Wes replied.

"with my hair short and a *sombrero*, I no be woman," said Maria.

"If you aim to travel with me," Wes said, "I want you to have clothes that fit. But if I get you a shirt that's the right size, there won't be any doubt about you bein' a woman."

Maria laughed. "I fix that."

On the packhorse was part of a bolt of cotton muslin intended for use as bandages. When they stopped to rest the horses, Maria partially untied the pack and brought out the muslin. Wes watched in silence as she ripped off a two-yard length of it. She folded it lengthwise until it was only a few inches wide. She then removed her shirt and wrapped her upper torso with the muslin. When she tied it securely, her chest was virtually flat. She then donned the shirt, buttoned it, and jiggled herself around. There was no tell-tale movement beneath the shirt, and she grinned triumphantly at Wes.

"Maybe you can become an *hombre*, after all," said Wes.

Chihuahua, Mexico, July 3, 1884

Long before reaching the town, Wes and Maria could see twin towers reaching into the western sky.*

"Is church, per'ap," Maria said. "My *padre* be here once, and he say they *elegante*."

The town was strung out, separated from the railroad and the depot. There were hills to the north and south. The streets were teeming with horse- and mule-drawn hacks, pack-laden mules, and crude two-wheeled carts drawn by donkeys. On the street leading to the railroad depot was an elaborate building that Wes eventually learned was the State Palace. To the rear of it was a *plazuela*, with a fine monument, and beyond that was the building whose twin towers they had seen from a distance. Across the railroad tracks, to the west, were the markets, shops,

*The Church of San Francisco. Begun in 1717, but not completed until 1789.

hotels, cafes, cantinas, and the shoulder-to-shoulder residences of the poor.

"I need *sombrero*," Maria said.

"You also need clothes that fit," said Wes. "Before we attract too much attention, I reckon we'd better find a store. You still aim to become an *hombre*?"

"*Sí*," she replied.

"I reckon I'd better buy myself some Mexican clothes," said Wes. "I feel pretty good behind this *Mejicano* stain of yours. I don't have *Mejicano* eyes, but changin' out of Texas duds might help."

They reached what appeared to be a mercantile, and it was somewhat isolated, likely because there was penned livestock. There was a pen of sheep, one of goats, and a third of pigs. A pair of mules looked over the rails of a makeshift corral. There were no horses, mules, wagons, or carts in sight, and the place looked deserted.

"This is an ideal place," Wes said. "Nobody else around. With any luck, maybe we can get in there an' out without bein' seen by anybody but the storekeeper."

They looped the reins of their horses around the hitching rail. Empty lay down next to Maria's black. While the dog hadn't become friendly to Maria, he had accepted her. With Maria leading, they entered the store. The old Mexican storekeeper was careful not to appear too curious. He allowed them to choose their purchases. Maria selected high-heeled riding boots, a loose-fitting cotton shirt, matching cotton trousers with a sash, and a wide-brimmed straw *sombrero*. Wes chose straw-colored trousers and matching shirt, and finally a wide-brimmed straw *sombrero*. He would keep his Texas boots. Maria paid for her purchases and Wes paid for his without a word being spoken. Quickly the storekeeper wrapped and string-tied everything in brown paper except the *sombreros.* Leaving the store, they mounted and rode in search of a lodging house or hotel. The lodging house they eventually chose was between the railroad and the street that seemed to house only cantinas, cafes, and bawdy houses.

"I speak," Maria said as they prepared to enter the lodging house.

The old Mexican woman wore a shawl that obscured everything except her wrinkled face. She looked at Maria, then at Wes, finally fixing her eyes on Empty, who eyed her with suspicion. She finally pointed to Empty.

"*Uno, dos, tres,*" she said.

Maria nodded, paying what she asked. They were led down the hall and shown to a room. There was no key. When they were alone in the room, Maria laughed.

"No *perro,*" she said, pointing to Empty. "He *hombre.*"

"I noticed that," said Wes. "If they serve grub here, he eats at the table with us. I reckon we'd better get into our *Mejicano* garb and find a place to stable the horses." Maria's new clothing was more in line with what a Mexican would wear. Her boots were simple, the shirt and trousers homespun.

Wes removed his hat, gunbelt, and boots. He then stepped out of his familiar Levi's and denim shirt, eyeing with some distaste the cheap Mexican clothing. It was loose-woven, a light tan in color, and appeared to be only a cut or two above burlap. The shirt fit well enough, and although he missed his belt, the trousers were adequate. The legs were long enough to conceal his Texas boots. The ungainly straw *sombrero* was the worst.

"This damn thing's as big as a wagon wheel," Wes complained.

Maria laughed. "Is *Mejicano*."

Wes gathered up his Texas clothing, including his hat. He wrapped it carefully in the brown paper in which the store had wrapped his Mexican garb. Maria brought him the too-big Levi's and denim shirt she had worn, and he included them in the package.

"This goes on the packhorse," he said. "Now we must find a stable."

"I ask," said Maria.

Dressed in Mexican clothing, a Colt belted around her lean hips, Wes had to admit the girl might pass as a young Mexican man. While he felt better about his own chances, he still was handicapped with blue eyes. Maria had gone in search of the old Mexican woman from whom they had rented the room, and when she returned, she knew of a stable where they might put up their horses. Leaving the packsaddle in the rented room, they then led their horses to a dilapidated livery barn a hundred yards down the rutted street. This was a poor section of town, and they saw nobody. Wes had tipped the cumbersome *sombrero* down over his eyes to lessen the possibility of his being recognized as an American.

"I reckon there's no point in goin' back to that room," Wes said. "Let's take a look at the town and maybe get some grub."

Empty trotted along behind them, suspicious of this strange place. Once they reached the narrow streets lined with cafes and cantinas, Wes began to breathe a little easier, for he and Maria were dressed in the same simple fashion as were the Mexicans. Patient mules drew two-wheeled carts along cobblestone streets. Within the carts were pigs and various fowl, while young boys herded small bunches of sheep and goats. Except for an occasional beggar, all the men seemed bound for some destination. Two women stood outside what was obviously a bordello. But one thing bothered Wes. He and Maria were armed, and the belted Colts immediately set them apart. While the Mexicans avoided them, three men on the other side of the narrow street did not. Two were Anglo, while one was a half-breed, and all were dressed like the border outlaws who had gunned down Nathan Stone back in El Paso. Each wore a tied-down revolver, and they did nothing to conceal their obvious interest in the pair of *Mejicanos* who were similarly armed. The 'breed said something, and his companions laughed.

"Don't look now," said Wes, "but we've been discovered. We might have gotten by in Mexican clothes, but our guns are givin' us away."

"What must we do?" Maria asked.

"Into that cantina," said Wes. "Maybe we can work our way out the back door."

But even as they entered the cantina, Wes turned his head just enough to see the trio crossing the street. The cantina was virtually deserted except for the little man behind the bar. Pointing to a keg on tap, Wes held up two fingers, and almost immediately before him were two glasses of vile-looking brew. There was the sound of boots on the wooden floor, as the three men entered the cantina. With his left hand, Wes took a gold coin from his pocket and dropped it on the bar.

"*Madre de Dios*," said the Mexican bartender.

He held up both hands as though to push Wes away, his eyes on the gold coin that lay on the bar. It glinted in the faint light from a window, and Wes learned to his horror that it wasn't a coin, but a coin-sized gold medallion. There was the unmistakable likeness of a dragon on the face of it. There was a sharp intake of breath as the significance of it struck Maria. She dropped behind a table as a slug ripped into the bar where she had been standing. Wes hit the floor, rolling to his left, his Colt blazing. Slugs crashed into the bar as the trio began gunning for Wes, but his first shot was true. One of the outlaws was hit in the chest, and when Maria fired from beneath the table, her shot killed another of the trio. Wes cut down on the 'breed, and when the slug tore into his upper torso, he dropped his weapon and bolted out the door.

"Come on," Wes gritted.

He caught Maria's hand and they ran down a narrow corridor to the living quarters behind the cantina. There had to be a back door! When they found it—despite their need for haste—Wes eased the door open and peered out. He was looking into a narrow alley, at the backs of other cantinas and shops. There were piles of refuse, empty bottles, and a few discarded tables and chairs with missing legs. From the corner of his eye, Wes caught some movement, but it was Empty, coming on the run.

"Whatever passes for the law in this town will be here *muy pronto*," Wes said. "Let's get out while we can."

They ran down the alley parallel to the street from which they'd entered the cantina, Wes hoping they might reach the lodging house before there was any organized pursuit. A door suddenly opened, revealing the curious face of a Mexican. But it disappeared just as suddenly when Wes drew his Colt. Aware of the danger, Empty ran ahead of them. When they reached the next cross-street, it appeared they had escaped the congested area of the shops and cantinas. Empty had turned back to the south, the direction from which they had entered the town, and the streets seemed deserted.

"*Sensato perro,*" Maria said.

"He's smarter than I am," said Wes. "When the shootin' started up front, he headed for the back door. Now he figures we're returning to the horses, and that's where he'll be takin' us."

"Per'ap we hide in the lodging house," Maria said.

"I'm hopin' you can," said Wes, "while I lead them on a wild goose chase. I'll take all three horses, and work my way back to the lodging house after dark. If they mount heavy pursuit, I don't want them gunning you down along with me."

"I wish to go with you," Maria said. "Per'ap I never see you again."

"We can't risk it," said Wes. "That damn coin I dropped in the cantina was our undoing."

"The image of a strange beast," Maria said.

"A dragon," said Wes. "It's their symbol, and since we're not part of the gang, they won't have to think long and hard to figure how and where we got it. By now they know about the seven dead outlaws in the arroyo."

Empty led them back to the livery barn by a series of twists and turns.

"Now," Wes said, "I want you to go back to the lodging house and stay there until I return for you. Keep the room dark. When they come looking for us, I want them to find tracks of three horses."

She didn't want to go, and Wes watched until she entered the house. He then stepped cautiously into the barn, but saw no one. Listening, he heard a deep snore. In a stall, on a pile of hay, he found the old hostler. Dead drunk, an empty bottle lay beside him, and that suited Wes. He wouldn't be able to tell the outlaws that Wes had taken the three horses and had ridden away alone. On an upturned wooden crate there was a lantern, and beside it Wes left a coin, careful that it was genuine. If each of the seven dead outlaws had been in possession of one of the devilish medallions, that meant there were at least six more of the golden emblems among the coins Wes had shared with Maria. Quickly, Wes saddled his grulla and Maria's black. The bay still resisted the packsaddle, but Wes calmed him enough to accept his burden. With the bay and the black on lead ropes, Wes rode south. He chose a trail across open ground, leaving abundant tracks for the outlaws to follow. Time enough to lose them once he had led them away from Maria. Once away from the town and into a concealing forest, Wes turned north, seeking the mountains he had seen earlier. He circled the town, always looking back, but there was no pursuit. That bothered him, along with the growing realization he could—and should—have brought Maria with him. Waiting for darkness, he sorted through the gold coins he had taken from the dead outlaws until he found four of the dragon's head medallions. Curious, he turned one over and found a number three. Quickly he looked at the others, and they were identical. He had no doubt the dragon's head symbolized the murderous outlaws, but what of the number—a three—on the opposite side? Uneasily, he waited until the shadows fell before making his way to the distant town. While he had left an obvious trail, there had been no pursuit. That, with Maria on his mind, was enough to arouse a sense of foreboding. Keeping to the shadows, Empty trotting alongside, he rode to the back of the lodging house. There he left the three horses, Empty remaining with them. The back door of the rambling old house wasn't even bolted, and he caught his breath when he stepped into the hall. The place was dark except for a wedge of light from beneath a single door—the door to the room where Maria was to be waiting. And Maria was there. What was left of her. On a nightstand beside the bed a lamp burned. Maria had been stripped and spread-eagled on the bed, her body a bloody mass of knife wounds. They had tortured her before finally slitting her throat. Wide open, her sightless eyes begged in mute appeal for mercy that had been denied. Her mouth hung open, her lips frozen in a silent scream of pain and terror. Wes ground his teeth in fury, cursing himself for a fool. On the nightstand—if he needed proof—was one of the gold medallions with the dragon's head. The bastards *wanted* him to know they had murdered Maria, and they hadn't followed him because they expected him to return. He knew then what he should have suspected. He had walked into a deadly trap! Empty began barking furiously, all the assurance he needed that the outlaws were waiting for him to break for his horses. Quickly he blew out the lamp. Even as he approached the window, it shattered in a tinkling crash. Lead slammed into the wall and sang off the bed's brass frame. There was but one way out, and that was through the door and into the hall. The old house had a second floor, and Wes remembered the stairway in the hall. On hands and knees he crept through the door, only to have the hall floor creak. Immediately, from the end of the hall, there was the roar from three different weapons. Lead whipping over his head, Wes fired three times at muzzle flashes. There were groans of pain, gaining him a few seconds to get to the stairs. They creaked badly, but his pursuers didn't know he had left the hall, and there was more shooting. Reaching an upper hall, Wes made his way toward the rear of the house. He hoped there might be a door leading to an upper balcony, but there was neither. Quickly he felt his way along the wall, searching for a door. Finding one, he stepped into a room where there was a window. But when he attempted to open it, the casing wouldn't budge. It seemed to be nailed shut. In the dim light from the window, he could see a bed, and beside it, a nightstand. Seizing the nightstand by two of its legs, he used it to smash the window, frame and all. There

were curtains, and the sudden draft sucked the loose
ends of them out the window. The room being at the
very rear of the house, the ceiling had begun to slope
downward with the contour of the roof. The window
was close enough for Wes, standing on the sill, to
grasp the edge of the tiled roof. But the breaking
glass had attracted the attention of the outlaws, and
as Wes scrambled for the roof, lead began ripping
into the side of the house.

"The bastard's on the roof!" one of the outlaws
shouted.

But Wes reached the roof, and the shouting below
had the desired effect. Men joined their comrades
below the smashed window. By the time Wes had
crept to the very end of the gabled roof, he was able
to step down to the roof that sheltered a back porch.
Empty was still barking from a distance, which told
Wes one or more of the outlaws had stayed with the
horses. The hound either saw or sensed Wes at the
roof's edge and came surging in, growling viciously.
Startled, the outlaw who had remained with the
horses began firing, but only got off one shot. Colt
in hand, Wes came down astraddle him, clubbing
him unconscious. In an instant, Wes was in the saddle, kicking the grulla into a gallop. His Colt in his
right hand, he seized the bay's lead rope in his left.
The black nickered, but with Maria gone, there was
no need for it. The outlaws rounded the corner of
the house and began firing. Wes fired only twice, for
he hadn't had time to reload and his Colt was empty.
He holstered the weapon and rode for his life.

*　　*　　*

"Damn it," said Wooten, chief of the outlaws, "he's gone."

"That ain't the worst of it," said one of his companions. "Klady, Snell, an' Hutchinson is dead, an' Tasby's hard hit."

"Anybody else hurt?" Wooten asked.

The Indian gunman, El Lobo, laughed.

"What's so damned funny?" Wooten demanded.

"Do not forget Zouks and Wroe, who die in the cantina," said El Lobo. "One of them by the hand of a *Mejicano* squaw."

"Kazman will have to be told of this," Wooten said. "He'll want to know just how in hell this slippery varmint managed to escape from a house and gun down three men, while ten of you failed to get a slug in him."

"Eleven of us," said one of the outlaws angrily. "You was here with us."

"El Lobo," Wooten said, "I want you on this hombre's trail at first light. Choose who you want ridin' with you."

"*Sí,*" said El Lobo. "I take Wanz, Votaw, Selmer, Eagan, Coe, and Mull."

"Damn," Votaw said, "why you takin' all of us?"

Again El Lobo laughed. "*Sencillio.* While this *muy bueno hombre* is killing all of you, per'ap I have the chance to kill *him.*"

"Wooten," said Eagan, "you aim to send *seven* men after one slippery gun-thrower?"

"If that's how many El Lobo needs," Wooten said. "He's *segundo* to this manhunt."

"I ain't takin' orders from no damn half-breed Indian," Selmer said. "By God, he was here tonight, an' I didn't see him firin' them twin cannons of his."

"I do not fire at shadows," said El Lobo contemptuously. "You ride with me, *gringo*, you do as I tell you."

"And if I don't?" Selmer said.

"I kill you," said El Lobo softly.

"Wooten," Coe said, "I'm with Selmer. I ain't ridin' with this cold-blooded bastard."

It was Wooten's turn to laugh. "It's up to you, El Lobo. Change his mind."

Like greased lightning, the Indian seized the front of Coe's shirt, standing him on tiptoe. Like magic, the muzzle of his right-hand Colt was under the frightened Coe's chin.

"Señor," El Lobo hissed, "you come with me *mañana*, or you die tonight."

"I . . . I'll go," said Coe.

Without another word, the Indian released Coe. He then faced Selmer, the starlight glinting off the Colt in his hand.

"I ain't likin' it," Selmer said sullenly, "but I'll go."

"That's settled, then," said Wooten, "Unless the rest of you got complaints. Just take 'em up with El Lobo."

None of the other outlaws said anything, but when they mounted their horses, Coe rode alongside Selmer, well behind El Lobo.

"The half-breed bastard," Coe hissed. "It'll likely be a long trail. That varmint might just damn well stop a slug that don't come from the hombre we're gunnin' for."

"Just what I'm thinkin'," said Selmer. "We got no

Mejicanos in our bunch, so why we got to stomach a mouthy half-breed Injun?''

Wes reined up in the hills north of town and satisfied himself there was no pursuit. He expected none until the dawn, and then he had no doubt they would be coming after him. If he continued to run, his vow of vengeance meant nothing, and his riding into Mexico would have been in vain. He must attack, forcing them to come for him, and when they did, show them no mercy.

"Empty," he said, "my time as a *Mejicano* is done."

From his pack he took the cowboy clothes and the flat-crowned Stetson he had placed there only hours ago. He thought of poor dead Maria and how thoroughly she had applied the stain that would soon be gone. He removed the *sombrero*, his gunbelt, and his boots. He then discarded the poorly woven Mexican clothing. Again wearing his own Stetson, his Levi's, and denim shirt, he felt better. He stomped his feet back into his boots, and as he was about to buckle his gunbelt, he thought of something. From the packsaddle, he took the *buscadera* rig—a gunbelt with twin holsters—that had belonged to Nathan Stone. He then took from the pack Nathan's second Colt, the one Maria had used to gun down four of the Sandlin gang. With a kind of reverence, He belted Nathan's rig around his own lean middle and placed one of the well-used colts in each of the holsters. Empty watched the procedure as though thoroughly familiar with it, perking up his ears when Wes spoke to him as Nathan Stone so often had.

"Old son, I hope I can become just half the man he was."

Already he had trained himself to draw and fire with either hand, and with the gunbelt riding low on his hips, he thonged down the holsters. He then practiced drawing, first one Colt and then the other, border-shifting them hand to hand. Finally, exhausted, he lay his head on his saddle and looked at the twinkling stars, silver pools in their faraway meadow of velvet. He thought of Nathan, of Maria, of the task that lay ahead. He even recalled the long ago days at the orphanage in St. Louis, and felt more alone than at any other time in his life. . . .

Chihuahua, Mexico. July 5, 1884

"Saddle up and ride," Wooten ordered, "and don't come back until you've caught up to the varmint that got away from us last night. I want his head in a sack."

Wanz, Votaw, Selmer, Eagan, Coe, and Mull mounted their horses. El Lobo was the last to mount, and he eyed his companions with obvious amusement. He led out, the others following. Selmer and Coe exchanged looks and then fixed their hate-filled eyes on the back of El Lobo.

Chapter 3

Even before it was light enough for his pursuers to take the trail, Wes had saddled the grulla, loaded the packhorse, and was on the move. He must conceal the packsaddle, for if his plans went awry and he was forced to ride for his life, the last thing he needed was a loaded packhorse on a lead rope. Reaching a small stream, he followed it into an arroyo with a huge promontory of stone at the far end. Water cascaded down the face of the rock, and Wes scrambled to the top. Looking down, he found the stone face behind the falling water wasn't solid, but concave. Taking food enough for himself and Empty, Wes wrestled the heavy packsaddle up the slope, concealing it behind the waterfall. Most of the surface over which he had climbed was stone, so he left no tracks. Returning to the pool at the bottom, he quickly built a small fire. There was no time for coffee, and some hastily broiled bacon became his and Empty's breakfast. If the outlaws got that far, they would know only that he had cooked a meal and watered his horses. But he doubled back the way he had come, parallel to his earlier trail. Being one against many, he would resort to an ambush, and he began looking for a likely place. His was a hit-and-run situation, for he couldn't remain in one position long enough for them to flank or surround him. While he would be on the run, his pursuers would be forced into a defensive role, for they had to contend with the constant threat of yet another ambush. In the foothills, he was unable to see the town, but a rising cloud of dust told him pursuit had begun.

"Empty," said Wes, "they'll be expectin' an ambush, so we'll have to choose the least likely place, if we're to take 'em by surprise."

Wes concealed both horses in a thicket, distant enough so they wouldn't nicker and give away his position. He then made his way back to a rise up which he expected his pursuers to ride, for there was little cover. There was only a wind-blown tree, and most of it had rotted away. Behind what remained, Wes bellied down with his Winchester where he could see down the long slope. Without an order, Empty had remained with the horses, for he hadn't forgotten similar situations he had faced with Nathan Stone. Wes could see the seven riders coming long before they were within rifle range. They were strung out in a V formation and there was something different about the point rider. While he didn't ride quite like an American, neither did he seem Mexican. Whoever he was, he was the enemy, and Wes had the man in his sights. But the very second he fired, he knew he had missed, for a strange thing had happened. Within the ranks of the outlaws, revolvers roared, and the lead rider pitched forward out of the saddle. Wes didn't question his good fortune, but began firing at the remaining outlaws. He quickly emptied three saddles, and while there was virtually no cover, the remaining three men piled off with their rifles. But Wes had a surprise for them. Slugs from his Winchester began kicking up dust beneath the hooves of the riderless horses, and they lit out in a fast gallop down the back trail. There was little doubt the spooked horses wouldn't stop short of their home corral. His adversaries reduced to three and afoot, Wes used the deadly Winchester to put the fear of God into them. Slugs flung dirt and rock into their faces, and they scrambled down the slope, intent on escaping with their lives. Wes could have gunned them down to the last man, but there was more to be gained by allowing them to stumble back to town afoot. It would do much to create an aura of mystery around the elusive *gringo* who killed like a merciless devil. When the shooting was over, Empty trotted out of the brush.

"I reckon we'd better have a look at the dead hombres," Wes said, "but it's more than I can expect that some of 'em would be the murderin' varmints from El Paso."

Warily, Wes approached the fallen men. The rider who had been gunned down by his companions lay facedown. While he had been hit twice in the back, the wounds were high up, and he might be playing possum.

"You're hard hit, *amigo*," Wes said. "Can you speak?"

There was no response. The man lay unmoving. Wes tried again.

"I'll help you if I can, but only if you do not resist."

"I . . . not resist," said El Lobo.

Wes rolled him over, and the front of his shirt was bloody. The slugs had passed on through, and if they hadn't nicked a lung, he had a chance.

"You need some doctorin'," Wes said. "I have medicine, bandages, and whiskey in my pack. I'm going for the horses."

While Wes had some misgivings about helping the wounded outlaw, the circumstances surrounding the shooting intrigued him. Why had the man's companions shot him in the back? He wasn't dark enough to be Mexican, and his facial features and eyes were those of an Indian. When Wes returned leading the horses, El Lobo had drawn his revolvers.

"Make up your mind," said Wes. "If you're just waitin' for a chance to kill me, then I'll ride on and leave you here to die. You know I didn't shoot you. Your *companeros* were responsible for that."

Slowly, raising his hands as high as he could, El Lobo released the revolvers, allowing them to fall to the ground. Wes took the weapons.

"I'm takin' you where there's water," Wes said. "I'll help you mount."

But the bay shied at the smell of blood, and by the time Wes had calmed the horse, El Lobo's eyes were closed. When Wes lifted him, he was a dead weight, and getting him belly-down across the bay horse was a fight. Wes was forced to ride alongside the bay, one hand gripping the wounded man's belt, so he wouldn't slide off. While they were only a few miles from the stream where the packsaddle was cached, it seemed much farther, for their progress was slow. Empty ran on ahead, while Wes kept a constant watch on his back trail. When they eventually reached the stream, Wes looked at the sun, estimating the time. It had been at least three hours since the gunfight, probably time enough for the trio of outlaws to reach town afoot. If they immediately mounted another force and came after him, his act of mercy toward this wounded outlaw could cost him his life.

"I don't like the odds, Empty," said Wes, "but I'll finish what I've started."

He built his fire small, put on a pot of water to boil, and went after the medicine and bandages in his pack. Finally, he removed El Lobo's shirt. The man's breathing was harsh and ragged. When the water began to boil, Wes cleansed the wounds front and back. He then folded lengths of cotton muslin into large square pads. One of them he placed over the wounds in the back, and the other over the exit wounds, just below the collarbone. He then drenched the pads with disinfectant. Suddenly the wounded man spoke.

"I come to kill you. Why you do this?"

"I'm not sure," said Wes. "I was about to drop you when your *companeros* shot you from behind. I reckoned if that bunch of coyotes hated you that much, there might be some good in you."

El Lobo's laugh was bitter. "There is none, *señor*. I am as vile as they."

"The *señorita*," Wes said. "She was tortured with a *cuchillo* and then murdered. Tell me the name of the bastard responsible for that."

"Wooten," said El Lobo. "He *segundo* in Chihuahua."

"Then I won't be leavin' Chihuahua until I settle

with him," Wes replied. "You'll need some time to heal from your wounds. Do you know of a place we can hole up where that bunch can't find us?"

"*Sí.* There are caves in the mountains to the north. El Lobo find. Rain come soon."

It was true, just as Maria had predicted, for the sky had already begun to cloud over.

"We'd better ride, then," said Wes, "because we'll have to take it slow. We'll be riding double, so the bay can carry the packsaddle. With any luck, the rain will wash out our tracks. But you'll have to guide me, because I don't know this country."

"*Sí.* El Lobo know. El Lobo tough, lak hell."

Wes noted with some relief that El Lobo was thinner, more wiry than he had at first appeared, so the grulla could bear the extra weight if they took their time. A little more than an hour into their journey, the rain came. Well before it ended, they had reached the cave El Lobo had in mind. It was roomy enough for the horses, there was water, and the entrance was concealed to the extent that it was lost to those who didn't know that it was there. Previous visitors had left a supply of dry firewood.

"*Indios* come here," El Lobo said.

"Thanks to the rain," said Wes, "we should be safe enough here."

A breath of cool air from the interior of the cave was proof enough of an escape for the smoke from a fire.

"I am Wes Stone," Wes said, by way of introduction. "Who are you?"

"I am El Lobo," said the wounded man.

"Nothing more?"

"Wolf, to my *amigos*. When I have any."

"I am surprised to find you riding with a band of outlaws and killers," said Wes. "I have the feeling you're a better man than that."

"What would you *have* me do?" El Lobo snarled. "My father is a Spaniard who return to his homeland on one of the great ships. My mother is an *Indio* who sell me into slavery when I am but ten summers old. I muck stables for a piece of bread and a pile of straw upon which to sleep. I am without a country."

His voice was cold, flat, emotionless. Startled by the manner in which the man's life paralleled his own, Wes said nothing. He took a pair of extra blankets from the packsaddle and passed them to El Lobo. He then set about building a fire, seeking the hot coffee he had been denied earlier in the day. By the time the coffee was ready, El Lobo slept. Wes crept to the secluded mouth of the cave and found the rain had ceased and the sun was no more than two hours high. In what was left of the day, there was little he could do. Better that he remain with the wounded man, for he would almost surely have a fever before the night was done. He would need one of the two quarts of whiskey Wes and brought along for just such a purpose.

Selmer, Mull, and Coe were limping toward town when the rain started.

"Damn it," Mull said, "if the two of you hadn't cut down on El Lobo, that varmint on the hill wouldn't of took us by surprise. I aim to see that Wooten hears about it."

"He won't hear about it from you," said Selmer.

Drawing his revolver, he shot the surprised Mull in the head.

Selmer and Coe walked on through the driving rain, and it was Coe who finally spoke.

"Five men dead, and that gun-throwin' bastard didn't get a scratch. It'll be almighty hard, gittin' Wooten to swallow that."

"He's got no choice," said Selmer, "an' neither have we. This damn *pistolero*'s got to be thought of as nine feet tall, a yard wide, an' hell on little red wheels with a gun."

"*El Diablo*, with horns, hooves, an' a spike tail," Coe said.

"That, an' more," said Selmer. "There was somethin' unnatural about him escapin' all of us at that lodgin' house last night. We got to build on that, else Wooten will have the both of us hung by the heels over a slow fire."

Namiquipa, Mexico. July 6, 1884

Jake Kazman was furious. For a long moment, he glared at Dantzler, Shatiqua, and Boudlin in tight-lipped silence. When he spoke again, he turned away from Dantzler, one of his lieutenants, and directed his wrath at Shatiqua and Boudlin.

"We're goin' over this one more time, by God. You're tellin' me you found seven men dead, with not a clue as to who gunned them down or why?"

"Honest to God," said Boudlin. "Nobody took the horses. We follered the tracks, but they was scattered seven ways from Sunday. Hell, they was all shod, and some of 'em was headed for Chihuahua."

"Hell's bells," Kazman roared, "that was likely the tracks of the killers. The two of you combined didn't have sense enough to trail them?"

"I've had enough of you rakin' my carcass," Shatiqua said. "Them hombres had been dead long enough for buzzards an' coyotes to nearly pick 'em clean. Whoever gunned 'em down had a three-day start. What good would it of done to foller 'em, knowin' we'd lose the trail? Hell, two hours after we found 'em, it was rainin' like pourin' it out of a boot."

"There's truth in what he's sayin', Jake," said Dantzler. "If the hombres that done the killings an' scattered the horses rode on to Chihuahua, maybe Wooten will have word of them."

It was something to consider, and Kazman turned thoughtful. When he spoke again, his anger had subsided.

"Even if Wooten's heard nothing, he should be told about the killings and the missing horses. There's somethin' more to this than meets the eye. I'll ride to Chihuahua and talk to Wooten."

"I reckon it'd be a smart move," Dantzler said. "It's almost like vengeance killings."

Jake Kazman said nothing more. An hour later, he saddled a horse and rode south.

As the night wore on, El Lobo became feverish. He mumbled in Spanish and reached for the revolvers that weren't there. Time after time, Wes dosed the wounded outlaw with whiskey. He had removed El Lobo's gunbelt and had returned the twin revolvers to their holsters. Curious, he examined the weapons.

They were matched .44-caliber Colts, with hair-
triggers, formidable weapons in the hands of a man
adept in their use. When his wounds had healed,
what would El Lobo choose to do about the men
who had shot him in the back?

"I sleep," El Lobo said, when he awakened the
next afternoon.

"Since yesterday afternoon," said Wes. "You've
been wrasslin' with a fever all night, and I've been
dosin' you with whiskey. You're on the mend."

"Head hurt lak hell," El Lobo said.

Wes laughed. "The whiskey. Sometimes the hang-
over's more painful than bein' shot. I have a pot of
hot coffee and grub when you're ready."

"Coffee," said El Lobo. "Much coffee."

He drank what remained of the coffee, and Wes
put the pot on the fire to boil more. Empty lay near
the cave's entrance, his eyes on El Lobo. Wes began
slicing bacon into a pan, knowing the wounded man
would be hungry once the whiskey had worn off. El
Lobo ate the food, downing the second pot of coffee
along with it. With only a nod to Wes, he then lay
down and slept another four hours. When he awakened, he struggled to a sitting position, getting his
back against the stone wall of the cave. When he
spoke, it wasn't a question, but a statement of fact.

"You ride the death trail, *señor.*"

"I have my reasons," said Wes. "So do you."

"*Sí,*" El Lobo agreed. "Selmer and Coe."

"And then?"

"I do not know, *señor,*" said El Lobo. "These hombres shoot me."

"You aim to make buzzard bait of them," Wes

said, "and I don't blame you. But when you do, the rest of the gang will be after your head, like they're after mine."

"Per'ap," said El Lobo, "and like you, I will not disappoint them. Have I the right to know why you wish to kill them?"

"I reckon," Wes replied. "It's no secret. Fact is, I want the varmints to know why I aim to gun them down to the last man. You know of the murder of Maria in Chihuahua, but there's more. Just a hell of a lot more."

Wes spoke for an hour, telling of the murder of his father, Nathan Stone, and of his vow to wipe out the Sandlin gang.*

"*Madre de Dios*," El Lobo said. "*El muerte* trail be your duty, a blood debt that must be paid. But you do not know the *hombres* you seek?"

"No," Wes said. "That's why I aim to wipe out the whole bunch, if I have to shoot my way from one end of Mexico to the other."

"Per'ap we ride the same trail, *señor.*"

"I must kill many," said Wes, "while you seek only two."

El Lobo laughed. "They kill me just as dead for shooting Selmer and Coe as they kill you for shooting many. *Comprende?*"

"I couldn't agree more," Wes said, "but you might be able to gun down Coe and Selmer without all the others comin' after you. That won't be the case if you ride with me."

"These *hombres*—this gang—are in all of Mexico,

*The Autumn of the Gun.

señor. He who is not one of them is against them. To remain in Mexico is to die."

"I don't aim to remain in Mexico any longer than it takes to smash this gang," said Wes, "and neither should you. We can then cross the border into the United States."

"I think there is no place for El Lobo in these United States. I not be welcome."

"I can make you welcome," Wes said. "Do you know of the Texas Rangers?"

"*Sí*," said El Lobo. "Since the war, many years ago, they are known as *los Tejanos Diablos*."*

"I was once one of them," Wes said, "and while they can do nothing to help me, they know of my reasons for being in Mexico. I'll make you a promise. Help me smash this band of outlaws, and you'll be welcome in the United States for as long as you wish to stay."

"It is a temptation, *señor*, to one who has no country of his own."

"You'll have a country," Wes said, "if we get out of here alive. What do you know of Sandlin, the leader of the gang?"

"Nothing," said El Lobo. "I hear the name, but nothing more. I join them when I am but seventeen summers. That be three summers past."

"That makes you two years older than me," Wes said. "How much do you know about the Sandlin gang?"

"There be many," said El Lobo. "Per'ap hundreds. They be in Hermosillo, Nogales, Guaymas, Santa

*The Texas Devils.

Rosalia, Namiquipa, Chihuahua, and many villages to the south which I do not know. There be many *segundos*. In Chihuahua is Wooten, in Namiquipa is Kazman. Of the many others, I do not know."

"We'll have to root the varmints out as we come to them," Wes said. "I reckon you'll know where to find Wooten and his bunch in Chihuahua?"

"*Sí*," said El Lobo. "You shoot two in the cantina, and four when you escape the lodging house."

"And three more out of the bunch that gunned you down," Wes said. "As far as you know, there's only the three who escaped my ambush and Wooten himself in Chihuahua."

"*Sí*," said El Lobo.

"*Bueno*," said Wes. "When you're able to ride, we'll start with them."

Chihuahua, Mexico. July 7, 1884

Jake Kazman listened incredulously as Wooten told him of the strange events of the past two days.

"Two men in the cantina," Kazman said.

"Three," said Wooten gloomily. "The 'breed was hit high up, but it nicked a lung."

"Four men that night, and four the next morning," Kazman said. "That's eleven dead men, in two days. There'll be hell to pay when word reaches Nogales."

"Well, by God," Wooten said angrily, "if you go takin' word to Nogales, don't forget to tell 'em about you losin' seven men an' a herd of horses."

"I'm in no hurry to get word to Nogales," said Kazman soothingly. "If all this is tied together somehow, it could be a vendetta, a conspiracy."

"Meanin' what?"

"Somebody's got a powerful mad on," said Kazman. "He gunned down seven men and then let the horses drift, an' that says he's after us. Maybe all of us. When word of this gets around, this hombre's got to look almighty tall, an' bulletproof."

"Or we'll look like damn fools," Wooten said.

"Now you're gettin' the drift," said Kazman. "Any trouble with the Mex law here over the shooting?"

"No," Wooten replied, "but the old Mex woman at the lodgin' house raised hell. I had to pay for the sheets an' for cleanin' up the room where the woman was killed."

"Keep it quiet about the woman bein' killed," said Kazman. "Don't even mention there *was* a woman involved. Two hombres gunned down three of your men in a cantina. From there, they escaped, and in a gunfight later that night, four more men were killed, without killing or capturing the hombres. But your story gets a mite thin when you send seven men after the killers and only two return."

"Damn it," Wooten snarled, "that's how it was. How do you aim to account for them horses that never made it to the border?"

"I'll be forced to tell the truth," said Kazman. "My boys was bushwhacked and their horses stole. One of Mexico's daily cloudbursts washed out the trail of the thieves doin' the killin'."

"The truth, hell," Wooten said bitterly. "You don't *know* the pair that rode in here an' give *me* hell wasn't the killers who cut down your men and scattered your horses."

"I don't know that they *was*, either," said Kazman.

"I'm tellin' you, I won't tell any more of this than I'm forced to. If this *is* some bastard set on bustin' up the gang, then he's got his work cut out for him. Let him make big tracks in Hermosillo or Guaymas, and his hell-raisin' here won't be so hard to believe."

Kazman and Wooten parted company, neither satisfied, both uncertain as to their next move.

Day after day, in the seclusion of the cave, El Lobo had practiced with the twin Colts, working the stiffness from his arms and shoulders. A week after he had been shot, he pronounced himself ready to ride.

"I cannot stand another hour in this cave, *señor*," El Lobo said.

"Damn it," said Wes, "stop callin' me *that*. It makes me feel like I'm your daddy. My name is Wes."

"*Sí*, Señor Wes," El Lobo said agreeably. "You may call me Wolf."

"*Sí*, Señor Wolf," said Wes.

For the first time since their meeting, they had occasion to laugh, and they did so. It would become a standing joke between them as they rode the *muerto* trails.

Chihuahua, Mexico. July 13, 1884

Selmer, Coe, and Wooten had spent yet another day seeking to add men to their diminished ranks, without results.

"It's no damn use," Selmer said. "We got to go to Nogales or Juarez for gunmen with sand enough to throw in with us."

"Yeah," said Coe. "We've had too many dead men. Even the Mexes that can use a gun are shyin' away from us. They're callin' this mystery gunman El Diablo."

"I'd rather face El Diablo than take the news of these killings to Nogales or Juarez," Wooten said gloomily. "They'll be lookin' to us for more horses to be sold in Texas, an' we don't have men for the job."

Near dusk, the trio returned to their lodging house. El Lobo watched them enter, and as quietly as he had arrived, he departed, a grim look of satisfaction on his rugged face.

"There's only three of them, then," Wes said when El Lobo had returned.

"I see no more," said El Lobo. "Wooten, Selmer, and Coe."

"I reckon you want Selmer and Coe," Wes said.

"*Sí*," El Lobo replied. "I show you where Wooten sleep."

They waited until well after dark, past the supper hour. The packsaddle had been left in the cave, and El Lobo rode the bay, leading Wes down alleys and byways. They reined up behind a darkened house, dismounted, and tethered their horses to a hitching rail. From the darkness, Empty materialized and took his position with the horses. Following El Lobo, Wes entered the hall of the house. Near the front door, a lit lamp sat on a table.

"Wooten," said El Lobo softly, pointing to a door.

"We'll be leavin' here on the run," Wes said. "How long?"

"*Uno momento*," said El Lobo. "No longer."

He pointed to the door of the adjoining room, placing his hand on the knob. Taking the knob of the first door in his left hand, Wes tried to turn it, but found it locked. El Lobo, faced with a similar situation, nodded. Simultaneously, they kicked in the doors and then stood to one side. Guns roared from within the darkened rooms, and chest-high, lead ripped through the open doorways. Wes and El Lobo had only to fire at muzzle flashes, and the roar of their Colts became a drumroll of sound. They paused just long enough to assure themselves there would be no return fire. They stepped out the back door, mounted their horses, and rode away.

Eventually El Lobo reined up.

"What is it?" Wes asked.

"I am not finish," said El Lobo. "Wait for me in the hills to the north of town."

Without further explanation, he was gone. Wes rode on, Empty loping beside him. In the hills, where he could still see the lights of the village, Wes reined up. In less than half an hour, he heard horses coming. Empty growled a warning, and a voice spoke from the darkness.

"El Lobo comes."

"Come on," Wes said.

He came closer, riding a black horse that was all but invisible in the faint starlight. The bay followed.

"I go for my horse, my saddle, and my Winchester," said El Lobo.

"*Bueno,*" Wes said. "We'll need the bay to carry the packsaddle."

Nobody dared venture into the bloody rooms of the lodging house until dawn. The constable came and, discovering the dead men were not Mexican, turned his back on the grim scene.

"*Por Dios,*" said the alcalde, when he arrived. "*Americano diablos.*"

In the late afternoon, a telegram arrived from Nogales, addressed to Dana Wooten. It demanded an immediate answer, but there was no address, and the *Mejicano* telegrapher shook his head. Even then, the Señor Wooten and his *companeros* lay dead, awaiting the digging of their graves. The old one crossed himself.

Chapter 4

El Lobo listened in silence as Wes told him of the killing of seven outlaws suspected of being part of the Sandlin gang, headquartered in Namiquipa.

"With seven gone," Wes said, "how many more are we likely to find in Namiquipa?"

"No more than five," said El Lobo. "One of these be Kazman, the *segundo*."

Having rested the horses, they mounted and rode on.

Since returning from Chihuahua, Jake Kazman had been closemouthed and surly. His remaining men—Dantzler, Shatiqua, and Boudlin—could only speculate as to the cause. The trio had been playing poker. At the sound of a galloping horse, they dropped their cards on the rickety table and stood up. Jake Kazman came out of the other room and peered out the cabin's window.

"Damn," Kazman said, "it's Turk Corbin."

As they all knew, Corbin was one of the lieutenants from Juarez, and he never, *never* rode the hundred and seventy miles to Namiquipa unless there was hell to pay. This time would be no different, for Corbin didn't beat around the bush.

"Telegrams to Wooten in Chihuahua have all gone unanswered," said Corbin. "What's the trouble down there?"

"Who says there's trouble?" Kazman demanded.

"The boss in Juarez," said Corbin shortly. "Ignore just *one* telegram from Juarez, and Wooten's hide wouldn't hold shucks. You know it, and he knows it. Now what do *you* have to say? You had eleven men. Where are the others?"

"Dead," Kazman said grimly. "Somebody bushwhacked 'em and took the horses they was bringin' in."

"And you did nothing," said Corbin in a dangerously low voice.

"I wasn't here at the time," Kazman said desperately, "but Dantzler sent Shatiqua and Boudlin to investigate. They—"

"Let them tell me what they found," Corbin said. "I don't want it secondhand from you."

He turned his cold eyes on the unfortunate pair, and they swallowed hard. Shatiqua managed to speak.

"They was ambushed in an arroyo an' looked to have been dead near three days 'fore we found 'em. Buzzards an' coyotes had been busy. Horses was gone."

"Horses leave tracks," said Corbin with scathing sarcasm.

"An' rain washes out them tracks," Boudlin added.

"We hadn't more'n started trailin' 'em when it rained for near two hours."

"I can't deny that," said Corbin. "Before the rain, what direction did the tracks lead?"

"Toward Chihuahua," Shatiqua said.

"There may be some connection between this and the unanswered telegrams to Wooten in Chihuahua," said Corbin. "I'm going there to see for myself, and I'll telegraph Juarez as to what I find. Juarez ain't goin' to like your holdin' back word of this ambush, Kazman, especially if it's got somethin' to do with the silence from Chihuahua. You'd best be comin' up with some answers. Damn good ones."

Corbin left the cabin, mounted his horse, and rode south. Nothing was said for a long moment as Dantzler, Shatiqua, and Boudlin turned accusing eyes on Kazman. Dantzler was the first to say what his companions were thinking.

"You just rode back from Chihuahua, an' you ain't said a word to us about what you learned. Somethin' *is* wrong, an' when Corbin figures it out, we'll all catch hell because we didn't report it. We got the right to know what you learned, and if you don't tell us, then there's enough of us to beat it out of you."

Each of the three had his hand near the butt of his revolver, and Kazman was careful not to make any foolish moves. When he began speaking, his words had a profound effect on his companions. The implications of what they were hearing hit the three of them like a bolt of lightning.

"My God," Dantzler said, "that explains why the horses was turned loose. Somebody's out to kill us. Every damned one of us."

"Looks that way," said Kazman.

"Damn you," Boudlin said. "Instead of keepin' this under your hat, you should have sent telegrams to Juarez an' Nogales. If we don't mount a force an' go after this bastard, he'll pick us all off, a few at a time."

"He's got a handle on it," said Shatiqua. "Wooten and his men are all dead, an' the *pistolero* that killed 'em will be headin' for the next nearest camp. That's us, sure as hell."

"Then we can't wait for help from Nogales or Juarez," Dantzler said. "If a killer's on the way, he'll be here today or tonight. We got to post a guard, an' I don't mean just at night. One of us oughta be on watch right now."

"I'll take the first watch," said Boudlin.

He was about to step out with his Winchester when a slug crashed into the door just inches from his head. He fell back inside, slamming the door, while his companions began scrambling for their weapons.

"That'll give 'em something to think about," Wes said, as he and El Lobo hunkered in some brush.

"Night come," said El Lobo. "They run like coyotes."

"They'll have to do it afoot," Wes said. "Soon as it's dark enough, one of us will slip over yonder to the corral and spook their horses."

"*Sí,*" said El Lobo. "I go."

Chihuahua, Mexico. July 15, 1884

The distance from Namiquipa to Chihuahua was more than sixty miles, and riding a tired horse, Turk

Corbin arrived after dark. He would stay the night, but even before he sought food and shelter, he went looking for Wooten and his men. He knew the old house where they roomed, but when he pounded on their individual doors, he got no response. It being well past the supper hour, they could be in the cantinas, he reasoned. But before he could leave the building, a door opened and he was facing a suspicious housekeeper.

"*Quien es?*"

"I look for the Señor Wooten," said Corbin.

"*Muerto,*" she mumbled, crossing herself. "*Muerto.*"

"The Señor Wooten's *companeros*?"

"*Muerto,*" she said, closing the door.

Turk Corbin shook his head. There had been thirteen men besides Wooten. Fearful of the outlaws, the town had long been buffaloed. Alphonse Renato, the figurehead constable, would have some answers. That is, if he knew what was good for him. But the door to the constable's office stood open, and Corbin found the pudgy constable in a cantina across the street.

"Renato," said Corbin, "I got some questions, and you'd better have some answers."

Corbin pointed across the street to the vacant office, and without a word the fearful Mexican left the cantina. Reaching the office, he sat down behind a battered desk. Corbin remained standing, and, his hand resting on the butt of his revolver, he spoke.

"What happened to Wooten and his bunch?"

"*Muerto,*" said the constable. "El Diablo."

Corbin spent an hour questioning, threatening, and shouting before eventually learning what the old constable knew. He learned of the cantina where Wes and Maria had shot three of Wooten's men, and he went there. The Mexican bartender recognized him and tried to escape into a back room, but Corbin stopped him with a word.

"You got some talkin' to do, bucko," Corbin said.

Corbin learned only that two men had entered the cantina, and that when three of Wooten's gang had followed, there had been shooting.

"Two *hombres* shot the three who followed, then," said Corbin.

"*Sí*," the Mexican bartender said. "*Dos hombres. Pistolas rapido.*"

Turk Corbin stabled his weary horse and took a room for the night. The information he had obtained was sketchy at best. He knew that three of Wooten's men had been shot in the cantina, and he knew that one of the "*hombres*" who had done the shooting had been a woman. Having captured her, Wooten had obviously used her to bait a trap for her companion, only to have it blow up in his face, costing him four more men. The killing of Wooten, Selmer, and Coe accounted for a total of ten men. What had become of the rest? All the more puzzling, Wooten and his companions had occupied two separate rooms, but appeared to have been simultaneously gunned down in their beds, an impossible feat for a single gunman.

"Damn it," Corbin snarled in the darkness, "who *is* this phantom killer, and is he one man or two?"

He lay awake far into the night pondering the problem, and the more he speculated, the less he blamed the Mexicans for being spooked. Of all the unanswered questions weighing on his mind, he narrowed it down to the three that bothered him the most: Who was this devilish killer? What was his motive? And how did he know so much about the Sandlin gang? It seemed he and his companion had ridden unerringly to the arroyo where they had gunned down seven men, and had gone from there directly to Chihuahua. Where might the killer strike next?

"Namiquipa!" he said aloud as the revelation hit him.

He kicked back the covers and got up, unable to sleep. Whatever was about to happen in Namiquipa would have happened long before he could return there. He decided the four would deserve whatever they got, for he believed he hadn't been told everything and that Kazman had known or suspected there was trouble in Chihuahua. Come dawn, he would telegraph to Juarez all he knew or suspected.

Namiquipa, Mexico. July 15, 1884

After the first slugs from Wes Stone's Winchester had driven Boudlin back into the cabin, there was only silence.

"Damn it," Shatiqua growled, "why don't they do somethin'?"

"They?" said Kazman. "There's just one man."

Dantzler laughed. "Hell, one man with a Winchester firin' from cover is good as an army. He's just waitin' for dark an' givin' us time to get spooked."

"We're not more than a mile from the village," Kazman said. "Somebody's bound to hear the shooting."

"Sure they will," said Dantzler, "but that bunch of Mexes won't care if we get shot to doll rags."

"Come dark," Shatiqua said, "I'm takin' my horse an' gittin' the hell away from here."

"Come dark," said Dantzler, "none of us will have a horse. If you aim to run for it, now's the time, but that stable's sixty yards away. It ain't likely you can outrun a slug from a Winchester."

"We don't know that he's still out there," Shatiqua said.

He turned the knob enough to release the latch and, with the toe of his boot, eased the door open just a little. Two slugs ripped into the upper half of the door, slamming it open and into the wall.

"Hell, he can't watch the front an' back door at the same time," said Shatiqua.

He tried the same tactic with the cabin's back door and received the same response.

"Well," Boudlin said, "now we know there's at least two *hombres* out there, and that cuts our chances—if we had any—in half."

In the brush, Wes grinned to himself. One of them had tried the back door, and El Lobo had given them something more to think about. They faced not one man, but two. The four men within the cabin were in serious trouble, and they knew it.

Kazman spoke. "I aim to find out who he is, and why he's after us."

"A lot of good that'll do," said Dantzler.

"You with the long gun," Kazman bawled. "Who are you, and why are you gunnin' for us?"

Just when it seemed there would be no response, the answer came.

"The name is Wes Stone. The Sandlin gang murdered my father in El Paso."

"You're barkin' up the wrong tree," Kazman shouted back. "None of us has ever been in El Paso."

"No matter," said Wes. "You're part of the Sandlin gang, and since I don't know the skunk-striped varmints that done the killing, I aim to gun down every last one of you, if I have to flush out every swamp and thicket in Mexico. You're all dead men."

Chihuahua, Mexico. July 16, 1884

Turk Corbin wrote a lengthy message to Juarez, including his suspicion that the killer or killers might strike next in Namiquipa. He directed the telegram to Rance Stringfield, who had the authority to issue orders to any Sandlin outpost in Mexico. He asked for an immediate reply, waiting until it arrived. The message was brief:

Return to Namiquipa and then to Juarez.

It was unsigned. Corbin mounted and rode north.

In Namiquipa, El Lobo waited until it was almost dark before making his move toward the stable. The four outlaws watched the gate, for it faced the cabin, and an intruder going after the horses would have to pass through it.

"Damn the luck," Boudlin growled, "there'll be a moon later tonight, but he won't be waitin' for that."

"I saw somethin'," said Shatiqua.

Through the window, he cut loose with his Winchester, and there was an immediate response as Wes fired at the muzzle flash.

"Oh, God," Shatiqua groaned, "I'm hit. Help me."

"How?" said Boudlin. "He got you, shootin' at a muzzle flash? What do you reckon he'll do to the rest of us when we strike a light?"

Shatiqua said no more.

"I can at least see how hard he's hit," Dantzler said.

Kneeling beside Shatiqua, he lit a match, shielding it with his hat. Blood soaked the front of the outlaw's shirt, and there was bloody froth on his lips.

"Well?" Kazman asked.

"He's dead," said Dantzler.

"Lord Amighty," Boudlin said. "He *did* see somebody. There goes our horses."

"That means nobody's coverin' the back door," said Dantzler. "Let's run for it."

"You damn fools," Kazman said. "Afoot you don't have a chance. They don't dare rush us, even in the dark. We ain't comin' out, you bastards," he shouted. "Come and get us."

Having spooked the horses, El Lobo had made his way back to Wes.

"They no run," said El Lobo. "We go in?"

"No," Wes said. "They're counting on that. I have another way of getting at them."

From his shirt, he took two sticks of dynamite, bound together, capped and fused. He lit a match and touched it to the short fuse. He held it only until he was sure the fuse had caught, and then flung it in an arc. There was a blinding flash and the cabin was only a pile of rubble. There wasn't a sound.

"Madre de Dios," El Lobo said. *"Dinamita."*

"There's more in the pack if we need it later on," said Wes. "Not quite as satisfying as gut-shootin' the varmints, but the results are the same. We'll wait a while and see if any of 'em crawl out of there."

The next afternoon, Turk Corbin reached Namiquipa. He reined up on a ridge, looking down at the wreckage that had been the cabin. Distasteful as the task was, he was forced to investigate, for when he reached Juarez, he would be forced to account for the four men. He found Shatiqua's body first, for he had fallen near the door. There were a few red particles of paper, powder-burned.

"Dynamite," Corbin said aloud. "Them that wasn't shot was blown to hell."

He moved enough of the debris to account for the remaining three men, and, there being nothing more he could do, he mounted and rode north. To Juarez.

Namiquipa, Mexico. July 17, 1884

"You know for sure there's outlaw strongholds at Guaymas and Hermosillo?" Wes asked.

"Sí," said El Lobo, "and there be others. Where or how many, I do not know."

"Which is closest, Guaymas or Hermosillo?"

"Hermosillo," said El Lobo. "Per'ap two hundred miles."

"A three-day ride," Wes said, "and we'd better get started. It's only a matter of time until what we've done catches up to us and these other camps are armed and waiting. Then, *amigo*, we ride with prices on our heads and the danger increases many times."

"*Sí*," said El Lobo. "You ride to avenge your father, while I ride for a country of my own."

Knowing the odds, accepting them, they rode west.

Ciudad Juarez, Mexico. July 16, 1884

Taking time only to see that his horse was stabled and cared for, Turk Corbin hurried to an old *hacienda* occupied by the outlaws. Corbin nodded to men that he knew, but his destination was the quarters of Rance Stringfield. He pounded on the door.

"Damn it," Stringfield bawled, "you don't have to knock it down. Come in."

Corbin entered and Stringfield rose from the table where he had been sitting and drinking coffee. He was a head taller than Corbin, and his face was grim. Any good humor that might have existed had vanished with Corbin's arrival. He said nothing, waiting for Corbin to speak. His manner irritated Corbin, and he began with a very pointed question.

"Have you alerted the rest of the outposts to the possibility of attack?"

"Why, hell, no!" Stringfield said irritably. "You know full well our grip on Mexico City and all of Mexico depends on the Mex government believing we are invincible, that we are in control. Anybody with the brains God give a goose ought to know that anything sent by wire can be picked up by anybody with an instrument. That, damn it, includes the Mexican government. Now what did you find in Namiquipa?"

"Kazman, Dantzler, Shatiqua, and Boudlin all dead," said Corbin. "Shatiqua had been shot. The others—along with the cabin—blown to hell with dynamite."

The startling news sobered Stringfield, and when he spoke again, his initial anger had abated.

"Did you look for sign?"

"Yes," said Corbin. "Boot tracks of two men. Three horses. One of them probably a packhorse. They rode out headin' west."

"Damn," Stringfield said. "Hermosillo?"

"It's the outpost nearest Namiquipa," said Corbin.

"Prepare a telegram to be sent to Packer at Hermosillo," Stringfield said. "Sign my name to it. Tell them to be ready for a surprise attack."

"Want me to tell them there's two kill-crazy *hombres*?"

"Certainly not," Stringfield roared. "You want all of Mexico knowin' we're fighting for our lives against two men? You are telegraphing Hermosillo only because there is no other way of warning them in time."

"What about Guaymas and Santa Rosalia? They're on the coast, south and southwest of Hermosillo. Ain't it time for that clipper from California, bringin' in them fancy ladies to them two strongholds?"*

"Turk, you're dangerously close to overstepping your authority," said Stringfield, "but you have some valid points. After you've wired Hermosillo, send the same message to both Guaymas and Santa Rosalia. I

*In the days of sailing ships, the clipper was a fast-moving oceangoing craft.

will contact Nogales, and it's their responsibility to warn the western outposts at Coahuila, San Felipe, and Catavina."

"What about the rest of the outposts, and the chief in Mexico City?"

"Remember what I said about overstepping your authority," Stringfield said. "Send the telegrams and leave the rest to me."

When Corbin had departed, Stringfield took pen, ink, paper, and an envelope from a desk drawer. He addressed the envelope to Dolan Watts, Nogales. The message he wrote consisted of four pages. Finished, he took the sealed envelope to one of his most trusted men.

"Take an extra horse and ride relays," said Stringfield. "Get this message to Dolan Watts at Nogales. Wait until he reads it, and if there's a reply, get it back to me just as soon as you can."

At Hermosillo, Burke Packer studied the strange telegram he had just received from Juarez. Packer accepted the warning as genuine, for the absence of any details told him far more than the brief message. Each of the outlaw chieftains had been warned never to use the telegraph to transmit potentially dangerous messages that might fall into enemy hands. Packer wasted no time in assembling his dozen men.

"Until further notice," said the outlaw chieftain, "I want two of you on watch, day and night. Splittin' it up, that's six four-hour watches. There'll be no smokin' after dark."

"What'n hell's the idee?" one of the outlaws demanded. "They ain't nobody in two hunnert miles but Mexicans, an' we got 'em convinced we're all first cousin to *el Diablo*."

Some of his companions laughed, but it quickly dribbled away to silence, for the grim look on Burke Packer's face didn't change.

"With all of us standin' watch," said another of the outlaws, "we ain't gonna be sendin' our quota of horses to Nogales."

"No matter," Packer said. "I don't know what the danger is, but it's real enough for Juarez to send me a warning telegram. It came from Rance Stringfield, and if it's strong enough to spook him, he'll be getting word to Nogales. All I can tell you is that we're to be prepared for an attack."

Hermosillo, Mexico. July 16, 1884

Wes and El Lobo had dismounted and were resting the horses a few miles east of the town. It was time to decide what their first move would be.

"What do you know about Hermosillo?" Wes asked.

"It is near the water, and the sailing ship come there," said El Lobo.

"It's near the ocean?"

"It not be the ocean," El Lobo said. "It be a finger of water that reach far inland, to the north of Sonora."*

"While I was in El Paso," said Wes, "the Sandlin gang was mostly robbing banks and stages, and rus-

*The Gulf of California, providing access to the Pacific Ocean.

tling cattle and horses on both sides of the border. From what I've heard, Mexico is a poor country. With no banks to rob, and with the border too far north for the rustling of cows and horses, what are these outlaws doing in towns like Hermosillo and farther south?"

"*Por Dios*," El Lobo said, "the robbing of banks and the rustling are as honest work when one knows of the evil these sons of *el Diablo* have visited on the villages of Mexico and its people. When there is no money, horses, or cows to steal, these Sandlin *bandidos* steal the young *señoritas* and sell them into a life of slavery, as *putas*."

"With water to the east and west, that's where the sailing ships come in," said Wes. "You're telling me that the Sandlin gang's involved in the selling of women into slavery to become prostitutes. I can take it from there. They're stealing Mexican *señoritas* and taking them far from their homes, and stealing white *señoritas*—probably from the United States—and selling them in Mexico."

"*Sí*," El Lobo said. "That, and per'ap worse."

"It can't get much worse," said Wes. "What else?"

"The *Diablo medicina*," El Lobo said. "It is like the *peyote* of the *Indios*, and it is used by the *medicos*, but it steals the mind. It comes from a flower and is smuggled out of Mexico."

"Opium," said Wes. "It's used in laudanum, and I brought two bottles of that with me. But you're right. Pure opium is dangerous, and before it eventually kills, it can and does steal the mind. I've heard that men and women sold into slavery were first forced to use opium until they couldn't escape from it. Do you know if men are sold as slaves?"

"*Sí,*" El Lobo said, "but not so much as the *señoritas.* Somewhere in Mexico there is a silver mine. Those *hombres* who dig are *Americano* and *Mejicano.*"

"Do you know who controls this mine? Is it the outlaws or the Mexican government?"

"I do not know," said El Lobo.

"We'll add that to the list of things we're unsure of," Wes said. "Before we ride into Hermosillo, we'd better find us a place to secure our supplies and the packhorse."

"*Sí,*" El Lobo agreed. "A place we can stand off many *hombres* with guns who wish to kill us."

"That, too," said Wes. "We'll be reachin' a point—if we haven't already—where they will be expectin' us, and we'll be ridin' for our lives. Before leavin' our supplies behind, I reckon we'd better fill our saddlebags with as much ammunition and food as we can. When we're pursued, we might be a while workin' our way back to our supplies, or we may not be able to return to them at all."

"*Sí,*" El Lobo said.

After several hours of searching, they were forced to conceal their supplies and the packhorse in a thicket near a small stream.

"Not worth a damn for defense, if we're on the run," said Wes, "but there's graze and water for the horse. We'll just have to take our chances, and if there's pursuit, we'll keep ridin', comin' back here if and when we can."

Unsure as to what awaited them, they rode toward Hermosillo.

Chapter 5

Hermosillo was strikingly different from Chihua-hua, its proximity to the ocean evident by the presence of many seagoing men. Nor did the Mexican populace dress in peons' clothing. There were well-dressed Mexican men, some accompanied by *señoritas* of some elegance. There were even a few single women on the street, and many of the men carried revolvers on their hips.

"We are not so different from the others, *amigo*," El Lobo said.

"We have an edge, then," said Wes, "unless they've been told what happened in Chihuahua and Namiquipa."

Suddenly Wes reined up. Ahead of them, hanging out over the boardwalk, was a vivid green sign with fancy gold lettering that said EL ORO CASA. In a circle was the head of the golden dragon.

"It is the image of the outlaws," El Lobo said. "*Casa* of the *puta*."

"A whorehouse," said Wes, "with the damn dragon at the front of it."

"They are powerful in Mexico," El Lobo said. "They do not have to hide."

"Stay with the horses," said Wes. "I'm goin' in there and see what I can learn."

El Lobo said nothing. Wes didn't see Empty. While the hound had accepted El Lobo, he didn't care for Mexican villages. The house looked somewhat forbidding, for curtains had been drawn. The image of the dragon out front had given Wes an idea. Quickly he dug into his pocket for a handful of gold coins, sorting through them until he found one of the medallions with the dragon's head. He pounded on the door, and when he had all but given up, the door opened. A hard-eyed Mexican woman looked at him as though trying to recall his face. He extended his hand, palm up, and when she saw the medallion with its dragon's head, she seemed to relax.

"*Sí*," she said, stepping aside so that he might enter.

Wes stepped inside, offering her no money. He dropped the medallion back into his pocket. The madam looked at him questioningly, and he realized she was waiting for him to make known his wants.

"A *señorita*," Wes said.

The woman nodded, and he followed her down a long hall. While he had taken a risk, he had learned something. The same medallion that had almost gotten him killed in the cantina in Chihuahua had gotten him into a Sandlin-controlled whorehouse in Hermosillo. The madam had accepted him as one of the gang, and here he might establish the truth of what El Lobo had told him about the Sandlin gang's involvement in white slavery. Without bothering to knock, his host opened a door and bade him enter. A young girl with golden hair lay on a bed. She was covered with a sheet and said nothing. Her eyes were cold and without expression. The door closed behind Wes, and he was alone with the girl. Suddenly she flung back the sheet, and he wasn't surprised to find her naked beneath it.

"Get out of your clothes," she said without emotion, "and do what you came to do."

"I only want to talk to you, to ask you some questions," said Wes. "Who are you, where are you from, and how did you get here?"

"I'm doing what I want to do," she said.

"I don't believe that," said Wes.

"I don't care a damn what you believe or don't believe," she hissed. "They send you here, I talk to you, then they come and beat me. I have nothing to say. Now get out!"

Another moment and she would have been screaming. Wes opened the door, stepped out into the hall, and made his way toward the door through which he had entered. There was no sign of the madam who had admitted him. He eased the front door open until he could see El Lobo and the horses across the street. Quickly, Wes crossed.

El Lobo laughed. "You *rapido, amigo.*"

"Nothin' but talk," Wes said, "and I didn't learn much. I used the dragon medallion to get in, and I was taken to a girl who is American, so you're dead right about the white slavery. But she told me nothing, except that she is beaten when she talks. She thought I'd been sent by the Sandlin gang to trick her into talking, and that she would be beaten."

"Now what we do?" El Lobo asked.

"I learned that the Sandlin gang comes here, evidently without charge," said Wes. "I reckon if we stake out this dragon-head whorehouse, sooner or later some of the gang will come here."

"How do we know them?"

"We don't," Wes said, "We'll have to judge by the look of them. Except for the outlaws, what kind of men are likely to come here?"

"Per'ap the rich *Mejicano*," said El Lobo.

"You stay here," Wes said, "and I'll go up the street a ways, where I can still see the door. We'll keep enough distance between us so that if one of us arouses suspicion, it won't involve the other."

Remaining on the same side of the street, Wes moved well away from El Lobo. There was open ground for a few yards, and several oaks had grown large enough to afford some shade. Wes left his grulla beneath one, while he sat down with his back to the other. He tipped his hat low over his eyes so that it might appear that he slept, while actually he was able to see all the way to the front of the whorehouse and beyond. But their vigil went unrewarded, and at dusk the same woman who had admitted Wes stepped out and lit a bracket lamp on each side of the door. In the gathering darkness, Empty made his way to Wes, concealing himself in the shadow of the trees. Wes shared his jerked beef with the hound, and the vigil continued. During the course of the evening, only three men entered the bordello, and in business dress; none of them had the look of outlaws. Finally, in the legitimate shops, lamps were extinguished and doors were locked. Eventually El Lobo came down the street leading his horse.

"I know those varmints have been to that house before," Wes said, "because I got in with one of those dragon-head coins. But where are they today?"

"Per'ap in the cantinas," El Lobo said.

"This town's considerably more tame than Chihuahua," said Wes. "Maybe we can have us a beer without a gunfight. Let's try that place over there with the rooster on the front door."

There were only a few patrons in the cantina, and with only four hanging lamps, there was little or no chance of recognition. El Lobo ordered beer for himself and Wes, and they took their mugs to a table in the corner.

"Tarnation," Wes said, "this is the strongest beer I ever laid tongue to."

"*Sí,*" said El Lobo. "Drink, and then we go."

Wes could only agree. Of the few men in the cantina, not one had the look of the outlaws they were seeking. They departed the cantina and were passing El Oro Casa when there was a scream of mortal terror from within the whorehouse.

"Come on," Wes said.

He slammed open the front door, El Lobo behind him. Lead tore into the doorframe and in the dimly lit parlor Wes fired at the muzzle flash. A second man fired, and a slug from El Lobo's Colt struck his gun hand. Dropping the weapon, he ran down the long, dark hall.

"It is him!" the madam screeched. "It is him!"

El Lobo caught her around the throat with his left arm and clubbed her unconscious with his Colt.

"*Madre de Dios,*" said El Lobo, "others come."

The girl with the golden hair lay facedown on the

floor, and when Wes rolled her over, he found her thin gown drenched with blood. It was the same girl he had spoken to earlier, and her throat had been slit. Her dead eyes looked into his, and he got to his feet.

"See what I find on the dead *hombre*," El Lobo said, extending his open palm.

In the dim glow from a single lamp was a familiar golden medallion with it's dragon's head.

"One of the varmints got away," Wes said. "We'd better run for it."

"*Sí*," said El Lobo. "Per'ap we follow him."

They stepped out the door just as the dazed madam sat up, rubbing her head. Almost immediately she began screeching, and as Wes and El Lobo ran for their horses, there was the sound of many voices. Empty was with the horses, growling a warning as the voices grew louder. Wes and El Lobo mounted on the run and were soon galloping away into the darkness.

At the outlaw camp, Wicks and Tobin were on watch when they heard a horse coming on the run. It was late, but others had heard it, too, and Burke Packer stepped out the door, waiting.

"Rein up," Wicks shouted, "and identify yourself."

"Rowden, damn it," came a voice from the darkness. "Vesper's dead, an' I'm hurt."

"Come on," Packer growled.

Rowden dismounted, and in the lamplight from the open door they could see blood dripping from the fingers of his right hand. Quickly he related what had happened.

"Two of 'em" said Suggs, "an' they outgunned you an' Vesper?"

"They took us by surprise," Rowden said defensively. "Vesper got off the first shot an' missed. The first *hombre* nailed him, an' the second one got me. I didn't see him for more'n a second, an' I swear to God I never seen him pull a gun. He was sudden as chain lightnin', an' he ruint my hand."

"Damn you and Vesper for a pair of fools," said Packer. "It's them two killers that Stringfield warned us about."

"That's what me an' Vesper thought when the madam told us this *hombre* had talked to the whore," Rowden said. "We was forcin' her to talk, an' she got away from us."

"So you allowed her to reach the parlor and scream her head off before you silenced her," Packer said.

"We didn't think—"

"You sure as hell didn't," said Packer. "Them two *hombres* staked out the whorehouse until you two showed up. You played right into their hands. Now the damn constable will be asking questions."

"Tell him the two gunmen busted into the whorehouse an' killed the woman," Rowden said. "Then when Vesper an' me went after 'em, they kilt Vesper an' wounded me."

"You shot the whore, then," said Packer.

"Uh . . . no . . ." Rowden said uneasily. "We used our knives, tryin' to make her talk."

"Rowden," said Packer, in a dangerous tone, "this constable may be *Mejicano*, but he's no fool. Two gunmen busted in, shot you and Vesper, and were gone within seconds. They wouldn't have had time to torture the woman with their knives, would they?"

"I reckon not," Rowden said with a sigh. "What can we do?"

"Come first light," said Packer, "we'll ride circles around Hermosillo until we find some sign of the varmints that done the shootin'. For now, I want you to tell me everything about them you can remember."

"I will," Rowden said, "but can't I have my wound took care of first?"

"Suggs," said Packer, "put some water on to boil. When it's ready, you and Yokum see to Rowden's wound."

Wes and El Lobo didn't speak until they reached the thicket in which they had hidden the packhorse and their supplies.

"They will trail us, *amigo*," El Lobo said.

"We have until first light," said Wes, "and it won't be easy, finding a place to conceal the packhorse and our supplies in the dark. They'll be trailing us, but we'll know which way they'll be coming. I reckon they'll be expecting an ambush, and we won't disappoint them."

Nogales, Mexico. July 17, 1884

Dolan Watts had read the lengthy message from Rance Stringfield many times, and he read it again, considering Stringfield's suggestion. Finally he sent for Skull Rudabaugh, his most trusted lieutenant.

"Read this, Skull," Watts said, handing him the letter.

Rudabaugh read it and returned it, waiting for Watts to speak.

"If this is as much a threat as Stringfield thinks it is," said Watts, "then every one of our outposts—including Mexico City—should know of it. I am considering sending a copy of this by sailing ship to each of our outposts along the coast, with a request that each of these outposts sends riders inland with the same information. What do you think?"

"I think it'd be easier and quicker to send every outpost a telegram," Rudabaugh said, "but Mexico City would raise hell and kick a chunk under it. I reckon you want me to do some ridin'. El Desemboque?"

"Yes," said Watts, "just as soon as I can make copies of Stringfield's letter. I'll send copies to San Felipe, Catavina, Santa Rosalia, and Guaymas. It'll be their responsibility to contact other outposts to the south."

"What about Hermosillo?"

"They may have been next in line after Namiquipa," Watts said, "and unless Stringfield sent a rider to warn them, it'll be too late."

"After delivering your messages to El Desemboque, I could ride to Hermosillo and see if anything's happened there," said Rudabaugh.

For a moment, Watts said nothing, thinking. Then he made up his mind.

"Do that, Skull. I'm sticking my neck out, following up on Stringfield's suspicions. I'd like to know how real this threat is before I get into it any deeper.

We have ships sailing from California with fancy cargo, and this is no time for trouble at any of our outposts along the coast."

Skull Rudabaugh nodded and departed, while Dolan Watts began preparing messages for delivery to the ship's dock at El Desemboque.

The outlaws at Hermosillo were active well before first light. Rowden's right hand was swollen and the bandage was stained with new blood. He had gained no favor with the rest of the outlaws and was sullenly nursing a tin cup of coffee.

"Dooley, Blake, Elkins, Mullins, and Hanson will ride with me," said Packer. "The rest of you will stay here, keepin' your eyes open and your guns handy. Tazlo, while I'm gone, you're in charge. If the constable rides out here askin' questions about last night, tell him he'll have to talk to me."

"What if he knows Rowden—"

"If anybody comes around asking questions," Packer said, "Rowden will make himself scarce. Won't you, Rowden?"

"Yeah," said Rowden sullenly.

Burke Packer and his five chosen men saddled up and rode out.

"There ain't that many horsemen in and out of Hermosillo," Packer said. "We'll circle the town, ridin' a hundred yards apart. We're lookin' for two riders, but they might have split up to confuse us. If you find tracks of one horse or two, sing out."

"What do you know of those mountains to the south?" Wes asked.

"There are mines and there are *Indios*," said El Lobo.*

"We'll take our chances with the Indians," Wes said. "Let's ride."

Wes and El Lobo reined up at an elevation where they could see their back trail for many miles. Empty was somewhere ahead of them, elated over having escaped the hated village.

"We might as well keep watch here until we see them comin'," Wes said. "It'll be a good time to rest the horses."

"*Sí*," said El Lobo. "We ride back to meet them."

"Maybe," Wes said. "They'll be expectin' an ambush, and I can't believe they'll come at us head-on. If they have any savvy at all, some of 'em will flank us east and west while the others appear to be followin' our trail."

"Cross fire," said El Lobo. "That be hell."

"That, and worse," Wes said. "We'll have to spring our ambush before the *hombres* flankin' us can move in close enough for an effective cross fire. They'll be expectin' us to retreat deeper into the mountains, and even if their cross fire fails, they'll still have some of their bunch waitin' for us."

El Lobo laughed. "We do not retreat."

"No," said Wes. "If they split up, tryin' to flank us, then we'll drive straight through 'em, back toward Hermosillo. We'll force the flankers to follow us and we'll be waitin' with a Winchester welcome."

"They come," El Lobo said, pointing.

_____

*The Yaqui and other hostile bands were a constant hindrance to working the mines.

Far away, losing themselves in distance and then reappearing, galloped six horsemen.

"Sometime, before entering the foothills, they should split up," said Wes. "Then we'll know what we have to do."

The six men reined up to rest their horses, and Burke Packer took the opportunity to give final orders.

"Before we reach the foothills, we'll split up. Dooley, I want you and Blake to swing wide to the east and then move forward. Elkins, you and Mullins will swing back to the west, followin' the same pattern. Hanson and me will follow their trail, forcin' them to spring their ambush."

"Maybe you got a death wish," said Hanson, "but I ain't."

"Hell, *somebody's* got to spring the trap," Packer said. "We'll hold back as much as we can, allowin' the others time to move in along the flanks. By the time they cut down on us, we'll have 'em in a cross fire. Even if that fails and they retreat, they'll ride into the teeth of our ambush. We'll have men behind 'em."

"You be right," said El Lobo. "They split up."

"Not much else they can do," Wes replied. "If they all came straight at us, we could cut them down to the last man. If their men can't get into position to east and west and set up a cross fire, they'll try to work their way in behind us. They're expectin' us to retreat farther into the mountains, givin' them a chance to set up an ambush of their own."

Even as Wes spoke, he could see the distant horsemen separating exactly as he had expected. It was a three-pronged offensive attack, and inexperienced defenders might well find themselves facing fire from three directions. But Wes and El Lobo—wise beyond their years—saw it for the obvious trap that it was.

"We ride lak hell, shoot lak hell," said El Lobo.

"Come on," Wes said. "We'll take the packhorse with us. By the time those *hombres* are in position to flank us or move in behind us, we'll be out of range. Then, by God, let them pursue *us*, if they've got the sand."

Packer and Hanson rode slowly, allowing their four companions to get in position for the flanking maneuver. They were still in the foothills, and the very last thing they were expecting was an attack by the men they were pursuing, for there was no suitable cover for an ambush. The first and only warning they had was the thump of hoofbeats, and in the next instant, Wes and El Lobo topped a rise.

"Hell's fire," Hanson bawled, "here they come."

"Cut them down!" Packer shouted.

But the two had been taken by surprise, and their first shots were hurried and wide. Wes and El Lobo held their fire until they were in range with their Colts. El Lobo fired first, and hard hit, Packer was flung out of the saddle. It was enough to spook Hanson, but he hadn't moved quickly enough. He was wheeling his horse to ride for his life when Wes fired. The horse galloped away, riderless, leaving Hanson belly-down, his life leaking out into the sand. Wes and El Lobo rode on, back toward Hermosillo.

Dooley and Blake were the first to reach their fallen comrades. Seconds later, Elkins and Mullins reined up.

"Hanson's dead," Dooley announced.

"Packer ain't," said Blake, "but he soon will be, if we don't git him to a doctor."

Elkins and Mullins caught the horses belonging to Packer and Hanson. Quickly the four loaded their fallen comrades on their horses and headed for town.

"Whoa," Dooley said, reining up. "We ain't usin' our heads. Them *hombres* is ahead of us. We could be ridin' into an ambush. We'd better circle and ride in from some other direction."

"We don't git Packer to a doc pronto," said Mullins, "he'll be dead."

"Won't do him a hell of a lot of good if we're all gunned down in an ambush," said Elkins. "Dooley's right. I say we circle around an' ride back to our place. One of us can ride through town an' fetch that Mexican sawbones next to the constable's office."

"I'll git the doc," Blake said. "The rest of you git back to camp and warn the others. That pair of gun-throwers could attack us there."

It was a sobering thought, and the three set out in a roundabout way for their outpost. Blake rode on toward Hermosillo, his Winchester at the ready.

Contrary to the outlaws' expectations, Wes and El Lobo had no intention of laying an ambush. Instead, they watched as one man headed for town, while the others—with their fallen comrades—rode away to the north.

"Three of 'em are takin' the long way home," Wes said. "I reckon they don't want the local law askin' bothersome questions about the two varmints ridin' belly-down."

"*Sí*," said El Lobo. "Per'ap they fear the ambush. We follow?"

"Damn right," Wes said. "Once we know where this bunch is holed up, we can lay all kinds of misery on them, while they can't get to us."

El Lobo laughed. "The cat and the mouse, no?"

"*Sí*," said Wes. "It's time word of us was gettin' back to the skunk-striped coyotes at the top of this outlaw totem pole. We want them to think of us as *el Diablo* in duplicate, nine feet tall, with lead-spittin' guns that never miss. I want the whole bunch of them—from the least to the greatest—afraid to close their eyes."

"We chase the dragon up a tree," El Lobo said.

Wes laughed. "Now you're gettin' the idea."

It was time to pursue the three outlaws. Wes and El Lobo rode out. Empty, ranging ahead, had already taken the trail.

Riding directly into town, Blake sought out Otero Hernandez, a Mexican doctor.

"I need you to come with me, doc," said Blake. "A man's been hurt."

"Hurt in what manner, *señor*?" Hernandez inquired.

"Horse throwed him," Blake said.

"Better you bring him here," said the doctor. "I have *carreta*."*

*Wagon.

"Better you come with me," Blake said. He drew his revolver, cocked it, and shoved it under the doctor's nose.

"*Sí*," Hernandez said, taking his bag.

Wicks and Tobin were on watch when Dooley, Elkins, and Mullins rode in, leading the horses bearing Packer and Hanson.

"My God," Tazlo said, "what happened?"

"Packer split us up," said Dooley. "Him an' Hanson rode straight in, but this pair of ring-tailed hellraisers didn't retreat into a cross fire. They rode straight at Packer an' Hanson, pumpin' lead. Hanson's dead as a Christmas goose, an' Packer may be. Blake rode through town to fetch a doctor."

Quickly they lifted Packer off the horse and moved him into the cabin. Stretching him out on a bunk, they opened his shirt.

"God," Suggs said, "he's hard hit, but at least he ain't breathin' blood."

"Man don't have to be lung-shot to die," said Tazlo.

"You'd better hope he don't," Rowden growled. "He left you in charge. I'd hate like hell to git stuck explainin' all this to Juarez or Nogales."

"I reckon you'll git a chance to explain that gunfight in town," said Tazlo. "You think Juarez and Nogales won't have to be told how it was that Vesper was shot dead and you was wounded, while them two gun-throwers escaped without a scratch?"

Rowden was spared the necessity of a reply by the arrival of Blake and the Mexican doctor. Hernandez stepped down from his wagon and tied his mule. Blake nodded toward the cabin door and the doctor entered. The men stepped aside, allowing him to reach the bunk where the wounded Burke Packer lay. His chest was a mass of blood, and Hernandez turned angrily to Blake.

"You said he was thrown from a horse!" the doctor said angrily.

"So I lied," said Blake. "Now you git busy. If he don't make it, we ain't gonna think too highly of you."

"I will do my best," Hernandez said gravely.

Wes and El Lobo followed at a great distance, for Empty had taken the trail of the outlaws and there was no danger of losing them. The cabin was several miles from the village. Wes and El Lobo reined up a considerable distance away, so that neither their horses nor those of the outlaws would reveal their presence. Keeping to the little cover that was available, they crept within rifle range of the cabin. Beyond the cabin was a corral in which a dozen horses picked at loose hay. Outside the cabin was a ramshackle wagon with a patient mule still in harness.

"Likely a doctor," Wes said. "One of us didn't shoot straight."

"*Madre de Dios*," said El Lobo, in mock horror, "what will they think of us?"

"Unlimber your Winchester," Wes said. "We'll just see to it that we don't lose any of their respect."

Shooting high, they each blasted half a dozen shots into the back of the cabin.

Chapter 6

Some of the lead ripped through the chinks between the logs, showering the outlaws with dust. Men bellied down on the floor, while Dr. Hernandez hunkered at the foot of Packer's bunk. They waited, expecting another volley, but none came.

"Damn them," Blake said. "They're tauntin' us."

"I reckon they got every right," said Tazlo. "Six of you went after 'em, an' you come back with Hanson dead an' Packer maybe dyin'. Worse, they follered you here, and there's no way we can defend ourselves from this rat hole. They can pick us off one or two at a time if we try to run for it, or they can trap us here till dark and burn us alive."

"Like hell," Elkins said. "Come dark, we can git to our horses an' run for it."

"Leavin' Packer here, I reckon," said Tazlo.

"Damn right," Elkins said. "I can't see totin' a dead body around, when we got a pair of pistoleers stalkin' us. Packer likely won't last till sundown. Right, Doc?"

"He has a chance," said Hernandez cautiously. "We know *mañana*."

"Tomorrow, hell," Mullins said. "We ain't got that much time."

"Oh, I reckon we got time aplenty," said Tazlo.

To prove his point, he stood back from the door, easing it open just a little. He then removed his hat and, holding it by the brim, exposed enough of the crown so that from a distance it might look as though a man were peering out. Almost immediately there was the bark of a Winchester and the hat was ripped out of Tazlo's hand.

"That tells me what I ain't wantin' to hear," Dooley said. "The bastards don't aim for us to get out of here alive."

"I can do no more for this man," said Dr. Hernandez. "Am I allowed to leave?"

Blake laughed. "I'd say it depends on them *hombres* with the Winchesters."

"You out there doin' the shootin'," Tazlo shouted. "There's a *Mejicano* doc in here, an' he wants out. Will you let him go?"

"He can go," Wes shouted back.

"Not so fast, Doc," Tazlo said. "First you tell us what more we can do for this man that's been shot. We're in no position to ride to town lookin' for you."

"Give him whiskey," said Hernandez. "There is nothing more anyone can do."

"Hell, we ain't got but two bottles of whiskey," Yokum said, "an' we'll likely need it ourselves."

They said nothing about payment for the doctor's services, and he, being allowed to escape with his life, didn't ask. Easing the door open, he stepped out. When there was no gunfire, he hurriedly untied his mule, mounted the wagon box, and drove away.

Nogales, Mexico. July 17, 1884

It was still early when Skull Rudabaugh rode out of Nogales, bound for El Desemboque. After posting the letters, Skull would be riding to Hermosillo, but the more Watts thought about it, the more uneasy he became. So far, two of the Sandlin outposts had been totally destroyed, and it appeared that Hermosillo might become the third. Nothing was being done to counter the devastating attacks, but what *could* be done? Guaymos was less than a hundred miles south of Hermosillo. There might yet be time to send a force from Guaymos, if the right man were in charge. Suddenly the inspiration he sought came to him. Skull Rudabaugh! Skull would be riding to Hermosillo after leaving El Desemboque, but Skull was just one man, and by the time he reached Hermosillo, it would be too late. But suppose skull took a sailing ship directly to Guaymos and then led a force from there to Hermosillo?

Guaymos had already been alerted to danger; now he must alert them to the arrival of Skull Rudabaugh and the need for men to ride to Hermosillo. Quickly he composed a telegram to Guaymos, and a second for Skull when he reached El Desemboque.

Riding at a slow gallop and resting his horse often, Skull Rudabaugh reached the dock at El Desemboque before dark. Fortunately, a sailing ship was loading for ports south. The telegrapher's shack was near the dock, and Skull tied his horse there. He was often there to intercept goods on incoming ships and was known to the telegrapher, who now beckoned to him.

"Telegram fer you."

Skull took the message. It was brief:

Post other messages as planned stop. Take ship to Gu-
aymos and personally deliver message to Stem Wurzback
stop. Tell Wurzback to send help to Hermosillo stop. You
will lead them stop.

The message was unsigned, but only Dolan Watts had known Skull was bound for El Desemboque. There was just time for Skull to book passage for himself and his horse. They would reach Guaymos during the night. If Wurzback didn't waste any time, there was a possibility that Skull and a force of fighting men might reach Hermosillo shortly after dawn. Skull could think of only one possible difficulty. There had always been bad blood between himself and Stem Wurzback, the Sandlin *segundo* at Guaymos. Stem would purely raise hell at the prospect of sending his men to Hermosillo with Skull leading them. There was no help for it, however, and Skull prepared himself for an unwelcome and probably ugly reception.

Within the outlaw cabin near Hermosillo, there was little conversation. The wounded Burke Packer lay unmoving, and only his ragged breathing told them he still lived. There was less than two hours of daylight remaining, and none of the men had any illusions as to what the night might bring. Blake said what they all were thinking.

"Soon as it's dark enough, we got to make a run for our horses."

"We do," Tazlo said, "then we'll have to get to 'em ahead of that jasper with the rifle. All he's got to do is spook the horses and we're dead men. We don't have enough water to make coffee in the mornin'. Give the sun two hours—if we're still alive—and it'll be hotter in here than seven kinds of hell, without water."

Burke Packer groaned and all conversation ceased. He cut his eyes to right and left as far as he could, and when he finally spoke, they could barely hear him.

"Hanson . . . ?"

"Hanson's dead," said Blake.

"The . . . ambush . . ."

"Wasn't no ambush," Blake said. "Them *hombres* went after you an' Hanson like hell wouldn't have it. They cut you down an' was gone 'fore we was in position to flank 'em or git behind 'em."

"Didn't . . . some of . . . you . . . trail them?"

"No," said Blake. "You was hard hit. We had to fetch you back here an' git a doc."

"So . . . you . . . lost them."

"Like hell," Tazlo said. "While Blake was fetchin' the doc, them two varmints tagged along behind Dooley, Elkins, an' Mullins. They're settin' out there with rifles, just waitin' for dark."

It was more than Packer could take. He spoke no more, lapsing into unconsciousness.

An hour before sundown, a rising wind herded dirty gray thunderheads in from the west. "We might have a chance, yet," Tobin said. "There'll be a storm tonight."

"At least it'll be too wet for 'em to burn us out,"

said Yokum. "It'll be their rifles agin ours, an' we got 'em outgunned."

"There's a storm buildin' over yonder," Wes said, "and that's the kind of cover this bunch is waitin' for."

"*Sí*," said El Lobo, "and storm come before dark, before we spook horses. Per'ap we use *dinamita*?"

"We may have to," Wes said. "While it's light, we can't get close enough to fire the cabin, and there's rain comin' before dark. Keep an eye on the cabin and see that none of 'em makes a run for their horses. I'll ride back for the packhorse."

The bay had been left where there was water and graze, and of necessity was closer to the village than Wes had liked. Now he regretted not having taken the animal with them, and while he trusted Empty's vigilance, the hound had his limitations. Uneasy now, he kicked the grulla into a fast gallop. Nearing the place where they had left the packhorse, he drew his Winchester from the saddle boot. Reining up, he dismounted, expecting Empty to come bounding to meet him. But there was no greeting, and he knew something was wrong. The bay horse and the pack-saddle were gone, and Empty lay near the stream, his head a mass of blood.

"Empty, old son," said Wes, his eyes dimming.

Kneeling beside the wounded hound, Wes found he was alive. Using his hat, he dipped water from the stream and poured it over Empty's bloody head. The dog opened his eyes and tried to rise, but could not. Wes was relieved to find he had only been creased by a slug. Bringing another hatful of water, he allowed Empty to drink. The hound struggled to sit up and, using his hindquarters for support, got shakily to his feet. He shook himself, spraying Wes with water.

"Stand right there," said Wes, "until I see to that wound."

In his saddlebag was a tin of sulfur salve. Empty stood patiently while Wes smeared enough of the medication on the gash to stop the bleeding.

"Now," Wes said, "we'll take it slow until you're steady on your feet."

Wes had no trouble finding the tracks of the bay, for it was being led. He followed the trail just far enough to learn he was headed toward town. There was little doubt that the trail would be lost among the cobbled streets, alleys, and byways of Hermosillo. With that in mind, Wes wheeled the grulla and rode back toward the outlaw outpost. Empty trotted alongside, rapidly regaining his strength.

El Lobo said nothing as Wes reined up and dismounted, for little explanation was necessary. There was no packhorse, no packsaddle, and the faithful *perro* had a serious head wound.

"No packhorse, no packsaddle, no grub, and no dynamite," Wes said. "The trail led straight toward town."

"Some poor *Mejicano* be rich *hombre*," said El Diablo.

"Yeah," Wes said. "Good thing we loaded our saddlebags with all the grub and shells we could. We can last a few more days."

Adding to their streak of bad luck, the rain blew

in before it was dark enough for them to spook the outlaws' horses.

"Plenty cover," said El Lobo. "They run like coyotes. *Mañana,* no trail."

"The same storm that covers them will cover us," Wes said. "When this storm really starts to blow, we'll stampede their horses. *Then* if they choose to run for it under cover of the storm or in the dark, they'll be afoot."

The storm grew in intensity, but it still wasn't good dark. Suddenly the door to the cabin opened, and Wes sent a Winchester slug screaming through it. Just as suddenly, the door was closed.

"Satisfied?" Tazlo asked as Blake slammed the door shut.

"If we don't git to them horses," said Blake, "you'll be laughin' out of the other side of your mouth."

"He's right," Mullins said. "This place ain't worth a damn for defense, and we'll be in big trouble if they stampede our horses. Packer left you in charge, and he's still out of his head. What do you aim to do?"

"Give it another ten minutes and it'll be dark," said Tazlo. "Wicks, Tobin, Dooley, Suggs, and Yokum, you'll go with me after the horses. We'll picket them here behind the cabin. I want the rest of you right on our heels, with your Winchesters, coverin' us. *Comprende?*"

"You ain't called me by name," Rowden said. "What are you expectin' of me?"

"Not a damn thing," said Tazlo. "With your arm

an' gun hand swole up bigger'n a corral post, what can you do?''

The situation was serious enough that nobody laughed. Rowden said nothing. The rain continued, driven by the wind, and when Tazlo judged it was dark enough, he opened the door, his comrades at his heels. Slipping and sliding in mud, they ran toward the horse corral.

Wes and El Lobo had begun working their way toward the horse corral when the cabin door opened. In the darkness and driving rain, the emerging men were no more than shadows.

''They come,'' El Lobo said.

Wes had already begun firing, and El Lobo cut loose with his Winchester. Immediately their muzzle flashes drew fire, and they dropped to their knees in the mud. But the return fire from the outlaws quickly diminished, for even with poor visibility, their adversaries had proven themselves dangerously accurate. Tazlo, Dooley, and Blake had been hit, and on hands and knees scrambled back toward the cabin. The others, intimidated, followed.

''That's enough,'' Wes said. ''We can't afford to waste ammunition. We nicked some of them, and I reckon they won't try anything foolish tonight. We'll give them time to get back inside, and we'll spook their horses.''

''Damn it,'' said Elkins, ''they're a pair of devils. I didn't see nothin' but their muzzle flashes, an' when I shot back, they wasn't there.''

"You got no kick comin'," Blake said. "At least you wasn't hit."

Blood dripped from his upper left arm, while Tazlo and Dooley had leg wounds.

"One of you stir up the fire, so's we got some light," said Tazlo. "We'll be needin' help with these wounds."

"I told you them bastards was straight outa hell," Rowden said with considerable satisfaction. "At least, you *hombres* knowed what you was gittin' into. Them two busted in, takin' Vesper an' me by surprise."

"By God," said Yokum, "I'm 'bout ready to agree with Rowden. We're up agin more'n just a pair of hell-raisers. They're out to kill us all."

Suddenly, above the roar of the storm, there were shots and shouts.

"There goes the horses," Rowden said.

Except for Burke Packer's ragged breathing, there was only silence as every man pondered the grim reality of what lay ahead. The horses were gone. When the storm and the night passed, *el Diablo*'s hombres would be waiting. With their deadly Winchesters . . .

Guaymos, Mexico. July 17, 1884

Somewhere in the village, a clock in a church tower struck eleven as Skull Rudabaugh led his horse off the ship and onto the dock. Mounting, he rode into the silent village. He expected the outlaws to have a man on watch, since they'd been sent a warning telegram, and he wasn't disappointed. They were headquartered in an old house in a run-down part of town, and the sentry sat on the front porch, a Winchester across his knees. He got to his feet when he heard the horse coming. Skull reined up.

"Who are you," the sentry demanded, "and what do you want?"

"I'm Skull Rudabaugh, from Nogales, and I have a message from Dolan Watts for Stem Wurzback. He's to receive it tonight."

"Like hell," said the sentry. "It's near midnight. He'd have my head an' yours. Come back in the mornin'."

"I'll take responsibility for wakin' him," Skull said, "but I've been ordered to get this message to him tonight. Them orders come straight from Dolan Watts at Nogales. If Stem don't like it, then let him complain to Watts."

"It's your funeral," said the sentry. "I'll wake him."

Wurzback finally appeared, minus boots and hat. The sentry took his place in the chair, while Wurzback sat down on the steps. When he spoke, it was without friendliness.

"Talk, Rudabaugh, an' by God, it'd better be good."

"There's a written message from Dolan Watts," Skull said. "I was about to post it at El Desemboque, but there was a telegram from Watts ordering me to deliver it. I reckon you got a warning telegram about a possible attack?"

"Yeah," said Wurzback, "I got it. We don't normally post a guard."

"I'm goin' to tell you what's behind that telegraphed warning," Skull said, "and then I have further orders from Dolan Watts."

Wurzback said nothing, and Skull presented the facts as quickly as he could. For a moment, Wurzback said nothing. Then he laughed.

"You're tellin' me them bull-of-the-woods outfits in Namiquipa and Chihuahua was wiped out by a pair of fast guns?"

"That's exactly what I'm tellin' you," said Skull, "and there's every reason to believe Hermosillo is next. Watts has ordered me to lead as many men as you can spare. We're to ride for Hermosillo just as quick as you can roust 'em out."

"No," Wurzback shouted. "By God, no! I ain't sendin' my outfit *nowhere* on your sayso, an' for sure not with *you* leadin' 'em."

"You don't like me, Wurzback, and I don't like you," said Skull, "an' there'll come a time when we'll have to settle our differences, but this ain't the time. Now you round up your bunch and get 'em ready to ride or I'll telegraph Watts at Nogales for authority to assume command of this outpost by whatever force may be necessary."

Wurzback got to his feet, but Skull had his thumb hooked under his gunbelt above the butt of his revolver.

"We'll ride," Wurzback said, "but not under your command. I'm leadin' my outfit, and I want that written message from Watts."

Without a word, Skull handed Wurzback the envelope, and Wurzback spoke to the sentry.

"Mayfield, wake everybody. Tell them we're ridin' in fifteen minutes. Nogales's orders."

Mayfield entered the house and Wurzback followed, leaving Skull Rudabaugh standing beside his horse. It wouldn't really matter if Wurzback insisted on being in control, unless the expedition ended in failure. In that event, Wurzback could also take the blame.

Hermosillo, Mexico. July 18, 1884

The storm passed well before midnight. Silver stars bloomed in the purple meadow of the sky. Wes and El Lobo continued watching the cabin, but there was little activity except for an occasional shadow visible through a window, the result of a low-burning fire. Inside the cabin, four wounded men slept fitfully, while the others didn't sleep at all.

"There's a chance the horses might drift back," Suggs said.

"Not if they run as far as the village," said Yokum.

"He's right about that," Rowden said. "After the *Mejicanos* have penned 'em up for a week, we'll never see 'em again. That weasel of a doc will spread the word that we're in trouble out here, and our reputation in town will be shot to hell."

"We're likely to be shot to hell along with our reputation," said Tobin. "We got one man dead and four with lead in 'em, while the bastards that done it ain't got a scratch. We got no horses, just a little water, and a pair of killers waitin' for us."

"Packer may be conscious, come mornin'," Rowden said hopefully. "Maybe he'll have a plan."

Wicks laughed bitterly. "If he has, I hope it's better

than his ambush that got him an' Hanson gunned down."

Guaymos, Mexico. July 18, 1884

A few minutes before midnight, twelve horsemen rode north, bound for Hermosillo. Stem Wurzback had taken control of his ten-man outfit, and Skull Rudabaugh had chosen to ride along in silence. The success of their mission—reaching Hermosillo in time—was of more importance than contesting Wurzback's leadership, but the issue was by no means resolved. Skull would see to it that Wurzback's act of insubordination was made known to Dolan Watts at Nogales, and if that failed, there were other ways.

"Rein up," Wurzback ordered. "Time to rest the horses."

"You're resting the horses a mite often," said Skull.

"My decision," Wurzback snapped.

"I'm keeping that in mind," said Skull. "If we don't reach Hermosillo in time, I'll see that Nogales holds you responsible."

Wurzback said nothing, but Skull noticed with some satisfaction that there were fewer and fewer delays. Riding at a slow gallop, they were within a few miles of Hermosillo when the first gray light of dawn touched the eastern sky. They bypassed the village, reining up on a rise from which they could see the outlaw cabin.

"Not a horse in the corral," Wurzback said. "That don't seem right."

"This pair of gun-throwers always stampede the

horses first," said Skull. "Does that tell you anything?"

"Packer and his bunch may be elsewhere," Wurzback said with as much sarcasm as he could muster. "Don't you reckon they'd take the horses?"

"No danger, then," said Skull. "Why don't you just ride down there and knock on the door?"

"Hello, the cabin," Wurzback bawled. "Burke Packer, are you there? This is Wurzback and riders, from Guaymos."

"This is Tazlo," came the shouted response. "Packer's hurt, and we're pinned down."

"Hell," said Wurzback, in surprise, "I don't see no—"

The crack of a Winchester seemed loud in the morning stillness. The slug burned the flank of Wurzback's roan, and the animal began crow-hopping. Wurzback was pitched ignominiously into the sand. There were more shots, and men cried out in pain. One of the riders caught Wurzback's horse. Disorganized, they galloped out of range, while Wurzback ran after them, lead kicking up dust at his heels.

"By God, I wouldn't have missed this for all the tea in China," said Skull Rudabaugh as Wurzback stumbled into their midst.

"Damn it," Wurzback shouted, "bring me my horse."

One of the men brought the animal, still skittish, and bleeding from a bloody gash on its flank.

"The situation down there ain't likely to change in the next few minutes," said Skull. "Your horse is hurt; see to his wound."

"Damn the horse," Wurzback snarled.

He had his foot in the stirrup when Skull hit him. He fell, and the already spooked horse danced away from him. Furious, Wurzback went for his gun, only to find himself looking into the muzzle of Skull's Colt.

"I wouldn't," said Skull. "You're here against orders from Nogales. The rest of you men should know that, before he starts somethin' he can't finish. Those *hombres* with the rifles are no shorthorns. The two of them wiped out the outposts at Namiquipa and Chihuahua. Mayfield, you were there standing watch. You heard me tell Wurzback about the killings at Namiquipa and Chihuahua, and you heard me relay the orders I brought from Nogales."

"Yeah," Mayfield admitted, "I heard."

"You men can ride with Wurzback or you can ride with me," said Skull. "I'm taking my orders from Dolan Watts at Nogales, and I'll be reporting to him. If you're sidin' me, move over here to my right and tell me your names."

Mayfield was the first, and the others followed. Tuttle, Boyce, Upton, Lowe, Savage, McDaniel, Willis, Handy, Pucket . . .

"Damn you, Rudabaugh," Wurzback said, "you'll pay for this."

"You're lookin' at it a mite cockeyed," said Skull. "It's me that's followin' orders, an' if there's any payin' to be done, it's you that'll be doin' it. Now, if you aim to ride along and add your gun to the fracas, welcome. If you don't, then ride out an' keep goin'. After I report to Watts at Nogales, there won't be room for you anywhere in Mexico."

*   *   *

After firing at the band of outlaws from Guaymos, Wes and El Lobo remained under cover, but the riders remained out of range of the Winchesters.

"I reckon we won't have to ride to Guaymos," Wes said. "The outlaws from there are over yonder on that rise, wonderin' what to do about us."

"We don't stay here," said El Lobo. "There be many, and they surround us."

"No," Wes agreed, "I reckon we'll have to retreat until we can think of some way of attacking without getting our ears shot off. We'll ride back into the mountains and force them to come looking for us. They'll be a day or two, licking their wounds. Maybe we can track down our packhorse, or at least find a place to buy grub."

Wes and El Lobo rode away while the outlaws from Guaymos were on the far side of the ridge. The men within the cabin were jubilant.

"By God," said Tazlo, "Juarez and Nogales must be organizing against these attacks. One of you go and hail the riders from Guaymos. Tell 'em the killers have backed off."

"Somethin' tells me we'd better ride through town and look for a general store," Wes said. "When that bunch comes after us, they may have even more hired guns. We got to add to our store of grub while we can."

"No packhorse," said El Lobo.

"No," Wes agreed, "but that might be just as well. If we have to run, a packhorse would only slow us down. Besides our saddlebags, each of us can carry maybe fifty extra pounds behind our saddles. What really bothers me is that we may not be able to find ammunition for our Colts and Winchesters."

"Per'ap we take shells from those *hombres* that wish us dead," said El Lobo.

Wes laughed. "I reckon they'd object to that."

"They no object if they be dead," El Lobo said.

The day was still young, and there were few people on the streets. El Lobo pointed to a long, low adobe building in the next block. The faded sign across the front was all in Spanish, and there was only a droop-eared mule tied at the hitch rail. El Lobo entered first, and by the time they reached the counter, the storekeeper was there to greet them. He was a balding little Mexican in a white apron, and he wasn't happy to see them.

"I am not open for business, *señors*."

"We pay," El Lobo said softly. "*Oro*." On the counter he dropped one of the gold medallions, and in the light from a single window, the dragon's head had never seemed more forbidding.

The little storekeeper's eyes darted to the tied-down Colts and then back to the unsmiling faces of the formidable men who stood before him.

"*Por favor*," he said. "I make the mistake. Satisfy your needs, *señors*."

"*Sí*," said El Lobo. He returned the dragon medallion to his pocket, replacing it with a pair of gold coins.

Chapter 7

By the time Skull Rudabaugh, Stem Wurzback, and the outlaws from Guaymas had ridden to the cabin, Burke Packer had regained consciousness. Rudabaugh took charge.

"If you ain't able to talk, Packer, I'll question these other *hombres*. I'm from Nogales, and we're organizing to counter these attacks."

"I can talk," Packer replied, "and it's my responsibility. I underestimated that pair of gunmen. They're curly wolves, and they aim to kill us all. Before we could flank 'em, they rode right over Hanson an' me. Hanson's dead, an' they near killed me."

"And you had how many men?" Skull asked.

"Five," said Packer, "an' I didn't reckon we'd need more. I told you I underestimated that pair of gun-throwers."

"I can accept that," Skull replied, "but how is it this pair of hell-raisers managed to find this place and trap you? Your four remaining men should have ridden them down."

"I was unconscious," said Packer. "I paid for my mistake."

Skull said nothing, shifting his eyes to each of Packer's men.

"Packer was hard-hit," Blake said defensively. "I lit out for town to git the doc, while the others brought Packer an' Hanson here."

"Simple enough, I reckon," said Skull. "The gunmen just followed you."

"That's how it was," Blake admitted. "Hanson was dead, an' we was tryin' to save Packer."

"So they stampeded your horses," said Skull.

"Yeah," Blake said. "Last night, durin' a storm. We tried to get to 'em first, but the bastards cut down three of us an' run off the horses."

Stem Wurzback laughed. "My God, what a feather-legged bunch."

"That's enough!" Skull shouted.

Some of Packer's riders had their guns half drawn, their vengeful eyes on Wurzback.

"This is no time to be fightin' among ourselves," said Skull, his eyes on Wurzback. "I reckon there's sense to what Packer's told us. These *hombres* are no ordinary gun-toters, and they're just a hell of a lot more than a man expects. That's how they wiped us out in Namiquipa and Chihuahua."

"We're gettin' nowhere standin' here palaverin'," Wurzback said, "while that pair's gittin' farther an' farther away."

Mayfield laughed. "They sure enough dropped your carcass in the dirt, an' as I recall, you was runnin' the other way."

Wurzback was furious when the rest of his riders laughed. Skull Rudabaugh spoke.

"We don't have to worry about losing that pair.

They'll find us, likely when we're not expecting them. As long as we're on the defensive, they'll stay one jump ahead of us, taking other outposts by surprise like they took Namiquipa and Chihuahua. I aim to telegraph Dolan Watts, at Nogales. While I can't tell him just how serious this situation is, I can tell him it calls for a grouping of men from our outposts all over Mexico. I'll be asking him to telegraph every outpost, asking them to send as many riders as possible, and we'll meet in Durango. From there, we'll send an army of men across Mexico."

"I like the sound of it," said Packer, "but it'll take months. Some of our outposts—Tampico, Poza Rica, Chilpancingo, Mexico City, and others—are hundreds of miles away."

"You're forgettin' somethin'," Skull said. "Thanks to the mines—iron ore, silver, and gold—there are railroads all over Mexico. Load men and horses into boxcars, and they can travel hundreds of miles in a matter of hours."

"You're takin' a hell of a lot for granted," said Wurzback scornfully. "Them railroads are government-owned. Do you aim to take command of them, too?"

"If necessary," Skull said. "I have some influence in Nogales, and Nogales can get to the right people in Mexico City, if need be. That's why Dolan Watts sent me here, gents. I have the authority to resolve this sorry situation in any manner I see fit. I can demand and get every damn locomotive and railroad car in Mexico, should I need them. If there are questions or doubts, let's hear them."

"One question," Blake said. "What are we goin' to do for horses?"

"Hermosillo's a fair-sized town," said Skull. "There must be wealthy *Mejicanos* with a horse or two they could be persuaded to contribute to the cause. When you're ready to go after them, you're welcome to borrow some of our mounts."

"I don't git my horse back," Wurzback said angrily, "somebody gits gut-shot."

"Wurzback," said Skull, "if anybody's gut-shot, it'll be you, and I'll personally take care of it. Now shut the hell up."

"I'm ready to go after them horses," Blake said. "Who'll go with me?"

All of Packer's able-bodied riders volunteered to go, and they rode out on borrowed horses, bound for Hermosillo. Skull Rudabaugh rode with them, prepared to send a telegram to Nogales, drawing the Sandlin outlaws from all over Mexico.

Nogales, Mexico. July 18, 1884

Dolan Watts studied the telegram he had just received from Skull Rudabaugh. While it was, of necessity, shy on detail, the enormity of what Rudabaugh had requested told Watts much. Jules Sumner, Watts's second-in-command, was aware of the crisis and of Skull Rudabaugh's mission to Hermosillo. Before making his next move, Watts met with Sumner.

"There's a hell of a lot ridin' on Rudabaugh's judgment," Sumner said after reading the telegram. "How far do you aim to go?"

"All the way to Durango," said Watts. "I'm wirin'

every outpost to send at least six riders, well armed, for an undisclosed mission. I aim to be there. You'll be in charge here, and I reckon I don't have to tell you we're operatin' under the utmost secrecy. I'll outline all this for Rance Stringfield and send a rider to Juarez. I'll want six of our most dependable men to ride with me."

"It's a mighty long ride," said Sumner.

"We'll ride to El Desemboque and take one of our packets to Mazatlán," Watts said. "From there we'll ride to Durango. We'll ride at dawn. You may not hear from me until our mission is accomplished, and don't use the telegraph unless you have to. This is a touchy situation."

"It's just hard to believe two *hombres* can raise so much hell," said Sumner.

"Believe it," Watts replied. "Just what they've done already is enough to discredit us, if word gets out. They must be stopped."

"Maybe you oughta put a price on their heads," said Sumner. "That would sweeten the pot, far as the gang's concerned."

"Maybe I will," Watts replied. "Five thousand dollars for each of them."

"Dead or alive?"

"Yes," said Watts, "but preferably dead."

Wes and El Lobo reached the foothills, and when Wes reined up, El Lobo reined up beside him.

"Damn it," Wes said, "I can't see ridin' to another town lookin' for more outlaws when that bunch from Guaymas came lookin' for us. It bothers me that they somehow got the word. That means other outposts may have been warned, and there may be more warnin's goin' out from Hermosillo. If I could get my hands on a telegraph instrument . . ."

"The telegraph talks to you?"

"I know it backwards, forwards, and upside down," said Wes. "I spent considerable time with the railroad. If the Sandlin gang's dug in all over Mexico, they must be usin' the telegraph."

"There be telegraph in Hermosillo?"

"I'd bet on it," Wes said. "Generally, where there's a railroad, there's a telegraph line."

"When dark come," said El Lobo, "per'ap we find this telegraph?"

"Exactly what I'm thinking," Wes said. "With any luck, the telegrapher will close up shop and leave the instrument. Half those outlaws are without horses, some are wounded, and I doubt they'll be ready to come lookin' for us before tomorrow. Maybe by then we'll know what their next move will be."

They rode on, and reaching an elevation where they could view the distant town, they unsaddled their horses and prepared to wait for darkness.

Reaching Hermosillo, Skull Rudabaugh parted company with Burke Packer's riders. He headed for the railroad depot and the telegraph office, while Packer's men went looking for new mounts to be acquired by whatever means might be necessary. The Mexican telegrapher sent Rudabaugh's message and accepted payment without comment.

"I'll wait for an answer," Rudabaugh said.

There was a trio of ladder-back chairs against one wall, and Skull sat in one of them.

"*Señor*, you are not permitted to remain in here," said the telegrapher.

Rudabaugh took from his pocket a gold medallion, offering it on the palm of his hand, the dragon head up. The telegrapher backed away, his hands raised as though he expected Skull to physically attack him. He retreated to the cubicle where the telegraph instrument was and remained there for an uneasy hour, until Skull's answer came. It was brief:

> Durango proposal accepted stop. Go there with riders from Hermosillo and Guaymas stop. Wait for orders.

There was no name, and none was necessary. Mounting his horse, Skull rode back to the outlaw cabin, prepared to counter any doubts. Only Stem Wurzback had doubts, and he wasted no time making them known.

"So you're aimin' to take half the riders from every Sandlin outpost in Mexico. That's leavin' 'em all at half strength, just invitin' this pair of killers to ride in and wipe 'em out, while ever'body else hunkers in Durango."

"Win, lose, or draw," Skull said, "it's my responsibility, not yours. You won't have to worry about your outpost bein' attacked. All your outfit and all of Packer's will be goin' to Durango as soon as Packer's able to ride."

"We all lay around here while that pair of killers just rides away," said Wurzback. "I think some of us oughta take their trail. At least we'd know where they are."

"That would be insubordination, and you know it," Skull replied. "If you ride out of here against orders from Nogales, don't bother comin' back."

Wes and El Lobo were far to the south of Hermosillo, and at a high enough elevation to see the Sandlin outlaws, should they attempt to ride out. But as sundown approached, their vigil had gone unrewarded.

"They're plannin' something," said Wes.

"*Sí,*" El Lobo agreed. "Per'ap telegraph talk to us."

Wes and El Lobo prepared their meal and doused their fire well before dark. Some of the lights of town had already begun to wink off when they saddled their horses and rode out. Empty trotted ahead. They reached the railroad several miles south of Hermosillo and followed it until they could see a few dim lights in the distance.

"Lucky for us the Mexicans build their railroads away from town," Wes said. "There's a good chance we can bust into the telegraph office and get away without anybody knowin' until morning."

Eventually, in the starlight, they could see the shadowy hulk of the water tank, and beyond that, the darkened railroad depot.

"You stay with the horses, within the shadow of the water tank," said Wes. "I'll take Empty with me. If there's any commotion, if I'm discovered, bring the horses on the run."

"*Sí,*" El Lobo replied.

Wes reached the shadow of the depot. The building faced the railroad track, and Wes slipped cautiously to the corner of the building, where he could see the front. Through the front window, a lamp glowed. Keeping within the shadow of the roof over-hang, Wes crept to the door. It was common for one man to serve as telegrapher as well as agent for the railroad and, in isolated areas, to have living quarters within the depot. There was but one way to find out. Wes knocked cautiously on the door, and when he received no response, he knocked again. Empty stood behind him, and there was no warning growl.

"Stay, Empty," said Wes.

Drawing the throwing knife from his boot, Wes slipped its thin blade between the edge of the door and the doorjamb. Releasing the latch, he entered without difficulty. The lit lamp proved a blessing, for on the desk next to the instrument was a substantial stack of papers. From his own experience with the railroad, Wes recalled that most telegraphers kept copies of messages sent and received. He dragged a chair over next to the lamp and began going through the dog-eared papers. The very first received mes-sage that he read bore the day's date, was scribbled in Spanish, and had been sent from Nogales. It had no signature, but the brief text told him much. It mentioned riders from Hermosillo and Guaymas, and an eventual meeting in Durango. Hurriedly, he looked for the original message to which the answer had been sent. He found it, written in English, recom-mending a coming together in Durango. Obviously the outlaws were using the telegraph as little as pos-sible. He replaced the sheaf of papers where he had found them and was about to leave the office when he was struck by inspiration so bold, so outrageous, he laughed aloud. With the outlaws attempting to conceal the devastating attacks on their outposts, suppose the telegraph lines were suddenly ablaze with the very news the Sandlin gang was trying so hard to conceal? Wes sat down before the telegraph instrument. Knowing nothing of the procedure in Mexico, running his fingers swiftly over the key, he requested permission to send. To his surprise, permission was immediately granted by an operator in Nogales. Wes quickly tapped out his message:

> Hombres of the dragon's head empire are gathering in Durango stop. Two gunmen seek to destroy the Sandlin outlaws stop. Outlaws in Namiquipa and Chihuahua are dead stop. All Sandlin riders ordered to Durango to search Mexico for these two hombres stop. Receiving operators are ordered to relay these words.

Wes signed off, and the operator in Nogales clicked out his signal that the message had been received. Immediately the instrument began to chatter, requesting permission to send. Wes granted it, and received the brief message:

> Identify yourself.

Wes answered with a single sentence.

> We are the two hombres who will destroy the Sandlin gang stop. Death to dragon.

He signed off, and before the instrument could respond, he found a pair of pliers and clipped the wire. From his pocket, he took one of the dragon's-head medallions and left it on the desk where the telegraph key had been. Hanging from a nail on the wall was a set of lineman's spurs—climbing hooks—and he took them. With the telegraph instrument and the climbing hooks, he stepped out the door, closing it behind him. Empty was waiting, and they soon were lost in the concealing shadows beneath the water tank.

"What telegraph say?" El Lobo asked.

"Plenty," said Wes. "Let's ride back into the hills and make camp, and I'll tell you."

Wes and El Lobo unsaddled their horses, and in the starlight, El Lobo looked wonderingly at the items Wes had taken from the telegraph office.

"They're callin' the gang together to come after us," Wes said.

"The telegraph say that to you?"

"Yeah," said Wes. "I found a copy of a message sent to Nogales by one of the Sandlin gang. It suggested that Sandlin riders from all over Mexico travel to Durango. Then there was an answer from Nogales directin' riders from Hermosillo and Guaymas to go to Durango and wait there for orders. Those messages have to involve the Sandlin gang. Nothing else makes sense."

"Why they don't talk about us on the telegraph?"

"We're hurting them," Wes said, "and we'll hurt them more when word gets out about what we've done in Namiquipa and Chihuahua. These outlaws, with their dragon-head coins, have a reputation, and everybody's afraid of them. What do you reckon will happen if all Mexico knows the Sandlin gang is on the run from just two *hombres* with guns?"

"*Comico*," said El Lobo. "They be disgrace."

"I used the telegraph to tell Mexico about the gang, and about us," Wes said, "and I brought the instrument with me. I'll have chances to use it again."

"How you do that? There be no wires to it."

"See these climbing hooks?" said Wes. "With them on my boots, I can climb any telegraph pole. When I patch the instrument into the line, I can send messages anytime."

"We ride to Durango?"

"I think so," Wes said. "The message I just sent will play hell with the Sandlin gang's reputation, and when they learn we can use the telegraph, we won't have to look for them. They'll be huntin' us with every man that can straddle a horse and use a gun."

Juan Pablo, Hermosillo's constable, had been called to the railroad depot the following morning, and he didn't relish the task that lay ahead. The cursed *gringos* bought and sold *señoritas* for *putas*, rustled horses, and laughed in his face, but this time they had gone too far. Taking the medallion with the dragon's head that Wes had left behind, Pablo mounted his horse and headed for the distant cabin occupied by Burke Packer and his riders. He was seen as he came over the rise, and half a dozen of the outlaws were waiting for him. He reined up, and since nobody asked him to step down, he remained in the saddle. With a sigh of resignation, he spoke.

"I speak to the Señor Packer."

"Packer ain't feelin' exactly prime," Blake said. "What do you want?"

Expecting trouble, Skull Rudabaugh stepped out the door.

"I'm Rudabaugh," said Skull, "and I'm in charge here. What do you want of us?'"

"I am not for certain, *señor*," Pablo said. "In the night, the telegraph instrument be taken and this be left in its place."

He dropped the medallion in the sand at Rudabaugh's feet, and the morning sun shone brightly on the dragon's head.

"I give you my word that nobody from here took your telegraph instrument," said Skull. "Was anything else taken?"

"*Sí*," Pablo replied. "Pliers and lineman's spurs."

"I don't know how the coin got there," said Skull, "unless somebody's trying to frame us. We have no use for any of the items taken. When we have need of the telegraph, we pay."

Pablo nodded and, without another word, rode away. Skull Rudabaugh returned to the cabin to face Burke Packer and Stem Wurzback.

"We heard," said Packer. "What do you make of it?"

"The same pair that's been givin' us hell broke into the depot and took the telegraph instrument," Skull replied, "and at least one of them knows how to use it. Why else would he have taken the pliers and lineman's hooks?"

"We're in trouble," said Packer. "If one of them knows the code, they can flood the country with anything they choose."

"Yeah," Skull agreed, "and by now Watts will have left Nogales, bound for Durango. There's nobody we can warn, except maybe Rance Stringfield in Juarez."

Stem Wurzback laughed. "Then you got to holler real loud or do some hard ridin', since you got no telegraph. This is all your fault, Rudabaugh. I'd of sent some riders after them two hell-raisers when they rode away from here. You let 'em go scot-free, givin' 'em time to break into the railroad depot last night."

"Wurzback," Skull said coldly, "when this is all finished, you and me are gonna take us a ride. Somewhere nice and quiet, where it's just you and me. Then we'll settle all our differences. Tomorrow at first light, we leave for Durango. Those of you recovering from wounds will have to make the best of it."

Austin, Texas. July 18, 1884

Texas Ranger Bodie West had been away. When he returned, his companion, Dylan Stewart, had some interesting news.

"Bodie," Stewart said, "this came in last night on the wire. We picked it up through the Juarez operator."

He handed West the message Wes Stone had sent the night before. West eased himself down in a ladder-back chair and read the message.

"That's one *bueno hombre*, with more than his share of sand," Stewart said.

"God Almighty," said West, "I'm surprised he's lived this long. I knew his daddy, and this is the very damn fool thing Nathan Stone would have done."

"You're right about that, from what I've heard," Stewart said, "but if this is who we're thinkin' it is, let's don't sell him short. He's got himself a gun-quick *compañero* ridin' with him, and in old Mexico, it takes some kind of *hombre* to accomplish that."

Juarez, Mexico. July 18, 1884

The telegram from Nogales—with word of the gathering in Durango—reached Rance Stringfield only minutes ahead of the message Wes Stone had sent the night before. Turk Corbin had brought both messages and waited in silence until Stringfield had read them.

"What do you make of all this, Turk?" Stringfield asked.

"Two weeks ago, this coming together in Durango might have been the thing to do," Corbin said, "but now I have my doubts. This pair of pistoleers is far more dangerous than any of us imagined, because one of them knows the code and can use the telegraph."

"Where did this message originate?" Stringfield demanded.

"The telegrapher here says it was sent from Hermosillo," said Corbin.

"Damn it," Stringfield shouted, "he should be able to reach the operator at Hermosillo and find out what's goin' on there."

"He tried," said Corbin, "but immediately after this message was received, the key at Hermosillo went silent. It's been silent ever since."

"Could the line have been cut?"

"No," Corbin said, "because contact has been made south of Hermosillo. But there's no answer from the operator at Hermosillo."

"Get in touch with railroad officials," said Stringfield. "They can order the next train that's southbound to stop and find out why the key's dead at Hermosillo."

"Now," Wes said, "how do we get to Durango?"

"Per'ap six day," said El Lobo. "We follow these mountains."*

"I've never asked you," Wes said, "but from what part of Mexico do you come?"

"San Ignacio," said El Lobo. "It be near the water, north of Mazatlán, per'ap one day ride to the west of Durango."

"I remember Mazatlán, from a map I saw once," Wes said. "Ships dock there."

"*Sí*," said El Lobo. "It is there the *bastardo* Spaniard who is my father boarded the sailing ship, never to return."

"Sorry," Wes said. "I didn't mean to remind you of that. Goin' back won't be easy on you, if . . . nobody's waiting."

El Lobo finished his coffee, set down the tin cup, and when he finally spoke, it was with a wistfulness.

"There was Tamara."

"Your intended?"

El Lobo laughed bitterly. "Tamara is pure, while El Lobo is the half-breed. Tamara Delmano is all I am not, and I am driven from her door as a *perro*."

"Tamara drove you away?"

"Tamara did not," said El Lobo. "It is her *rico* father, Hernando Delmano."

"You should have fought for her," Wes said.

*The Sierra Madre.

"For why?" said El Lobo. "San Ignacio say I am no good, Hernando Delmano say I am no good, my own mother say I am no good, so I ride away. I sell my gun to outlaws and my soul to *el Diablo*."

"You're not selling your gun to outlaws now," Wes said, "and you're a long way from *el Diablo* havin' your soul. We'll be near San Ignacio, and Tamara will be older now. Why don't you call on her?"

"Older," said El Lobo. "Per'ap *esposa*."

"You don't know that," Wes said. "Her highfalutin old daddy sounds like the kind that'll keep her unmarried until he picks some varmint that suits him. See Tamara, and if she's willing, take her with you to the United States."

"*Por favor, amigo*, do not tempt me," said El Lobo. "It is the destiny of a fool to have only his dreams."

"Wrong," Wes replied. "It is the destiny of a fool to live with his dreams only as long as he's satisfied with 'em. If you want Tamara and she wants you, there won't be anything or anybody in Mexico big enough to stand in your way."

"Per'ap you be right," said El Lobo.

He said no more, nor did Wes. Both knew that they might never leave Mexico alive, that if their bones were left to bleach forever beneath the hot desert sun, then all their dreams were for naught.

Hermosillo, Mexico. July 19, 1884

Twenty-two men, led by Skull Rudabaugh, rode south, bound for Durango. Passing through the village, they found it deserted, but from behind closed doors, some Mexican inhabitants of Hermosillo breathed sighs of relief. Others, however, suppressed their anger as they beheld their horses being ridden away by the outlaws.

"Madre mía," said Constable Juan Pablo. *"Madre mía."*

Chapter 8

Rance Stringfield had sent for Turk Corbin, and when Corbin arrived, he had disturbing news.

"I just got word from the railroad officials," Corbin said, "and they've learned why the telegraph at Hermosillo has been silent. The instrument was stolen, probably by the same gent that sent the message givin' us hell. He also took a set of climbin' hooks."

"Then the hell-raising has only started," said Stringfield. "They can climb a pole anywhere in Mexico and telegraph anything that suits their fancy."

"With the telegraph government-controlled," Corbin said, "we ought to get some help from the military."

Stringfield laughed. "The military doesn't care a damn for us. The only reason *they're* not givin' us hell is that they're still out of favor with the people, and have been since the war."

"Hell's fire," said Corbin, "that was near forty years ago."

"Three times under Santa Anna's military dictatorship left a lasting impression," Stringfield said. "Our organization could never have survived under a strong military, but as it is, in return for their hostility, they seem to feel the Mexican people deserve whatever they get."

"And that includes us," said Corbin. "Who do you aim to send to Durango?"

"You," Stringfield said. "Take five men of your choosing. Brodie Fentress is *segundo* there."

"Will he be in command?"

"No," said Stringfield. "Dolan Watts from Nogales is responsible for this gathering in Durango, and I expect him to take charge."

"You want me to report back to you?"

"I think not," Stringfield replied. "After this recent trouble with the telegraph—and with our enemies in possession of an instrument—I think we should leave it alone. We'll allow Watts to make decisions regarding the use of the telegraph."

"Yeah," said Corbin. "Before this is done, I got an idea we'll all be cussing the telegraph. I'll get some men together, and we'll leave tomorrow."

Durango, Mexico. July 23, 1884

The outlaw stronghold was actually twenty-five miles west of Durango, a day's ride from Mazatlán. Dolan Watts and his men reached Mazatlán in the late afternoon.

"We'll take quarters here for the night," Watts said. "If you go to the cantinas, limit your drinks. We'll leave for Durango at first light."

Mazatlán, with ready access to the Pacific ocean, hosted many sailing ships, and as a result boasted several hotels of some elegance. There were newspapers from· half a dozen Mexican towns, but none from Hermosillo. But there was one from Durango, and Watts bought a copy. There was a possibility that the arrival of many riders had stirred curiosity and that there might be some mention of it in the newspaper. But Watts was unprepared for the startling spread that greeted him. Covering half the front page, the headline read:

EL DIABLO PISTOLAS COME, BANDIDOS DIE

It began with the text of the devastating telegram Wes Stone had sent from Hermosillo, which had prompted an investigation at Namiquipa and Chihuahua. Suddenly, in light of the newly discovered vulnerability of the Sandlin gang, people were talking. There were accounts of the killings of the outlaws at Namiquipa and Chihuahua, and the Mexican doctor at Hermosillo had told of wounded outlaws held captive in a cabin by just two men with deadly rifles. They had escaped only when the El Diablo Pistolas had allowed them to, and had immediately ridden away. The Mexican agent at the depot had testified to the theft of the telegraph key and was virtually certain it had been taken by the El Diablo Pistolas, since their telegram had been sent from there. The more Watts read, the more damaging it became. There was an editorial praising the unknown El Diablo Pistolas for accomplishing what Mexico's *soldados* had been unable or unwilling to do, and openly urging the Mexican people to shelter and secure the renegades when possible. Yet another story speculated that, since the El Diablo Pistolas had taken the telegraph instrument, there would be other revealing telegrams. With that possibility in mind, the newspaper promised to remain in constant touch with the telegraph office. Watts dropped the paper on the hotel bed and went after copies of other newspapers. To his horror, their accounts were much the same, and some had gone ever further. The Mazatlán paper carried a story in which a prominent citizen of San Ignacio—Hernando Delmano—accused outlaws of stealing young Tamara, his only daughter. Playing off Delmano's accusation, the newspaper suggested that the regular disappearance of young girls was, indeed, the work of outlaws, and that the *señoritas* were being sold into slavery. Some of the papers had boldly taken from Wes Stone's telegram the dramatic words, *Death to the dragon.* Dolan Watts wadded the papers, dropping them at his feet. He had once believed the Sandlin gang, with its dragon dynasty, all but invincible. Now he was beset with uncertainty, dogged by an emotion unfamiliar to him. For the first time, Dolan Watts was afraid.

Los Mochis, Mexico. July 23, 1884

"What do you know of this place?" Wes asked. "Are Sandlin outlaws holed up here?"

"I do not know," said El Lobo. "If the telegraph speak the truth, per'ap they be gone to Durango."

"I'd like to get my hands on a newspaper," Wes said. "I can't believe the Sandlin gang is powerful enough to keep the lid on. Especially after I sent that telegram. There's a dock and there's ships, so one more strange *hombre* shouldn't seem out of place.

Empty doesn't like towns, so I'll leave him with you."

"*Sí*," said El Lobo. "Per'ap these papers be worth the risk."

El Lobo watched Wes ride away, unaware that what he would soon learn would change the course of his life and sear into his very soul his hatred of the Sandlin gang.

Wes reined up in the hills above the town and saw nothing to arouse his suspicions. Several ships were docked, and he could see tiny figures as men scurried about unloading them. In the distance to the north was a distant finger of land. But beyond that—and before him—was an endless expanse of sky-blue water. The Pacific Ocean. Kicking the grulla into a trot, Wes rode on. The town, when he reached it, seemed dramatically different from inland Mexican towns. There were goods for sale everywhere, and open markets sheltered only by a makeshift roof. Dark-eyed *señoritas* looked at him, but he wasn't the only man wearing guns, and thus attracted no undue attention. There were newspapers from Los Mochis, Mazatlán, and Durango. Wes bought copies of all three. Before leaving, he rode part of the way through town and made a discovery. On one end of a building that might have been a warehouse, there was a sign, TELEGRAFO.

"Telegraph," he said aloud. "First one I've ever seen where there wasn't a railroad."

He rode on and was soon in the foothills. With a convenient telegraph line, it might be a good time to send another telegram before they rode on. He found

El Lobo with his back to a tree, his eyes on the distant blue water.

"You didn't even turn your head," Wes chided. "Suppose it hadn't been me."

"I trust the *perro*," said El Lobo. "He sleeps."

"There's a telegraph office," Wes said. "Before we ride on, I ought to track down the line and send another telegram. But I can do that in the morning. Let's find a place to make camp. I want to fan through these newspapers before dark."

They rode until they found a stream, and there they unsaddled their horses.

"I fix grub," said El Lobo. "You read papers."

Wes unfolded the paper from Durango first, and caught his breath.

"Let the grub wait," Wes said, "and look at this."

El Lobo hesitated, and it occurred to Wes that he might not be able to read.

"Go ahead with the grub," said Wes, "but keep your ears open. I'll read it to you."

He began reading, and El Lobo ceased what he was doing and listened. He laughed, and when Wes had finished the lengthy account in the Durango newspaper, he began reading the copy from Mazatlán. When he reached the story in which Hernando Delmano had accused outlaws of stealing Tamara, he paused, not believing his eyes.

"You stop," said El Lobo.

"I didn't know if I should read any more or not," Wes said, "but this is something I think you should know. Listen."

El Lobo listened, spellbound. When Wes had finished, El Lobo was gritting his teeth, a hand resting on the butt of each of his Colts. When he finally spoke, Wes could scarcely hear him.

"*Madre de Dios,*" he hissed, "they take her for a *puta. Por Dios*, I kill them. I kill them all."

"I know how you feel," Wes said, "but you should first find and save Tamara. Killing the outlaws can wait."

"Tamara be *puta*," said El Lobo bitterly.

"You don't know that," Wes said, "but even if she *is* a whore, it's no fault of hers. If she still wanted you, would you turn away and forget her?"

El Lobo looked at Wes, and his dark eyes were like points of flame. His mouth worked, but he couldn't speak. He dropped his eyes toward the toes of his boots.

"Well," said Wes, "would you? Would you turn away and forget her? Does El Lobo allow his foolish pride to suck the life from his dreams?"

"No!" El Lobo shouted. "No! I find her, and I kill the *bastardos* that take her."

"Tomorrow, then," said Wes, "we'll ride as fast and as far as we can. I think first we must talk to her father, Hernando Delmano."

"He no talk to me," El Lobo said. "I am not pure."

"So what?" said Wes. "That won't mean a damn thing if you can rescue Tamara. I'll be ridin' with you."

Wes extended his right hand, and at first it seemed that El Lobo wouldn't accept it. When he finally did, his dark eyes lit with what could only be joy, and he spoke.

"*Bueno amigo, muy bueno companero.*"

Los Mochis, Mexico. July 24, 1884

Wes and El Lobo rode south at first light, bound for Mazatlán. Wes intentionally rode down into the foothills paralleling the bay. El Lobo looked at him questioningly.

"We'll travel at a lower elevation," Wes said. "It'll be easier goin', and when we're far enough from town, I aim to send another telegraph message. I can do that while we rest the horses."

While El Lobo had said nothing, Wes knew he was impatient. The one thing Hernando Delmano hadn't said in the newspaper story was how much time had elapsed since Tamara had disappeared. It all depended on how swiftly the outlaws smuggled their human cargo out of Mexico. The only real hope Wes had was that the girl had been taken within the last three or four days. The turmoil his telegraph message had caused might have delayed the sailing ship that would have taken Tamara away. They followed the meandering telegraph line until it was time to rest the horses. El Lobo watched with interest as Wes took the telegraph key from his saddlebag and attached the climbing hooks to his boots. Swiftly he climbed a pole and patched the instrument into the wire. He asked for and received permission to send, and without knowing with whom he had made contact, sent his message:

El Diablo Pistolas warn the Sandlin outlaws stop. We are coming for you stop. Death to the Dragon.

Quickly Wes broke the connection, climbed down the pole, and returned the equipment to his saddlebags.

"What telegraph say?" El Lobo asked.

"It told the Sandlin gang we're comin' after them," said Wes. "That first message got so much attention, I felt like we owed 'em another. I figure the newspaper people will be roosting pretty close to every telegraph office in the country. If this second message hits as hard as the first, that bunch of owlhoots in Durango ought to be pretty well spooked by the time we get there."

El Lobo said nothing. They mounted and rode on, stopping only to rest the horses. It was near sundown when they unsaddled their horses and made camp near a spring. There was a light wind from the south, and from somewhere in the distance a dog barked.

"Easy, old son," Wes said when Empty's hackles rose.

"Not be Mazatlán," said El Lobo. "Per'ap this time *mañana*."

After supper, they stretched out, heads on their saddles, and listened to their horses cropping grass.

"I reckon it's none of my business," Wes said, "but you've never told me your given name. I can't imagine your ma naming you El Lobo."

He was silent for so long, Wes thought he had become angry. Finally he laughed.

"My mother call me Palo Elfego, after my wandering father. I hate the name as much as I hate him. I take the name Wolf—El Lobo—for myself."

"I can't say I blame you," said Wes. "The name becomes you."

They rode out at dawn, and soon they could see a village below.

"More sailing ships," Wes said. "What town do you reckon this is?"*

"Not know," said El Lobo.

Durango, Mexico. July 25, 1884

When Dolan Watts and his men reached the outpost at Durango, more than five hundred of the Sandlin outlaws had gathered there. While most of the men paid no attention, the arrival of Dolan Watts was noted with interest by Brodie Fentress and Denton Rucker. Fentress, *segundo* of the Durango outpost, and Rucker, his second in command, waited for Watts and his men to dismount.

"So *you're* the daddy of this snake-stompin'," Fentress said. "I reckon you've seen the papers an' know what the telegraph's spreadin' all over the country."

"Yeah," said Watts. "How many of our outfits are here?"

"Less than half," Fentress said sourly. "What do you aim to do about the others?"

"Wait for them," said Watts, just as sourly. "Do you have a better idea?"

"No," Fentress replied, "but Black Bill Trevino likely will. He's on his way here from Mexico City."

"Then let him come," said Watts recklessly. "I'll step aside and he can appoint anybody he chooses—includin' you—to take command of this outfit. Somethin' had to be done, and if the rest of you don't

*Culiacán, roughly halfway between Los Mochis and Mazatlán.

like the moves I've made, then by God, I'll back off.
Do it your way."

Before Fentress could respond, there was the
thump of hoofbeats, a rider coming at a fast gallop.
He swung out of the saddle, a wad of newspapers
in his hand.

"Brodie, the Durango paper just come out, and
there's another telegram from them *hombres* that's out
to get us."

Silently, Fentress took the paper and unfolded it.
The entire front page was devoted to the mysterious
duo who had begun the destruction of the Sandlin
gang. In addition to the threatening text of the second
telegraph message, there was the text of the first,
along with all the damning information that had appeared previously.

"By God," said Rucker, "if this goes on, gunnin'
down these two *hombres* will be the least of our troubles. We'll have to fight all of Mexico."

"That's the truth if I ever heard it," Fentress said.
"These Mexes used to be scared to death of us, and
now they're laughing at us. Where in tarnation do
we start lookin' for the pair of varmints that started
all this?"

All eyes were on Dolan Watts, and he had no
answers.

San Ignacio, Mexico. July 25, 1884

Wes and El Lobo reached the village in the late
afternoon, and El Lobo pointed out the Delmano resi-
dence. By Mexican standards, it was a mansion. De-

spite El Lobo's obvious interest in Tamara Delmano, he seemed reluctant to face her father.

"Come on," Wes said, "and let's get this behind us. The worst he can do is ask us to leave."

They dismounted and, leading their horses, approached the big house with the white columns and spacious grounds. They had been seen. The grim man who stood waiting for them was dressed in black, his arms folded across his chest.

"That be Hernando Delmano," said El Lobo.

Their welcome was much as El Lobo had predicted.

"Palo Elfego, you are not welcome here," Delmano said.

"I come only for word of Tamara," said El Lobo, "and then I go. When she be taken by outlaws?"

"Five days ago," Delmano said. "Now go."

"You don't show much concern for your daughter," said Wes. "What kind of man are you?"

"A private one," Delmano said, "and I do not welcome strangers who interfere where they are not wanted. Who are you, and what is your business here?"

"I am here with my *amigo*," said Wes, "and his concern is my own. We seek to find and rescue your daughter, Tamara. Not for your sake, but for hers."

"Then go," Delmano said, "and take with you my pity for your unfortunate choice of friends."

Wes and El Lobo had no choice. Mounting their horses, they rode back the way they had come. While Delmano's hostility had come as no surprise, El Lobo was obviously dejected.

"I only want to save Tamara," said El Lobo, "and still he hate me."

"That old *busardo* needs some holes poked in him, lettin' the pride leak out," Wes replied. "If we can return Tamara to him, maybe it'll change his feelings toward you."

"I not know where to look for her."

"In the last four or five days, we've raised hell and kicked a chunk under it," said Wes, "and I'm thinkin' that might have slowed the slave trade some. Tamara may still be in these parts. Maybe in Mazatlán."

"Per'ap," El Lobo said without much enthusiasm.

"We'll start in Mazatlán," said Wes. "If there's a whorehouse and it's under the control of the Sandlin gang, then maybe we can learn something there."

El Lobo said nothing. Now that the search for Tamara Delmano had begun, he seemed fearful of what they might discover.

Mazatlán, Mexico. July 25, 1884

Wes and El Lobo reached Mazatlán in the late afternoon. It was larger than any of the coastal towns they had passed along the way, and four sailing ships were at the dock. One of them was being loaded for departure. A Mexican flag fluttered from its mast.

"That could be a slave ship gettin' ready to leave," Wes said. "I reckon we got no time to lose. Let's find that whorehouse."

It was a time when such places were prominent, usually found in a part of town with an abundance of cheap cafes, run-down rooming houses, and cantinas. Mazatlán was no different. The place was a two-story affair near the waterfront, and a faded sign proclaimed it the CASA DE SEÑORITAS.

"It's late enough in the afternoon," Wes said. "They should be ready for business."

Wes pounded on the door with the butt of one of his Colts, while El Lobo waited uncertainly behind him. When the madam finally appeared, she eyed the duo suspiciously, but Wes had his foot in the door before she could close it.

"It is the time of the *siesta*," she objected.

"The *siesta* just ended," said Wes. "We're lookin' for a particular *señorita*."

She was still doing her best to close the door when Wes extended his hand. In his palm was one of the dragon medallions, and it produced the desired effect. Without a word, the woman allowed them to enter, and then closed the door behind them. She then spoke a single word.

"*Señoritas?*"

"Yes," Wes said. "We want to see all of them."

"No *comprender*."

Wes drew his right-hand Colt and placed its muzzle under her chin.

"All the *señoritas*," said Wes. "*Comprende?*"

"*Sí*," she replied.

She turned as though to mount the stairs, and in the split-second her back was to Wes, she drew from her bosom a .41-caliber derringer. She whirled, and there was barely time for Wes to seize her wrist with his left hand. The pocket pistol roared, dropping dust and plaster from the ceiling. His Colt still in his right hand, Wes slammed the muzzle of it against the woman's head. She slid to the floor, unconscious.

"That shot may bring the law," said Wes. "We may not have much time, but we'd better bind and gag this old *señorita*. Never trust a woman after she's tried to kill you."

Quickly they bound the woman with cords cut from window blinds, and El Lobo tore enough from the bottom of her long dress for a gag.

"I don't know Tamara," Wes said, "so you'll have to visit all the *señoritas*. Come on."

They took the stairs two at a time and found themselves looking down a long hall. Wes knocked on the first door, but there was no response. A knock on the second door went unanswered.

"Damn it," said Wes, "we don't have time to be polite."

He turned the knob of the first door and, finding the room empty, tried the second door, only to find another empty room. In the third room, a girl had drawn a sheet over her head. Wes yanked it off, but El Lobo shook his head. The naked girl wasn't Tamara. Quickly they found three more women, none of whom was the girl El Lobo sought. There were just two more doors at the end of the hall. One of the rooms was empty, but in the last one, an American girl with auburn hair sat on the edge of a rumpled bed. She wore nothing, and her face was buried in her hands. It seemed her very soul had been taken from her, and only when she lifted her head did her eyes go wide with the shock of recognition.

"Wes!" she cried. "Wes!"

She was pitifully thin, and when she got to her

feet, she stumbled and fell. Shocked for only an instant, Wes was by her side.

"Renita," he cried, "I left you in El Paso. How . . . why . . ."

He helped her to her feet, and she sank down on the bed, weeping wildly.

"Your woman?" El Lobo asked softly.

"My woman," said Wes.

"I go," El Lobo said. "Keep watch."

He fully understood the danger, for a shot had been fired, and at any moment their presence in the house might be discovered. Wes took Renita by the shoulders and shook her. There was no time for hysterics, and she gradually became aware of their precarious position.

"We have to get out of here," Wes said. "Where are your clothes?"

"In El Paso," she said between sobs, "but what does it matter? I've been here too long. I've been used. I've been made a whore, and nothing will ever be the same. I can't expect you to pretend it never happened."

"I won't pretend it never happened," said Wes, "but there's one thing that won't ever change. You're the same girl I left in El Paso, and you're being here is no fault of yours. Whatever's been done to you, I still want you. Has it changed your feelings for me?"

"Oh, dear God, no!" she cried. "I . . . I just thought . . . I'd lost you forever . . . because of . . . of what . . . I've become."

"Then dress yourself in whatever you can find," said Wes. "I'm taking you with me."

"Go with me while I look in some of the empty

rooms," she said. "There must be something I can wear."

"You're thinner than when I first found you in El Paso," said Wes. "Have they been starving you?"

"I've been starving myself," Renita replied. "Since the day they took me, I've prayed that I could die. Who is that . . . riding with you?"

"He used to be one of the outlaws I came to kill," said Wes, "until they tried to kill him. He calls himself El Lobo, but his real name is Palo Elfego. We came here looking for Tamara Delmano, a Spanish girl the outlaws stole away from San Ignacio. El Lobo wanted her, and I reckon she wanted him, but her daddy—Hernando Delmano—is a prideful old varmint that gave El Lobo the gate. We've been givin' the Sandlin outlaws hell, and we had the notion that maybe Tamara was still in Mazatlán, that they hadn't taken her away."

"Perhaps she was one of the two girls brought here," Renita said. "One of them was Mexican, but the other could have been Spanish. They were kept here three days and were taken away yesterday. The two men who brought them here said they were to be broken in before taking them aboard. I believe he was referring to a ship, because that's how I was brought here. I was taken west in a wagon, to the Gulf of California, and we sailed from there."

In a closet in one of the vacant rooms, Renita found some long dresses, one of which wasn't large enough to swallow her.

"I have nothing to wear under it," she said.

"No matter," said Wes. "Somehow we'll have to

get you a horse, and if we're able to manage that, I reckon we can find you some britches and a shirt."

"Some shoes or boots, too?"

"We'll try," Wes said. "Come on, and let's get out of here."

Descending the stairs, they found El Lobo keeping watch at the front door. The Mexican madam lay where they had left her, but she was conscious, and her dark eyes fairly glittered with hatred. On impulse, Renita seized the hem of the woman's long dress, drawing it almost over her head.

"Let her feet loose," said Renita. "She has something I can use.'

Mystified, Wes did so. Renita peeled off the madam's underdrawers and, raising her own skirt, wriggled into them. El Lobo watched with interest, a twinkle in his eyes.

"I don't like straddling a horse in a dress with my behind bare," Renita said.

Wes bound the madam's ankles, and they left the house. Empty had remained with the horses, and nothing seemed amiss.

"El Lobo—also known as Palo Elfego—this is Renita," said Wes. "From what she's told me, two girls were kept here for three days, and then possibly taken to a ship. One of them was Spanish and might have been Tamara Delmano."

"El Lobo thanks you," he said, bowing. "There is hope for Tamara."

"Damn right," said Wes. "Let's ride."

Chapter 9

Renita riding with Wes, the three of them reached the foothills above the harbor. In the distance, men were still loading the ship flying the Mexican flag.

"That one's gettin' ready to sail," Wes said, "but if it's a slaver, why are they loading other cargo?"

"The one that brought me had other cargo," said Renita. "I was locked in an iron cage on a lower deck with the freight."

"We'll have to board her," Wes said. "It'll soon be dark."

"I go," said El Lobo.

"You're not going alone," Wes said. "You don't know how many armed men you may be facing. Getting yourself killed won't help Tamara. Renita, we'll have to find a safe place to hide you."

"No," said Renita, "I don't want to be left alone. I want to go with you. I'll stay with the horses, and you can leave Empty with us."

"*Bueno*," El Lobo said. "*Señorita sensato.*"

Wes couldn't argue with that. Being in hostile territory, Renita would be safer with Empty and the horses than she would be in the mountains alone.

The vessel bearing the Mexican flag was the last in a line of four anchored near the dock. As darkness fell, there was the dim glow of a lantern on the prow of the ship being loaded.

"They may be sailing tonight," said Wes. "We don't have any time to spare."

They reined up several hundred yards from the dock, in the shadow of a warehouse whose far end faced the bay. Four men wrestled barrels and crates from the warehouse to the ship that was being loaded.

"Renita," Wes said, "you and Empty will stay here with the horses. El Lobo, you and me have to get inside that warehouse while all four of those *hombres* are somewhere between it and the ship. We'll buffalo them two at a time, and we should be able to board the ship before they come to their senses. But once aboard, we don't know how many of the outlaws we'll be facing. No shooting if it can be avoided. If there's no other way, we'll go over the side and swim for it. Ready?"

"*Sí,*" El Lobo said.

Keeping within the shadow of the building, they crept as near the front of the warehouse as they dared. Wes watched the dockworkers until he had some idea as to how long it took two of the men to deposit their cargo on board and return to the warehouse. As two of them approached the ship with their load, the second pair headed for the building. Wes nudged El Lobo, and as the men stepped through the door, Wes and El Lobo were behind them, each with a Colt in his hand. Both men were unconscious following swift blows to the head. Wes and El Lobo dragged them away from the door and waited for their companions to return. But the returning pair were curious.

"*Hola*," one shouted. "*Perezoso perros.*"*

They paused, reassured only after El Lobo uttered some convincing swear words in Spanish. When they entered, Wes took one and El Lobo the other, leaving them with their unconscious comrades.

"Let's go," said Wes. "We don't have any idea what's ahead of us, and we may not have much time."

They ran across the dock, thankful that the gangplank was in shadow. Apparently the upper deck was devoted only to cargo. Recalling what Renita had said about being locked in a cabin on the lower deck, Wes began looking for a way down. When he found it, there was only a dark hole, with a ladder. Somewhere below, there was a light, and Wes started down, El Lobo right behind him. Wes dropped the last few feet to the lower deck, and it was all that saved him. There was a roar, a muzzle flash, and lead sang off one of the iron rungs of the ladder. Wes drew and fired just as El Lobo dropped to the deck behind him. There was a groan and the sound of a gun striking the deck. El Lobo had drawn his Colt, but there were no more shots. The two captive women were imprisoned in an iron cage at the far end of the lower deck. There were two narrow bunks along one wall, and a slop jar, and nothing more. The two women had been stripped, and there were scabbed-over sores on their bare backs where they

*Lazy dogs.

had been beaten. One of the girls was clearly Mexican, while the other could have been American. It was the latter who spoke.

"Palo! Palo Elfego!"

"Tamara," said El Lobo. "I have come for you."

"Palo," she cried, "it is too late. I have been defiled."

Wes was going through the pockets of the dead outlaw. He found a handful of gold coins, several of which bore the image of the dragon. Among them was a key. Quickly he inserted it in the lock, opened the barred door, and swung it wide. Without a word, the Mexican girl sprang out the door, ran to the distant hatch, and disappeared up the ladder. There were shouts from somewhere above, evidence enough that the dockworkers had come to their senses and were sounding the alarm. To Wes, it seemed that Tamara was in shock, for she gripped the iron bars of the cell door and stared at El Lobo as though he had risen from the dead.

"Pry her loose from those bars and let's get out of here," Wes said. "If we're trapped on this lower deck, there'll be hell to pay."

His harsh words broke the spell. El Lobo seized the naked Tamara and, shoving her ahead of him, ran toward the iron-runged ladder that led to the upper deck. El Lobo gave Tamara a shove, starting her up the ladder, but her bare feet slipped and she would have fallen if El Lobo hadn't caught her.

"Damn it," said Wes desperately, "get up there, and I'll lift her up to you."

In an instant, El Lobo was up the ladder.

"Now," Wes said to the naked girl, "raise your

arms over your head so he can reach them. I'll lift you as far as I can."

Wes lifted her, and she was limp, as though she had no strength. But she lifted her arms, and El Lobo was able to reach them. Wes scrambled up the ladder, and none too soon, for there was the thump of boots on the wooden dock and shouts of excited men. Wes drew his Colt and fired over their heads, only to have his fire returned.

"In among the freight," Wes shouted.

He led the way, while El Lobo and Tamara followed. They ducked behind barrels and crates as lead sang over their heads.

"We'll have to go over the side, into the water," said Wes.

Wes quickly discovered they were on the wrong side of the deck, for there was a ship anchored next to them, and someone aboard had lit a lantern. They now had to make their way across the deck to the other side, where there was only open water.

Just for a few seconds, they were forced to leave the cover of the stored freight, and to gain them an edge, Wes shot the lantern out of somebody's hand. There were shouts of pain as men were showered with burning oil. It bought them enough time to cross the deck to the opposite rail.

"Over the side," Wes ordered.

El Lobo wasted no time. He seized Tamara and they went over the rail, disappearing in the blackness below. Wes followed, counting on the possibility their pursuers might not immediately realize they had left the ship. Wes treaded water until he got his bearings. The ship they had just departed was anchored near the end of the dock, and with nothing between him and the shoreline, Wes began swimming. He soon caught up to El Lobo and Tamara and was relieved to find the girl swimming on her own. Evidently, the cold water had been a shock. The light from the open door of the warehouse was a welcome beacon, and they reached the shore a hundred yards below it. There was still much activity aboard the ship, allowing Wes, El Lobo, and Tamara to circle the warehouse and come in behind it. The night wind seemed cold, and Tamara's teeth were chattering. There was a welcome growl from Empty and a sigh of relief from Renita. When she could see them in the dim starlight, she realized the girl they had rescued was stark naked.

"She's freezing," Renita said. "What happened to her clothes?"

"She wasn't wearing any," said Wes, "and we didn't have time to look around. We had to shoot a guard, and with that bunch shootin' at us, we barely escaped."

El Lobo had removed a blanket from his bedroll and had wrapped it about the grateful Tamara. The two seemed strangely silent, neither having spoken since Wes and El Lobo had first found the girl imprisoned aboard the ship. He hoped it was a temporary condition, perhaps stemming from shame on Tamara's part and awkwardness on El Lobo's.

"Let's ride," Wes said. "We have to find us a place to hole up, dry out, and cook some grub."

They rode slowly, both horses carrying double. Reaching the foothills, they gave up the idea of finding shelter, for there was no moon. Eventually they came upon a creek and followed it to a secluded hollow. There was evidence of other fires, and even some wood, and they soon had a small fire going. Tamara Delmano sat hunched in her blanket, staring into the fire, and none of them quite knew what to say to her. Renita sat on the other side of the fire, equally silent. Wes was about to say something when El Lobo spoke.

"Per'ap we find wood for fire."

"Yeah," Wes agreed. "It won't be easy in the dark. Empty, stay."

El Lobo waited until they were well away from the fire before he said what was on his mind.

"What we do, *amigo*? How we hunt outlaws with *desnudo señoritas* who have not the horses?"

"I wish I knew," Wes said. "I thought after we rescued Tamara we might return her to her father's house, until this fight with the Sandlin gang is done. But that was before I had Renita on my hands. *Pronto*, we're likely to have every outlaw in Mexico on our trail. Gettin' ourselves killed was our business, but it's not fair, us draggin' Tamara and Renita down with us."

"Per'ap they decide," El Lobo said.

"Maybe you're right," said Wes. "They have every right to hate this bunch of outlaws. We have to make plans, and we can't as long as they're not talking to us. Let's find a little more wood for the fire and tell them about El Diablo Pistolas."

In Mazatlán, after the furious madam had been freed, she had gone looking for the Sandlin outlaws. Drawn by the shouting and shooting, she found the five outlaws on the dock. One of their number—Shelton—was dead, and had just been carried off the ship.

"You *idiotas* have allow El Diablo Pistolas to steal the *Americano puta*, leaving Madam Izona bound and humiliated. Now one of you is dead. Swenson, they have take the *putas* from the ship?"

"Yeah," the outlaw admitted. "Hell, we drew lots, an' Shelton lost. Wasn't room for more'n one of us down there. Bailey, Rinks, Mannon, an' me was havin' a few drinks. As for your damn house, we just git the whores for you, so much a head. It ain't up to us to see they don't git loose an' run off."

A crowd had gathered, some of whom had heard the angry madam speak of El Diablo Pistolas. Somebody laughed, others shouted obscenities, while several called for the town's constable. Madam Izona stomped off into the darkness, leaving the outlaws in a situation not to their liking. Without a word, Bailey seized the dead Shelton's arms, while Swenson took his feet, and they all disappeared into the night.

While Wes had confidence in Renita, he had no idea where he or El Lobo stood with Tamara Delmano. While she was grateful to them for having rescued her from a fate worse than death, would she be content to ride the vengeance trail with El Lobo? Or would she prefer to return to her home in San Ignacio? But *could* she return? There was the disturbing possibility that if she returned, naked but for a blanket, Hernando Delmano would turn her away. There was no delaying it any longer, and Wes began.

"Renita, you know I have sworn to destroy the

Sandlin gang, because they murdered my father. I
hadn't planned on you being here, risking your life
as I risk mine, but there is no other way. I've started
something I'll have to finish. Tamara, I am saying
this mostly for your benefit, because you're in the
same dangerous position. El Lobo—or Palo Elfego,
as you know him—was shot in the back and left for
dead by the same outlaws I've sworn to destroy. For
that reason—and for what they've done to you—he
rides this vengeance trail with me."

"*Sí*," El Lobo said. "They are evil. They must die."

"My *amigo* is in a painful position, Tamara," said
Wes, "for you have a choice. Unlike Renita, you have
a home and a father to which you can return, or
you can remain with Palo—El Lobo—and risk being
gunned down with the rest of us. In fairness to you,
it must be your decision."

"It is not my decision," Tamara said, in a surprisingly firm voice. "It is Palo's. He is not bound by his
words aboard the ship."

"You hear the truth aboard the ship," said El Lobo
simply. "I will die for you, but I be *perro*, taking
you from your *casa* and your father, to face the guns
of outlaws."

"I have no house and I have no father," Tamara
said. "I wish to return to San Ignacio for my clothing
and my horses, and then I will ride with you. To my
death, if I must."

"*Madre de Dios*," said El Lobo.

"Then we'll return to San Ignacio tomorrow,"
Wes said.

"If you have more than one horse," said Renita,
"could I perhaps ride one?"

"You may," Tamara said. "I have a second saddle, as well."

Durango, Mexico. July 27, 1884

The ranks of the Sandlin gang had swelled to more than seven hundred men. One of the new arrivals was Black Bill Trevino, one of the lieutenants from Mexico City. Despite the criticism of some of the *segundos,* the massive manhunt proposed by Dolan Watts was approved by Trevino. After consulting with Watts, he and Trevino went before the gathering to explain their proposed strategy.

"Mexico City likes the plan Watts has come up with," Trevino said, "and they agreed to the rewards he suggested. There's a five-thousand-dollar reward on the head of each of these *hombres* callin' themselves El Diablo Pistolas."

"Alive or dead?" a dozen voices inquired.

"That's the rub," said Trevino. "Mexico City wants 'em alive. They want to force the bastards to talk, to find out who's behind these killings. Watts has worked out a plan to start the manhunt."

"One *segundo* to every ten men," Watts said. "So far, these hombres have done all their hell-raisin' to the north of here, and that's where we're takin' this manhunt. We'll fan out across Mexico, from Mazatlán to Zacatecas to Tampico. Then we'll move north."

The proceedings were interrupted by the arrival of a horseman. He ignored everyone else and spoke directly to Brodie Fentress. Fentress, in turn, made an announcement to the others.

"This is Swenson, from Mazatlán," said Fentress.

"Late yesterday, two men busted into Madam Izona's house and took one of the American whores. Last night, they boarded a ship, murdered one of our men, and took two *señoritas* bound for California."

One man laughed, others shouted, and somebody began firing his revolver.

"Quiet, damn it," Black Jack Trevino bawled. "If these are the two *hombres* causing all the trouble, we have to box them in before they move farther south."

"That's what I thought," said Dolan Watts, "but this changes things. Mexico is shaped like a big horn, the tip of it to the south. Instead of pushing north, where we'd be forced to cover three times the territory, why not drive them south? While our use of the telegraph is limited, we still might alert our outposts to the south that these hunted men are moving in that direction."

"Hell," somebody shouted, "that cuts down our chances of gittin' the reward."

"Reward be damned," said Black Jack Trevino. "If we don't stop these marauders, you and the rest of us may find our reward at the business end of a rope. Why were there only five men in Mazatlán?"

"After Watts sent telegrams to different outposts, six of 'em had been sent here for the manhunt," Brodie Fentress replied.

"Then send them back to Mazatlán," said Trevino.

"I'll do better than that," Fentress replied. "I'll send ten more, with my lieutenant, Denton Rucker, as *segundo*. We know that pair of gunmen didn't reach and leave Mazatlán afoot. By God, if there's a trail, Rucker and my boys will find it."

"Bueno," said Trevino. "The rest of you *segundos* gather your men and prepare to move out."

In a matter of minutes, Denton Rucker had his men mounted and they rode out for Mazatlán. Not quite sure of their status, Swenson, Bailey, Rinks, and Mannon followed.

San Ignacio, Mexico. July 27, 1884

Wes and El Lobo had no idea what to expect as they neared the huge Delmano house on the wooded rise. They sneaked looks at Tamara, and she seemed composed. As before, when they drew near, someone had told Delmano of their coming. He waited, as grim and unsmiling as ever. When they were within speaking distance, Wes and El Lobo reined up. Wes spoke.

"Mr. Delmano, we have brought your daughter home. She has something to say."

"I have no daughter," Delmano said stiffly. "None of you are welcome. Now go."

Clutching the blanket about her, Tamara slid off El Lobo's horse and began walking toward the house.

"You . . . *puta* . . . you whore," Hernando Delmano shouted, "go."

"I will go," said Tamara calmly, "but not without my clothing and my horses."

"Then take what is yours," Delmano hissed, "and do not return."

He stepped aside, allowing Tamara to enter the house, making no move to follow. He stood there in furious silence, without inviting Wes, El Lobo, or Renita to dismount. When Tamara emerged from the

house, she carried a large canvas bag. She was
dressed in riding clothes and boots, and secured by
a chin thong, a flat-crowned hat rode her shoulders.
Surprisingly, a gunbelt circled her narrow waist, and
in the holster was a .31-caliber Colt.

"Come with me to the stable," she said.

She chose to walk. Wes and El Lobo kicked their
horses into a trot, following. Hernando Delmano remained where he was, watching them go. Delmano
had many horses, but when they reached the stable,
two of them nickered in recognition. Tamara
dropped her bag of personal possessions, entered the
stable, and let out a pair of blacks. They were mares,
looking identical, each with a white blaze on its face.

"They're beautiful," said Renita.

"*Madre de Dios*," El Lobo said. "*Bonito.*"

"I've never seen a more perfectly matched pair,"
said Wes. "My God, in Texas they'd bring a thousand dollars apiece."

"I would not sell them for ten times that," Tamara said.

"I don't blame you," said Wes. "Where are the
saddles?"

Wes nodded to El Lobo, and the two of them followed Tamara to a tack room. From a rail, they removed the saddles she pointed out, while she
gathered bridles and saddle blankets. Almost as an
afterthought, she took a pair of saddlebags for each
horse.

"If you ain't pushing your luck," Wes said, "we
could use some grain."

"Come," said Tamara. "We will take some."

Tamara found four empty burlap bags. Wes and

El Lobo filled each of them half full, tying the necks with rawhide thongs. Each bag was then divided, balancing half its contents in each end, so that it rode easily behind the saddle.

"Anything else?" Wes asked.

"There is nothing more," said Tamara.

She passed the reins of one of the blacks to Renita, and the four of them mounted. As they rode away, Hernando Delmano watched them go. Wes sneaked a look at Tamara and, from the firm set of her mouth and half-closed eyes, realized what the parting was costing her. But she didn't look back, and when El Lobo's admiring eyes met hers, she tried to smile.

Mazatlán, Mexico. July 28, 1884

When Denton Rucker and his twenty men reached the village, they sensed a change. The Mexicans stared at them, whispering among themselves. The ship flying the Mexican flag was gone. Rucker turned to Swenson and his three companions.

"You gents was here when that pair of hell-raisers showed up. Surely you can tell us somethin' about which way they went."

"Hell," said Swenson defensively, "it was dark as the inside of a cow."

"Not when they took the American girl from the whorehouse," Rucker replied. "You told Fentress it was still light."

"We wasn't told to watch Madam Izona's whorehouse," Bailey said.

"He's right," said Drayton, one of the six who had

been sent ahead to Durango. "We was told when a ship come in with American women, we was to take 'em ashore after dark an' git 'em to Madam Izona's place. When there was Mex *señoritas* to be took away, we was to take 'em first to Madam Izona's. After dark, we moved 'em to the waitin' ship an' stood watch over 'em until the ship sailed."

"And five of you couldn't manage that," Rucker said. "Where the hell was the rest of you, while your pard was bein' gunned down?"

"We was in a cantina," said Swenson. "We took turns, one at a time. There wasn't no room for five of us on the lower deck, anyhow."

"I got an idea," Rinks said, "if the rest of you will shut up so's I can talk."

"Talk, then," said Rucker. "These other three ain't told me a damn thing."

"There's a chance," Rinks said, "that them *señoritas* that was took off the ship might lead us to that pair of gun-throwers. One of them gals we brought in was more Spanish than Mex, an' her daddy owns a big house in San Ignacio. You reckon they ain't took her back to her daddy?"

"There's a chance," said Rucker, "and we got nothin' better. Let's ride."

Leaving San Ignacio, there was no conversation. Wes and El Lobo led out and, keeping within the mountains, rode south. Only when they stopped to rest the horses—almost an hour later—was there any conversation. For the sake of the two women, Wes felt an explanation was necessary.

"The Sandlin gang is pretty well all over Mexico,"

Wes said, "but we know they're comin' together in Durango for a manhunt. What we don't know is whether they'll move to north or south."

"There had long been talk of these outlaws," said Tamara, speaking of them for the first time. "They have always been feared because their leaders are part of the very soul of Mexico's government. Unlike the old days, when Santa Anna's dictatorship was strong, the military is no longer in favor. Corrupt politicos have stolen the offices of government, and they answer only to the thieves and murderers who put them there. If one is to destroy a serpent, the head must be severed, and the head of this outlaw serpent is in Mexico City."

"*Por Dios*," said El Lobo in admiration.

"You would ignore the individual outlaw strongholds, then, and ride straight to headquarters in Mexico City," Wes said.

"I would," said Tamara, "if I were serious about destroying the Sandlin gang."

"I reckon the Sandlin gang's takin' us serious enough," Wes said, irritated. "We wiped out two of their outposts to the last man, and they're gatherin' right now in Durango to begin a manhunt lookin' for us."

"Wes," said Renita, "You and Palo have done so much, it . . . it's a miracle. You rescued me, and then you rescued Tamara. What bothers me, and I think what bothers Tamara, is that these outlaws are gathering—perhaps by the hundreds—to come looking for you. So far, you have been the attackers, and the outlaws have been on the run. Now that's about to change. I'll be with you to the end, but there are hundreds of them, and so few of us."

"These are my feelings, also," Tamara said, her eyes on Renita. "When these outlaws come after us with guns, we can kill only a few of them before they ride us down, while the evil men who rule the country are safe in Mexico City. Destroy these leaders, and the hundreds who gather in Durango will flee like frightened coyotes."

"*Sí,*" El Logo agreed, his dark eyes aflame.

"By God," said Wes, "you're talkin' sense."

"These thoughts are not my own," Tamara said. "I listened to my paternal grandfather, who spoke out against the outlaws. But he was old, and he died last year."

"*Por Dios,*" said El Lobo, "what happen to the Señor Hernando Delmano?"

"The Señor Hernando Delmano is a coward," Tamara said. "He took all my grandfather fought for, and he has done nothing."

"That's not entirely true," said Wes. "He told the newspaper in Mazatlán you'd been taken by outlaws. Otherwise, Palo and me never would have known."

"*Sí,*" El Lobo agreed.

"I do not know why he bothered," said Tamara. "You heard him greet me as a *puta*, a whore. Five men carried me away to a whorehouse, where I was stripped and violated. I fought, and I still bear the stripes where I was beaten, while in my father's eyes I am unclean. Damn him and his unbending pride. I welcome you, Wes Stone, and you, Palo Elfego, and I applaud your vows of vengeance. You must not fail. I swear, upon the memory of my grandfather, that I will ride with you to the end, even if it be death."

"That's how I feel," Renita said, "but you said it so much better than I did."

"I'm not always right," said Wes, "and I have to admit I've been a mite unsure about how we should handle that bunch of outlaws gatherin' in Durango. I reckon we owe your grandfather for some sound advice. We'll have to make some plans, but we can't do that until we know what we're up against in Mexico City. I'd say, from those clouds buildin' up in the west, that we're in for some heavy rain. If we ride the rest of the day and most of tonight, it should conceal our trail. Tamara, how far are we from Mexico City?"

"From Mazatlán," Tamara said, "it is almost six hundred miles."

"Then let's ride," said Wes. "Startin' right now, we'll totally change our tactics. We'll keep them from knowing where we are. When we strike again, we'll do it with enough force to bring down some of the big coyotes."

There was approval in the eyes of Renita and El Lobo, while Tamara actually laughed. She, with her black hair and dark eyes, was a beautiful girl. El Lobo would be a lucky man if he was still alive when the shooting was done.

Chapter 10

San Ignacio, Mexico. July 28, 1884

Before Denton Rucker and his riders reached San Ignacio, the storm broke, drenching the landscape for almost two hours.

"There goes our chance of picking up a trail," Rucker observed sourly.

"Yeah," Said Swenson, "but we still might learn whether or not them *hombres* has been here. Hernando Delmano lives here, and he don't know for certain who it was that made off with his *señorita*. We can always tell him we're a posse of upstandin' citizens that's lookin' for the varmints."

It was just nervy and audacious enough to strike them as funny, and some of the men slapped their thighs with their sodden hats.

"I reckon it's worth a try," Rucker conceded. "We'll let you handle it, Swenson, since it was you and your bunch that allowed the women to be taken from the ship."

"That's far enough," said Delmano, when the riders were within speaking distance. "What do you want?"

"We heard your daughter was took by outlaws," Swenson said, as seriously as he was able, "an' we're lookin' for the varmints that done it. Can you tell us anything that might be a help?"

"I have nothing to say," said Delmano. "Now go."

"We just aim to help, if we can," Rucker said.

"I don't want your help," said Delmano. "You are trespassing."

"By God, why don't you call the law?" one of the outlaws said angrily.

Rucker wheeled his horse and rode away, the others following. Not until they were well away from the Delmano house did they rein up.

"Well," Rucker demanded, "anybody else got any bright ideas?"

"Maybe Watts is right," said Swenson. "If this pair we're huntin' is already this far south, why would they suddenly turn around and ride north?"

"Hell," Rucker growled, "I don't know."

"They got one woman from the whorehouse, and one of the two they freed from the ship," said Bailey. "Maybe that's what they was after."

"Oh, for God's sake," Rucker said, disgusted, "use your head. Would *you* fight your way to Mazatlán, riskin' your neck for a pair of whores? Even if that was true, they had no cause to wipe out our outposts at Namiquipa and Chihuahua. There's somethin' just a hell of a lot more serious behind these attacks."

"Since we ain't found a trace of them whores," said Mannon, "I'd say we're lookin' for four riders instead of two. That bein' the case, they had to find two more horses somewhere. Maybe we could ask around and—"

"Learn exactly nothing," Rucker finished. "Everybody will be just as closemouthed as old Delmano was. For all we know, he may have given them the horses they needed. We've been beaten at every turn by this nervy pair of hellions, and we've done nothing about it. They've captured the imagination of the Mexicans, and unless we can change that, we're finished."

"That's damn scary," Swenson said. "We goin' to ride back to Durango an' admit we come up dry?"

"No," said Rucker. "I don't know about the rest of you, but I like Mexico, with its ready money and freedom from the law. We got to find that pair of troublesome bastards and salt 'em down before they do any more damage. We're ridin' south, and I think we'll follow the shoreline. At least as far as Tepic, keepin' an eye on the telegraph line."

"We'll remain in the mountains as far south as we can," Wes said. "It should be far easier to keep an eye on our back trail and to find a place to hole up at night. We'll have to be careful of our cook fires, or eliminate them altogether. Tamara, how far should we follow the coast before turning inland toward Mexico City?"

"I am not sure," said Tamara. "I know at some point there is a trade route—a wagon road—that crosses the mountains. It leads from the ocean to Mexico City."

"Another reason to ride this mountain range," Wes said. "Let's just hope this trail has been used enough that we don't miss it."

Empty generally ranged on ahead, but their third day on the trail, he fell behind.

"The *perro* know something we do not," said El Lobo.

"I think you're right," Wes said. "The rest of you keep goin'. I'll be riding our backtrail for a while."

Wes dropped back and found Empty waiting for him. The hound trotted back the way they had come for several miles. Then he veered down the mountainside toward the distant blue water of the Pacific. At first Wes saw nothing, for the foothills below were densely wooded. Finally he fixed his eyes on a clearing and waited. Eventually his patience was rewarded when the first horsemen appeared. He watched as they emerged from the trees, counting them as they crossed the clearing. Empty sat beside him.

"*Bueno, amigo,*" he said, ruffling the hound's ears. "That's all we need to know."

Wes caught up to El Lobo, Tamara, and Renita as they were resting their horses.

"They come?" El Lobo asked.

"Twenty-one of them," said Wes. "They're ridin' along the coast, likely following the telegraph line. We've spoiled the varmints. They think if they follow the wire far enough, they'll find us. I reckon we'll have to find another way of lettin' 'em know we're around."

El Lobo laughed. "*Sí.* When it be dark, we stampede their horses."

"Damn right," Wes said. "All the way back to Mazatlán."

"It is a wise move," said Tamara approvingly. "It will do much to discredit them."

"I'm so glad we don't have to fight," Renita said. "I don't even have a gun."

"I have another," said Tamara. "It was my grand-father's, and you are welcome to use it if you wish."

Tamara and Renita had much in common, and Wes watched as they slowly but surely became friends. Of all the clothing Tamara likely possessed, she had brought only what was suitable on horseback. She had an extra pair of riding boots, and generously gave them to Renita, along with clothing more suited to the saddle. While the fit was still a bit large, it was better for Renita than riding barefoot in an ill-fitting long dress from a whorehouse. They rode until almost sundown before unsaddling their horses. Supper was a hurried affair.

"There'll be a moon tonight," Wes said, "and we have to get ahead of it. Tamara, you and Renita will remain here. We'll need Empty with us."

"I feel useless," said Renita, "like I should be doing something."

"That is much the way I feel," Tamara said.

"Both of you will get your chance," said Wes. "But for now, there's no two *hombres* anywhere in Mexico better at spookin' horses than El Lobo and me. Eh, Wolf?"

"*Sí*," El Lobo agreed. "It will be long walk to Mazatlán."

Wes and El Lobo rode out an hour before moon-rise. Empty seemed to know exactly what had been planned, for he led them unerringly to within a mile of the outlaw camp. Confident with their number, the men had made no effort to conceal their fire, and on a bed of glowing coals sat two large coffeepots. The horses had been picketed to the north of the camp.

"Perfect," said Wes softly. "We won't be stampeding the horses through the camp, so they won't have a chance to catch any of them. First we'll cut them loose."

Swiftly, silently, they moved among the horses, touching an occasional flank to calm the animals. When all were loose, they returned to their own horses. They were almost in position, between the outlaw camp and the horses, when several of the loose animals began to nicker.

"Hey," an outlaw shouted, "there's trouble with the horses!"

But the alarm came too late. Wes and El Lobo kicked their mounts into a fast gallop, and shouting, they charged. The loosed horses galloped away to the north. Although they had no targets, the frustrated outlaws had begun firing, and the fusillade further spooked the stampeding horses.

"Damn it," Swenson complained, "we should of posted a guard. Rucker, you ain't no great shakes as *segundo*."

"There's twenty-one of us," said Rinks. "Who'd ever have thought they'd have the nerve to slip in this close?"

"It's the only sensible thing they could have done," Rucker conceded. "We're a bunch of damn fools for not expecting it. They couldn't be any more rid of us if we were dead."

"Now what, Mr. *Segundo?*" Swenson asked.

"We begin hoofing it back the way we come," said Rucker shortly, "and you'd better all be hopin' we catch up to them horses before they drift back to Mazatlán or Durango. If word of this gets out, Mexicans will be throwing rocks at us."

Wes and El Lobo drove the horses north for more than an hour.

"That's near forty miles," Wes said, "and they'll drift back to their home corrals on their own. That bunch will find it slow going, afoot and totin' their saddles."

"*Sí*," said El Lobo. "This be more *comico* than shooting them."

"I think so," Wes agreed, "and more effective. These varmints have prospered here in Mexico because everybody's been afraid of them. Now they're being made to look like fools by just two *hombres*."

It was very late when Wes and El Lobo returned to their own camp.

"Wes and El Lobo comin' in," said Wes softly.

Only then did Tamara and Renita arise from cover, and in the moonlight Wes noted that Tamara had her revolver cocked and ready. She eased the weapon off cock, returning it to the holster.

"You were gone so long, we were starting to worry," Renita said.

"It took a while," said Wes. "We ran their horses at least forty miles north. They'll drift the rest of the way to their home corrals long before the Sandlin bunch can catch up to them."

"It is a satisfying victory," Tamara said.

"Yeah," said Wes. "It'll play hell with their reputation when word of it gets around. I wonder if I shouldn't spread it a little faster by sending another telegram."

"It's a temptation," Renita said, "but that will just warn the others. The next time you go to stampede the horses, they'll be waiting for you with guns."

"*Por Dios*," said El Lobo, "that be right. The telegraph must not talk."

Tamara laughed. "You are wise warriors. These men who are afoot have been shamed. If they do not speak of this, it is a thing you may do again and again."

Toluca, Mexico. July 28, 1884

Headquarters for the Sandlin gang had quietly been moved from Mexico City to the village of Toluca, several miles south. Here, in a board room within an elegant mansion, a dozen men met to pursue the gang's involvement in drug running, white slavery, rustling, prostitution, and other nefarious activities. About to call the meeting to order, Cord Sandlin looked upon the twelve hard-eyed men who had become known as Sandlin's Disciples. There was Jarvis, Canton, Tafolla, Zouka, Sumar, Knado, Handley, Wittrus, Moke, and Undilay. All were Americans, wanted for various crimes. Finally there were Hidalgo and Ximinez, both holding influential positions within the Mexican government.

"I had hoped this meeting would not be necessary," Sandlin said. "It has to do with the troublesome pair who apparently destroyed our outposts at Namiquipa and Chihuahua."

"We authorized payment of ten thousand dollars

in rewards," said Jarvis, and sent Black Bill Trevino to Durango to oversee the manhunt. What more can we do?"

"I'm not quite sure," Sandlin replied. "That's the purpose of this meeting. I have some disturbing news from Mazatlán. Two men showed up at Madam Izona's, slugged her, and took an American girl. That same day, after dark, these two boarded a ship preparing to sail for California. They shot and killed one of our men and escaped with two women who had been secured on a lower deck. One of them went over the side and disappeared."

"So two men made off with three whores, and one of them disappeared," Canton said. "Who's gonna connect that to us, and how can it be proved?"

"The damn newspapers," said Sandlin. "The *hombre* that was gunned down on the ship was searched before our outfit could get to him, and one of our dragon's-head coins was found in his pocket. Not only have we been linked to prostitution and slave trading, we've again been humiliated by just two men. People no longer fear us. Instead, they laugh, and if it continues, we're finished."

"I was promised protection," Hidalgo said. "I think per'ap it is time I withdraw."

"*Sí,*" said Ximinez. "Because of you and your promises of wealth, we betray the trust of the Mexican people."

Sandlin laughed. "You sold out, and you're in this neck-deep, just like the rest of us. Nobody withdraws. There's enough evidence to send every damn one of us before a firing squad ten times over, and if I go, I promise you, I won't go alone."

"If these *hombres* were last in Mazatlán," said Jarvis, "they must be coming south. If they're hell-bent on destroying us, then they must be comin' here."

"I've been waiting for some of you to reach that conclusion," Sandlin said.

"I reckon you've already reached it," said Sumar, "so why the hell did you go along with organizin' this manhunt in Durango?"

"With hundreds of men available, I believed we might capture this pair before they got to us," Sandlin said. "Now—after their activities in Mazatlán—I believe they are on their way here."

"That was a damn fool idea, orderin' 'em captured alive," said Wittrus. "You should of offered a reward for 'em dead."

"I must agree with you," Sandlin said. "We don't know if they're acting on their own, or if they're part of a conspiracy, but they must be stopped. I have another plan, and this one is costly, because it does not involve any of our men."

"Our bunch ain't made much of a showin', so far," said Jarvis. "Talk."

"I favor hiring as many professional gunmen as we can find. Killers, to put it bluntly. Each is to be paid a thousand dollars in advance, and five thousand more for each of the two men when he can prove he has killed them. Can we find ten such killers?"

"*Sí*," Ximinez said. "Per'ap more."

"Put out the word, then," said Sandlin. "I want them on the streets of Mexico City tomorrow."

"*Sí*," Ximinez said. "You have the gold?"

"I have it," said Sandlin grimly.

"*Bueno*," Ximinez said. "It be done."

"This pair of *hombres* we're after can shoot like hell wouldn't have it," said Sandlin. "You must be damn sure that when some of your gun-throwers get salted down, it can't be laid at our door."

Mazatlán, Mexico. July 30, 1884

When Black Bill Trevino and Dolan Watts had dispatched groups of men all across south-central Mexico, Brodi Fentress spoke to Trevino.

"I'm ridin' to Mazatlán to see what I can learn firsthand."

"Rucker, your *segundo*, went there just three days ago with twenty men," Trevino reminded him.

"All the more reason for me to follow," said Fentress. "They must've learned something, or we'd have heard from them. If they've discovered a lead, we're wasting a hell of a lot of time and men elsewhere."

Fentress rode out, reaching Mazatlán just in time to witness the arrival of most of the horses Rucker and his men had been riding. They came drifting in from the south, looking lost, and immediately drew the interest of various people. People who, Fentress suspected, had watched the twenty-one men ride out. Somewhere, Rucker and his men were afoot. Or dead. Fentress began hazing the horses, seeking to gather them, but it was a difficult task, bordering on the impossible. He looked around, seeking help, but there was not a man in sight. The curious Mexicans had vanished like frightened quail. With a sigh, Fentress went about driving the horses back the way they had come.

Thirty miles south of Mazatlán, Rucker and his companions stumbled along on aching, blistered feet. They had long since abandoned their saddles.

"Damn it," Swenson complained, "I say some of us should go after the horses while the rest wait here. We can draw lots."

"Or we can send volunteers," said Rucker. "You can be the first. Who wants to go with him?"

"Hell," said somebody in disgust, "let ever'body go after his own horse. We're all at fault for not havin' the brains to keep watch over the horses."

"That's the truth," Rucker said. "Nobody's feet are more blistered than mine, and you don't hear me whinin'. Now shut up and keep hoofin' it."

A few minutes before sundown, Fentress, driving ten horses ahead of him, met the bedraggled men. All of them, including Rucker, seemed speechless.

"I couldn't gather them all," said Fentress, "and the Mexes were too amused to help. Ten of you will have to ride back and find the others, and you'd better not waste any time. Our reputation's suffered to the extent that the rest of your mounts may belong to somebody else before you can claim them."

"Hell, that's a good thirty-five or forty miles each way," Swenson complained, "an we got no saddles."

"Then you'll ride bareback," said Fentress in a dangerously brittle tone. "Those of you who claim these ten horses, mount up and get started."

Slowly, ten men came forward, one of whom was Swenson. Some of them mounted with difficulty, lacking saddles and stirrups, but eventually they rode away toward Mazatlán.

"Now," said Fentress, "how the hell did a salty bunch like you end up on foot, with your horses wandering loose in town?"

"No excuse," Rucker said. "It was still early, and we hadn't posted a guard over the horses. They scattered 'em to hell and gone."

"Damn near all the way to Mazatlán," said Fentress. "They wouldn't have drifted that far on their own. Now, where would you say the bastards are that spooked them?"

"Somewhere to the south," Rucker said.

"How do you know?" Fentress asked. "Were you trailing them?"

"No," said Rucker. "We were followin' a hunch. Stayin' near the coast, using the trees for cover, I don't know how the hell they spotted us. Just the two of them, it's almighty close to unnatural, what they can do."

"Well, they're not phantoms," Fentress said. "If they're southbound, there has to be a trail. Once you have the rest of your horses, I want you to find that trail and stay with it for as far and as long as it takes you."

"Most of those *hombres* you sent after the horses wasn't from my Durango outfit," said Rucker. "I'd not be surprised if they just keep ridin'."

"I would," Fentress said, "because I aim to catch up to them. One way or another, you'll have horses sometime tomorrow."

With that, Fentress rode away, bound for Mazatlán.

*   *   *

"I'm tempted to just keep ridin'," Swenson said to his nine companions as they rode uncomfortably toward Mazatlán. "Hell, I didn't tie in with this outfit to ride all over Mexico huntin' gun-happy *hombres* with a grudge."

"I'm wanted on the other side of the border," said Bailey, "and I can't imagine you bein' lily white."

Rinks laughed. "Me neither. If ever'body wantin' to hang Swenson was brung together in a bunch, they'd have to git in line an' take a number."

All the others laughed, and Swenson said no more. It was just as well, for soon there was the thud of hoofbeats. They reined up and waited until Fentress reached them.

"I reckoned you might need some help roundin' up them horses," Fentress said.

The morning after stampeding the horses, Wes, El Lobo, Tamara, and Renita mounted and rode south. They remained in the mountains, and there was always the blue Pacific to the west. Occasionally the foothills became less wooded and they could see small villages along the distant coast.

"The dragon does not follow," El Lobo said.

"They haven't had time to recover their horses," said Wes. "We dealt them a blow, leaving them afoot, but they now know we're riding south. They'll be after us."

"Oh, God," Renita said, "I hope they don't figure out where we're going."

"If they haven't, they will," said Wes. "While we've discredited them all over Mexico, we haven't touched the varmints at the highest level. They've got to suspect that'll be our next move unless they stop us."

"Many will pursue us," Tamara said, "but you know the dragon well. His fangs are mighty, and they run deep. The real danger lies ahead."

"There'll be more rain sometime today," said Wes, "so by the time they're mounted, they won't find a trail to follow. We should reach Mexico City well ahead of them. It all depends on what we find waiting for us there."

When Fentress and his ten companions reached Mazatlán, they had no trouble finding the missing horses. Mexican men watched in silence as they gathered the horses. They did not offer to help, nor did they seem afraid, and that bothered Fentress.

"Now," Fentress said, when the horses had been recovered, "get the hell back to the rest of the men. There'll soon be another outfit followin' you."

Fentress couldn't be sure of that, but it was a threat calculated to force the outlaws to return the horses to their footsore companions. Rucker would take it from there. With that assurance, Fentress rode to Durango. Another change in plans was in order.

"Well, by God," said Black Bill Trevino when Fentress reported to him, "we've sent men east, all the way to the gulf. There's near six hundred strung out across south-central Mexico, and now we learn the bastards we're after are ridin' along the Sierra Madres."

"Hell, I'm just telling you what's happened," Fentress said angrily. "I didn't cause it."

"We don't have time to fight among ourselves," said Dolan Watts. "We gambled and lost. Now I think we all know where these pistoleers are bound."

"Yeah," Black Bill said. "They're on their way to Mexico City, and there's not a damn thing we can do about it."

"You can use the telegraph," said Fentress. "If you can't get the message across to Hidalgo and Ximinez, then I can."

"Don't smartmouth me," Trevino shouted. "If any messages are sent, I'll send them. It's my responsibility, not yours."

"Thanks," said Fentress, his voice dripping sarcasm. "I'll keep that in mind."

Trevino saddled his horse and rode into Durango. Strong on his mind were his orders against using the telegraph, but a pair of dedicated killers were on their way to attack Sandlin's border empire in a manner that might well destroy it.

The sun was three hours high when Swenson and his companions returned with the needed horses.

"By God, it took you long enough," Rucker said.

"You got your damn horses," said Swenson. "Don't you start bully-raggin' us."

"Mount up," Rucker ordered. "Let's go after our saddles."

Their saddles and supplies were where they had been left.

"We been ridin' all night," said Swenson, "and I ain't goin' nowhere until I eat. Damn it, I'm starved."

"No more so than the rest of us," Rucker said grimly. "We have to make up for lost time. Now saddle up."

Swenson turned away, but only for a moment. He whirled to face Rucker, and there was a gun in his hand. But Rucker was ready for him. He fired once, and Swenson's gun sagged, blasting lead into the ground at his feet. He stumbled backward, and when his knees buckled, he fell. The wind caught his hat and sent it cartwheeling away. The rest of the outlaws watched in silence, some of them swallowing hard.

"I gave an order," said Rucker. "If any of the rest of you have ideas that conflict with it, speak up."

Without a word, the men began saddling their horses.

"There's Swenson's horse and saddle," Bailey said.

"Saddle his horse and bring it along on a lead rope," said Rucker.

"You want we should bury Swenson, so's the coyotes can't git at him?" Rinks asked.

"Leave him lay," said Rucker. "Coyotes won't bother one of their own."

They rode away, Rucker leading them deeper into the Sierra Madre. Eventually they found the remains of a campfire and the tracks of four horses.

"It's got to be them," Bailey said. "They must have that pair of whores with 'em."

"We never did figure out what happened to the Mex gal that escaped from the ship," said Mannon.

"That makes no difference now," Rucker replied. "We'll trail them as far as we can before dark."

"You mean before the rain washes out their tracks," said one of the outlaws.

There was no denying the truth of that, and the outlaws had been following the tracks less than an hour when the rain began.

"Damn the luck," Rucker said. "We can't follow their tracks, but we know they're on their way south. We'll keep to the crest of these mountains until we pick up their trail again."

Chapter 11

Toluca, Mexico. August 1, 1884

Hidalgo and Ximinez, the Sandlin gang's contacts within the upper echelons of government in Mexico City, had traveled under cover of darkness to Toluca, where they reported to Sandlin.

"We have sent word to the *hombres* who sell their *pistolas*," Ximinez said, "and they have accepted the gold."

"Who are they?" Sandlin asked.

"You do not know them," said Hidalgo.

"I've laid out ten thousand dollars to these scum," Sandlin said. "Damn it, what are their names?"

"One should be careful, lest his tongue dig his grave," said Ximinez. "These scum, as you refer to them, are dangerous men. They are Kalpana, Shawanna, Barbonsio, Ryashia, Picado, Zopilote, Quemada, Santos, Esteban, and Jaspeado."

"The first five I've never heard of," Sandlin said.

"Kalpana is Spanish," said Hidalgo. "Shawanna, Barbonsio, and Ryashia are *Indios*, and Picado is *Americano*. The others are *Mejicanos* and half-breeds."

"You sure they won't take our money and vamoose?"

Ximinez laughed. "In their own way, they are honorable enough. They have all served time in prison. Most were sentenced to be executed and were saved only by compassion of certain . . . ah . . . officials within the government. Hidalgo and me believed they might at some time prove useful. That time is come, and they will not forget. There is, per'ap, one small difficulty. These two *hombres* to be . . . ah . . . executed, how do we know them?"

"I have received a carefully worded telegram from Durango," Sandlin said. "Nobody's seen either of these men and lived to talk, except a whorehouse madam in Mazatlán. One is an American, the other a mix of Spanish and Indian, both with *buscadera* rigs."*

"Some help, per'ap," Hidalgo said. "Nothing more?"

"They may have two women with them," said Sandlin. "For some reason, they freed a pair of whores in Mazatlán. One from a whorehouse, the other from a ship that was bound for California. And for whatever it's worth, they have gotten their hands on some of our dragon pieces, using them to their advantage."

"The dragon image is of no use in identifying them," Ximinez said. "Our *hombres* use these pieces."

"No more," said Sandlin. "Not until this troublesome pair is dead. I've issued orders that none of our outfit is to use the dragon piece until further notice. Your *pistoleros* have only to watch for the dragon sign. Nobody will be using it except the *hombres* who are to be gunned down."

*A gunbelt with right and left holsters, for twin revolvers.

"Ah," Hidalgo said, "it is the touch of genius one does not often find in *Americanos*."

"*Americanos* have thin hides," said Sandlin. "Don't push your luck."

Ixtapa, Mexico. August 4, 1884

"There's a village down yonder, and a ship's dock," said Wes. "It's the first dock we've seen in two days. We could be gettin' close to that trail that crosses these mountains to Mexico City."

"I think so," Tamara replied. "I pray that it has seen enough use that we do not cross in unknowingly."

Wes grinned, appreciating Tamara's perfect English. He thought El Lobo was a little intimidated because of his own limitations.

"Down there, across that clearing," said Renita after they had ridden a short distance. "That looks like a road, or at least a trail."

"It looks mighty like a road," Wes said, "and it's plain enough. If it continues across these mountains, maybe it's what we've been looking for."

"If it's the road we seek, perhaps there will be someone we can ask," Tamara said.

The "road" proved to be only a pair of well-defined ruts, but it apparently did cross the mountains through a narrow pass. Almost immediately there was the distant rattle of a wagon on its way up the mountain road.

"Not likely it's part of the Sandlin gang in a wagon," said Wes. "Maybe it's somebody hauling freight. Let's find out."

El Lobo had his hands near the butts of his Colts when the wagon, drawn by a team of mules, emerged from a stand of trees. The wagon was piled high with what appeared to be freight, and its two occupants were Mexicans in wide-brimmed *sombreros*. One held the reins while his companion held a shotgun, and it was he who first saw the riders.

"Por Dios, bandidos!" he shouted.

"En paz," said Wes, raising his hand with the peace sign, two fingers up.

Tamara spoke to them rapidly in Spanish, and the shotgun was laid aside. Trotting her horse closer to the wagon, Tamara continued to speak. At ease now, the Mexicans seemed to be answering her questions. When she was finished, they stood and removed their *sombreros*. Tamara back-stepped her horse, raised her hand in farewell, and the Mexican clucked to his team. The wagon rattled on its way, and Tamara joined her companions.

"Excelente," El Lobo said approvingly.

"That was smooth," said Wes.

Tamara laughed. "I told them you and Palo are El Diablo Pistolas and that we ride to Mexico City. This is the road, and they bid us *vaya con Dios.*"

"You took a terrible chance," Renita said. "They might tell of having seen us."

"They will not tell in any way that harms us," said Tamara. "They say the Mexican people are praying for us, and urge us to ride carefully. This is the way to Mexico City, but when I spoke of it, they said the dragon waits in Toluca."

"Then we may be barkin' up the wrong tree, ridin' to Mexico City," Wes said.

"I do not think so," said Tamara, "or they would have told us. Perhaps Toluca is a nearby village."

"When I ride with the outlaws at Chihuahua, I hear the name Toluca," El Lobo said.

"Then we'll ride on to Mexico City," said Wes. "Just because the Mexican government is headquartered in Mexico City there's no reason the Sandlin bunch can't be holed up in another place. In fact, that makes perfect sense. The last thing the outlaws would want is to have their link to the Mexican government revealed."

"I think the people know of it," Tamara said, "but they are afraid. They do not know how to oppose it, and that is why they wish us well."

"Then if we can expose the whole rotten mess," said Wes, "we can accomplish even more than we set out to do. We can smash the Sandlin gang, and in so doing, give these people back their country."

"*Sí,*" El Lobo said. "*Mejicanos* make monument to us."

"Shame," said Tamara. "That is selfish."

"Damn right," Wes said, going along with her humor. "I'll settle for just gettin' out of Mexico alive."

Durango, Mexico. August 4, 1884

When Brodie Fentress reported to Dolan Watts and Black Bill Trevino, he told them only that Rucker and his men had picked up the trail of four riders, two of which were believed to be the men bent on the destruction of the Sandlin gang. He chose not to reveal that Rucker—his lieutenant—had foolishly failed to have the horses watched and that as a result he and all his men had been afoot for two days.

"So they are headed south," Black Bill Trevino said. "How do you account for the two extra horses?"

"I'd say the two extra mounts account for the pair of whores they stole in Mazatlán," said Fentress.

"Since you're the *hombre* with the answers," Watts said, "why is this pair of hell-fire and brimstone pistol-toters got a couple of whores ridin' with 'em?"

"Why not?" said Fentress. "It's just possible these females are sisters—or even wives—of the *hombres* that's been givin' us hell. There's some reason they've got it in for us. Selling women for whores is a lowdown, stinking business, and I've never favored it."

Watts laughed. "Well, if you've done gone and got religion, you can leave anytime. I don't see any leg irons on you."

"That's enough," Black Bill Trevino said. "We got trouble enough without any fights among ourselves. Now that we know the men we're after are ridin' south—probably to Mexico City—what are we gonna do about the near six hundred men scattered all the way from Mazatlán to Tampico?"

"Nothing we can do," said Watts. "They've been told to work their way south, but to not go beyond Mexico City."

"Just a damn shame to waste all that force," Trevino said, "when we're all but certain the men we're after are somewhere between here and Mexico City. I'll likely catch hell for such a miscalculation, but I did wire them a description of the *hombres* that busted into the whorehouse in Mazatlán."

"Hell, that's more than we had," said Fentress. "It's time they stood up on their hind legs and done some snake-stompin' of their own."

"I'd agree with that," Trevino said, "but for one thing. This pair of hell-raisers have proven that, with a little encouragement, the Mexican people will turn on us. Let somethin' bust loose exposing our people in the upper levels of government, and it could result in a military coup. We've been tolerated by the military because they've been out of favor with the Mexican people. Let these people forget the dictatorships of Santa Anna and join hands with the military, and we're finished."

Ixtapa, Mexico. August 6, 1884.

Every day since Denton Rucker and his men had recovered their horses, there had been rain. No sooner had they found the trail they were seeking than thunderheads rolled in and drenched the land. When they reached the road that crossed the Sierra Madres, the wagon ruts were full of water, and there wasn't a sign of a track.

"Well," Bailey said, "do we keep ridin' south or do we foller this wagon road?"

"We'll ride east along the wagon road," said Rucker. "This road looks well traveled. If we meet somebody, we'll ask if this is the way to Mexico City."

They had stopped in the wagon road to rest their horses, when they heard a wagon coming up the mountain. By the time the two Mexicans saw the riders, they could only slow their freight wagon and come warily on. Rucker trotted his horse back to meet them, his hands raised to show he meant no harm. In his best Spanish, he spoke to them, asking if the road they traveled led to Mexico City.

"No *comprende*," said the Mexican who held the reins.

His companion said nothing, but tilted the muzzle of his shotgun toward Rucker.

Rucker repeated his question and received the same response. The Mexican with the shotgun laid its ugly muzzle across his knee, pointing it directly at Rucker's middle. There was little Rucker could do except ride away, and he hastily did so. He joined his waiting companions, and they watched the wagon rumble out of sight.

"Nervy bastards," said Rinks, "and they didn't even know us."

"They know us," Rucker said, "and they know who we're after. That gun-throwin' coyote and his telegrams has played hell with our reputation."

They rode on, being careful not to catch up to the wagon and its testy *Mejicanos*.

Half an hour and many miles later, the Mexican with the shotgun spoke. "*Bastardos*. They follow *El Diablo Pistolas*."

"*Sí*," his companion replied. "May *El Diablo* soon welcome them to his *hacienda*."

Mexcio City. August 7, 1884

"We'll wait until after dark before riding into town," Wes said. "El Lobo and me will visit a few cantinas and perhaps learn something."

"I do not feel I am being useful," said Tamara.

"Neither do I," Renita said. "Can we do nothing more than stay with the horses and wait?"

"That be important," El Lobo said.

"It is," said Wes. "The Sandlin gang should know by now that we're through shooting up isolated outposts. I think they'll be looking for us to show up here, and that means the danger is double. I haven't spoken of this before, because it didn't seem necessary. Now it does. There's a chance that El Lobo and me will run into some of the Sandlin gang, that we may not be able to get back to the horses. We may be shot or captured. It's important that we not lose the horses, and it's even more important that neither of you fall into the hands of the outlaws. If it becomes obvious that we've been captured, or if we're forced to run for it, take the horses and ride. Hole up somewhere, and if you can't find us, then wait for us to find you. If we're gunned down, hide out during daylight hours and follow the north star at night. Try to reach the border. There's a Texas Ranger station at San Antonio. Ask for Bodie West. He knows I'm in Mexico, and he knows why I came. So if I cash in, I'll want him to know. Tell him Tamara is to be welcomed in my name.

"Wes," Renita said, near tears, "I want to see the Sandlin gang destroyed, but not at the cost of your life."

"I stood over my father, Nathan Stone, while the life leaked out of him," said Wes, "and I took an oath—a blood oath—to destroy the varmints responsible for his death. If I fail to do that, I couldn't live with myself. You must understand."*

*The Autumn of the Gun.

"I . . . I'll try," Renita said softly.

"*Bueno, valiente hombre,*" said El Lobo.

"*Muerte antes deshonra,*"* Tamara said. "Wes and Palo, *vaya con Dios.*"

They waited for darkness to fall, and there was little conversation, for it seemed there was nothing more to be said. They rode in from the south, avoiding well-lit streets, seeking the less affluent side of town where there were dingy cantinas, open-front cafes, and the smell of roasting meat. They reached a cross street, and three buildings down was what appeared to be a hotel or boardinghouse.

"If there's an alley behind those houses," Wes said, "We'll leave the horses there."

Empty didn't like towns, and he sought the shadow of the buildings. Halfway down the block was the dark maw of an alley that ran behind the buildings fronting the cross street. The dim glow of an occasional lamp bled into the alley, but that was all.

"We'll leave the horses here," said Wes. "Renita, Tamara, don't forget what I've told you. Empty, stay."

Just for a moment, Wes took Renita's hand. El Lobo spent a similar moment with Tamara and then followed Wes down the alley. Reaching the street, they walked close to the buildings, keeping within the shadows. Ahead of them was a cantina, its door lit by a single bracket lamp. Wes opened the door and stepped inside, El Lobo following. The Mexican cantinas, unlike saloons, didn't encourage patrons at

---

*Death before dishonor.

the bar. Instead, there were many small tables, each with four ladder-back chairs. White-aproned waiters moved quietly among the tables, leaving full bottles, removing empty ones. Wes and El Lobo took a table in a corner of the room, where they could see the front door, as well as the curtain that concealed what might be a back exit. One of the waiters glided over, and Wes nodded to El Lobo.

"Pulque," El Lobo said.

They were brought a bottle and two glasses. El Lobo poured three fingers of the potent liquid in each of the glasses, while Wes looked around the room. There were only a few patrons, two of which looked vaguely familiar. El Lobo sipped his drink, and, not wishing to appear conspicuous, Wes tried his own. The stuff was like liquid fire, and he broke into a wheezing cough.

"God Almighty," he grunted, "what *is* this stuff?"

El Lobo laughed softly. "Hundred and forty proof."

Unbidden, one of the waiters brought a glass of water. Wes gulped it gratefully, and thereafter took only small sips of the fiery liquid, seeming not to notice his companion. El Lobo had recognized the two men who seemed familiar to Wes as the pair of Mexican freighters they had met on the road to Mexico City. When the men left the cantina, El Lobo followed. Once they were on the street, in the shadows, one of the Mexicans spoke.

"El Diablo Pistolas?"

"*Sí*," said El Lobo.

"Hidalgo, Ximinez, *Mejicano politicos*," said the

Mexican. "These *hombres* serve the dragon. *Rapido pistolas matar. Oro. Mucho hombres.*"

He said no more, and the two hurried away. El Lobo returned to the cantina and for the next few moments concerned himself with emptying his glass. His elbows on the table, he spoke so softly, Wes could barely hear him.

"These are the *Mejicano* freighters we meet on the trail. They say *Mejicano politicos* Hidalgo and Ximinez serve the dragon. They hire fast guns, pay in gold."

"So the Sandlin gang is sendin' hired guns after us," Wes said, "and we have no way of knowin' who they are."

"*Sí,*" said El Lobo.

"Let's get out of here," Wes said. "That pair of *hombres* at the table near the bar was almighty interested when you left the cantina with those freighters."

Wes beckoned to one of the waiters, digging into his pocket for a coin to pay for the drinks. For only an instant, among the coins in the palm of his hand was one of the coins with the dragon's head. The waiter accepted a coin in payment and, when he turned away, nodded almost imperceptibly to the pair of men of whom Wes had been suspicious. Wes and El Lobo had no warning, and all that saved them was the dimness within the cantina and the haste of the gunmen. The two fired simultaneously, and before they could fire a second time, Wes and El Lobo had upended a pair of tables and were returning the fire. But the odds changed rapidly when two more gunmen burst through the front door.

"*Cuidado, amigo!*" El Lobo shouted.

He scrambled around the end of the bar, and Wes followed, lead clipping chairs and tables all around them. Their only chance lay in reaching the back door. If there *was* one. Bursting through the curtain, they came face-to-face with one of the barmen bearing a sawed-off shotgun. El Lobo shoved the gun's muzzle aside, slugging its bearer with the muzzle of his Colt. Wes leaped aside just as the shotgun roared, and the charge struck some of the gunmen who were pursuing. There were shouts of pain and the sound of a body striking the floor. There was no light except that which leaked through from the cantina, and the back door was barely visible. It was also locked.

"Hit it!" Wes grunted.

El Lobo slammed his shoulder against the door, and it barely moved.

"Stand 'em off," said Wes, "and let me try."

El Lobo drew both Colts and began firing, while Wes attacked the door. Once, twice, three times he put his shoulder to it before he felt it give. The gunmen were returning El Lobo's fire, and a slug struck Wes in the left arm above the elbow. Wes drove his right shoulder into the door, and it splintered just as El Lobo's Colt's clicked on empty. Just as they stepped into the alley, there was the thud of boots on cobblestones. Guns flamed in the darkness, and El Lobo grunted in pain. Wes drew his right-hand Colt and, returning the fire, had the satisfaction of hearing one of their pursuers cry out in pain. It had some effect on the others, and when his Colt clicked on empty, Wes holstered it. Blood dripping off the fingers of his left hand, he used his right to draw his left-hand Colt. Once, twice, three times he fired at muzzle flashes. El Lobo stumbled and almost fell.

"How bad, *amigo?*" Wes asked.

"The leg," El Lobo grunted.

"Lean on me," said Wes. "We must make it to the horses."

There was no longer any sound of pursuit, but somewhere ahead there was the *clop-clop-clop* of hooves.

"Damn," said Wes in despair.

Suddenly there was that friendly rumble from Empty's throat that he often used to announce his presence. Wes drew a deep breath and paused, aware that Tamara and Renita were bringing their horses.

"We heard shooting," Renita said, "and we believed you needed your horses."

"You couldn't have been more right," said Wes. "At least four gunmen jumped us. El Lobo has a leg wound, and I have a bloody left arm. Can you mount, *amigo?*"

"*Sí*," El Lobo said. "I lose much blood."

"We must get away from here and back into the hills," said Wes. "We have to find a place to hole up and treat our wounds."

But El Lobo was leaning against his horse, reloading his Colts, and Wes followed his example. Making their way out of town, they rode slowly, hoping not to attract unwanted attention. They needed hot water to cleanse their wounds, but they dared not risk a fire, for they knew not how many gunmen were looking for them. Somewhere ahead of them, a mule brayed.

"Rein up," Wes ordered. "Could be trouble."

"Perhaps not," said Tamara. "*Quien es?*" she asked softly.

"*Amigos,*" came the reply. "El Diablo Pistolas?"

"*Sí,*" Tamara replied. "*Daño. Medico.*"

"*Seguir,*" said the voice from the darkness.

"He wishes us to follow," Tamara said. "He is one of the teamsters who spoke to us on the road to Mexico City."

"We owe them our lives," said Wes. "But for them, we would never have gotten out of that cantina alive. Tell him we'll go with him."

Tamara spoke in swift Spanish, and the second Mexican soon appeared with the team of mules and the wagon. The Mexican who had spoken to Tamara joined his companion on the wagon box, and the wagon rumbled off into what appeared to be dense woods. But the *Mejicanos* knew where they were going, and the wagon progressed without difficulty. When they reached a swift-running creek, the *Mejicano* handling the team reined up. Trotting her horse alongside the wagon, Tamara asked a question and one of the teamsters answered.

"We are to ride our horses in the creek," Tamara said. "They believe that with the dawn, the killers will follow."

"I can't argue with that kind of thinking," said Wes. "Where are they taking us?"

"To a place of safety, where your wounds can heal," Tamara said.

Wes, El Lobo, Tamara, and Renita trotted their horses into the creek, and the wagon rattled along beside it. They rode for what seemed like many miles before there was finally a dim light somewhere ahead. There was the braying of numerous mules, which suggested this was more than just a *peon*'s cottage. At the bidding of their hosts, they left the creek and approached an enormous barn. Adjoining was a six-rail-high corral in which more than a dozen mules picked at hay. The light they had seen from a distance proved to be a single lantern hanging near the barn's entrance. The two *Mejicanos* climbed down from the wagon box and approached the barn on foot, while Wes, El Lobo, Tamara, and Renita waited. A Mexican hostler came out of the barn and the teamsters spoke to him in rapid Spanish for a few moments. The teamsters then mounted their wagon box and drove away. Approaching the riders, the Mexican hostler spoke.

"*Señors, señoritas*, I am Pablo. Ride your horses into the barn. I will see to them. But first we must conceal you from the *Diablo* dragon. Then Shekeela will care for your wounds."

The center of the barn was open, with stalls down both sides, and Pablo paused at one of the stalls at the very end. Kicking aside loose hay, he revealed an iron ring in what proved to be a wooden floor. Steps led down into the darkness. Pablo took a lantern from a wooden peg, lit it, and led the way down the steps to a musty room. It was large enough for five bunks. On a table sat a small charcoal stove, and on the floor a bin of charcoal. The bunks were no more than wooden frames with latticed—criss-crossed—rawhide strips several inches wide. There were clean blankets on each of the bunks. Pablo sat the lantern on the table, and from a wooden bucket poured water into a blackened iron pot. He then sloshed a little oil from the lantern on to the charcoal and lit the stove.

"Shekeela come," said Pablo. "I tend to horses."

He lifted the door with his shoulders, stepped out, and let the door carefully down.

"Damn," Wes said. "After those Mex teamsters went out of their way to bring us here, we didn't even thank them."

"I thanked them," said Tamara, "but they wanted no thanks. They wish us success."

"That water will be boiling soon," Renita said. "If Shekeela's coming to doctor your wounds, you should be getting ready."

"My shirt's ruined," said Wes, removing it.

All eyes then turned to El Lobo and the bloody right leg of his trousers.

"Get out of them," Wes said. "How else can we doctor that bloody hip?"

El Lobo actually blushed, while Tamara and Renita laughed delightedly. The overhead door was lifted, and Shekeela appeared with a medicine kit. Tamara said something to her in rapid Spanish, and she laughed, her dark eyes on El Lobo.

"*Desnuda*," said Shekeela. "*Mucho hombre, eh?*"

Sheepishly, El Lobo stepped out of his trousers. He was left with only his shirt, and it wasn't long enough to spare him embarrassment. Shekeela pointed to one of the bunks, and he obediently stretched out on it.

Word of the failed ambush had made its way back to Hidalgo and Ximinez, and Picado, one of the hired guns, had brought it.

"Santog is dead," said Picado. "Kilt by the barkeep's shotgun, when he was buffaloed by one of the *hombres* we was after. Guigman, Estebanand, and Jaspeado is bad wounded."

"Five of you," Hidalgo said in disgust, "and still they do not die."

"We done the best we could," said Picado. "There'll be another time."

"*Sí*," Ximinez said. "These *malo, Diablo hombres* kill the rest of you."

"I can't speak for the others," said Picado angrily, "but if you reckon you can do any better, then grab a gun and go after these hell-raisers yourselves."

Chapter 12

Mexico City. August 9, 1884

Arriving in Mexico City, Black Bill Trevino did the very thing he had been cautioned not to do. He called on the Señor Hidalgo.

"You have been told not to come here," Hidalgo said stiffly.

"Yeah," said Black Bill, "we got to be careful not to dirty your honorable carcass, but we got no time to go through channels. Them hell-raisin' *hombres* is headin' this way."

Hidalgo laughed, and it wasn't a pleasant sound. "They are here. The Señor Sandlin is offering rewards for them. He pays ten *pistoleros* to find and kill them. *Comico.*"

"What's so damn funny about that?"

"These Diablos Pistolas shoot their way out of a cantina and escape. Five of these *malo pistoleros* cannot stop them. One be dead, others wounded."

"They escaped?" Trevino roared. "Didn't nobody have the brains to trail them?"

"It is dark when they escape," said Hidalgo, "and they ride south. Come the dawn, there is no trail."

"By God," Trevino snarled, "there's *always* a trail. I'll talk to Sandlin."

"Please do," said Hidalgo, "and do not return here."

But Trevino was unable to speak to Sandlin. He had to settle for Jarvis, *segundo* and the second in command.

"Damn it," Trevino said, "how can this pair keep slippin' through our hands? Are they bulletproof?"

"No," said Jarvis. "The five gunmen that braced them in a cantina got in some telling shots. The two escaped, but not without wounds."

"If they're hurt, they'll find a place to hole up," Trevino said. "We got to ransack all the huts and villages within fifty miles until we find 'em."

"Denton Rucker and nineteen men arrived from Durango," said Jarvis, "and they're all fanned out to the south of here, searching. Feel free to join them."

"I aim to," Trevino said. "Tell Sandlin it's time to come down off the throne and put an end to this."

It was after sundown, coming on dark, when Trevino found Rucker and his outfit by the smoke from their supper fire. Rucker hadn't liked the way Trevino had virtually taken over at Durango, and when Black Bill reined up, Rucker said nothing.

"That pair of gun-throwers was wounded," Trevino said, "and they got to be holed up somewhere. We'll find 'em if we got to rip down every shack, barn, and village."

"I don't recall asking for your advice or your help," said Rucker coldly.

"No matter," Trevino replied, just as coldly. "This

threat's got to be stopped or we'll all get invited to the same ball, dancin' on the business end of a rope.''

It was a sobering thought, and Rucker responded with a little less hostility.

''We reckoned the best way for 'em to hide their trail was to take the wagon road out of town. We follered that, lookin' for tracks leavin' it. Maybe ten miles out, we found the tracks of mules, a wagon, and four horses leadin' down to a creek. The mules and wagon follered the creek, while the four riders took their horses into it.''

''They gotta come out of that creek somewhere,'' Trevino said.

''You think we don't know that?'' said Rucker. ''It was near dark when we picked up the trail. We aim to try again at first light.''

It was a perfectly logical response, and Trevino could think of nothing to say. There was a prolonged silence, and when nobody offered Trevino coffee, he took a tin cup from his saddlebag and helped himself. All of Rucker's outfit knew Black Bill Trevino was close to Sandlin, yet Trevino had told them nothing of the outlaw leader's plans. Bailey said what the others were thinking.

''You ain't told us nothin' about what Sandlin aims to do. We rode in from Durango, an' all we was told was that Sandlin's hired a bunch of fast guns, and that five of 'em lost their edge in a failed ambush. Jarvis done Sandlin's talkin', an' told us to git out here and beat the bushes for them escaped gunslingers.''

''Hell, you know as much as I do,'' Trevino growled. ''Jarvis sent me here to join in the search.''

"I've heard talk that Sandlin owns one of them sailin' ships anchored at Tampico harbor," Rucker said. "Is there any truth to that?"

"I dunno," said Trevino uncertainly.

"Think about it some," Rucker replied. "Ever since them *hombres* struck at Namiquipa, things has been goin' sour. If ever'thing just goes plumb to hell, you reckon Sandlin aims to pick up the pieces?"

"I don't know what Sandlin aims to do," said Black Bill, "but I'm sure of one thing. If your kind of talk gets back to him, he'll have your head in a sack."

Rucker laughed. "I'll risk it. You won't tell him, because you'll be thinkin' of Sandlin's sailin' ship anchored over yonder at Tampico."

Trevino said nothing, but his grim expression and the fire in his eyes suggested that Rucker had come painfully close to the truth.

"We can't remain here any longer," Wes said after their second day under Pablo's old barn. "They'd murder Pablo and Shekeela for taking us in."

"But Palo's leg wound hasn't healed," said Renita, "nor has the wound in your arm."

"No help for that," Wes said. "We'll ride out at dawn."

"*Sí*," said El Lobo. "They be coming for us."

"Yes," Tamara agreed. "They will search every house, every barn, every village. There are hundreds of them."

But when Shekeela brought them their supper, she didn't share their caution.

"They not find you here," she protested.

"Sooner or later," Wes said, "they'll find where we left the wagon road. While we all rode our horses in the water, they'll know we reached the creek following the wagon. They have only to follow the wagon tracks here to the barn. While tracks of our horses were lost as we left the creek, there are four horses in the barn. Pablo is a seller of mules. He couldn't account for the horses. They would know."

"*Sí*," Shekeela admitted sadly. "They are *Diablos*. They would know."

The four riders left Pablo's barn before good daylight, guiding their horses into the creek. But no sooner had they done so than there was a shout from a distant ridge. They had been seen! There was a clatter of hooves as mounted men charged down the slope. Not quite within range, they began firing, some of them with Winchesters. Slugs kicked up dirt at the very heels of their horses.

"Renita," Wes shouted, "you and Tamara ride for it. El Lobo and me will hold 'em off to give you a start."

"No," said Renita, "I won't leave you."

"Nor will I," Tamara said. "I will remain with Palo."

"God help us," said Wes under his breath.

They swept over a rise, and of a single mind, Wes and El Lobo swung out of their saddles. Each had a Winchester.

"Ride, damn it," Wes shouted at Renita and Tamara.

Neither of the women had a rifle, and there was

little they could do. They rode on, as Wes and El Lobo prepared to meet the oncoming riders.

"Cut down as many as you can, as quick as you can," Wes said. "If we empty enough saddles, maybe we can discourage the others."

Wes and El Lobo held their fire until the riders were well within range. They fired almost simultaneously—once, twice, three times—and six horses galloped riderless. The pair of deadly Winchesters kept spitting lead, and before they got out of range, three more of the outlaws were hit. Lead stung some of the horses, and they lit out wildly back the way they had come. Only Black Bill Trevino charged ahead, a revolver in his hand, but he dropped it when lead ripped into his shoulder. Another slug struck his horse, and he was flung bodily out of the saddle. He was cursing his companions when they finally regrouped and caught up with him.

"By God," Trevino bawled, "what's with you cowardly varmints?"

"There's just a thin line between brave an' stupid," said Mannon. "Wouldn't hurt you to look around an' be sure which side of that line you're on."

Black Bill struggled to his feet, saying nothing. One of the outlaws had caught up one of the riderless horses and passed the reins to Trevino.

"You're welcome to take over this outfit, Trevino," Rucker said. "There's eight dead men, and Rinks is hard hit. You've just had a little taste of what these two *hombres* can do, even when they're outgunned. Far as I'm concerned, they're nine feet tall and a yard wide. A man that ain't afraid of dying takes just a hell of a lot of killing."

"Tell that to Sandlin," said Trevino.

"I reckon I won't ever get that close," Rucker replied. "Let him find it out as best he can."

Trevino didn't respond, for there was the sound of galloping horses, and six hard-eyed riders approached. Looking at Trevino's bloody shoulder, some of them laughed.

"Who the hell are you?" Trevino demanded.

"Ah, *señor*," said a grinning Mexican, "I am Zopilote. Beside me is Picado and Quemodo. The *Indios* are Shawanna, Barbonsio, and Ryashia. We come to save you from El Diablo Pistolas. The few of you that remain."

Denton Rucker laughed. "You must be what's left of that *malo* bunch that got shot up in the cantina."

"I would call you a fool, *señor*," said Zopilote, "but I do not esteem you so highly."

"Somebody get a fire goin' and boil some water," Black Bill said. "I got a wound that needs tending."

The six newly arrived gunmen back-stepped their horses.

"Hey, buzzard-face," Trevino shouted, "where do you think you're going? We ride when I'm ready, and I ain't ready."

"We do not take orders from you, nor do we ride with you, *señor*," Zopilote replied. "Do not push your luck."

The Mexican carried a thonged-down revolver on each hip, and his thumbs rested on the butts of the weapons. Black Bill Trevino's face colored, but he said nothing, for he had not recovered his dropped Colt. Turning their backs in contempt, the six gunmen galloped their horses away. There was nervous laughter from some of the men, and nobody had yet started the fire.

"Damn it," Trevino shouted, "I said start a fire and boil some water."

"We got no time to wet-nurse you," said Rucker coldly. "You got a horse and you're not worth a damn to us wounded. Ride back to town and find yourself a doc."

"You ain't heard the end of this," Black Bill snarled.

"Thanks for the warning," said Rucker. "I'll watch my back. The rest of you mount up. We got some ridin' to do."

"Rinks ain't dead," Mannon said. "What do you aim to do about him?"

"Nothing," said Rucker, "unless you want to put a bullet through his head. He's been gut-shot, and it's just a matter of time. Now let's ride."

Black Bill Trevino laughed, while the ten remaining outlaws mounted their horses. But the men eyed Rucker with anger and distrust, each aware that he might have received the same heartless treatment as the unfortunate Rinks. A tiny spark of rebellion had been kindled.

Wes watched the western horizon hopefully, for the daily thunderstorm appeared to be in the making. His companions shared that hope.

"If the rain will hold off long enough for us to find a place to hide," Renita said, "we can escape them."

"That's about the only chance we have," said Wes. "That was just one bunch of the varmints. We don't know how many more may be looking for us."

"Infierno," El Lobo said in disgust. "The wolf does not hide from coyotes."

"He does when the coyotes have Winchester fangs," said Wes. "We shot our way out of this because they *expected* us to run. Next time they'll know better, and if we stand our ground, we'll find ourselves surrounded *muy pronto."*

The shelter, when they found it, was only an overhang along a creek, but the growth that shrouded the creek banks was dense. They rode their horses in the water, leaving no trail. Thunder rumbled in the distance and a west wind brought the smell of rain.

"We will be secure for today and tonight," said Tamara.

The rain came, drenching the pursuers and washing out the trail they followed. The six gunmen took it in stride, prepared to wait out the storm and pick up the trail if and when they could. But Denton Rucker and his riders were frustrated.

"We'll never find 'em now," Bailey complained. "When this rain's done, we'll have to go lookin' for their trail all over again."

"Yeah," said Rucker sourly, "but we got other business to attend to. We know where they was holed up after that shootin' in town, and it's time we made believers of these damn *Mejicanos* that's sidin' with them against us."

With Rucker leading the way, they rode back to the modest cabin where Pablo and Shekeela lived.

"Bailey, you and Mannon set fire to the barn," Rucker ordered. "The rest of you shoot every mule in the corral."

The thundering of Winchesters and the slaughter of the mules brought the expected response. Pablo and Shekeela came running from the house.

"Please," Pablo cried.

He spoke no more, for Denton Rucker fired and the heavy slugs flung him on his back in the dirt. Shrieking in terror and fury, Shekeela ran toward the fallen Pablo, but she never reached him. Rucker turned the deadly Winchester on her, and she collapsed in a lifeless heap. Rucker stomped into the little cabin and, finding a coal-oil lamp, slammed it against a wall. He dropped a match in the spilled oil, and the flames quickly took hold. He and his ten followers mounted their horses and rode toward town, never looking back. But their cowardly acts hadn't gone unnoticed. Juan, a friend of Pablo's and an occasional visitor, had been approaching the cabin when he had heard the outlaws coming. In hiding, he had watched, horrified.

"*Diablos, bastardos,*" he said, crossing himself.

The bodies of Pablo and Shekeela must be attended to, but he was old and he must have help. He and his people knew of the two valiant men who had so often bested the evil dragon, and now its disciples were destroying all who stood in its way. Mounting his mule, he rode away at a gallop, for there were many in town who must know of this foul, evil deed. The dragon must pay.

Toluca, Mexico. August 9, 1884

After a doctor had seen to his wound, Black Bill Trevino wasted no time in calling on Jarvis, one of Sandlin's lieutenants.

"That's how it is," Trevino said, after telling Jarvis of the slaughter of half of Denton Rucker's men. "Rucker's bunch didn't get off a shot, and they held back while I rode after the gun-throwin' varmints myself."

"And you allowed the pair of them to escape," Jarvis said.

"Allowed, hell," said Trevino. "They had Winchesters and all I had was a Colt. They cut down on me and nicked my horse before I was in range."

"Stay off the street," Jarvis warned. "We have a meeting tonight."

Trevino had been gone only a short time when a courier arrived from Mexico City. The message he brought from Hidalgo was short and urgent.

Presidente calls for investigation. *Soldados* possible.

Jarvis hurriedly conferred with some of Sandlin's disciples, and while they had no idea what had prompted an investigation or what it might involve, a possible police action by soldiers would be serious indeed. The pending meeting became all the more important, and Señors Hidalgo and Ximinez would have to do some explaining.

"I have already received a report on your action this morning," Jarvis said when he was confronted by Denton Rucker. "A loss of nine men, with nothing to show for them. I think you'd better back off until I've had a chance to . . . ah . . ."

"Talk to Sandlin," said Rucker bitterly.

"Maybe," Jarvis said. "See me tomorrow."

Uneasily, Rucker returned to his men. They were looking to him for answers, and he had none.

For the first time, Sandlin's disciples met without their leader.

"This morning," said Jarvis, "I had a message from Señor Hidalgo. He's told me only that the president is demanding an investigation of some sort and that soldiers may be involved. I reckon all this involves us in some way, so why don't you spell it out for us, Hidalgo?"

Hidalgo got to his feet, and but for Ximinez, there wasn't a friendly face in the room.

"Today," Hidalgo said, "A *Mejicano* and his *señora* were murdered, their animals shot, and their buildings burned. There was a witness, and he is calling it an act of revenge. We have been accused, for these *Mejicanos* have been hiding the pair of *Diablo* gunmen we seek and have been unable to find."

"Tell your president he's barkin' up the wrong tree," said Jarvis. "These *Mejicanos* were likely shot by the very gunmen they've been hiding."

"No," Hidalgo said. "Eleven men did the killing and the burning, and afterward they returned to town. The *presidente* is aware of these two *hombres* we seek, and he is in no way sympathetic to us."

"So that's how it is," said Jarvis. "Your president don't give a damn if these two varmints kill us or if we kill them. His concern is for the poor *Mejicanos* who get caught in the line of fire."

"*Sí*," Hidalgo said. "The *Mejicanos* complain by the hundreds, and *el presidente* finds the support he needs. He seeks the authority to deploy the *soldados* in a police action."

"Damn," said Jarvis, "how much time do we have?"

"Two weeks, per'ap," Hidalgo replied. "No more."

"Then we must find and eliminate these two gun-throwers before the soldiers move in," said Jarvis, "and there must be no more killing of *Mejicanos*, for any reason."

"*Sí*," Hidalgo said, "but I fear the damage has been done."

"Maybe you're right," said Jarvis, "and I think I know who's responsible for that. I'm calling this meeting adjourned. Hidalgo, you and Ximinez can go. I have a job for everybody else."

Hidalgo and Ximinez wasted no time in departing. Canton, Tafolla, Zouka, Klady, Handley, Wittrus, Moke, and Undilay waited expectantly. Jarvis spoke.

"Canton, you're in charge. Denton Rucker and the *hombres* ridin' with him got us into this when they gunned down that pair of *Mejicanos*. I'll tell Rucker I'm sending the eight of you to replace the men he lost and that you're to resume the chase. Then when you're well away from town, I want you to show Rucker and his bunch the error of their ways."

The decision of Mexican officials to use soldiers to quell the killings had far-reaching effects. The telegraph carried the word to every military outpost in Mexico, and in Juarez, Ranch Stringfield took it as a warning. He packed a few personal belongings and cleaned out the safe, most of whose contents didn't belong to him. He filled saddlebags with gold and, mounting a fast horse, rode north. Into Arizona.

Toluca, Mexico. August 10, 1884

Denton Rucker and his remaining ten men were surprised when they were met by the eight riders Jarvis had sent them.

"I'm takin' charge," Canton said. "Jarvis gave the order."

Rucker's men looked at one another, not liking this new development.

"You tell Jarvis we're ridin' back to Durango," said Rucker. "I ain't takin' his orders or yours."

Canton and his men tensed, their hands on the butts of their revolvers, but they were still in town. Slowly they relaxed, and Canton spoke.

"Insubordination don't set well with this outfit. There's no place for any of you. Not in Durango or anywhere else in Mexico. Ride for the border, and keep ridin'."

Unwilling to turn their backs, Rucker and his men back-stepped their horses, getting as far from Canton and his riders as they could. Finally they wheeled their horses and rode away at a fast gallop.

"By God," Bailey said, "if the time an' place was right, they'd have gunned us down."

"That's the feelin' I got," said Rucker."

"We ain't goin' back to Durango, then," Mannon said.

"You can suit yourself," said Rucker, "but I don't plan to. All things being equal, I ain't one to run out on a fight, but I won't dodge lead from both sides.

I'll risk hanging in Texas if my only other choice is bein' shot in the back in Mexico."

There was a rumble of agreement from the rest of the men, and when Rucker rode out, they followed.

"Damn it," Jarvis said, when Canton reported to him, "they knew what was coming. I want all of you to be watchin' for other groups arriving from Durango, and I want them kept out of town. The last thing we want them knowing is of the decision to use soldiers."

"If you know how to reach Sandlin, you'd better be gettin' at it," said Canton. "When all this bunch rides in from Durango, there'll be may be six hundred men within ridin' distance of town. You reckon they won't attract some attention? Hidalgo and Ximinez will be havin' conniption fits."

"Yeah," said Tafolla, another Sandlin lieutenant, "all it'll take is for one or more of these *hombres* to pull a gun, and we'll have them soldiers down on us."

"Just do what I said," Jarvis growled. "Keep watch in the hills to the north and tell all the arriving outfits they're not to come into town. Sandlin's orders."

"Hold it," said Wes. "Riders coming."

The six riders crossed the creek within sight of where Wes and his companions had reined up. It was the morning after their successful escape from Rucker's outfit.

"They be Sandlin outlaws, or hired guns?" El Lobo wondered.

"Hired guns," said Wes. "Sandlin outlaws usually travel in packs of ten or more."

"Then why do we not ambush them?" Tamara asked.

"Per'ap there be more," said El Lobo.

"He's right," Renita added. "We saw only six, but there may be many more, all close enough to hear the shooting."

"That's why we're going to trail them," said Wes. "They're riding away from town. If they're looking for us, we'll let them find us, but not until we're ready for them."

Empty ran on ahead, aware they were trailing the mounted men who had so recently crossed the creek.

"The *perro* follows the trail," El Lobo said.

"He'll see that we don't ride upon them unexpectedly," said Wes. "We'll give them a little more distance and then El Lobo and me will get ahead of them."

"It's always you and El Lobo," Renita complained. "When are you going to let me and Tamara prove ourselves?"

El Lobo laughed.

"It is no laughing matter," said Tamara. "These outlaws made whores of us. We owe them something."

"I won't argue with that," Wes said, "but you're armed only with Colts, and they're for close quarters. You'll need Winchesters, and you must know how to use them."

"We dare not venture into town," said Tamara. "How are we to get these weapons?"

"I figure these six hombres we're trailing will be well-armed," Wes replied. "Once we are finished with them, they won't complain if we take a pair of Winchesters and as much of their ammunition as we can use."

They rode on, reining up when Empty came trotting back to meet them.

"The *perro* warns us," said El Lobo.

"They've stopped for some reason," Wes said. "Maybe to rest their horses. It's time we circled around and planned a reception for them. Renita, you and Tamara remain here. I don't want either of you doing anything that could get you killed. Keep your eyes on our back trail. When we open the ball ahead, there could be other riders close enough to hear the shooting. If you see or hear other riders coming, get out of sight pronto."

Wes and El Lobo swung wide, Empty taking the lead. It was a procedure that Empty knew well, for many times he had guided Nathan Stone during similar maneuvers.

Half a mile ahead, the six gunmen prepared to mount after resting their horses.

"We come too far," said Shawanna, one of the Mexican-Indian riders.

"Per'ap," Zopilote conceded, but he made no move to turn back.

They had ridden not more than a mile when there was the sudden bark of a Winchester, and the flat-crowned hat was snatched off Zopilote's head.

"If you're lookin' for us," Wes shouted, "you've found us. We're givin' you more of a chance than you'd give us. Raise your hands and dismount, slowly.

"Ah, *señor*," said Zopilote, "you would spare us, knowing we come to kill you?"

"We would," Wes replied, "if you'll give up your weapons and your horses."

"*Por Dios*," said the gunman, "you would have us walk the many miles back to town, in disgrace?"

"That," Wes said, "or you can die right here."

"You leave us no choice," Zopilote said. "We dismount."

"Do not trust them, amigo," said El Lobo quietly.

It was good advice, and before Wes could respond, the six gunmen spilled out of their saddles. Each had pulled a Winchester from the saddle boot, and even with no cover, they bellied down and all hell broke loose.

Chapter 13

Wes and El Lobo, firing from cover, had an edge. Shawanna and Barbonsio died in the first volley.

"*Retiro*," Zopilote shouted.

The Mexican seized the reins of a horse. One foot in the stirrup, clinging to the side of the animal Indian-style, he managed to escape. But his comrades weren't so fortunate, for the shooting had spooked the rest of the horses. Ryashia, Picado, and Quemodo sprang to their feet and charged, their Winchesters spitting lead. It was an act of desperation, and they were cut down quickly.

"We do not get them all," El Lobo said. He spoke with some reproach, for he had not favored challenging the gunmen.

"It's my fault, damn it," said Wes, "but I don't favor gunning a man down without warning, in cold blood."

"Even when those *hombres* wish to do it to you?" El Lobo asked.

"Even then," said Wes. "Let the one who escaped tell the others we gunned down five of them without taking a hit. It'll give the rest something to think about. Now, since these coyotes won't be needin' 'em anymore, let's take a pair of Winchesters for Renita and Tamara.''

Wes and El Lobo took two Winchesters and all the ammunition they could find, which would interchange with Winchester or Colt. They then mounted their horses and rode back to join Renita and Tamara.

"We could have shot the one who rode away," Tamara said, "but we obeyed you."

"I'm glad you did," said Wes. "Let him take word to the dragon that hiring extra guns won't stop us."

"We still haven't accounted for the rest of that bunch that came after us as we were leaving Pablo's barn," Renita said.

"No," said Wes, "and that bothers me. They would have lost our trail during the rain, and likely had one hell of a mad on. They must have seen us leaving Pablo's place, and I'm afraid they may have gone there to take their revenge."

"It is the kind of evil these sons of *el Diablo* would do," Tamara said.

They soon learned their suspicions were well founded. There were only ashes where the barn and cabin had stood, and along the creek were several mule-drawn carts and a few saddled mules. The Mexicans gathered there saw them coming and hastily began backing away.

"*Amigos*," Tamara cried. "El Diablo Pistolas."

She trotted her horse toward them, speaking in Spanish, and one—a gray-haired old man—responded. After Tamara spoke to him, he turned to the others and, speaking rapidly, dispelled their

fears. Tamara then spoke to Wes, Renita, and El
Lobo.

"This is Juan," she said, pointing to the old one.
"He was approaching Pablo's house when the outlaws attacked. He quickly concealed himself and his
mule and witnessed the murder of Pablo and Shekeela. They are buried near the creek, and these are
friends who have come to pay their respects."

"Tell them they have nothing to fear from us,"
said Wes. "Tell them we will see that the killers pay
for what they have done to Pablo and Shekeela."

Quickly Tamara repeated what Wes had said, and
it was Juan who spoke for them all.

"*Sí*," Juan said grimly. "*Matar. Vaya con Dios.*"

There was nothing more Wes and his companions
could do, so they rode away.

"Dear God," said Renita, "those poor people died
because they were kind to us."

"Yes," Tamara said, "and if it is the last thing we
do, we must see that they have not died in vain."

"*Sí*," said El Lobo.

"From now on," Wes said, "we'll take the fight to
them. By now that bunch gathered in Durango
knows we're ridin' south, and they should be headed
this way. I think we'll begin searching the hills north
of Mexico City. I doubt all those *hombres* will be permitted in town, and that means a camp similar to
the one near Durango."

"Tamara and me have Winchesters now," Renita
said.

"I know," said Wes, "but how well can you handle them?"

"I don't know," Renita admitted, "but I intend to find out."

"I can shoot as well as any man," said Tamara.

El Lobo looked at her with some amusement, but it swiftly faded, for her dark eyes were a sea of grim, fiery defiance.

"Keep your Winchesters fully loaded, then," Wes said, "and let's ride."

Toluca, Mexico. August 11, 1884.

Jarvis paced the study of the Sandlin mansion, irritated by Sandlin's habit of keeping him waiting. There was something mysterious about Cord Sandlin, something that didn't quite ring true, and it had begun bothering Jarvis more and more. There was no feeling or compassion within the outlaw band, but it seemed that Sandlin carried the lack of it a step further, to excess. Rarely did Sandlin smile, and even then it never reached the ice-blue of the eyes. Jarvis had never gotten beyond the study, and he wondered what secrets might be concealed within the mansion. There was no sound, but Sandlin was suddenly in the doorway, appearing in an almost ghostly manner.

"I know the Mexican government intends to use soldiers to stop the killing," Sandlin said. "I want to know why, and what action you have taken."

"Denton Rucker and his outfit killed a pair of *Mejicanos* and burned their place," said Jarvis. "Some old Mexican saw the killings and blamed them on us. When I tried to rid us of Rucker and his bunch, they rode out. Bound for the border, I reckon. Our Mexicans—Hidalgo and Ximinez—are havin' conniption fits. Canton and the rest of our bunch is in the hills north of Mexico City. I gave orders in your name to halt all the riders comin' in from Durango."

"A wise move," Sandlin said. "Hundreds of armed men riding into town would hasten the use of soldiers. What progress has been made toward riding down the men who would destroy us?"

"None," said Jarvis. "They shot their way out of a cantina. One of the ten gunmen you hired was killed and three others wounded. The pair of men we're after—along with two of the whores they freed in Mazatlán—were hidden in a barn by a *Mejicano* and his wife. Rucker and his bunch spotted 'em ridin' out and went after them. Rode headlong into an ambush and lost nine men."

"By God," Sandlin said, "such stupidity should not go unrewarded. The rest of them should be backed up against a wall and shot."

"That's close to what I had in mind," said Jarvis, "but they got wise."

"Damn it," Sandlin said, "I can't be away for two days without everything going to hell. What do you suggest we do with this army of men gathering to the north of Mexico City?"

"I don't know," said Jarvis. "But whatever you choose to do, you'd better do it *muy pronto*. This hairy-legged bunch ain't the kind to hunker out in the woods when there's cantinas within spittin' distance."

"So the soldiers are only part of the problem," Sandlin replied.

"Maybe the smallest part," said Jarvis. "If you aim

to use this bunch that's ridin' in from Durango to continue the manhunt, you'll have to do it before the soldiers take over. If you don't, our bunch will become the hunted."

"When Black Bill Trevino arrives," Sandlin said, "I want him here. As I recall, he was sent to Durango to organize this manhunt. I want to know why our outfit is scattered all over southern Mexico in a fruitless search, while the troublesome pair we're seeking are raising hell here among us."

"Black Bill's already here," said Jarvis, with some relish. "He rode out and joined up with Rucker's outfit in time to ride into that ambush. He charged a pair of Winchesters with a revolver and was wounded. Knocked out of his saddle without firin' a shot. Rode back to town and found himself a doc. I reckon he's here somewhere."

"Find him," Sandlin said grimly. "Is there nothing Hidalgo and Ximinez can do to halt the use of the military?"

"Nothing they're *willing* to do," said Jarvis. "Before this is done, I won't be surprised if the two of 'em run like scared coyotes."

"I think not," Sandlin said. "When all or most of the men have arrived from Durango, inform me immediately and I will speak to them. We will conclude our manhunt and these men will return to their outposts before the soldiers take the field."

"*Bueno*," said Jarvis. "That's the kind of move it'll take to save us."

Jarvis turned to go and, reaching the door, looked back. Sandlin was gone.

*   *   *

Black Bill Trevino sat in a cantina nursing a drink and a foul temper. The appearance of Jarvis did little to improve his disposition, for Jarvis had long enjoyed a more favorable position within the empire than had Black Bill.

"Sandlin wants to see you," Jarvis said.

"Thanks for nothin'," said Trevino. He gulped the remainder of his drink, got to his feet, and departed. Watching him go, Jarvis felt a little sorry for him. Cord Sandlin didn't tolerate failure.

A Mexican servant escorted Black Bill Trevino into the study where he had been only a few times before. He waited, uneasily clenching and unclenching his fists. He was startled at Sandlin's sudden appearance.

"Sit down," Sandlin commanded.

Trevino sat, uncertain. Almost immediately a servant appeared with a tray and a pair of drinks. Sandlin took one and nodded to Trevino.

"Thanks," said Black Bill, "but I just had a drink."

"Then have another," Sandlin snapped. "You're going to need it."

Sandlin's eyes bored into Trevino's, and he almost spilled his drink. He tossed it down in a single gulp, the potency of it causing him to cough and wheeze. He wiped his eyes on the sleeve of his shirt, but his belly felt strange. Sandlin said nothing, but the cold, hard eyes never left Trevino's face. Suddenly a pain ripped through his vitals, doubling him up. There was a second gut-wrenching pain, and Black Bill fell to the floor, groaning in agony. Lying on his back, his pain-stricken eyes met Sandlin's.

"Damn you," Trevino gasped. "Poison . . . is . . . a coward's way . . . of killin' a . . . man. . . ."

"Perhaps," said Sandlin to the lifeless body, "but it is swift, clean, and with virtually no danger. When you are found, there will be no marks on you."

Leaving the burned-out cabin and barn of Pablo and Shekeela, Wes and his three companions rode northwest.

"We must keep far enough to the west that we don't run into any of them," Wes said. "After dark, with Empty guiding us, we'll ride east a ways and see if we can locate their camp."

"Do not forget," said Tamara. "When you ride after the outlaws, I do not wish to be left out."

"Nor I," Renita said.

"Neither of you will be," said Wes. "When they all come together, there may well be hundreds of outlaws. It'll likely take all of us to stampede their horses."

El Lobo laughed. "*Sí*. To Durango, per'ap."

"It will be a fitting disgrace," Tamara said, "and it will further encourage the Mexican people."

"That's exactly what we want," said Wes. "I doubt we'll ever track down and kill all these varmints. The next best thing is to force them out of Mexico and back into Texas, to face a rope or the guns of Texas lawmen."

"*Sí*," El Lobo said. "We follow, kill them there."

"That makes sense," said Renita. "At least we won't be fighting the whole gang at the same time."

"We're still a long way from driving them out of

Mexico," Wes said, "but it's something to look forward to."

Well before moonrise, Wes and El Lobo rode out, Empty leading. They would find the outlaw camp, learn where the horses were picketed, and return for Renita and Tamara. While El Lobo said nothing, Wes had his misgivings, but eventually the women would become involved in the fight. The stampeding of the horses would be a good night's work. There would be much time and opportunity for shooting before the dragon was beaten.

"We lose the *perro*," said El Lobo.

"Empty will find us when he's ready," Wes replied. "He won't let us get too close to the outlaws."

"Him *amigo*," said El Lobo. *"Perro mucho hueso."*

Wes laughed. "Empty looks a mite bony, but it's the way of his kind. He looks half starved right after he's been fed. He belonged to my father, Nathan Stone, and I'll thank God every day I'm alive that he took to me."

"The *perro* sees much of your father in you," El Lobo said. "The Señor Nathan be *uno bueno hombre.*"

They had stopped to rest the horses when Empty returned.

"We'd better leave the horses and continue on foot," said Wes. "Empty's a good judge as to how close we can ride without giving ourselves away."

Wes and El Lobo picketed their horses and, with Empty leading the way, crept carefully through the underbrush. They had to be cautious, for the wind was against them. The supper fires had burned down to ashes, and Wes counted half a dozen beds of live coals, as the night wind touched them.

"Horses not be all together," El Lobo said softly.

"Damn rotten luck," said Wes. "With the horses picketed in six bunches, there's no way we can spook them all at once."

"There be four of us," El Lobo said.

"It'll take some doing," said Wes. "It'll depend on you and me gettin' in close enough to free all the horses."

"Tamara one bunch, Renita one bunch," El Lobo said. "Other, you and me."

"It's a long shot, Wolf," said Wes. "I'll have to stampede a herd of horses through a camp of armed men, combine them with a second bunch, and then spook the lot of 'em. So will you. There's a damn good chance one or both of us will be shot."

"*Hombres* sleep, no *luna*," El Lobo said.

"That's about the only chance we have," said Wes. "We'll wait until the moon's down and they're all asleep. But there may be sentries watching the horses."

"El Lobo fix."

El Lobo didn't fear sentries, for he could move through the darkness like a shadow, his lethal bowie knife dealing silent death.

"Let's go, then," Wes said. "We'll need to explain this to Tamara and Renita. I want them to do exactly as they're told. Nothing more."

As he had expected, Wes found Tamara and Renita eager to take part in the spooking of the horses.

"There are six camps," Wes said, "and six different groups of horses. El Lobo and me will slip in among the horses and cut them loose. These camps are pretty well strung out, one adjoining the other. Renita, you and Tamara will stampede the horses belongin' to the two groups of horses farthest east. You'll stampede them to the north. El Lobo and me will each try to run two groups of horses to the west, and eventually north."

"You take all the danger upon yourselves," said Tamara. "To stampede two herds of the horses, each of you must drive one herd through an outlaw camp before reaching the second herd."

"*Sí*," El Lobo said. "It is the only way."

"It's not worth it," said Renita, "if one or both of you are killed."

"We don't aim to be," Wes said. "El Lobo will go after the sentries before we loose the horses, and we'll wait until the outlaws are asleep before we begin the stampede. We'll want to drive the horses as far as possible, leaving the whole bunch of them afoot. After El Lobo and me have driven the four bunches a mile or so to the west, we'll turn them to the north. All or most of these men are from some outpost to the north of here, and with any luck, all these stampeded horses will head for their home corrals."

"It is a beautiful plan," said Tamara. "Where are we to meet you when the stampede is done?"

"Once we're shy of the outlaw camps," Wes said, "we'll try to run our horses to the northeast. They should mingle with your horses, and we'll all come together at the tag end of the stampede. Watch for Empty. He's done this before, and he'll bring us together if we get separated."

"When we stampede the horses, should we fire our guns?" Renita asked.

"No," said Wes. "I think we'd better save our ammunition. Just screech as loud as you can. Besides, there's a muzzle flash when you shoot at night, and that provides targets for return fire."

Well after midnight, when the moon had set, Empty led them back to within a mile of the outlaw encampment.

"Renita, you and Tamara wait here until we come for you," said Wes.

"It be long walk," El Lobo observed.

"*Sí*," said Wes, "but they're downwind from us. Any closer, and their horses would be nickerin' their heads off."

"We'll have to ride in close for the stampede," Renita said. "Suppose their horses begin to nicker before we're in position?"

"It's a chance we'll have to take," said Wes. "Once we're ready to hit them, we'll have to move fast. Their horses have to be off and running before those outlaws can roll out of their blankets and go for their guns."

Leaving their horses with Tamara and Renita, Wes and El Lobo set out on foot. When they were within several hundred yards of the first group of horses, they halted. Ahead of them, there was an intermittent wink of light as a man on watch drew on his quirly.*

"*Espera*," El Lobo said.

In an instant he was gone. He well knew that if one of the outlaw camps had a man on watch, it was likely there would be one or more sentries at all of them. Wes waited for what seemed an hour, and El Lobo reappeared as abruptly as he had vanished.

*Hand-rolled cigarette.

"*Hombres* on watch no watch," said El Lobo.

"Horses picketed?"

"*Sí*," El Lobo replied. "Close."

"We have our work cut out for us, then," said Wes. "I'll work my way around to the farthest bunch of horses, while you start here. If it all goes sour and we're discovered, get away as quickly as you can and return to our horses."

Wes made his way to the farthest of the outlaw camps and in the starlight counted eighteen horses. He paused when some of the animals raised their heads, continuing only when they had resumed grazing. The night wind touched the ashes of a supper fire, and a single live coal winked like an amber eye in the darkness. Wes moved in among the horses, touching a flank to calm an animal that seemed uneasy, slashing picket lines as he went. He marveled at the thoroughness of El Lobo, for not a trace of the sentries remained. A dead body—or just the smell of blood—would have been sufficient to spook the horses. Making his way to the next picketed horses, he counted fourteen. By the time he had freed the third bunch—a dozen—El Lobo was by his side. It was time to return for Renita and Tamara. Empty ran on ahead, announcing their coming.

"All the horses are loose," Wes said. "Tamara, I'll position you and Renita just south of the farthest two bunches of horses. The very second you hear El Lobo and me yelling, gallop toward those horses, making all the noise you can. Once the horses are on the run, stay behind them for a while. We want to run them as far north as we can."

"It is a wise move," said Tamara, "but these are only a few of the outlaws."

"Less than a hundred," Wes said, "but we have to start somewhere. After we've put enough of them afoot, we'll have the varmints afraid to sleep."

Leaving El Lobo near the first of the outlaw camps, Wes guided Renita and Tamara to the north. Once they were well beyond the farthest camps, they circled back to the south.

"Renita," said Wes, "this is your position. You can barely see the grazing horses from here."

"I see them," Renita said.

Wes rode on, Tamara following, until they could see the grazing horses near the last of the outlaw camps.

"Sit tight," said Wes, "until El Lobo and me start raising hell. When you join in, give it all you've got."

Wes rode back to El Lobo, and they circled to the southwest, coming in to the south of the remaining four bunches of horses. Their timing had to be exact, for each of them had to drive a bunch of horses through an outlaw camp, uniting it with the bunch of horses on the other side. They would then attempt, after stampeding the combined herd to the west, to head them north. Hopefully, their four bunches would combine with the two that Renita and Tamara would stampede. Wes counted slowly to a hundred, allowing El Lobo to reach his position.

"Hieeeeyaaah," Wes shouted, kicking his grulla into a fast gallop.

There were immediate shouts, sounding like echoes of his own, from his companions. Some of the loosed horses nickered in fear, spooking the others, and they were all off and running. Sleeping men, rudely awakened, scrambled to escape flying hooves. Wes ran his first bunch of horses into the second, and then the combined lot into the two bunches El Lobo had stampeded. Thus three groups of the sleeping outlaws were in the path of the entire thundering herd. Struck by hooves, men cried out in pain. Others responded in the worst possible manner, firing into the darkness and spooking the horses all the more. Soon the sound of the galloping horses was lost to distance. When they began to slow, Wes and El Lobo got ahead of them, turning the leaders north. They had pushed them not more than three miles when they converged with the bunches stampeded by Renita and Tamara.

"*Por Dios,*" Tamara cried, "never have I enjoyed anything so much."

"Nor I," said Renita. "It worked just as you planned. They shot at everything but us."

"We took them by surprise," Wes said. "If there had been more horses, we couldn't have pulled it off."

"*Mucho suerte,*" said El Lobo.*

"They've lost their horses and some men," Wes said. "They'll be more careful now."

The night was full of angry, cursing men, but they grew somber when they found the bodies of six of their companions who had been on watch. Each of the unfortunate sentries had bled to death from a slashed throat.

Some of the outlaws were about to venture forth on foot in search of their horses when Jarvis and

*Much luck.

Sandlin arrived. Jules Sumner, Skull Rudabaugh, and Burke Packer were part of the unhorsed bunch, and none of them was in a mood for embarrassing questions from Jarvis or Sandlin. But with their horses gone and their camp a shambles of smashed coffeepots and trampled blankets, little explanation was necessary.

"By God," said Jarvis, "when will you men learn to stand watch over your horses?"

"There were six men on watch," Skull Rudabaugh snapped, "and every one of 'em had his throat slit. You reckon you could have done any better?"

"Jarvis," said Sandlin, "perhaps he has a point. One can only go so far with precautionary measures. We have underestimated the resourcefulness of these men who have set out to destroy us. All of you gather around, for I have something to say."

Many of the men had never met Sandlin, and Jarvis felt an introduction was in order.

"This is Cord Sandlin," Jarvis said.

It all seemed a bit ridiculous, and somebody laughed, but Sandlin ignored it.

"Within the next several days," said Sandlin, "the rest of the men who were gathered in Durango should be here. All of you will then cover every inch of these hills surrounding Mexico City and Toluca until you discover and destroy this pair of marauders. Forget any orders given you about taking them alive. They're to be shot on sight."

"What about the pair of whores they took from Mazatlán?" one of the men asked. "Do we got to shoot them, too?"

"Yes," Sandlin said. "Kill them all."

"I reckon we got no room to complain," said Burke Packer, "but we got no horses. I doubt we can find this many horses in all of Mexico."

"Perhaps that won't be as much a problem as you think," Sandlin said. "Bear in mind that we have men riding in from Durango. How many, Jarvis?"

"Five hundred or more," said Jarvis.

"I can't imagine these men not gathering those loose horses," Sandlin said. "If they don't have sense enough to know something's wrong here, they'll answer to me."

"We're goin' to wait for them, then," said Jarvis.

"We are," Sandlin replied. "We're going to end this foolish conflict once and for all."

Many miles to the north, the stampeded horses were grazing alongside a creek. They lifted their heads and watched the approaching horsemen, more than fifty strong.

"This is an almighty lot of horses to just be wanderin' around loose," one of the outlaws observed.

"Too many," said a *segundo*. "We'll round 'em up and take 'em with us. Some of our outfit that's ahead of us may be afoot."

Chapter 14

Sandlin's prediction came to pass more quickly than any of them expected, for the next morning following the stampede, more than fifty men rode in from the north. Before them they drove the missing horses.

"Excellent," Sandlin said approvingly.

"They got past six sentries last night," said Jarvis. "What's to stop them from doing the same thing tonight or tomorrow night?"

"It won't happen again," Sandlin said, "if every damn rider in this outfit has to stand watch over his own horse. Perhaps that will be enough incentive for us to find and kill this troublesome pair of phantoms."

Dolan Watts had ridden from Durango, and he spoke directly to Sandlin.

"There's at least a hundred and fifty men here. What are we waiting for?"

"The rest of the men from Durango," said Sandlin. "We're going to deploy them all in a massive manhunt, ending this standoff once and for all."

"I was afraid of that," Wes said as he and El Lobo looked down on the outlaw rendezvous from a distant ridge. "Men riding in from Durango caught up and returned the horses we ran off last night."

"That still don't be all the *hombres*," said El Lobo.

"No," Wes agreed, "and by stampeding the horses again, we'd only be endangering ourselves for nothing. They'd only be caught up by outlaws riding in from the north."

"Per'ap we stampede the horses into the town," said El Lobo.

"It's a temptation," Wes replied, "but after last night, they'll double and redouble the watch. Our risk would be much greater."

Wes and El Lobo returned to their camp, where Renita and Tamara waited, bearing the unwelcome news of the returned horses.

"Oh, damn it," said Renita. "It all worked so perfectly last night."

"Dare we try it once more?" Tamara wondered.

"El Lobo and me don't favor it," said Wes. "We saw a pair of riders come in from the south, and I'd not be surprised if one of them was Sandlin. He's likely to have the entire camp on watch tonight just hopin' we'll try to equal what we did last night."

"If we don't go after them, they will be coming after us," Renita said. "What are we going to do now?"

"We'll let them make the next move," said Wes. "Striking at night and leaving some of them afoot is nothing more than harassment. Except for the sentries El Lobo eliminated, and the men trampled by horses, we didn't hurt them last night. We'll keep a close watch on them so we'll know what to expect.

I believe they're waiting for the arrival of the rest of their bunch from Durango."

"Then they look for us," El Lobo said.

"Yes," said Wes. "This is building toward some kind of finish. When they turn all their guns on us, we must counter their move in a way that will hurt them most."

"I think you are considering such a move," Tamara said.

"I am," said Wes, "but you'll have to thank El Lobo for giving me the idea."

"I only say we should stampede the horses through the town," El Lobo said.

"That wouldn't quite do it," said Wes, "but suppose we take it a little farther and lure all Sandlin's outlaws into Mexico City? We know the Mexican people hate the dragon, for we saw their anger as they stood over the graves of Pablo and Shekeela."

"*Madre de Dios*," Tamara cried. "We force the evil ones to fight in the very streets of the capital city. No more can the *policia* turn their heads."

"Per'ap they kill us," said El Lobo, "and the *policia* no give a damn."

"You're likely right," Wes said. "The Mexican authorities wouldn't ordinarily care if we live or die, but the turning point may have come when Sandlin's outlaws murdered Pablo and Shekeela. We're no longer a bunch of damn fools with a mad on. We are leading the fight for freedom from the hated Sandlin gang, and this is showin' all the earmarks of a revolution. I have read of them, and the cause must become greater than those who are willing to die for it. Less than fifty years ago, a hundred and eighty men held out against an army of more than five thousand for thirteen days. They died game, leaving behind a legacy that became a rallying cry for all the Republic of Texas."

"*Sí*," Tamara cried. "*Remember the Alamo* was the beginning of the end for Santa Anna and his cursed dictatorship."

"This will become our Alamo, if we can capture the confidence and imagination of the Mexican people," said Wes.

"*Sí*," El Lobo said, "and if we cannot?"

"We'll be as dead as those *bueno hombres* at the Alamo," said Wes, "with one big difference. Nobody will give a damn."

"It's the only way," Renita said. "There are hundreds of Sandlin's outlaws gathering here, and perhaps hundreds more we don't know about. There are too few of us and too many of them. It's the way to destroy them without killing them."

"*Sí*," said Tamara. "Let us discredit and disgrace them. Then the Mexican people will rebel and drive them out of Mexico."

"That's our plan, then," Wes said, "with one exception. If it's the last thing I ever do, I aim to see Cord Sandlin dead."

North of Mexico City. August 14, 1884

Over the next two days, the rest of the Sandlin gang that had congregated in Durango rode in. In the afternoon, before supper, Sandlin prepared to speak to them.

"Don't forget the soldiers," said Jarvis. "You'd better tell the men to stay out of Mexico City and Toluca."

"I can't very well tell them that without giving a reason," Sandlin replied, "and I don't want them knowing the soldiers are coming. Six hundred of us against a pair of gunmen is all the odds any man could ask for. But bring in the Mexican militia and those odds just go to hell."

"I agree," Jarvis said, "but suppose these *hombres* we're chasing hole up in town? I wouldn't want to tell our bunch they can't go in after 'em."

"Nor would I," said Sandlin, "but that's a chance we'll have to take."

Amid cheers from the gathered outlaws, Sandlin outlined his plan. They would ride at dawn and, flushing their quarry, shoot to kill.

"We couldn't get an accurate count," Wes said when he and El Lobo had returned from scouting the outlaw camp, "but there must be between five and six hundred. Maybe more. They'll be riding soon. Likely at dawn."

"Then we lead them into town," said Renita. "But where do we go from there?"

"Where we're likely to get the most attention," Wes said. "To the statehouse. To the presidential palace. We'll hole up there."

"I have seen it only once," said Tamara, "and there are many guards. *Soldados.*"

"*Bueno*," Wes replied. "Let Sandlin's boys pour some lead into Mexican soldiers. That ought to rile up the rest, along with the Mexican people."

"*Peligro*," said El Lobo, his eyes on Tamara.

"Danger is a mild word for it," Wes said. "It'll be hell with the lid off. It'll be a gunfight to end all gunfights. I don't know how to say this without it comin' out all wrong, but this is man's work. Tamara, I can't allow you and Renita to buy into this."

"Perhaps," said Tamara coldly, "for the sake of safety we should ride back to Mazatlán and become whores again."

"*Por Dios*," El Lobo said, "you not mean that."

"I do mean it," said Tamara, her eyes boring into his. "There are just certain things a woman can do, and being a whore is simple enough. Is it more desirable to become old before one's time, rotting away with a vile disease, than to die for a worthy cause, with a gun in the hand?"

"*Cuernos de el Diablo*," El Lobo groaned, at a loss for words.

"I reckon that's how you feel, too," said Wes, his eyes on Renita.

"Yes," Renita said. "I lay naked in a whorehouse for three months, used by crude, dirty men. Can death be any more terrible than that? I don't think so."

Wes sighed, and when he looked at El Lobo, Palo shrugged his shoulders. They had no defense against these abused, bitter, determined women.

"It's settled, then," said Wes. "We'll ride in with Winchesters and Colts fully loaded. Let's find a telegraph line and I'll send one more message. That should open the ball."

Wes climbed a pole, patched into the line, and sent a brief, startling message.

El Diablos Pistolas challenge the guns of the dragon in the streets of Mexico City at dawn.

Wes grinned as he thought of his late father, Nathan Stone. He believed it was the very thing Nathan would have done, for it was a diabolical act. If the outlaws accepted his challenge and rode in, their very presence branded them for what they were. On the other hand, if they didn't show, their absence would drive yet another nail in the coffin of public opinion.

"*Bueno*," said El Lobo. "When the wire talks, will they come?"

"Yes," Wes replied. "We know Sandlin has bought off at least two men within the Mexican government. They're safe enough as long as the robbing and killing takes place somewhere else, but what will they do when all hell busts loose in the streets of their own capital city?"

El Lobo laughed. "Run like coyotes, save own carcass."

"That," said Wes, "or begin shouting for soldiers."

"*Sí*," Tamara agreed, "and that would be perfect. Once the soldiers are called against the Sandlin gang, the Mexican government can no longer pretend the outlaws do not exist."

"When the wire talk to the *Mejicanos*," said El Lobo, "per'ap they send *soldados* after us."

"That's possible," Wes said. "We'll have to avoid them until the Sandlin gang gets up the nerve to ride in."

*   *   *

The telegram stirred up an immediate ruckus in the statehouse.

"*Por Dios*," Hidalgo groaned, "this must not happen."

"Send a courier to Sandlin at Toluca immediately," said Ximinez. "Tell him he and his men must ignore this foolish taunt. Their coming here would justify the use of soldiers and bring them upon us all the sooner."

The courier reported back to Hidalgo, and Hidalgo again conferred with Ximinez.

"Sandlin rode out three days ago," Hidalgo said, "and the servants do not know when he will return."

"Jarvis?"

"Jarvis rode with him," said Hidalgo.

"Many men ride in from Durango," Ximinez said. "Perhaps Sandlin is with them."

"But we do not know where they are," said Hidalgo, "and darkness is almost upon us. What are we to do?"

"We can only pray that Sandlin and his men do not see that telegraph message. What can these El Diablos Pistolas do if Sandlin and his men do not accept their challenge?"

"Perhaps create enough disturbance to bring the soldiers down on us a week early," Hidalgo said.

Wes and El Lobo had ridden back to a point where they could observe the outlaw camp, and had watched it until darkness had fallen.

"One thing bothers me," Wes said when he and El Lobo again joined Tamara and Renita. "From within an hour after I sent that message until dark, we watched their camp, and there were no riders to or from town. If Sandlin's there in the camp, there may not have been any way of his getting my message."

"They no be in town," said El Lobo.

"Not unless we get their attention some other way," Wes said.

"I'm half afraid to ask what you have in mind," said Renita.

"I am not," Tamara said. "They will come, if I must ride naked on a horse and have them follow me."

El Lobo groaned and Wes laughed. While Renita said nothing, she wasn't in the least shocked.

"I reckon we can get their attention easy enough," said Wes. "We can ride over there at first light and part their hair with some Winchester slugs."

"You and El Lobo, I suppose," Renita said.

"No," said Wes. "There won't be time for us to come looking for you and Tamara, so we'll all be going. After we've parted their hair with some Winchester slugs, they'll be on our trail like hell wouldn't have it. We'll likely be dodging lead before we reach town."

"If we are going to fire to attract their attention," Tamara said, "let us shoot to kill."

"*Sí*," said El Lobo. "That attract their attention."

Wes said nothing. While he had some doubts about Renita, he certainly had none as far as Tamara was concerned. She had a hard edge to her, and it seemed to become more cutting the longer they pursued the outlaws.

*   *   *

Sandlin's outfit was down to the morning's final cups of coffee, and some of the men had already begun saddling their horses. Suddenly there was the thunder of Winchesters, and four men fell. Others scrambled for their rifles, only to have the firing cease.

"Mount up!" Sandlin shouted.

The command was unnecessary, for this was something every man understood. Having been fired upon, they must retaliate. Sandlin and Jarvis hastened to saddle their horses as the outlaws kicked their horses into a fast gallop.

"This could play hell," said Jarvis. "We've lost control of them."

"Not necessarily," Sandlin said. "They're after the killers we want."

"Yeah," said Jarvis, "but suppose those killers head for town."

"Then we're in trouble," Sandlin said. "Let's ride."

"Well," said Renita, her eyes on Wes, "are you satisfied that I can handle a rifle?"

"You're considerably better with it than I expected," Wes replied, "but this time we were shooting from cover. From here on, there may be no cover, and God only knows how many guns will be returning our fire. Now let's ride."

"*Sí,*" said El Lobo. "They come."

"Let them," Tamara said grimly. "We will kill them all."

When it became obvious they were headed for town, Empty veered away. In all his earlier travels with Nathan, and finally with Wes, he had learned to make himself scarce when lead began to fly.

Beyond the spires of several cathedrals was the statehouse dome, and Wes headed for it, his companions following.

"In behind the building," Wes shouted.

There was a courtyard surrounded by head-high brick walls, and they galloped their horses into it. While their pursuers were coming, riding hard, there was a more immediate danger. Zopilote, the Mexican gunfighter, appeared under the arch, in the entrance to the courtyard. With him was Kalpana, the Spaniard.

"Ah, *señors*," Zopilote said, "we shall try your courage when you do not shoot from ambush. Kalpana, the *Indio* is yours."

Wes and El Lobo had but a split second to respond, for even as the Mexican spoke, he and Kalpana had gone for their guns. Wes fired once, and Zopilote's shot was wide, for he had been hard hit just above the belt buckle. Kalpana's first shot went over El Lobo's head, screaming off the courtyard wall. El Lobo fired, and the Spaniard stumbled, seeming surprised at the blood welling from the hole in his chest. He collapsed near Zopilote, their bodies blocking the courtyard entrance. Only seconds had elapsed, but the pursuing outlaws had already begun their assault on the courtyard.

"Here they come!" Wes shouted.

He opened the ball by emptying two saddles, and the rest of the outlaws began piling off their horses, Winchesters in their hands. The courtyard walls provided protection, but they were a hazard as well, for a ricochet could be as deadly as a direct hit. The outlaws quickly took advantage, mounting their horses and firing over the wall. Lead screeched off the walls, slamming into the courtyard's stone floor.

"Against the walls," Wes shouted.

It was their only defense as long as the attackers fired over the wall, pouring lead into an opposite wall. Even then, the fragmented lead came dangerously close. Only when some of the outlaws charged the courtyard entrance did the defenders fire. A dozen men died in quick succession, and the rest backed off, content to fire over the walls, seeking a ricochet.

"Back off," Sandlin shouted. "Cease fire."

But his commands went unheeded amid the roar of Winchesters and the shouts of the attackers. Security from within the statehouse—half a dozen Mexican soldiers—charged into the courtyard, shouting for attention. Two of them died almost immediately, and a third was hit before he reached the safety of the statehouse.

"*Madre de Dios*," Hidalgo cried from his office on the second floor, "we are ruined."

"Speak for yourself," said Ximinez. "I know nothing of this."

The battle raged for an hour, and while none of the defenders had been hit, they had accomplished little. Suddenly there were shouts from the outlaws, firing ceased, and there was the sound of thundering hooves.

"They're riding away!" Tamara cried.

"I reckon they got a reason," said Wes, "and here it comes."

Mexican soldiers swarmed into the courtyard, armed with rifles with fixed bayonets. Having little choice, Wes and his companions raised their hands. Their Colts and Winchesters were taken and they were marched through the courtyard to the statehouse. Several soldiers led their horses away. Beneath the statehouse was a cavernlike area that served as a jail. Wes and his companions were taken down a flight of stone steps. One of the soldiers unlocked a pair of cells. Wes and El Lobo were forced into one, while Tamara and Renita were locked in the other. The soldiers had spoken not a word, and when they had closed the outer door, the cells were in darkness.

"Damn it," Renita complained, "there's no chamber pot, and no light to find it even if there was one."

Tamara laughed. "It is dark, and there is the floor."

"*Por Dios*," said El Lobo, "we be dead."

"Not immediately," Wes said. "We accomplished what we set out to do. I just hope our confidence in the Mexican people is justified. If our scheme goes all to hell in a handbasket, we could find ourselves at the mercy of a Mexican court."

"*Sí*," Tamara agreed, "and for revolutionaries, there is but a single sentence."

"I'm afraid to ask what it is," said Renita.

"You wanted to be a part of this, so you might as well know the worst," Wes said. "In Texas they believe in rope justice, but Mexico has a tradition all its own. They prefer to back you up against a wall, facing a firing squad."

"It's still better than a Mexican whorehouse," said Renita defiantly.

"Sí," Tamara said, "and as long as I am alive, I do not give up."

"No horse, no gun, *mucho soldados*," said El Lobo.

"Tamara's right," Wes said. "We don't know what they aim to charge us with, if anything. Some of the guards from the statehouse were hit, but that was the doing of the Sandlin gang."

"Sí," said El Lobo, "but the Sandlin gang escape. We do not."

"I reckon we'll know come morning," Wes said.

Hidalgo and Ximinez, seeking to salvage something from the chaos following the gunfight in the courtyard, quickly went before Renaldo Gonzales, a Mexican magistrate.

"These *hombres* be killers," Hidalgo argued. "It is they who murdered poor Pablo and the Señora Shekeela."

"There are witnesses to this terrible thing?" Gonzales asked.

"Sí," said Hidalgo.

"Por Dios," Gonzales said, "if there is such proof, they will die against the wall."

Ximinez said nothing until the pair had left the office of the magistrate. "You lie," he said to Hidalgo. "You know the old one who witnessed the killing of Pablo and Shekeela will not name these *hombres* the *soldados* capture. There is no such proof."

"Sí," Hidalgo agreed, "but I do not name the witness. In Mexico, where life is cheap, what is one's word worth? I will buy a witness. More, if they are needed."

"There is still the matter of the Señor Sandlin and

his men," said Ximinez. "Can you deny it was they who besieged the courtyard and murdered the *soldado* guards from the statehouse? *El presidente* is furious."

"The Señor Sandlin and his men do not be in custody," Hidalgo said. "These killers have been captured, and there are witnesses to their crimes. *Madre mia*, is that not enough to satisfy the state?"

Mexico City. August 18, 1884

After two days of languishing in their cells with only bread and water, the captives were removed and taken to court. Magistrate Renaldo Gonzales wasted no time.

"Your names, *señors*."

"I'm Wes Stone," said Wes, "and this is Palo Elfego."

"You stand accused of murdering Pablo and Shekeela Ortega," Gonzales said. "How do you plead?"

"Not guilty," said Wes.

"There is a witness who disagrees," Gonzales said. "Pasquido?"

Pasquido, not looking at the prisoners, described the murder and identified Wes and El Lobo as the killers.

"He's a damn liar," Wes shouted. "We didn't do it."

"I do not believe you," said Gonzales. "At sunrise, one week from today, the two of you will be executed by firing squad."

"Old man," Tamara said, "you are a fool. Cord

Sandlin's band of outlaws committed these murders. Do you fear them?"

"You *Mejicanos* are a bunch of cowards," said Renita. "Why don't you send us before the firing squad as well? Or do you fear being known as a woman killer?"

"*Señor* magistrate," said one of the guards, "you did not sentence the *señoritas*. What are we to do with them?"

"An oversight," Gonzales said angrily. "I sentence the insolent ones, for as long as they shall live, to the prison laundry."

"Damn it," said Wes to Renita and Tamara, "why didn't you stay out of it? If you'd gone free, you might have been able to help El Lobo and me."

"We still will help you," Tamara vowed. "I do not give up. Ever."

"Nor I," said Renita.

It was their last opportunity to talk. Wes and El Lobo were placed in one wagon, and Tamara and Renita in another. They were then taken to the prison, a forbidding structure of stone in which the enemies of Santa Anna were once left to die. There were three levels. To the lower one—a dungeon— Wes and El Lobo were taken. On the second level was the kitchen, the laundry, and a sleeping room with bunks for a dozen guards. Quarters for the female prisoners—when there were any—were on the third level, with a barred door at the head of the stone stairs. Tamara and Renita were taken there and locked in a cell.

"We're in one hell of a mess," Renita said. "Now what do we do?"

"We find a way to escape," said Tamara.

"These bars look awful strong," Renita said. "If you have even a hint of a plan, I'd be interested in hearing it."

"The guards are all men," said Tamara. "Does that suggest anything to you?"

"Maybe," Renita said, "but I wish there was another way, short of becoming a whore again."

"There is no other way," said Tamara, "for there is not enough time. Wes and Palo are to be put to death a week from today. If I must, for these few days, I will sell my body for Palo's life. Will you not do as much for Wes?"

"You know I will," Renita said. "What can I sell that hasn't already been taken many times?"

"Well spoken," said Tamara. "These two guards are young men. We will allow them to take us until they are no longer suspicious. Then we will kill them."

"Kill them? How?"

From down the back of her shirt, attached to a leather thong, Tamara drew out a two-edged, wicked dagger.

"It won't be easy concealing that when you're naked," Renita said.

"I will not remove my shirt," said Tamara. "Few men seem interested in a whore's upper body."

"That will take care of one of them," Renita said, "but I have no weapon."

"The knife kills silently," said Tamara. "When I have freed myself, I will then free you. But you must make him mount you so that his back is exposed, and you must somehow keep his attention. If he suspects anything, or if he hears me approaching, then all is lost. We will not have another chance."

"Never fear," Renita said. "I'll give this one all I've got. If we can get our hands on their guns and the keys to this place, we can free Wes and Palo."

In the gloom of the dungeon, Wes and El Lobo weren't nearly as optimistic.

"The *Mejicanos* hate the Sandlin outlaws," said El Lobo, "and we seek to destroy the Sandlin outlaws. Why we be in *juzgado, amigo?*"

Wes sighed. "I hate to admit it, but I might have miscalculated. As long as we were free, giving Sandlin's bunch hell, the *Mejicanos* were all for us. Now the dragon's still out there on the loose, and we're sentenced to death."

"Per'ap we escape," El Lobo said. "We give Sandlin outlaws hell again, then *Mejicanos* be with us."

"I'm all in favor of escaping," said Wes, "but how? We could die here like rats in a hole, except that a week from now they aim to execute us."

"I not believe Tamara allow that to happen," El Lobo said. "She strong."

"So is Renita," said Wes, "but they're locked up, too."

"There be old Injun saying: One not be dead until one be dead," El Lobo said.

"That old Injun was never locked in a dungeon and was likely a damn fool," Wes replied.

"Do not speak ill of your *amigo*," said El Lobo.

Chapter 15

The day after the sentencing of Wes and El Lobo, word of the trial reached relatives and friends of Pablo and Shekeela Ortega. Juan, the actual witness to the murders, wasted no time in creating the very backlash Wes had hoped for.

"Those who kill are free to kill again," Juan said. "This execution must not be. Let us march on the *casa* of *el presidente*. Let us demand freedom for El Diablos Pistolas."

The old man spoke with truth and conviction, and all those who owned or were able to borrow a mule began riding to outlying villages, crying for justice, for an end to the ruthless outlaw reign. On the third day they began gathering on the outskirts of town, many of them afoot, armed only with their anger and sense of injustice.

"*Madre de Dios,*" Hidalgo said. "What does this mean?"

"It means the witness you bought is about to earn his gold," said Ximinez.

Tamara and Renita had no trouble seducing their guards, Ganos and Onate. Once the barred door at the head of the stone stairs was locked, nobody could gain entrance to the second level. When the guards brought their supper, Tamara and Renita wore only their shirts. Ganos looked at Tamara, raising his eyebrows.

"*Modesto*," Tamara said.

Onate peered at Renita in the dim light of the cell. "*Modesto?*"

"*Sí*," said Renita.

"Eat," Ganos said. "We return."

"That was easy," said Renita, when the pair had gone. "They are so young, it's almost a shame to kill them."

"Fishing is always easy," Tamara said, "when one uses the proper bait. Though they are young, they are our captors. Do not forget that."

When the pair returned, they said nothing, for the message had been clear enough. Onate led Renita down the dimly lit cell block, leaving Tamara alone with Ganos. In less than half an hour, Tamara and Renita were alone in their cell and their guards had returned to their alcove at the head of the stairs.

"I feel terrible," Renita said.

"Why?"

"Being forced into a whorehouse is one thing," said Renita, "but choosing to perform as a whore is . . . well . . . different."

"It is no different than killing another so that you may live," Tamara said. "One does what one must do. My body has been used, but my soul is pure."

"Tomorrow night, then?" said Renita.

"I think we will allow them to take us a second time," Tamara said. "The third time, they die."

*   *   *

The third day after Wes and El Lobo had been
taken to prison, a delegation headed by Juan met
with an aide of the magistrate, demanding an audi-
ence with Renaldo Gonzales.

"The Señor Gonzales is very busy," the aide
protested.

"*Sí*," said Juan. "We will wait."

Their persistence paid off, and Gonzales was finally forced to meet with them. There was a grim
look on his face when they departed, and he spoke
harshly to his aide.

"Go to the statehouse and tell the Señor Hidalgo I
will see him in my quarters and that he is to come
immediately."

Ximinez looked up as Hidalgo stumbled into his
office.

"I have been summoned to the office of the magistrate," Hidalgo said desperately. "*Por Dios*, what am
I to do?"

"Then you must go," said Ximinez pleasantly,
"and I think you must take your bought witness
with you."

"But I do not know him or where to find him,"
Hidalgo protested.

Ximinez shrugged, forcing Hidalgo to face the fury
of Gonzales alone. It wasn't long in coming, for the
magistrate was waiting.

"You have made a fool of me and of this court,"
Gonzales shouted, pounding the desk with his fist.
"Where is this witness, this *perro*, who has perjured
himself before me?"

"I . . . I do not know," said Hidalgo. "He came to me. . . ."

"I will tell you where he is," Gonzales roared. "He is in the cantina where you found him, and he has recanted his testimony. For leniency, he has admitted his perjury, for which he was paid. By you, Señor Hidalgo."

"No," said Hidalgo, sweating. "I only wished to see justice done."

"Then you will understand why you are being taken into custody," Gonzales said. "*El presidente* is demanding a hearing, and I would suggest you be prepared to defend yourself. Guards!"

The two guards who had been waiting in an inner office emerged, leading the speechless Hidalgo away. Gonzales immediately summoned his aide.

"Prepare the necessary orders freeing the Señors Stone and Elfego. I will see them in my office tomorrow."

"What of their *señoritas?*"

"They will be freed also," Gonzales said.

But Tamara and Renita were about to make their own bid for freedom. Ganos and Onate, becoming more confident, had switched partners. Ganos led Renita away, while Onate remained with Tamara. As usual, the affair was conducted in silence, and Renita did her best to capture the attention of Ganos. He might see Tamara from the corner of his eye as she entered the cell. Unbidden, Tamara stretched out on her back on one of the bunks, her hands behind her head. She waited for Onate, not daring to bring the knife into play until she was sure she could complete the deadly act. Slowly, imperceptibly, she drew the knife with her right hand. Then, with all her strength, she drove it into Onate's back. He grunted only once, and his body relaxed. Tamara withdrew the knife and rolled him off on the floor. She then took his revolver and pistol belt, to which was attached a ring of keys. Quickly she dressed and, the still-bloody knife in her hand, crept stealthily down the cell block. Reaching the cell occupied by Ganos and Renita, knife poised to strike, Tamara dropped Onate's gunbelt. Ganos tensed and tried to roll away from Renita, but she threw her arms around him until Tamara plunged the knife into his back. Renita released him and he fell to the floor on his back. For a sickening moment, as the life drained out of him, his eyes met hers.

"Oh, God," Renita cried. "Oh, God, what have we done?"

"We have bought our freedom," said Tamara. "Get dressed. We must go."

Tamara removed the gunbelt from the dead Ganos and passed it to Renita. Removing the ring of keys, she buckled Onate's gunbelt around her waist. Reaching the head of the stone stairs, Tamara tried different keys until one of them unlocked the barred door. Their footsteps echoed hollowly on the stone as they crept down to the first level. It was dark, for here were the administrative offices, the kitchen, and the laundry, mostly unused since the last days of Santa Anna. If there were other guards, they would be in the cell block below ground, where Wes and El Lobo had been taken. There were barred doors at the head of the stone stairs, and there was only the dim light from a single bracket lamp.

"Try the keys," Tamara whispered. "I will have a gun ready should someone come."

There were more than a dozen keys, and one by one, Renita tried them all.

"Oh, damn it," said Renita in desperation. "None of them fit."

"One of them must," Tamara said. "Let me try."

But all their efforts were in vain, for none of the keys unlocked the massive barred doors.

"What are we going to do?' Renita cried. "How can we save Wes and Palo?"

"We cannot with these keys," said Tamara. "We must escape and think of something else. Come."

There was a final barred door trapping them within the prison, and they were down to the last of the keys before the door creaked open. Tamara locked it behind them, and in the distance they could see the lights of Mexico City. Suddenly there was a rustling in the greenery that surrounded the prison, and Tamara cocked the revolver.

"Don't," Renita whispered. "It's Empty."

The hound had followed Wes as far as he could and had waited without food. Now he recognized Tamara and Renita and made his presence known.

"Perhaps he can lead us to our horses," Tamara said.

"He won't leave as long as Wes is here," said Renita.

Empty followed for a short distance, but when they looked back, they could no longer see him.

There was no moon, and the twinkling stars only seemed to make the darkness all the more intense.

"There should be a stable near the statehouse," Tamara said. "If we cannot find our own horses, there will be others."

The statehouse had closed, but as they neared the courtyard, they heard footsteps. Concealing themselves in the shadows, they watched as a sentry made his rounds. Finally the nickering of a horse led them to the stable they sought, for it was convenient to the statehouse. A single lantern hung above the entrance.

"Step into the light and ask if there is someone inside," Tamara said. "I will remain in the shadows with a gun."

Renita stood beneath the lantern and spoke softly. "Is there someone here?"

"*Si, señorita. Quien es?*"

An aged Mexican appeared, and quickly Tamara stepped into the light, revolver cocked and ready to fire. Frightened speechless, the old hostler raised his hands.

"Don't be afraid," Renita said. "We only want our horses."

"*Ligero,*" said Tamara, pointing to the lantern above the door.

"*Sí,*" the hostler said. From inside the door he produced a second lantern, and lit it with unsteady hands. He then backed into the stable, holding the lantern for them to see their way. Tamara kept her eyes on him, holding the gun, while Renita looked for their horses.

"I've found them," Renita cried. "The saddles, too."

"Saddle them quickly," said Tamara. "Are there horses for Wes and Palo, as well?"

"Yes," Renita said.

"Saddle them," Tamara said. "We will take them with us."

Renita wrestled with the saddles, discovering their Winchesters had been returned to the saddle boots. She led the saddled horses near the open door, and Tamara spoke to the hostler.

"It is time you slept, *padre*."

The old hostler swallowed hard and nodded, for she had emphasized her words with the muzzle of the pistol. Tamara and Renita led the saddled horses quickly from the stable, pausing in the shadow of some trees.

"If he cries for help, are you going to shoot him?" Renita asked.

"Of course not," said Tamara. "I wish to see how much time we have."

They waited a few moments longer and, when there was no sign of the hostler, led the horses down a tree-lined street where no lights showed.

"We're free," Renita said. "Now what?"

"I am not sure," said Tamara. "I know only that we must escape the town."

They rode southwest and, only minutes after leaving the town behind, were able to see several fires in the distance. Facing the wind, they smelled roasting meat.

"The outlaws," Renita said.

"I do not think so," said Tamara. "Not so close to the town. Wait for me."

"*Quien es?*" a voice inquired, and Tamara spoke.

"Señoritas de El Diablos Pistolas."

"Sí. Juan know."

Juan and his companions gathered around, speaking excitedly in Spanish. Realizing they were among friends, Renita rode in leading the two extra horses. She listened, not understanding all the Spanish, until Tamara told her what had been said.

"The Mexican people have rebelled, forcing the court to rescind the conviction of Wes and Palo. They will be freed tomorrow."

"Dear God," said Renita, "where does that leave us?"

"As fugitives, I think," Tamara said. "Somehow we must unite with Wes and Palo."

"Yes," said Renita. "We have their horses."

"That," Tamara said, "and we still must destroy the Sandlin gang. Let us dismount. Juan and his people have invited us to eat and to stay the night."

Mexico City. August 19, 1884

Wes and El Lobo had no idea why they were removed from the prison and were again taken to the magistrate's courtroom. Gonzales wasted no time, for he wished to be done with the disagreeable task.

"You, Wes Stone, and you, Palo Elfego, are being freed. It has been proven to my satisfaction that the witness who testified against you perjured himself. You are free on the condition that you will leave Mexico and never return. A military escort will follow you north to the border and see you into the United States."

"There are the *señoritas*," said Wes. "What of them?"

"They murdered their guards last night and escaped," Gonzales said. "When we find them, I shall see that they are tried and executed. They took your horses as well as their own. We will provide you with mounts as far as the border, and your weapons will be returned to you there."

Not believing their good fortune, Wes and El Lobo turned to go. Waiting for them were four Mexican soldiers. Outside there were six horses, four of them belonging to the soldiers. Wes and El Lobo each mounted one of the extra horses. One of the soldiers drew his saber and pointed north. Having no choice, Wes and El Lobo rode out, their four escorts following. They had ridden only a few miles when they encountered another party of Mexican soldiers, a dozen strong. Wes and El Lobo watched while the two groups conferred. It was obvious they were being discussed, for one of their escorts pointed to them.

"What *soldados* be doing?" El Lobo wondered.

"They're looking for the Sandlin gang," said Wes. "They've turned us loose, and now they have to find somebody to replace us. It'll be a mite hard on us, huntin' the Sandlin gang, with the Mexican soldiers hunting them, too."

"*Sí*," El Lobo agreed. "We be in Texas, without horses."

"Don't count on that," said Wes. "Tamara and Renita are out here somewhere, and they have our horses."

"Madre de Dios," El Lobo said, "they kill two *hombres.* How they get so close?"

"I don't want to know," said Wes, "and I don't think you do, either."

Wes, El Lobo, and their escorts resumed their journey and the second party of soldiers went on their way. The sun was past noon-high and they were seventy miles north of Mexico City when they stopped near a creek to rest the horses. Suddenly, from a stand of scrub oak a hundred yards away, a rifle spoke. Like an echo of the first, others joined in the one-sided fight, cutting down the soldiers. Unarmed, Wes and El Lobo had only a hummock of ground for protection, a few feet from the creek.

"Por Dios," said El Lobo, "the Sandlin gang."

"Some of them," Wes said, "and with us unarmed, there'll be enough."

Winchester lead kicked dirt in their faces, and there was little they could do. Their own weapons were in a soldier's saddlebag, and there was only open ground between them and the side arms the fallen soldiers carried.

"They soon get behind us," said El Lobo.

It was a logical move, for there were six of the Sandlin outlaws, but the odds changed quickly. From behind them, a pair of Winchesters opened up, and three of the outlaws went down in the first volley. Two more were cut down trying to reach their horses, and a third died with his foot in the stirrup.

"We've a pair of *amigos* that's almighty good with a Winchester," said Wes, dusting himself off.

El Lobo said nothing. He and Wes waited until

Tamara and Renita reined up, and it was Tamara who spoke.

"Do you *hombres* approve of our shooting?"

"*Sí,*" El Lobo said.

"The pair of you can ride with me anytime," said Wes, "but why the hell did you kill the guards and break jail, when they aimed to set us free?"

"Damn you, Wes Stone," Renita said angrily, "we didn't *know* you were going to be set free. For all we knew, the both of you were to be executed. We're being hunted as murderers, and after risking our lives to save you, this is the thanks we get."

"Sorry," said Wes. "I reckon I wasn't thinking. After today, we'll all be hunted as murderers. That bunch in Mexico City will never believe we didn't somehow kill those four soldiers."

"There be six dead outlaws," El Lobo said.

"True," said Wes, "but it's unlikely Mexico City will search this far for four missing soldiers. When the horses wander back, with our weapons missing from the saddlebags, I expect El Lobo and me to be branded as killers for sure. This time they won't bother with a trial. We'll be shot on sight."

"*Sí,*" El Lobo agreed.

"We have learned one thing," said Tamara. "The Sandlin outlaws attack the soldiers."

"That could work in our favor," Wes said, "if we can stay out of the hands of the soldiers until they clash with the outlaws. When these four *hombres* turn up missing, the military may want us as bad as or worse than the Sandlin gang."

Wes and El Lobo recovered their Colts from the saddlebags of two of the dead soldiers. Mounting their own horses, they rode south, Tamara and Renita following.

Toluca, Mexico. August 19, 1884

Rarely did Ximinez visit the mansion Cord Sandlin occupied, so it came as a surprise to Sandlin when the Mexican rode in.

"I presume you have an important message," Sandlin said.

"Of the utmost importance," said Ximinez. "Señor Hidalgo has been arrested and has told all he knows. I escaped only because I did not return to the statehouse. I have told them nothing, and I will not. I depend on you for protection. You owe me."

"I promise they'll never take you," Sandlin said. "Let us drink to your loyalty."

Sandlin took one of the glasses a servant brought, passing the other to Ximinez. The Mexican downed his drink in a single gulp, leaning back in his chair. Suddenly his body went rigid and his hands gripped the arms of the chair. His mouth worked, but there were no words. He turned hate-filled eyes on Sandlin, and the outlaw leader spoke.

"I said they would never take you. I keep my word."

A full-fledged scandal rocked the statehouse. Señor Hidalgo had admitted to his longtime involvement with the Sandlin gang, and in so doing had implicated Ximinez, who had mysteriously disappeared. Thus encouraged, witnesses came forth testifying to a variety of crimes committed by the Sandlin gang.

Mexican officials, from the smallest villages to the largest cities, had become suspect. Mexican soldiers clashed almost daily with bands of outlaws, and there were rumors that the Sandlin gang in northern Mexico was no more, that men from within its higher echelons had quietly crossed the border into Texas. There were daily meetings at the Sandlin mansion in Toluca, and while controversy raged, Sandlin seemed unperturbed.

"We're losing men," Jarvis reported, "especially in the north. There are more soldiers riding the border, and no horse herds have crossed, north or south, since this fighting with the military began."

"I am aware of that," said Sandlin. "The Mexican government has requested the help of the United States. All ships flying Mexican colors sailing into or out of American ports are subject to search and seizure."

"That doesn't bother you?"

"Of course not," Sandlin said. "I can and will curtail all activity indefinitely. There are no specific charges against me. These peasants who blame all their troubles on the Sandlin gang are unable to name any specific culprit, and it's for these ignorant masses the military is putting on a show."

"In a town with ten whorehouses, the law closes one of them," said Jarvis.

"Exactly," Sandlin replied. "That's to satisfy the good citizens. As long as the soldiers are battling the outlaws, who can fault them or their politicians beating the drums?"

"We've lost our contacts within the Mexican government," said Jarvis. "Hidalgo will be damned lucky if they don't stand him against the wall."

"He and Ximinez were good investments," Sandlin said. "Neither of them could blame a specific crime on us. They only succeeded in incriminating themselves, and that goes a long way in vindicating us. While we took advantage of their positions and their weakness, we are in no way to blame for them. Remember, it's the Judas who sells out that bears the disgrace. It rarely ever dirties the hand bearing the silver or the gold."

But while the Sandlin empire seemed secure, much of the spoils were secretly taken aboard a fast clipper ship anchored in Tampico bay. Twice a month, the vessel sailed to a secluded harbor in South America. . . .

"I have heard, even before we began this vendetta, of a clipper ship owned by Sandlin," Tamara said. "My grandfather knew an outlaw who swore this ship is anchored in Tampico bay."

"How long ago?" Wes asked.

"Three years, I think," said Tamara. "Grandfather believed that when the time came, Sandlin would board that ship and sail to some foreign port to enjoy his ill-gotten gains."

"That's not as far-fetched as it sounds," Wes said. "This empire of Sandlin's is headed for hell on greased skids. He's got to be losing men, yet it seems like nothing has any real effect on the bastard."

"Per'ap we sink the ship," said El Lobo.

"If there *is* one," Wes said, "that might be the one way to destroy Sandlin."

"With the soldiers looking for us, as well as the outlaws, what more can we do in Mexico City?" Renita asked. "Suppose we go looking for this phantom ship."

"It will not be easy," said Tamara. "Grandfather said it flies false colors."

"We go to Toluca," El Lobo said. "We follow Sandlin to this ship."

"Those Mexican freighters spoke of Toluca," said Wes, "but we don't know Sandlin or where he's holed up."

"Sandlin has a mansion there," Tamara said. "Juan, the old one, spoke of it. Sandlin does not hide."

"Then El Lobo's idea is a good one," said Wes. "We'll find us a place to hole up in or close to Toluca. Then we'll watch the Sandlin house. We'll follow anybody leaving there, at least until we know where he's going. Where is Tampico, Tamara?"

"To the north," Tamara said. "It is a port on the Gulf of Mexico."

"We'll ride at night," said Wes. "Do you know how we can find Juan?"

"Yes," Tamara said. "When I last spoke to him, he promised his help."

"If he knows where Sandlin's place is, that's all the help we'll need," said Wes.

"But how will we watch Sandlin's house, when the outlaws and the soldiers are looking for us?" Renita asked.

"We'll have to come up with a plan after we've seen the place," said Wes. "Juan may have some ideas."

They waited for darkness before they rode any closer to Mexico City, and it was near dawn when they reached the shack that Juan called home. Quickly Tamara told him what they wished to know.

"I take you," said Juan, pointing to Wes and El Lobo.

"I wish to go," Tamara said.

"And I," said Renita.

Juan shook his head. He led them to a ramshackle barn that leaned drunkenly to one side, and within the barn was a two-wheeled wooden cart. Juan pointed to the cart, and there was barely room for Wes and El Lobo to get into it. Taking a hay fork, Juan began throwing hay into the cart until Wes and El Lobo were covered. He then went for his mule and hitched the animal to the cart. Wes and El Lobo sneezed, and Tamara laughed.

"No come," Juan said, his eyes on Tamara and Renita.

He touched the mule's flank and the animal lurched into motion, the cumbersome cart creaking along behind him.

"*Por Dios,*" said El Lobo, "How far be Toluca?"

"*Silencio,*" Juan said.

Tamara and Renita led all four horses well away from Juan's place, hiding the animals where they were unlikely to be seen.

"I hope Toluca's not too far," Renita said. "It's got to be awful cramped in that cart."

"Juan knows what he is doing," said Tamara.

The cart rumbled on, and only once did Juan speak, when he had stopped to rest the mule.

"The *casa* stands alone. When we are before it, I will again rest the *mulo*."

It seemed forever before the cart creaked to a halt. Wes and El Lobo peered through a tangle of straw at a magnificent house with six white columns supporting a second-floor balcony. The nearest building appeared to be a livery barn, and hay could be seen in the loft above. Juan clucked to the mule and the cart creaked on its way. It was near noon when they reached Juan's place. Thankfully, Wes and El Lobo crawled through the tangle of hay and out of the cart. Tamara and Renita had been watching for them.

"The house stands alone," Wes said. "There's no place to hide except what looks like a livery barn."

"Perhaps we can watch from there," said Tamara. "Juan, what do you think?"

"I fix," Juan said.

Chapter 16

"I wish Juan would hurry," Renita said. "He's in danger as long as we're here. I can't forget what happened to Pablo and Shekeela for taking us in."

"The situation's changed since then," said Wes. "With the military going through the motions of battling the Sandlin gang, neither should have the time to harass Juan."

"Per'ap they no expect us to be so near the town," El Lobo said.

"Juan is respected among his people," said Tamara. "What he can accomplish may well surprise you."

Darkness had fallen when Juan returned, riding his mule.

"*Señorita*," he said, pointing to Tamara, "I talk, you listen."

Tamara had a better command of Spanish than any of them, but when he began speaking rapidly, even Tamara had trouble understanding him. He rattled along for a quarter of an hour, and when he was finished, Tamara translated.

"Juan has arranged for us to conceal the horses in the stable near Sandlin's mansion. Wes, you and Palo will keep watch on the Sandlin house from the stable's loft. Beyond the stable—a distance from the Sandlin place—there is a boardinghouse. Juan's kin owns it. Renita and me will become servants there for as long as there is a need. Wes, you and Palo will take your meals there twice daily, but you must come and go under the cover of darkness. Juan and his people are in much danger should any of us be discovered. Juan says it is all he can do."

"*Por Dios,*" El Lobo said. "It is enough."

"It's more than enough," said Wes. "Juan, how can we thank you?"

"*Es Nada,*" Juan said, shrugging his stooped shoulders.

"Wes, Juan will go with you and Palo to the stable," said Tamara. When he returns, he will see Renita and me to the boardinghouse."

"*Caballos,*" Juan said.

Juan mounted his mule. Wes and El Lobo mounted their horses and, leaving Tamara's and Renita's mounts, followed Juan. The old Mexican avoided all lit byways, bringing them to the end of the stable farthest from the Sandlin house. A young Mexican swung the barn doors open, allowing them to enter. The doors were quickly closed. A lantern was lit.

"This be José," said Juan. "He no talk."

Juan stuck out his tongue and made a slicing motion with his hand. José grinned at them, apparently accustomed to Juan's crude introduction. Wes and El Lobo dismounted and José took the reins of their horses. Juan pointed to the hay-filled loft above and to a wooden ladder leading to it. First Wes and then El Lobo extended their hands, and Juan took them.

He then let himself and his mule out, closing the barn doors behind him.

"Water," said El Lobo. "I hear spring."

The sound was the overflow from a horse trough made from an enormous, hollowed-out cedar log. Water was fed in through a smaller log, split and hollowed out.

"It took some kind of genius to figure that out," Wes said. "The source would have to be high enough for gravity to bring the water in."

Suddenly there was a sound behind them, and both men whirled, their hands on the butts of their Colts. José stood there grinning, pointing to himself and then to the rig that brought fresh water into the barn.

"A grand piece of work, José," said Wes. "I've never seen anything like it."

José beckoned to them, and they followed him up wooden steps and into a tack room with a wooden floor. There was a crude table, with a bench on each side. On the table was a large wooden bowl of roasted meat. In a brown jug was a potent brew that proved to be mescal. José pointed to the jug. Wes took a swallow and passed it to El Lobo. Nodding to them, José sat down on one of the benches and attacked the meat. Wes and El Lobo sat on the other bench and, having had no food since early morning, sampled the meat.

"*Madre de Dios*," El Lobo said, "what this be?"

"Roast goat," said Wes. "I've had it a time or two and it's always tough. Somethin' like cuttin' a hunk out of your saddle and chewin' on it."

José just grinned and reached for another piece of goat.

"If the place Juan's taking us is near the stable where Wes and Palo will be," Renita said, "why didn't all of us go together?"

"I do not know," said Tamara. "Juan has his reasons."

When Juan returned, Tamara and Renita mounted their horses and followed him. He again avoided lit areas, coming in behind the boardinghouse. There appeared to be no more than a dozen rooms, all of them on one level. The kitchen still smelled of freshly baked bread, and the Mexican woman who greeted them had more than a little gray in her hair.

"Anna Marie," Juan said, by way of introduction.

"He do not talk much," said Anna Marie, who proved to be a little more comfortable with English.

Without another word, Juan left the kitchen, closing the door behind him.

"Where's he going?" Renita asked.

"He take your horses to the stable," said Anna Marie. "Come, there is food."

"Wes and Palo must be hungry, too," Renita said.

"They eat," said Anna Marie. "There plenty roast goat."

Their host sat them down to a table on which there was fresh bread, milk, and, apparently, more roast goat.

"Anna Marie," Tamara said, "how much has Juan told you about us and what we are attempting to do?"

"Enough," said Anna Marie. "Shekeela was my sister."

It was an awkward moment. Tamara and Renita reached for some roast goat and said no more.

Wes and El Lobo were about to climb up to the loft when the barn doors creaked open. Both men relaxed, for it was Juan, bringing Tamara's and Renita's horses. José took the reins, and without a word Juan departed, closing the barn doors behind him. Wes and El Lobo found the loft well supplied with hay, and there were cracks through which they could see the Sandlin house.

"Nobody find us now," El Lobo said.

"At this point," said Wes, "I think the military probably wants us more than Sandlin's bunch. I don't know that any of the Sandlin gang ever got a good look at any of us, but we can't say that for the military. We must avoid them."

It was still dark outside when Wes and El Lobo were awakened by a thumping, like a horse was kicking its way out of a stall. Instead, they found José looking up at them from a circle of lantern light. He motioned them down and led them out the barn doors farthest from the Sandlin house. The moon had long since set, and dawn wasn't too far distant. It soon became evident what José had in mind. Approaching a house that was totally dark, José knocked three times on the back door. When it was opened, the three of them entered and the door was closed. They were led to a room in which a single lamp burned. Each of the several windows were covered with blankets. Tamara, Renita, and a Mexican woman began bringing in food. Wes and El Lobo noticed, with some relief, there appeared to be no roast goat.

"Wes, Palo," said Tamara, "this is Anna Marie."

"Eat," Anna Marie said. "You must go while the darkness hides you."

"Wes," said Renita when Anna Marie returned to the kitchen, "Shekeela was Anna Marie's sister."

"I hate it for her sake," Wes said, "but we have her—along with Juan and others of his kin—to thank for us being alive. When I first came to Mexico to destroy the Sandlin gang, I was mad as hell, and I thought my hate for them would be enough. El Lobo and me rode around gunning down outlaws, but there was always more. Stomp on a rattler's tail all day, and he'll just go right on bitin' you. You have to go for the head, and for the first time, that's what we're about to do."

"Yes," said Tamara. "When Sandlin's Border Empire crumbles from the top, it will not matter how many outlaw camps remain or how many within the Mexican government have sold out."

Conversation ceased. Wes and El Lobo had to return to the stable's hayloft while the darkness concealed them. The meal was soon finished, and the trio returned to the safety of the stable.

"One thing we forget," El Lobo said. "We not know who leave the Sandlin house in the dark."

"I haven't forgotten," said Wes. "While it's possible Sandlin could be removing things at night, it's something we can't help. If we're figurin' it right, the military can't come up with any single crime they can charge to Sandlin. You can't arrest an *hombre* for having his goods hauled somewhere else. Even to a ship in Tampico harbor."

"So there be no reason to work in the darkness."

"None that I can think of," Wes said. "That's why the Mexican people are with us. They know—as we do—what Sandlin's Border Empire has done to them, but there is no legal way to destroy it. If we can't do it, Sandlin will be here forever."

"Why it not be legal to shoot *bastardos* who are so in need of it?"

"That's kind of how it is in the American West," said Wes, "and I hope I'm not there to see it change."

Suddenly there was a growling below, and José appeared at the head of the ladder.

"That's Empty," Wes said. "He followed us here."

Wes beckoned José away from the ladder and climbed down. José cautiously followed. Wes ruffled Empty's ears, and the hound only looked at José with interest. Struck by inspiration, José went into the tack room and returned with two large hunks of roast goat. One of these he offered to Empty, and after sniffing it suspiciously, he wolfed it down. José offered him the second piece, and it quickly followed the first. José raised his empty hands. There was no more roast goat.

"Empty," said Wes, "this is José. He is a friend, an *amigo*."

Empty stalked around José, sniffing him, and the Mexican had the good sense to at least seem unafraid. Finally there was that friendly rumble that wasn't quite a growl, and the hound lay down in a corner on some hay. Reassured, José grinned, and Wes climbed the ladder back to the loft.

Toluca, Mexico. August 21, 1884

"The Mexican brass is claiming victory over the infamous Sandlin outlaws," Jarvis told Sandlin. "There hasn't been a fight for two days now."

"Splendid," said Sandlin. "We want it to appear that we're beaten. When all the dust has settled, there'll be only you, Canton, Tafolla, Zouka, Sumar, Klady, Wittrus, Moke, and Undilay. There'll be no more meetings until I give the word. Only you are to come here, and you will come and go only under cover of darkness."

"Sounds like a smart move to me," Jarvis said, "but what will I tell the others?"

"No more than what I've told you," said Sandlin. "If you encounter any of the rest of the outfit—*segundos* included—tell them we're finished in Mexico. If they continue to clash with the military, they do so at their own peril."

"For them of us that's to stick," Jarvis said, "how long before we reorganize?"

"That I can't tell you," said Sandlin. "We've had too much negative publicity, and that fight in the courtyard was the last straw. We may be three months away from resuming any activity."

"Some of the boys won't like that," Jarvis said. "That damn manhunt cut us all down to the bone."

"That's not my problem," said Sandlin coldly. "Those who can't survive a dry spell are welcome to move on."

"I reckon that includes me," Jarvis said.

"Yes," said Sandlin, "that includes you. There is no room for sentiment within this organization."

Jarvis said nothing, but after he left the house, he paused in the darkness, thinking. What he hadn't told Sandlin was that the men Sandlin had named were already restless, and their trust in Sandlin had dwindled to a spark. There was speculation that Sandlin was preparing to run for it, and what Sandlin had just said would only add more fuel to the fires of discontent. It was late, but Jarvis decided to call a meeting of the disciples, and as he alerted them one by one, he got no argument.

"That's Sandlin's words," Jarvis told them, in the dimly lit back room of a cantina.

"I don't like the sound of it," said Canton. "Hell, I only took enough money to put a roof over my head and to keep me in booze and grub. Sandlin owes me. By God, I ain't settin' on my hunkers for no three months waitin' for some cash to dribble down."

"Me neither," Tafolla said.

"I reckon we'd better take a vote," said Jarvis. "Them that can't abide this order of Sandlin's, stand up."

There was a scraping of chairs, as all eight men got to their feet. Jarvis kicked back his chair and stood with them.

"Speak up," Jarvis said.

"I think Sandlin's getting ready to vamoose," said Canton, "leavin' us high and dry."

"Them's my sentiments exactly," Tafolla said.

Zouka, Sumar, Klady, Wittrus, Moke, and Undilay agreed unanimously.

"Now that we're all of the same mind," said Canton, "what are we goin' to do?"

"We can take turns watching the Sandlin mansion," Jarvis said. "I've heard Sandlin's got access to a fast clipper ship, that it's anchored in Tampico bay. We need to know if there's any truth to that, and if there is, we'll know the direction Sandlin aims to run."

"If there is such a ship, Sandlin won't never get on it," said Undilay. "I'll be standin' there with a cocked Colt, waitin' to shoot the double-crossin' bastard."

"By God, you'll have to get in line," Klady said.

"Watching the house won't be easy," said Jarvis, "with it standing alone. The closest other building is that stable, owned by an old Mex."

"Forget him," Handley said. "The old varmint won't even let us stable our horses in there."

"This will be for nothin' if Sandlin pulls out at night," said Wittrus.

"I don't consider that likely," Canton said. "Sandlin's always had a thing about gold, and it'll take a wagon to move it any distance. I don't remember there bein' any decent road from here to Tampico. Can anybody say I'm wrong?"

"It don't make sense, havin' this ship at Tampico," said Sumar. "Hell, there's a pretty good wagon road south, all the way to the Pacific, and it ain't near as far as Tampico."

"No," Jarvis conceded, "but there's no major Pacific port any closer than Mazatlán. In Tampico, what's one more clipper ship? It's a busy port, and it would be well worth the greater distance, not having this ship attract any unwanted attention. If there is such a ship, it'll be in Tampico bay."

"I reckon we can agree on that," said Zouka. "Now, how can we watch Sandlin's place without bein' seen and identified?"

"There can't be more than one man," Jarvis said. "If we can't use the stable, I can't think of but one other place close enough, and that's a cantina."

"Yeah," said Moke, "and there ain't a window in the place."

"Damn it," Jarvis said, "you won't be inside. Dress yourself like a poor Mex, tilt a *sombrero* over your face, and hunker outside like you're soakin up sun."

"In that case," said Canton, "you can't have a horse. What poor Mex could afford a horse? That calls for a mule, without a saddle."

"No, by God," Wittrus said. "It ain't civilized, a white man ridin' a mule, with or without a saddle."

"Civilized or not, it makes sense," said Jarvis. "All of us will have to wear the same kind of *peon* clothes, wear the same *sombrero*, and ride the same mule. It has to look like the same lazy Mex is there, day after day."

"Suppose I'm on watch," Handley said, "and I see Sandlin loadin' a wagon? Damn it, I ain't about to ride all the way to Tampico on a mule, with or without a saddle."

"If you see Sandlin doin' anything suspicious—like loadin' a wagon—then follow just long enough to be sure of the direction," said Jarvis. "There'll always be another of us just waitin' to side you. The two of you can then mount your horses and follow."

"I'll take the watch tomorrow, then," Canton said. "Who's got a mule I can borrow?"

Nobody had a mule, and some of the men laughed.

"See me at dawn," said Jarvis. "I'll find a mule."

Toluca, Mexico. August 22, 1884

From their position in the stable's loft, Wes and El Lobo could see the front and both sides of the Sandlin mansion. While they couldn't see the front of the house, they could see the entrance to a distant cantina, and it was there that they first noticed some activity. What appeared to be a poor Mexican reined up his mule, dismounted, sat down with his back to the adobe wall, and tilted his *sombrero* over his eyes.

"He no *Mejicano*," El Lobo said.

"How can you tell?"

"No can ride *mulo*. He used to horse, saddle, stirrup. Dismount hard," said El Lobo.

"Now that you mention it," Wes said, "there is something odd about him. Why does a man arrive a good three hours before a cantina opens, and why does he choose this particular cantina? The sun shines everywhere."

"*Sí*," said El Lobo. "Per'ap he look for somebody."

"*Amigo*," Wes said, "you have a habit of getting at the truth of a matter. I'd bet a horse and saddle he's watching the Sandlin mansion."

"Why? He no *soldado*."

"We may not be the only ones who suspect Sandlin's about to make a run for it," said Wes. "I'd say some of the *hombres* here in Toluca are looking for a double-cross. If Sandlin's inner circle is watching him, then our suspicions are well founded."

"*Sí*," El Lobo said. "We watch everybody."

As the day wore on, the "Mexican" never left his position before the cantina.

"*Por Dios*," said El Lobo, "no food, no water."

"It'll be interesting to see if he shows up tomorrow," Wes said. "If he does, or one dressed like him, then we'll know Sandlin's bunch is watching the house."

A few minutes before sundown, the "Mexican" stood up, stretched, and very clumsily mounted the mule. El Lobo laughed. When it was good and dark, José thumped on the wall, his way of telling them it was suppertime. Empty bounded ahead, for he knew they were going to the house to eat. Tamara and Renita became very excited when they learned that some of Sandlin's own men might be watching the house.

"It is more than we could have hoped for," Tamara said. "How can Sandlin not be brought down, with so many of us joining the fight?"

"We don't yet know for sure," said Wes, "but we should tomorrow. If there's another phony Mexican over there tomorrow, I believe we can safely say he's watching the Sandlin house."

For three days, Wes and El Lobo watched the Sandlin mansion without seeing anyone arrive or depart. Each day, the nondescript "Mexican" showed up outside the cantina.

"That settles it," Wes said. "Somebody's watching that place besides us."

"Per'ap Sandlin be gone when we come," said El Lobo.

"I'm startin' to wonder," Wes said. "We'll give it another day."

On the morning of the fourth day, a woman emerged from the mansion. Going to a carriage house, she led out a horse and harnessed it to a buckboard. She then mounted the box and drove away toward the business district of the town.

"Sandlin's *señorita*," said El Lobo. "We follow?"

"I don't think so," Wes replied. "There's nothing in the buckboard. Let's see what our *amigo* does over yonder by the cantina."

The "Mexican" near the cantina didn't leave his post. Two hours later, the buckboard returned. The woman backed the vehicle into the carriage house, unharnessed the horse, and returned it to its stall. She then took her parcels and entered the house.

"We still do not know if Sandlin be there," said El Lobo.

"No," Wes said, "and I don't know how we can find out."

Tampico, Mexico. August 26, 1884

Aboard the *Aguila*, a clipper ship anchored in Tampico bay, Captain Agar studied the telegram he had just received. It said:

Sail immediately per my instructions and do not return.

There was no signature, and none was necessary. Renaldo, first mate to the five-man crew, said nothing. Agar passed him the telegram, and after reading it, he grinned.

"It's what we been waitin' for, eh, Cap'n?"

"Yeah," Agar said. "It means what we got on board is our last payload."

"I never would of thought we'd be trusted this far," said Renaldo. "Why you reckon Sandlin ain't sailin' with us?"

"Who knows?" Agar replied. "This particular plan was to come into play only if Sandlin couldn't get away without bein' followed. So much the better for us. Now we ain't got to bother disposin' of Sandlin. We're still sailin' to South America, but to a port of our own choosin'."

"Haw, haw," said Renaldo, "this'll be the sweetest double-cross in the history of the world. What do you aim to tell the rest of the crew when we bypass Sandlin's port?"

"Nothin'," Agar said. "Once we're in port, they're expendable."

Renaldo laughed, but had he been more observant, he wouldn't have liked the crafty look in Captain Agar's hard eyes.

Cord Sandlin paced the floor impatiently. The telegram to Tampico had been the least favorable of three possible plans, but Sandlin wasn't sure the Mexican government hadn't staked out the *Aguila*. The moment the craft prepared to sail, it might be boarded and searched. While there was no way the vessel or its cargo could be traced to Sandlin, the gold would be confiscated, and that would be regrettable.

But the Sandlin house held many secrets. Beneath the first floor was a cellar, and only Sandlin knew of the concealed tunnel that led to a vault containing millions in gold. There was a means—if circumstances warranted it—of collapsing the tunnel and sealing off the chamber. There was food, water, ventilation, and a means of escape of which only Sandlin was aware. There the gold would be secure until it could safely be removed.

"Damn it," Canton said, "I don't believe Sandlin's in that house. He's managed to find some female to stay there, figurin' to throw us off the trail. Jarvis, you got to go back to that place and be sure we ain't watchin' an empty house."

"I got no reason for goin' back there," said Jarvis. "You know what Sandlin said, and I ain't wantin' a tongue-lashing."

"You know what the varmint's doin'," Undilay said. "We been told to lay low for the next three months, and that's what Sandlin's doin'. By God, one of them servants is goin' out for grub, and nobody—includin' us—will lay an eye on Sandlin."

"Yeah," said Wittrus, "and me not knowin' if Sandlin's in there or not just rubs me the wrong damn way. Why don't we ride in after dark and shoot up the place?"

"If that's the best idea you got," Jarvis said, "why don't you ride over there and do it in broad daylight?

All it'll do is draw attention to Sandlin, and that three-month wait will stretch into never."

"Yeah," said Canton, "if we aim to hang on here, we can't do anything more to stir up the military and these old Mexes that's been raisin' hell."

"So we go on settin' next to a cantina watchin' the house, not knowin' if Sandlin's in there or not," Zouka said.

"That's how it is," said Jarvis. "We got to do it Sandlin's way or we're on our own."

"I think we're on our own, anyway," Klady said in disgust. "Hell, Sandlin's stringin' us along, so's we don't stir up trouble here in town. Let the dust settle, and Sandlin will run for it."

"Klady's right," said Tafolla. "We ain't gettin' another *peso* out of Sandlin. We're all supposed to get fed up and ride on, leavin' Sandlin with all the loot."

"All the more reason why I don't aim to ride on," Jarvis said. "I'll be here until I get some satisfaction. I won't fault any man wantin' to move on."

"Ah, hell," said Klady, "I reckon I'll stick it out. I can't see lettin' Sandlin have it all without a fight."

Swallowing their anger and disgust, they all agreed to stay, taking turns watching the Sandlin mansion.

"There has to be a way to smoke Sandlin out of there," Wes said while he and El Lobo were having breakfast.

"We only need proof that Sandlin is there," said Renita. "Couldn't someone go there and ask?"

"*Sí*," El Lobo said, "but for why?"

"I will speak to Juan," said Tamara. "Perhaps he will know how we can do it."

"Juan will be here tonight," Anna Marie said.

"*Bueno*," said Wes. "Tomorrow we'll do something, even if it's wrong."

Chapter 17

Wes and El Lobo spent another fruitless day watching the Sandlin house. When it was dark enough, they made their way to Anna Marie's boardinghouse for supper and found that Juan was already there.

"I have spoken to him," Tamara said, "and there is a way we can get into the Sandlin house. Not you and El Lobo, but Renita and me. Once each week, two *señoritas* go there to clean. This time—the day after tomorrow—we will replace those *señoritas*."

"Too dangerous," said Wes. "Both of you are white-skinned, and Renita has almost red hair."

"We fix that," Anna Marie said.

"Yes," said Tamara. "Anna Marie knows of a brew—a stain—that will brown us so that we look Mexican. Renita will wear her hair in a bun, covering it with a scarf."

"I know of the stain," Wes said, recalling how Maria Armijo had once transformed him, "but Renita's slow with the Spanish."

"I know that," said Renita. "Tamara will speak for us."

Wes had no further objection, and Juan grinned at

them all, proud that he had offered a solution to their problem.

"I'll see that the *señoritas* you replace are paid," Wes said.

"We thought of that," said Tamara, "but Juan refuses. He says if we destroy Sandlin, that is enough."

"Get in house," El Lobo said, "what you do?"

"If we are not to arouse suspicion," said Tamara, "we will have to clean the house. If we only learn that Sandlin is still there, we will know our watching and waiting has not been in vain."

"*Bueno*," Wes said, "but there's a chance you may discover other useful things. Look for a safe, or a sealed-off room you're not allowed to enter. The important thing is to get a look at Sandlin. So far, none of us knows what the varmint looks like."

"*Sí*," El Lobo said, "and there be the *señorita* that go, come, and do not go again."

"He's right," said Wes. "I'd forgotten about her. She *has* to be in that house somewhere."

"There are many mysteries within the Sandlin mansion," Tamara observed. "Revealing them will perhaps hasten the end of this evil empire."

"Just don't get careless," said Wes. "Don't talk one to another, because those walls may have ears. If there's so much as a chance you may be discovered, get out of there."

Yet another day passed without anyone entering or leaving the Sandlin mansion, and by suppertime Wes and El Lobo were more than ready for Tamara and Renita to enter the house the following day. To their surprise, when they reached Anna Marie's, Tamara and Renita were completely transformed. All skin that might be seen—including their feet and ankles—looked Mexican. Renita had her auburn hair in a tight bun, concealing it entirely with a colorful scarf. Both women wore plain, long *peon* skirts to their ankles. Anna Marie beamed, proud of her handiwork, while the mute José looked at them with amazement.

"By God," said Wes, "I don't believe even Sandlin can see through that, if neither of you stumble. You're well prepared, but just don't forget the danger involved."

"We are even better prepared than you think," Renita said. "Look."

She and Tamara drew their skirts waist-high, and each had a Colt revolver secured to the inside of one thigh. José grinned, while Anna Marie laughed delightedly.

"I've never seen a Colt carried in that position before," said Wes. "It must be mighty uncomfortable."

"A little," Tamara admitted, "but one can stand discomfort for a while, if one's life is at risk."

"You can't walk to the Sandlin place from here," said Wes. "How will you go?"

"Juan thought of everything," Renita said. "The usual cleaning women are taken there in a wagon. The same wagon will come for us here, well before daylight, and will return to Sandlin's place for us at sundown. We won't be back here until after dark tomorrow."

"Tarnation," said Wes, "is *everybody* in these parts related to Juan?"

"Some only *amigos*," Anna Marie said, "but all hate the evil empire."

Wes and El Lobo were watching the Sandlin house the following morning when Renita and Tamara arrived. They used the big brass door knocker, and when the door opened, the person who opened it very carefully avoided being seen. Wes and El Lobo sighed. It would be a long day.

"*Buenos dias, señor*," said Tamara in perfect Spanish.

Sandlin—if the man *was* Sandlin—nodded, saying nothing. They followed him down a long hall, and he stepped aside when they reached the kitchen. He was assuming they knew where the mops, brooms, and cleaning supplies were. Tamara swallowed hard and, with Renita following, crossed to the farthest end of the kitchen, where there were double doors. They both breathed a huge sigh of relief when they opened the doors to reveal the necessary cleaning equipment and supplies. Rare for the time and place, built into the kitchen counter was a huge sink, and above it, a pump. Daring to look back, Tamara found Sandlin gone.

"We are alone, I think," Tamara said.

"My God," said Renita in a whisper, "this is such a huge place. Where do we start?"

"You sweep the kitchen floor and I will mop," Tamara replied softly. "Then we each will take brooms and sweep the rest of the house."

They saw Sandlin only once more during the day, and again were met with brooding silence. While there was water in the kitchen, they had been offered no food, and dared not look for any. They were listening eagerly for the rattle of the wagon, and when at last it approached, they left the house.

"Damn," said Renita, "I never worked so hard in my life."

"Nor I," Tamara said, "but we dared not give Sandlin a reason to suspect us."

"If that really *was* Sandlin," said Renita.

"I am not impressed," Tamara said. "For an outlaw, leader of the evil empire, I was expecting . . . something more."

They climbed into the wagon without looking back at the house. The old Mexican said something to the mule, and the wagon lurched into motion. They would have to wait until after dark before returning to Anna Marie's. Wes and El Lobo arrived for supper, to find that Tamara and Renita had not returned.

"Tarnation," Wes said, "I hope nothin' went wrong."

They all breathed sighs of relief when at last they heard the wagon coming.

"*Madre de Dios*," said Anna Marie, when at last Tamara and Renita entered. "We were fearful—"

"Nothing much happened," Renita said, "except we worked our behinds off. That, and this damn Colt has rubbed the inside of my left thigh raw."

"What about Sandlin?" Wes asked impatiently.

"If it *was* Sandlin," said Tamara, "we saw him twice. Neither time did he speak."

"No *señorita?*" El Lobo asked.

"We saw no one except the *hombre* who's supposed to be Sandlin," said Tamara.

"Why you think this *hombre* not be Sandlin?" El Lobo asked.

"I do not know why we have our doubts," said Tamara.

"I think I do," Renita said. "I just remembered something that took a while to sink in. This . . . this Sandlin is just too pat, too slick, and no razor's ever touched those cheeks or that chin."

"That," said Tamara, "and this *hombre* is terribly short. Never have I seen boots with three-inch heels."

"*Mejicanos* be short," El Lobo observed.

"This *hombre* does not have *Mejicano* coloring or features," said Tamara.

"Maybe Spanish or South American, then," Wes said.

"I do not think so," said Tamara. "We have not heard the voice. But perhaps the next time we shall."

"Next time," Renita said, "we'll try harder to learn something about the house. There is what might be a door to a basement, and there were several rooms with doors locked."

"These rooms with locked doors are all on the second floor," said Tamara. "Perhaps one of us can watch near the head of the stairs while the other investigates."

"How old this Sandlin be?" El Lobo asked.

"I don't know," said Renita.

"Very young," Tamara said. "Much younger than I had expected."

"For the first time," said Wes, "I'm startin' to wonder if Sandlin *is* the leader of this gang."

"If not," Renita said, "then who is?"

"I don't know," said Wes, "but why would the

leader of a band of outlaws allow himself to be whip-sawed into a situation like this? We believe there is a clipper ship waiting in Tampico bay, but Sandlin—if this *is* Sandlin—has made no move in that direction. If we are thinkin' straight, then Sandlin has a fortune stashed somewhere. If it's not in the house, it must be, all or part, on the ship, and somebody's responsible for moving that ship. This has all the earmarks of a double-cross, if Sandlin's countin' on that ship."

"*Madre mía,*" El Lobo said, "if Sandlin does not escape to the ship, why we watch the house?"

"Tamara," said Wes, "are you *sure* there is such a ship?"

"My grandfather was sure," Tamara said angrily, "and I believed him."

"Tamara," said Renita consolingly, "we're not doubting there is a ship. I think what we're trying to discover is where the ship fits into all this. Could it be that Sandlin has purposely used these rumors about the ship, while planning to escape some other way?"

"That's what I was gettin' at, Tamara," Wes said, "but my choice of words was poor. Every day we've watched Sandlin's mansion, there's been a man in Mexican garb lazing up against a cantina, watching the house. El Lobo and me believe that's the doing of Sandlin's gang, that their thinking has been runnin' neck-and-neck with ours. They're expecting Sandlin to try and slip off to Tampico, to that waiting ship. I won't be surprised if Sandlin has seen to it that they know of the ship. Trouble is, they've run headlong into the same stone wall that we have. Like us, they believe Sandlin has a pile of gold that must be taken to Tampico. But suppose there's only a small part of Sandlin's loot on that ship."

"That does not mean it is in Sandlin's mansion," said Tamara. "I had heard of the ship more than three years ago. Sandlin's spoils could have been taken to another port, a little at a time."

"Sandlin could have moved only enough gold to keep the rumor alive," Wes said. "The crew taking that ship to another port would need a reason not to just take Sandlin's loot and disappear. They've likely been expecting Sandlin to run, bringin' along the rest of the loot. At the right time, a well-placed slug could do away with Sandlin, and the body could be thrown overboard."

"But if Sandlin avoids the ship," said Renita, "all the gold that's been removed by the ship's crew will be taken by them. Like you said, a double-cross."

"A double-cross Sandlin may have expected and counted on," Wes said. "Suppose the Mexican government isn't as stupid as they sometimes appear, and that they know of this Sandlin ship in Tampico bay. All they'd have to do is board the ship, confiscate the loot, and tell the Mexican people the Sandlin gang is no more. For proof, they'd have the ship and its small store of outlaw gold. Sandlin would then be free to escape Mexico at some future time, when his gang has disbanded and ridden away, when the soldiers are satisfied the outlaw threat is no more."

"*Madre de Dios*," cried Tamara. "If what you say is true, Sandlin could wait months or years before making a move. If indeed the Mexican government takes the ship and some of the outlaw gold, they will have no more interest in the Sandlin gang. We waste our time waiting for Sandlin to run. I will take my *pistola* and shoot the *bastardo* through the head when next I see him."

"It might come to that," Wes said, "but let's not be hasty. Like you and Renita have pointed out, we don't really *know* the person in the house is actually Sandlin. We'll go on watching the place until you and Renita spend one more day there. You must, if possible, learn for a certainty that it really *is* Sandlin in the house."

"We shoot Sandlin, the *soldados* come after us," said El Lobo.

"Not necessarily," Wes said. "That's why we'll go on watching the house for a little longer. If we're right about the ship and it's seized by the Mexican government, they'll be satisfied the Sandlin outlaws are finished."

"They not give a damn if we shoot Sandlin," said El Lobo.

"That's how I see it," Wes said. "They won't be in a hurry to reopen old wounds by reminding all of Mexico that they never actually went after the leader of the outlaws."

"They can't come after us without giving us credit for exposing the Sandlin gang," said Renita. "You and El Lobo didn't kill your soldier escort, and those two prison guards were molesting Tamara and me. We only protected our honor."

El Lobo tried not to laugh, but it was a lost cause. Wes joined in, and they slapped their thighs with their hats. The silent José and Anna Marie were torn between the mirth of Wes and El Lobo and the angry, hurt looks on the faces of Tamara and Renita. Empty growled suddenly, loud enough for them to hear him outside. Wes and El Lobo had their hands near the butts of their Colts when Juan spoke. Anna Marie unlocked the door and the old Mexican entered. Obviously, he wondered what they had accomplished, and Tamara quickly told him, adding that they must visit the Sandlin mansion one more time. But Juan had a message, and it wasn't good news. He spoke rapidly in Spanish, and when he had finished, Tamara translated.

"Juan says the Señor Sandlin has sent word to Juan's kin that the *señoritas* are not to come to the house again."

"Damn," said Renita, "he saw through us. I didn't think we were all that bad."

While Juan may not have understood the words, he sensed the indignation, and again he spoke to Tamara in rapid Spanish.

"Juan doesn't believe Sandlin was suspicious of us," Tamara said. "Sandlin doesn't just not want us, he doesn't want *any señoritas*."

"That tells us something," said Wes. "Sandlin's about to make some kind of move. We must get back into that house."

"Then we must wait for Sandlin to leave," Renita said.

"Perhaps there is a secret entrance to the house," said Tamara. "What of the *señorita* who left the house and returned there? We saw no sign of her."

"If there is a secret entrance," Renita said, "why did the mysterious *señorita* not use it when leaving and returning?"

"Maybe two reasons," said Wes. "First, to anyone watching, it appears there is at least one other in the house besides Sandlin. Second, any other means of entering or leaving the house may have been devised for use just once, when Sandlin makes a run for it."

"We waste time watching the Sandlin house," Tamara said.

"Maybe," said Wes, "but I don't aim to leave Mexico until I know Sandlin's dead."

"*Sí*," El Lobo said. "We wait."

"At least," said Renita, "the next time someone leaves the house, I believe one or both of you should follow."

"*Sí*," Tamara said.

For an instant, in Tamara's dark eyes, Renita observed something that Wes and El Lobo did not. Tamara had something in mind that she wasn't quite ready to share, for she had found and had taken a key from a drawer in the Sandlin mansion.

After days of watching the Sandlin mansion without result, Sandlin's former disciples were ready to give it up. Then a story appeared in Mexico City's weekly newspaper that changed everything. Jarvis discovered it first and immediately called together his companions.

"There was a ship anchored in Tampico bay," Jarvis said, pointing to the front-page story in the newspaper. "The captain and the crew was gettin' ready to sail when the Mexican government moved in and seized the ship. The military's crowin' its fool head off, claimin' to have struck the Sandlin gang a death blow."

"By God," said Canton, "that means we get nothin'. Not three months from now, not ever. How could Sandlin have been so damn careless?"

"Maybe he wasn't," Zouka said, looking at the newspaper Jarvis had passed among them. "You think if all Sandlin's loot was on that ship, somethin' wouldn't of been said about how much gold there was?"

"You may have somethin' there," said Jarvis. "I figure the Mex government will play this up for all it's worth so they can get shut of this Sandlin affair once and for all. It is mighty strange they didn't say anything about the recovered loot. Makes you wonder if there wasn't all that much, and they're makin' the most of the recovery without saying how much was recovered."

"Jarvis," Klady said, "this just kills that order Sandlin give you about us keepin' shy of that house. He owes every man of us, and he knows damn well we're countin' on what's ours. Now, by God, we're bein' told the Mex government's took it all. If I got to go by myself, I'm shovin' this newspaper in Sandlin's face and demanding an accounting."

"Hell, you won't be by yourself," said Tafolla. "I'm goin', too."

Jarvis, who normally might have tried to restrain them, did not, for their cause was his own. He had but one thing to say.

"Let's wait till sundown, when it's almost dark. Call attention to Sandlin, and we draw attention to ourselves. It's as much to our advantage as to his, havin' everybody believe the Sandlin gang is no more."

"Yeah," said Wittrus, "you're right. Now, if we got to gut-shoot the bastard, nobody will miss him."

The newspaper story has been widely read, and Juan wasted no time in taking a copy of the paper to Anna Marie's.

"*Por Dios*," Tamara said, "this is much like Wes believed it might be. They take the ship, but they do not say how much gold there is."

"Just enough for the military to boast they've taken Sandlin's ship and his gold," said Renita.

Juan rattled off some rapid Spanish, and Tamara translated.

"Juan agrees," Tamara said. "He believes the ship is a decoy, that there is just enough gold to allow the *soldados* to boast of having destroyed the outlaw gang."

"Ask him to take this newspaper to the stable, to Wes and El Lobo," said Renita. "It's important that they know, in case something happens at the Sandlin house."

Quickly Tamara spoke to Juan, and he nodded. Taking the newspaper, he headed for the stable. Empty growled, and through a crack in the wall of the loft, Wes and El Lobo could see Juan coming. They soon descended the ladder and were waiting when the old one entered the barn. Wordlessly, he passed the newspaper to Wes, while El Lobo looked over his shoulder.

"You be right," El Lobo said. "They don't say how much gold."

"No," said Wes, "and that tells me it's not enough to get excited about. But it sounds like the Sandlin gang's out of business once and for all, and that will help the military and the Mexican government save face."

"Now what we do?" El Lobo wondered.

"We go on watching Sandlin's place," said Wes. "If we're right and some of his gang is laying low, this may bring them out in the open. If I was in their place, I'd be raising hell, and I'd start right over yonder at Sandlin's mansion."

"*Sí*," Juan said approvingly.

When Juan had left the barn, Wes and El Lobo again climbed the ladder to the loft.

"I think we'll stay here for as long as we can see the Sandlin house," said Wes. "Even if these outlaws *are* ready to give Sandlin hell, I don't expect them in daylight. It won't be to their advantage to start a fight just when everybody's been told the gang's finished."

"The *hombre* from the cantina be gone," El Lobo observed.

"They don't need him anymore," said Wes. "There'll be no fast ride to Tampico."

Toluca, Mexico. August 31, 1884

A few minutes before sundown, Jarvis and his followers saddled up and rode out for Toluca. Seeking to draw as little attention as possible, they rode in behind the mansion, leaving their horses there. On foot, they approached the massive front door, and ignoring the brass knocker, Jarvis used the butt of his Colt.

"I'd bet my horse and saddle the varmint don't answer the door," Klady said.

"You won't find no takers here," said Tafolla sourly.

Proof of that became evident as Jarvis continued pounding on the door without result. Finally he tried the knob, only to find the door securely locked.

"This place is bound to have other doors," Handley said. "Let's try 'em all."

They did so, only to find every door locked.

"Well, hell," said Undilay, "let's smash a window."

"That won't help," Jarvis said. "This place is a damn fort. Every window is barred."

Even in the dusk, they could see the vertical iron bars.

"Damn it," said Moke, "he ain't gittin' away with that."

Beside the carriage house leaned an ax, and Moke seized it. He swung it with all his might against one of the barred windows. There was the crash of broken glass, followed by the bellow of a shotgun. The blast struck Moke chest-high, and what was left of him was flung half a dozen feet.

"God Almighty," said Zouka, "let's get out of here. That'll draw attention."

But some of the men had drawn their weapons, and approached the fatal window from the sides, out of the line of direct fire.

"Nobody's in there," Jarvis said. "The scattergun's rigged to a trip wire."

"Yeah," said Canton, "and the rest of the windows and doors may be wired the same way. Any more of you with ideas of breakin' in will have to do it without me."

One of their number having been cut down without warning had a sobering effect on the survivors. They quickly mounted their horses and vanished into the night.

"No can see," El Lobo said, following the shotgun blast.

"No," said Wes, "but listen."

Sound carried in the still of the evening, and they could hear the creaking of saddle leather as men mounted, and finally the sounds of them riding away.

"Nobody shoot back," El Lobo said.

"Likely nothin' to shoot at," said Wes. "It's dark enough. Let's slope on over there and at least see what happened."

Empty thought Wes and El Lobo were going to supper, but quickly changed direction when they started toward the distant Sandlin house. They circled around until they found the window that had been broken, and even in the starlight they could see the remains of a dead man. Suddenly there was the *snick* of a hammer being eared back.

"Do not move, *señors*," a voice said. "You are covered."

"We've done nothing," said Wes. "We were near and heard the blast of a shotgun. We came to see what had happened."

"Per'ap we may all learn what 'appen, *mañana*," the voice said. "For tonight, *señors*, it be the *juzgado*. Release your belts and drop your guns. Quickly."

While the Sandlin mansion was somewhat isolated, the jail was within walking distance, for Toluca wasn't a large village. Wes became aware that Empty was following them.

"Empty," said Wes, "go. Return to Renita. Go."

"*Silencio*," their captor said.

The jail—such as it was—had but two cells. Wes and El Lobo were forced to enter, and the Mexican came in after them. He beckoned with the muzzle of the shotgun for Wes and El Lobo to enter one of the cells. He then closed and locked the door, placed their gunbelts in the drawer of a battered desk, and turned back to face them. A lit lantern hung just inside the door. Their jailor was short, fat, and a tarnished star hung drunkenly from the lapel of a coat that was several sizes too small.

"Suppertime be over," he said. Blowing out the lantern, he departed, closing the door behind him.

"Damn," said Wes, "if I wasn't so old, I'd cry."

"Per'ap we both cry," El Lobo said. "You send the *perro* away before he know where we be going."

But old habits were hard to break, and as long as Empty could see Wes, he followed. Only when Wes and El Lobo entered the jail did the hound make his way back to Anna Marie's and begin scratching at the door. Cautiously, Anna Marie opened it, and Empty came in. He whined, a distressful sound that said something was wrong and he could do nothing to fix it. José had come to supper, not knowing where Wes and El Lobo had gone or their reason for going.

"Thank God," Renita said. "Empty, take us to Wes."

"Please be careful," said Anna Marie. "I send José for Juan, if you wait."

"Send for Juan, please," Tamara said, "but we cannot wait."

Empty quickly got ahead, paused until they caught up, and then headed unerringly toward the Sandlin mansion. But before crossing the cobbled street, he veered away toward the lights of Toluca.

"Oh, God," said Renita, out of breathe, "what could have happened to them?"

Tamara said nothing, for they were nearing the village, and their destination soon became obvious. Small though it was, there was no mistaking the jail. It was nothing fancy, for there was no glass in the cell window.

"Wes," Tamara whispered. "Palo."

"In here," said Wes through the small barred window.

"Please tell us what happened," Tamara said.

Quickly Wes did.

"Anna Marie has sent for Juan," said Renita.

"*Bueno*," Wes replied. "This Mex is a local constable or something, and I don't see how he can blame the killing on us, for neither of us had a shotgun. He must have arrived about the same time we did."

"Wait until the morning," said Tamara. "Juan will know how to get you out."

That seemed the best way, so Tamara and Renita started back to Anna Marie's.

"I'm sorry they have to spend the night in jail," Renita said.

"Perhaps it is for the best," said Tamara, "for they

would not like what we do. In the morning, we are going into the Sandlin mansion.''

"Suppose Sandlin's there."

"You have a gun and I have a gun," Tamara said.

Chapter 18

Surprisingly, when Juan arrived and Tamara explained the situation to him, he seemed distressed. He spoke rapidly in Spanish.

"Juan does not know this constable in Toluca," Tamara said. "He will try to have Wes and Palo released sometime tomorrow, but he says we must go."

"I'm sorry we've had to involve Juan in all this," said Renita. "He's done so much for us. We couldn't have lasted this long without him."

"Juan understands," Anna Marie said. "He believes you have done all you can do, and wishes you *vaya con Dios*."

Only when Tamara and Renita had retired to the little room they shared did Renita ask Tamara to explain her plan for entering the Sandlin mansion.

"I have a key," said Tamara. "While we were there, I found it in a desk drawer."

"But you don't know what it's for," Renita protested. "There are so many doors in that house, we may never find the right one. Especially if your key doesn't fit one of the outside doors."

"In my father's house there is an outside door with a key very much like this one," said Tamara. "If it does not fit the front door, then perhaps the back door. There is a side door that opens to the carriage house, as well."

"Do you really intend to shoot Sandlin?"

"Much depends upon Sandlin," Tamara replied. "If this Sandlin is anything like I am expecting, then I will kill him without remorse."

Renita shuddered, for in Tamara's dark eyes was a terrifying resolve that could not be denied. Yet, with Wes and El Lobo in the clutches of the law, and Juan telling them they must go, how else could they prevent Sandlin escaping scot-free?

"I know where we can get some dynamite," Canton said. "Drop a few sticks of that through them windows, and no more Sandlin."

"And no more gold," said Jarvis.

"I don't care," Canton said. "I'll give up my share of any Sandlin loot just for the satisfaction of blowin' Sandlin to hell and gone. There's nothin' lower than a damn double-crosser."

"I'm of the same mind," said Zouka. "Let's wipe Sandlin and his mansion off the face of the earth and ride to Texas."

There were shouts of angry agreement. Only Jarvis had reservations, and they were not strong enough to provoke a fight, so he said nothing. Sandlin had gone too far.

"C'mon Klady, and help me fetch the dynamite," Canton said.

Austin, Texas. September 1, 1884

Texas Rangers Bodie West and Dylan Stewart were having breakfast.

"So you don't know if the kid's alive or not," said Stewart.

"No," said West. "All I know is that since he rode south, the Sandlin gang seems to have gone to hell on greased skids. The last telegram he sent—the last one we know of—he challenged the outlaw gang to a fight in the streets of Mexico City. Can you imagine such a thing? I've been wondering if even Nathan Stone would have done that."

"Sounds like the boy's standin' in his daddy's shadow," Stewart said. "I hope he don't get himself killed, livin' up to his old man's reputation."

"There's been no further word of him," said West. "The last I've heard of the Sandlin affair was a newspaper account of the Mexican government having seized a ship belonging to Sandlin, along with some outlaw loot. Not a word about Wes Stone."

"He may have been in some way responsible for the seizure," Stewart said. "Maybe the Mexican government took all the credit, puttin' themselves in a better light. You know, since Santa Anna's military dictatorship, the *soldados* have been thought of as maybe several cuts below a sand rattler."

Wes sighed. "I just hope I don't have to telegraph Byron Silver and tell him Wes is dead. Silver took it mighty hard when Nathan was killed, and I know he's had high hopes for young Wes."

"I've heard some impressive tales about the days Stone and Silver rode together," said Stewart. "Stone should have had a position with the Federals, along-side Silver."

"Nathan didn't want it," West said. "He rode with Silver, but he wasn't bound by the same rules. Young Wes is the same way. Have you ever noticed that a man most willing to die for a cause never earns a dime from it?"

Toluca, Mexico. September 1, 1884

"Come on," said Tamara. "It'll be light in another hour. We must be inside the house before then."

"'Suppose we go through all this," Renita said, "and then find your key fits none of the outside doors."

"Then we can do nothing," said Tamara, "but I will not be content to do nothing as long as there is a small chance."

They were unable to leave the house without Anna Marie hearing them, and Tamara told the Mexican woman of their plans.

"There is much danger," Anna Marie said. "Juan would forbid it."

"That's why Juan wasn't told," said Renita.

"*Sí*," Tamara replied. "When Juan learns of it, Sandlin will be dead."

"Or you will be dead," said Anna Marie. "*Vaya con Dios.*"

Sandlin hadn't slept. Obviously, the order Jarvis had taken to the disciples had been soundly ignored, robbing Sandlin of the time needed to quit Mexico with the outlaw gold. With one of their number dead as a result of last night's visit, Sandlin had little doubt that the lot of them—including Jarvis—would return. They were the kind, when they learned their share of the loot had been denied them, who would do all in their power to see that Sandlin never left Mexico alive. Quickly Sandlin gathered a few personal items. There was an oilskin pouch of matches, for along the escape tunnel were small charges of dynamite to collapse the tunnel after Sandlin had passed through it. The ticking of the clock on the mantel seemed loud in the stillness. Less than two hours remained. . . .

Tamara and Renita had scrubbed all the stain from their bodies and had exchanged the long Mexican dresses for their riding clothes. They again wore their Colts belted around their middles when they left Anna Marie's. To their surprise, Empty was waiting for them and bounded on ahead. They passed the stable where Wes and El Lobo had spent fruitless days on watch, and looming in the distance was the Sandlin mansion.

"Lord," said Renita, "it always looks so dark and forbidding. I've never seen a light in there. How will we find our way around in the dark?"

"It will be light by the time we enter the house," Tamara said.

Suddenly Wes sat up on his bunk. El Lobo was peering through the small barred window in the adobe wall.

"Juan is here," said El Lobo.

Juan had two mules hitched to a double tree and

backed up to the jail wall. Secured to the double tree was a length of chain, and by climbing upon the back of one of the mules, Juan had passed it around two of the bars. He said nothing, for it was obvious he was helping them break jail. It would soon be daylight, and Juan worked rapidly. Softly he spoke to the mules, and they leaned into their harness. At first nothing happened, but as Juan again spoke to the mules, there was a grating sound. When the bars ripped loose, a good portion of the wall collapsed with a rumbling crash.

"*Madre de Dios,*" El Lobo said.

"Let's vamoose," said Wes. "If that didn't wake the town, nothing will."

Juan didn't even try to recover the chain. He loosed it from the double tree and, with a word to the mules, vanished in the predawn darkness. Somewhere there was a shout, and not too far away someone lit a lamp or lantern. Wes and El Lobo ran, avoiding the cobblestone street, keeping within the shadows of trees. Taking a more direct way, they soon reached the stable. There they stopped to catch their breath before making their way to Anna Marie's.

"I reckon we'll have to run for it now," Wes said. "I just hope Juan don't get himself strung up for busting us out of jail."

"Nobody see Juan," said El Lobo. "Per'ap we get strung up for busting out of jail."

Reaching Anna Marie's, Wes rapped frantically on the door. Anna Marie peered out.

"How you get loose?"

"Juan busted us out," Wes said. "We'll have to run for it. Where's—"

"Your *señoritas* go to the Sandlin *casa*," said Anna Marie. "Much danger."

"My God, yes," Wes groaned. "Come on, Palo."

"There's no point in all of us riding," said Jarvis. "We'll cut the cards, and the four drawing the lowest numbers will throw the dynamite. Fair enough?"

"No," Zouka said. "I want to throw some of that dynamite."

"Cut the damn cards," said Wittrus.

Jarvis shuffled the cards and, holding them face-down, allowed each man to draw one.

"By God,"—Zouka cackled, drawing a deuce—"I'm goin'."

Zouka, Tafolla, Klady, and Wittrus drew low cards. Quickly they saddled their horses. Jarvis and Canton passed each of the men four sticks of dynamite bound together, capped and fused.

"Don't waste any time, if you aim to ride with the rest of us," Jarvis said. "Within an hour, we aim to get the hell out of here."

"We'll be here *pronto*," said Klady. "When all this dynamite blows, I reckon all them *soldados* will have to get off their hunkers and look busy."

"Light them fuses," Canton said, "and count to three. From there you got no more than seven seconds before the dynamite blows."

The four rode away, and Jarvis sighed. It would be a long ride north to the border.

When Tamara and Renita reached the Sandlin

place, Empty remained well away from the house. Boldly, Tamara tried the key, and the massive front door didn't budge. Renita followed her around to the back door, where they encountered the same dismal failure. They crept around to the far side, where there was a door that led from the mansion to the carriage house. Despite her show of confidence, Tamara was nervous. She dropped the key, and it was still dark enough that she had trouble finding it. Muttering some choice words in Spanish, she recovered the key. It turned easily, and the door opened soundlessly. Tamara allowed Renita to enter and then, stepping inside, closed the door behind her. A short corridor led to a second door, which was closed.

"I feel like our luck is running out," Renita whispered.

"Perhaps," said Tamara softly, "but this is our last chance. We must enter that door, if we are to search the rest of the house."

Tamara had barely touched the door handle when the door swung open. Both women froze when a cold voice spoke.

"Come in. I have been expecting you. You can't see me, but I can see both of you, and you're covered. Don't do anything foolish, and you shall live a few minutes longer."

Only when their eyes became accustomed to the gloom could Tamara and Renita see the person speaking to them. They were looking into the ugly snout of a sawed-off shotgun, but more startling was the face belonging to the deep, cold voice.

"My God," Renita cried, "you're a . . . a woman."

"Yes. I am Cord Sandlin. Cordelia, if you prefer."

She stood up, dressed in a flat-crowned black Stetson, black embroidered jacket, and divided riding skirt. Black riding boots completed her attire. She beckoned with the shotgun toward the stairs.

"Where are you taking us?" Tamara asked.

"To a room upstairs I have prepared for you," said Sandlin. "I suspected you, and left the key where you could find it. Now the two of you are going to pay the price for your part in the destruction of my Border Empire. Move."

Slowly Tamara started up the stairs, Renita following. Sandlin stayed just far enough behind that Renita couldn't turn and seize the shotgun. It was now light enough that they could see without difficulty. There was a room near the head of the stairs, and the door stood open.

"In there," Sandlin ordered.

Tamara and Renita entered and then turned to face their captor.

"You will never leave Mexico alive," said Tamara angrily.

Sandlin laughed. "Do you not believe that I have expected this moment and prepared for it? Beneath these stairs we just climbed, there is a vat of coal oil to which is attached a slow-burning fuse. I will lock the door to this room, and when I am safely away, the house will burn. Need I say more?"

"You heartless bitch," Renita shouted, "may you burn in hell."

"Perhaps," said Sandlin, without emotion, "but the two of you will burn first."

Sandlin stepped out, closed the door and, using a key, locked it. On a table near the head of the stairs stood a lamp. It had been filled with coal oil for this very occasion, and Cordelia Sandlin raised the globe and lit it. The basement beneath the house, and the tunnel that would lead her to safety, would be dark, and the lamp would be necessary.

"Come on," said Klady as he and his three companions approached the mansion from the rear. "Let's be done with this. I'll take a window back here. The rest of you pick one on the front and sides."

"We all throw at the same time," Tafolla said. "One of us will have to signal."

"Then shout when you're ready," said Klady. "The rest of us will throw at the sound of your voice."

"Dear God," said Renita, "there are bars on the window. There's no way out."

"We will have some time before the fire reaches us," Tamara said. "We must find a way out of this room."

She charged the door, hurling herself against it, but it held.

"Fire away," Tafolla shouted, throwing his bundle of dynamite toward a window.

The four charges blew, but not quite together, each sounding like an echo of the last. Glass shattered in the windows, the foundation cracked, and sections of the lower wall fell away. Inside, Cordelia Sandlin had reached the foot of the stairs, and the concussion flung her senseless to the floor. The lamp shattered and flaming coal oil soaked the plush carpet. The flames spread quickly, getting ever closer to the supply of coal oil beneath the stairs. Their vengeance complete, the four riders galloped away as the wind sucked gusts of smoke through the broken windows of the Sandlin mansion.

Wes and El Lobo were in the barn, saddling their own horses and those of Tamara and Renita when the charges of dynamite exploded. They left the barn on the run, leading the two extra mounts.

"*Por Dios*," El Lobo shouted. "It burns."

Already the flames were licking out the lower windows of the Sandlin mansion. There was another minor explosion, and the flames roared higher. Within the house, Cordelia Sandlin came to her senses only to find herself surrounded by flames. She got to her knees, her clothing afire, and the heavy banister from the stairs collapsed on her. She screamed.

"My God," Wes groaned, "Tamara and Renita are in there. One of them screamed."

Wes and El Lobo rode around the house, seeking a means of entering, but there was no way. The lower portion of the house was in flames. Suddenly there was the sound of shattering glass. Wes and El Lobo looked up, into the frantic faces of Tamara and Renita, trapped behind the bars of the window.

"Hold on," Wes shouted. "We'll try to get you out through the roof."

Seizing his lariat, Wes built a loop and dropped it over the chimney, which was still intact. El Lobo had already found the ax near the carriage house.

"I'm goin' up," said Wes "When I get up there, send up the ax. Then get the horses away from here."

"But *amigo* . . ."

But Wes was already struggling up the side of the burning house, praying the stone chimney wouldn't crumble from the heat. El Lobo quickly looped the end of the rope about the handle of the ax, and the moment Wes reached the roof, he drew up the ax. Already the horses had begun to nicker and shy away from the flames. El Lobo seized the reins and led the animals away. He could see the terrified faces of Tamara and Renita at the window, and already tendrils of smoke swirled out of it.

"Wes be on the roof," El Lobo shouted.

Wes tried to reach the portion of the roof above Tamara and Renita, for there might not be time enough to enter the second floor of the house and seek out the room.

"This way, *amigo*," El Lobo shouted.

Frantically, Wes swung the ax. When he finally broke through the roof, he coughed and choked as smoke was whipped into his face.

"Wes," Renita cried. "Wes."

Desperately, she reached as high as she could, but he couldn't get to her.

"There must be something you can stand on," Wes shouted.

Dimly, he could see Tamara struggling to move a dresser or chest of drawers. Renita threw her strength to the task, and when they climbed onto the furniture, Wes was able to reach their hands. He lifted out Renita and then Tamara as flames swept into the room from which they had just escaped. There were shouts, and villagers stood across the road from the burning house, pointing to the rescued and the rescuer on the roof. Suddenly flames shot through the hole Wes had chopped in the roof.

"Come on," he shouted.

They struggled across the roof to the chimney, and Wes made a loop in the loose end of the rope.

"Get that over your head and under your arms," he ordered Tamara.

When she had done so, he lowered her over the edge of the roof. El Lobo was waiting for her. Quickly he slipped the rope over her head. Wes withdrew it and sent Renita over the edge. Once Renita was down, Wes slid down the rope. El Lobo had brought the horses as near as he dared to the burning house, and now he struggled to hold them. The others were already mounted, and as Wes swung into his saddle, the chimney collapsed. As they rode away, somebody shouted, and behind them there was a crash as the roof of the house fell in.

"You're a pair of damn fools," Wes said angrily when, miles away, they dared stop to rest the horses. "A few more minutes, and you'd have been goners."

"We went after Sandlin," said Tamara defiantly. "It was our last chance."

"We learned something nobody else knew," Renita said triumphantly. "Cord Sandlin was really Cordelia Sandlin, a woman."

"Tarnation," said Wes, "then the woman who left the house and returned was—"

"Sandlin," Renita finished, "and she died in the fire she intended for us."

"How do you know?" El Lobo wondered.

"When part of the house fell, we heard her scream," said Tamara. "Somehow, she was caught in the fire."

"However the fire started," Wes said, "it might not have been her doing. While we were in the barn saddling the horses, there were four quick blasts that might have been dynamite."

"Yes," said Renita. "It shook the house, broke windows, and came just after Sandlin had locked us in that room. She would have had only enough time to get down the stairs, but no more."

"The concussion might have knocked her out," Wes said, "and if she happened to be carrying a lit lamp or lantern . . ."

"I wished her a place in hell," Renita said, "but it was a terrible way to die."

"We came to destroy the Sandlin gang," said Wes, "and I reckon this closes the book, except for those varmints who threw the dynamite."

"We did not kill Sandlin," Tamara said, "but I do not feel cheated. It is fitting that Sandlin was destroyed by the remnants of the Sandlin gang."

"*Sí*," El Lobo agreed. "Now do we get out of Mexico alive?"

"We'll have to ride careful," said Wes. "I think we'd better find a place to hole up for the rest of the day, and do our riding at night. There can't be much of that jerked beef left in our saddlebags."

"Per'ap not," said El Lobo, "but the box that talk to the telegraph wire still be there."

Wes laughed. "Tarnation, I can't believe the soldiers left that. Before we leave Mexico forever, I reckon—"

"El Diablos Pistolas will send one last message," Renita finished.

"We must be careful, and not become overconfident," said Tamara. "Those who set off the dynamite—the last of the Sandlin gang—may be somewhere ahead of us, or perhaps behind us."

"If they're smart, they're ahead of us," Wes said. "El Lobo and me had to rescue you and Renita from that burning house, so they had a head start."

The four rode mostly at night, sharing the little jerked beef that remained. And true to his word, a hundred miles south of Juarez Wes climbed a telegraph pole. He sent a final, brief message.

Cordelia Sandlin is dead and El Diablos Pistolas say adios to Mexico.

Austin, Texas. September 7, 1884

Texas Ranger Bodie West slapped his thigh with his hat and roared.

"What's got into you?" Dylan Stewart asked as he entered the office.

"Look at this," said West. "By God, the kid did it."

Stewart read a copy of the telegram and grinned.

"That ties in with the word from Toluca that the Sandlin house was destroyed," West said, "but there was no mention of Wes."

"You'd better telegraph Byron Silver," said Stewart.

"I already did," West replied. "He sails today, bound for Corpus Christi."

El Paso, Texas. September 8, 1884

Wes took rooms at Granny Boudleaux's boarding-house for himself, Renita, El Lobo, and Tamara.

"Now," Wes said, "I'm ridin' to town to send a telegram to Ranger Bodie West in Austin. It won't seem right, payin' for my telegrams."

Wes sent the telegram and waited for an answer. It arrived within minutes, and said:

Come to Austin immediately stop. Twenty-one coming.

The message was unsigned.

"We're ridin' to Austin," said Wes when he returned to Granny Boudleaux's.

"For why?" Granny demanded. "You no give me time to get used to you not being dead. You get the drifting foot worse than your daddy."

Austin, Texas. September 15, 1884

When Wes and his companions reached Austin, Silver was already there. West led the way to Silver's hotel, and they met in his hotel room. Wes performed the introductions.

"Tamara and me, we have no home in Mexico," El Lobo said.

"Any friends of Wes Stone's are friends of mine," said Silver. "Welcome to Texas and the United States of America. Walk on the right side of the law, and this will be home as long as you want to claim it."

"*Sí*," El Lobo said. "Remember the Alamo."

"By God," said West, "he's a Texan already."

"I'm glad you and Wes are *amigos*, Palo," Silver said. "Because of what you have been able to accomplish in Mexico, there's something I want to ask of you. Something akin to what I so often asked of your father, Wes."

"Lay it on the table, then," said Wes.

Silver dropped two coins on the table. One was a double eagle, the other a golden medallion. On one side was the head of a dragon, on the other, the number two.

"God Almighty," Wes said.

"The dragon lives," said El Lobo.

"I'm afraid so," Silver said, "and if something isn't done, this nation's going broke. Do you see anything wrong with that double eagle?"

Wes felt the coin, dropped it on the table, and El Lobo repeated the procedure.

"It's counterfeit," said Silver. "It looks real, it rings true, but it's worth only a few cents. Best we can tell, the damn things are being cast in New Orleans, Denver, Carson City, and San Francisco."

"Those are all towns where there are U.S. mints," Wes said.

"Yes," said Silver, "and it's a continual slap in the face. But the dragon is involved in other crimes, much the same as in Mexico. Here there is one big difference. You will have the full cooperation of my office and the U.S. government. You won't have to worry about soldiers threatening to have you executed. Will the two of you side me?"

Wes looked at Renita, while El Lobo turned to Tamara.

"I will not object, but I will not be left behind," Tamara said.

"Nor I," said Renita.

"I'll be honest with you," Silver said. "There will be times when Wes and Palo will be forced to work alone. That is the nature of this assignment. Can you accept that?"

"This is mine and Palo's adopted country," said Tamara. "We will do what must be done, accepting what must be accepted."

"I can't do any better than that," Renita said.

"Then I'm buyin' the steaks," said Silver. "The biggest in Austin. Then we will seek a means of slaying this golden dragon once and for all."

"*Sí*," El Lobo said. "The *bastardo* have thick hide."